"A HIP, BRISK
PAGE-TURNER."
—*Us Weekly*

"CAPTURES THE
READER WITH BULLET
SWIFTNESS."
—*Denver Post*

"A GREAT READ...HIS
BEST WORK YET."
—*Los Angeles
Features Syndicate*

"BOTTOM LINE:
WEST WING ZING."
—*People*

PRAISE FOR *THE FIRST COUNSEL* AND BRAD MELTZER

"Nothing gets in the way of the adrenaline jolt Meltzer delivers like a master." —*Kirkus Reviews*

"Meltzer is fast on his way to becoming one of America's fiction stalwarts."

—*Tampa Tribune-Times*

"Move over, John Grisham and David Baldacci. Brad Meltzer's just elbowed his way into your megastar company." —*Fort Worth Star-Telegram*

"Ups the ante for legal thrillers with its intricate plot and clever, complex characters. Most impressive is Meltzer's knowledge of every nook of the White House. With all its grand history and mystery, the mansion comes alive. The White House hasn't seen this much action since . . . well, you know." —*People*

"Curl up in front of a fire with [this] edge-of-your-seat thriller." —*Cosmopolitan*

"The Washington color and scenery and the unusual cast of characters take it a step above your average page-turner and will keep you reading until the last startling conclusion." —*Booklist*

more . . .

"The writer's skill here is obvious."

—*Denver Post*

"Meltzer is so good."

—*Entertainment Weekly*

"A riveting look at life inside the White House. Meltzer's book will keep you guessing until the end."
—*Greensboro News & Record* (NC)

"One critic has predicted that Meltzer would be 'the next John Grisham'; there's no need for that, for Meltzer does quite well being Brad Meltzer."

—*Richmond Times*

"Another winner . . . engrossing and suspenseful."

—*Library Journal*

"Meltzer has mastered the art of baiting and hooking readers quickly into a fast-moving plot."

—*USA Today*

"Meltzer's latest thriller is the kind of book that makes you want to stay up late, get up early, and take a long lunch hour—whatever it takes to find out what happens next."

—*Ohio News Journal*

THE
FIRST
COUNSEL

ALSO BY BRAD MELTZER

Dead Even

The Tenth Justice

BRAD MELTZER

THE FIRST COUNSEL

WARNER
VISION
BOOKS

An AOL Time Warner Company

WARNER BOOKS EDITION

Cover design by Shasti O'Leary

Warner Vision is a registered trademarks of Warner Books, Inc.

Warner Books, Inc.
1271 Avenue of the Americas
New York, NY 10020

Visit our Web site at
www.twbookmark.com.

For information on Time Warner Trade Publishing's online publishing program, visit www.ipublish.com.

An AOL Time Warner Company

Printed in the United States of America

Originally published in hardcover by Warner Books.
First International Paperback Printing: September 2001
First U.S. Paperback Printing: December 2001

10 9 8 7 6 5 4 3 2 1

For Cori,
my First Counsel,
my First Lady,
my First Love

And for my sister, Bari,
for never tattling when we were little,
and for always reading my mind as we grow up

ACKNOWLEDGMENTS

I wish to thank the following people, whose love and support never fail to inspire: As always, my First Lady, Cori, who is an endless source of patience and inspiration—especially as I continually drive the two of us to the limits of sanity. From pre-book plotting to final-form editing, she is everything at every moment: friend, hand-holder, advisor, editor, partner, lover, soulmate. I love you, C—if it weren't for you, this book wouldn't exist and neither would I; Jill Kneerim, my agent, for one of the kindest, most rewarding friendships I've ever known. Of everything I've been fortunate enough to experience as a writer, one of the best rewards was finding Jill. Her endless faith continually helps us keep it all in perspective, and we wouldn't be here without her; Elaine Rogers, whose tremendous energy brought new definition to the term gangbusters; Sharon Silva-Lamberson, Stephanie Wilson, Nicole Linehan, Ellen O'Donnell, Hope Denekamp, Lindsey Shaw, Ike Williams, and everyone else at the Hill & Barlow Agency, who keep the machine running and are among the nicest people I've encountered.

I'd also like to thank my parents, for giving me everything they never had, for teaching me to lead with my heart, and for knowing exactly when to be my mom and dad. You're both incredible; Noah Kuttler, whose never-ending patience affects all my work and whose insight forces me to reach my own potential; Ethan Kline, whose astute observations are among the first I turn to, and whose friendship and trust are simply awe-inspiring (thanks for the big one, E); Matt and Susan Oshinsky, Joel Rose, Chris Weiss, and Judd Winick continue to be a brain trust I never want to be without. They read, react, suggest, and always keep me laughing.

Since the White House prides itself on secrecy, I owe immense thank-yous to the following people who let me sneak in: Steve "Scoop" Cohen, for . . . well . . . for being Scoop. From the brainstorming of the plot, to the research, to the nitpicky details, Scoop was the master of ceremonies. He is fearless and insightful, and without his creative instinct, this book wouldn't be the same. Thank you, buddy; Debi Mohile, whose keen eye kept me honest on (almost) every page and whose great sense of humor always made it a pleasure. No one knows the White House like Debi. Thanks for putting up with me; Mark Bernstein, one of the nicest people around, for showing me the rest of the way firsthand and for reminding me the value of old friends; Lanny Breuer, Chris Cerf, Jeff Connaughton, Vince Flynn, Adam Rosman, and Kathi Whalen, who went beyond the call of duty and never failed to use their imaginations to answer tons of my inane questions; Pam Brewington, Lloyd Cutler, Fred Fielding, Leonard Garment, Thurgood Marshall Jr., Cathy Moscatelli, Miriam Nemetz, Donna Peel, Jack Quinn, Ron Saleh, Cliff Sloan, John Stanley, and Rob Weiner, who were the rest of my White House team, and in giving their time, gave me so many of the great details and stories; Larry Sheafe and Chuck Vance, who were the nicest Secret Service guys anyone could ask for; the one

First Daughter who was kind enough to share her experiences in the bubble (for nothing more than the good of fiction), thanks again!; Dr. Ronald K. Wright, for his amazing forensic advice; Pat Thacker, Anne Tumlinson, Tom Antonucci, Lily Garcia, and Dale Flam for help with the details; Marsha Blanco (who's just incredible), Steve Waldron, Chuck Perso, Carol Rambo Ronai, Sue Lorenson, Dave Watkins, Fred Baughman, John Richard Gould, Rusty Hawkins, Philip Joseph Sirken, and Jo Anne Patterson, for welcoming me into The Arc organization and the mental retardation community (www.thearc.org for more information). Rarely have I been so inspired and so utterly humbled. And, of course, to my family and friends, whose names, as always, inhabit these pages.

Finally, I'd like to thank all of the talented and wonderful people at my new publisher, Warner Books: Larry Kirshbaum, Maureen Egen, Tina Andreadis, Emi Battaglia, Karen Torres, Martha Otis, Chris Barba, Claire Zion, Bruce Paonessa, Peter Mauceri, Harry Helm, and all of the incredibly nice people who made this book a reality and always make me feel like part of the family. Special thanks also go out to Jamie Raab, not only for her editorial input, but for being one of our biggest supporters. Her warmth and energy never cease to amaze. Finally, I want to thank the two editors who worked on this book, Rob Weisbach and Rob McMahon. From the very start, Rob Weisbach lent his creative talents to every level of our publishing experience, and we wouldn't be here without him. His influence can be felt on every page, and though I've said it before, I'll say it again: Rob has real vision and we've always been blessed to be a part of it. I owe him my career and I cherish his friendship. At Warner, Rob McMahon is a true gentleman who picked up our proverbial ball and ran with it. We couldn't be luckier. His editorial comments were insightful beyond belief and he always pushed me to reach beyond what I thought was possible. Rob, we'd be lost without you. So to Rob Weisbach and Rob McMahon, I will always appreciate your energy, but I am far more thankful for your faith.

I resented a lot about the White House.
Then I realized I could adjust or I could adjust.

> Luci Johnson
> Daughter of Lyndon Baines Johnson

You don't live in the White House,
you are only exhibit A to the country.

> President Theodore Roosevelt

I remember miserable nights of nightmares.

> Susan Ford
> Daughter of Gerald Ford
> On her time as First Daughter

THE
FIRST
COUNSEL

CHAPTER 1

I'm afraid of heights, snakes, normalcy, mediocrity, Hollywood, the initial silence of an empty house, the enduring darkness of a poorly lit street, evil clowns, professional failure, the intellectual impact of Barbie dolls, letting my father down, being paralyzed, hospitals, doctors, the cancer that killed my mother, dying unexpectedly, dying for a stupid reason, dying painfully, and, worst of all, dying alone. But I'm not afraid of power—which is why I work in the White House.

As I sit in the passenger seat of my beat-up, rusty blue Jeep, I can't help but stare at my date, the beautiful young woman who's driving my car. Her long, thin fingers hold the steering wheel in a commanding grip that lets both of us know who's in charge. I could care less, though—as the car flies up Connecticut Avenue, I'm far more content studying the way her short black hair licks the back of her neck. For security reasons, we keep the windows closed, but that doesn't stop her from opening the sunroof. Letting the warm, early-September air sweep through her hair, she leans back and enjoys the freedom. She then adds her final personal touch to the car: She turns on the radio, flips through my preset stations, and shakes her head.

"This is what you like?" Nora asks. "Talk radio?"

"It's for work." Pointing to the dashboard and hoping to be cool, I add, "The last one has music."

She calls my bluff and hits the last button. More talk radio. "You always this predictable?" she asks.

"Only when I—" Before I can finish, the shriek of an electric guitar pierces my eardrum. She's found her station.

Tapping her thumbs against the steering wheel and bobbing her head to the beat, Nora looks completely alive.

"This is what you like?" I shout back over the noise. "Thrash radio?"

"Only way to stay young," she says with a grin. She's kicking my shins and she loves it. At twenty-two years of age, Nora Hartson is smart. And way too confident. She knows I'm self-conscious about the difference in our ages—she knew it the first moment I told her I was twenty-nine. She didn't care, though.

"Think that's going to scare me off?" she had asked.

"If it does, that's your mistake."

That's when I had her. She needed the challenge. Especially a sexual one. For too long, things had been easy for her. And as Nora is so keenly aware, there's no fun in always getting what you want. The thing is, that's likely to be her lot in life. For better or worse, that's her power. Nora is attractive, engaging, and extremely captivating. She's also the daughter of the President of the United States.

As I said, I'm not afraid of power.

The car heads toward Dupont Circle, and I glance at my watch, wondering when our first date is going to end. It's quarter past eleven, but Nora seems to just be getting started. As we pull up to a place called Tequila Mockingbird, I roll my eyes. "Another bar?"

"You gotta have at least a little foreplay," she teases. I look over like I hear it all the time. It doesn't fool her for a second. God, I love America. "Besides," she adds, "this is a good one—no one knows this place."

"So we'll actually have some privacy?" Instinctively, I check the rearview mirror. The black Chevy Suburban that followed us out of the White House gate and to every subsequent stop we made is still right behind us. The Secret Service never lets go.

"Don't worry about them," she says. "They don't know what's coming."

Before I can ask her to explain, I see a man in khakis standing at the side entrance of Tequila Mockingbird. He points to a reserved parking spot and waves us toward him. Even before he pushes the button in his hand and whispers into the collar of his struggling-to-be-casual polo shirt, I know who he is. Secret Service. Which means we don't have to wait in the long line out front—he'll take us in the side. Not a bad way to bar-hop, if you ask me. Of course, Nora sees it differently.

"Ready to rain on his parade?" she asks.

I nod, unsure of what she's up to, but barely able to contain my smile. The First Daughter, and I mean *the* First Daughter, is sitting next to me, in my crappy car, asking me to follow her under the limbo stick. I can already taste the salsa.

Just as we make eye contact with the agent outside the Mockingbird, Nora rolls past the bar, and instead heads to a dance club halfway up the block. I turn around and check out the agent's expression. He's not amused. I can read his lips from here. "*Shadow moving,*" he growls into his collar.

"Wait a minute—didn't you tell them we were going to the Mockingbird?"

"Let me ask you a question: When you go out, do you think it's fun to have the Secret Service check out the place before you get there?"

I pause to think about it. "Actually, it seems pretty cool to me."

She laughs. "Well, I hate it. The moment they walk in, the really interesting people hit the exits." Pointing to the Suburban that's still behind us, she adds, "The ones who *follow* me, I can deal with. It's the advance guys that wreck the party. Besides, this keeps everyone on their toes."

As we pull up to the valet, I try to think of something witty to say. That's when I see him. Standing at the front entrance of our newest destination is another man whispering into the collar of his shirt. Like the agent who was standing outside the Mockingbird, he's dressed in Secret Service casual standards: khakis and a short-sleeve polo. To call as little attention to Nora as possible, the agents try their best to be invisible—their attire is keyed to their protectee's. Of course, they think they blend in, but last I checked, most people in khakis don't carry guns and talk into the collars of their shirts. Either way, though, I'm impressed. They know her better than I thought.

"So, we going in or what?" I ask, motioning toward the valet, who's waiting for Nora to open her door.

Nora doesn't answer. Her piercing green eyes, which were persuasive enough to convince me to let her drive, are now staring vacantly out the window.

I tap her playfully on the shoulder. "So they knew you were coming. Big deal—that's their job."

"That's not it."

"Nora, we're all creatures of habit. Just because they know your routine—"

"That's the problem!" she shouts. "I was being spontaneous!"

Behind the outburst, there's a pain in her voice that catches me off guard. Despite the years of watching her on TV, it's the first time I've seen her open her soft side, and even though it's with a yell, I jump right in. My playful shoulder-tap turns into a soothing caress. "Forget this place—we'll find somewhere new."

She glares angrily at the agent near the front door. He grins back. They've played this game before. "We're out of here," she growls. With a quick pump of the gas, our tires screech and we're on to our next stop. As we take off, I again check the rearview mirror. The Suburban, as always, is right behind us.

"They ever let up?" I ask.

"Goes with the territory," she says, sounding like she's been kicked in the gut.

Hoping to cheer her up, I say, "Forget those monkeys. Who cares if they know where you—"

"Spend two weeks doing it. That'll change your tune."

"Not me. My tune stays the same: *Love the guys with guns. Love the guys with guns. Love the guys with guns.* We're talkin' mantra here."

The joke is easy, but it works. She fights back the tiniest smile. "Gotta love those guns." Taking a deep breath, she runs her hand across the back of her neck and through the tips of her black hair. I think she's finally starting to relax. "Thanks again for letting me drive—I was starting to miss it."

"If it makes you feel better, you're an excellent driver."

"And you're an excellent liar."

"Don't take my word for it—look at the lemmings behind us; they've been smiling since you peeled out from the club."

Nora checks the rearview mirror for herself and waves at two more of the khaki-and-polo patrol. Neither smiles, but the one in the passenger seat actually waves back. "Those're my boys—been with me for three years," she explains. "Besides, Harry and Darren aren't that bad. They're just miserable because they're the only two who are actually responsible for me."

"Sounds like a dream job."

"More like a nightmare—every time I leave the House, they're stuck watching my behind."

"Like I said: dream job."

She turns, pretending she doesn't enjoy the compliment. "You love to flirt, don't you?"

"Safest form of intense social interaction."

"Safe, huh? Is that what it's all about for you?"

"Says the young lady with the armed bodyguards."

"What can I say?" she says with a laugh. "Sometimes you've got to be careful."

"And sometimes you've got to burn the village to save it."

She likes that one—anything that brings back some challenge. For her, everything else is planned. "So now you're Genghis Khan?" she asks.

"I've been known to ravage a few helpless townships."

"Oh, please, lawboy, you're starting to embarrass yourself. Now where do you want to go?"

The forcefulness turns me on. I try to act unfazed. "Doesn't matter to me. But do the monkeys have to follow?"

"That depends," she says with a grin. "You think you can handle them?"

"Oh, yeah. Lawyers are well known for their ability to beat up large willing-to-take-a-bullet military types. There's a whole 'Fisticuffs' section on the bar exam . . . right after the 'Rain of Pain' essay."

"Okay, so if it's not going to be fight, we're going to have to go with flight." She hits the gas and my head snaps back into the headrest. We're now once again flying up Connecticut Avenue.

"What're you doing?"

She shoots me a look that I can feel in my pants. "You wanted privacy."

"Actually, I wanted foreplay."

"Well if this works, you're gonna get both."

Now the adrenaline's pumping. "You really think you can lose them?"

"Only tried once before."

"What happened?"

She shoots me another one of those looks. "You don't want to know."

The speedometer quickly shoots up to sixty, and the poorly paved D.C. roads are making us feel every pothole. I grab the handle on the door and prop myself up straight. It's at this moment that I see Nora as the twenty-two-year-old she really is—fearless, smug, and still impressed by the rev of an engine. Although I'm only a few years older, it's been a long time since my heart's raced this fast. After three years at Michigan Law, two years of clerkships, two years at a law firm, and the past two years in the White House Counsel's Office, my passions have been purely professional. Then Nora Hartson slaps me awake and starts a flash fire in my gut. How the hell was I supposed to know what I was missing?

Still, I look back at the Suburban and let out a nervous laugh. "If this gets me in trouble . . ."

"Is that what you're worried about?"

I bite my lip. That was a big step backwards. "No . . . it's just that . . . you know what I mean."

She ignores my stumbling and gives it more speed.

Stuck in the silence of our conversation, all I can hear is how loud the engine is revving. Up ahead is the entrance to the underpass that runs below Dupont Circle. The small tunnel has an initial steep drop, so you can't see how many cars are actually ahead of you. Nora doesn't seem to care. Without slowing down, we leap into the tunnel and my stomach drops. Luckily, there's no one in front of us.

As we leave the tunnel, all I can focus on is the green light at the end of the block. Then it turns yellow. We're not nearly close enough to make it. Again, Nora doesn't seem to care. "The light . . . !"

It turns red and Nora jerks the wheel into an illegal left turn. The tires shriek and my shoulder is pressed against the door. For the first time, I actually think we're in danger. I glance in the rearview mirror. The Suburban is still behind us. Never letting go.

We race down a narrow, short street. I can see a stop sign ahead. Despite the late hour, there's still a steady stream of cars enjoying the right of way. I expect Nora to slow down. Instead, she speeds up.

"Don't do it!" I warn her.

She takes notice of the volume of my voice, but doesn't reply. I'm craning my neck, trying to see how many cars there are. I see a few, but have no idea if they see us. We blow through the stop sign, and I shut my eyes. I hear cars screech to a halt and the simultaneous blaring of horns. Nothing hits us. I turn around and watch the Secret Service follow in our wake . . .

"What're you, a psychopath?"

"Only if I kill us. If we live, I'm a daredevil."

She refuses to let up, twisting and turning through the brownstone-lined streets of Dupont Circle. Every stop sign we run leaves another chorus of screaming horns and pissed-off drivers. Eventually, we're tearing up a one-way street that crosses back over the main thoroughfare, Connecticut Avenue. The only thing between us and the six lanes of traffic is another stop sign. With a hundred feet to go, she slams on the brakes. Thank God. Sanity's returned.

"Why don't we just call it a night?" I offer.

"Not a chance." She's scowling in the mirror, staring down her favorite agents. They look tempted to get out of the Suburban, but they have to know she'll take off the moment they do.

The agent in the passenger seat rolls down his window. He's young, maybe even younger than me. "C'mon, Shadow," he yells, rubbing it in by using her Secret Service code name. "You know what he said last time. Don't make us call this one in."

She doesn't take well to the threat. Under her breath, she mutters, "Cocky jock asshole." With that, she punches the gas. The wheels spin until they find traction.

I can't let her do this. "Nora, don't . . ."

"Shut up."

"Don't tell me to—"

"I said, shut up." Her response is a measured, low snarl. She doesn't sound like herself. We're barreling toward the stop sign and I count seven cars crossing in front of us. Eight. Nine. Ten. This isn't like the side streets. These cars are flying. I notice a tiny bead of sweat rolling down the side of Nora's forehead. She's holding the wheel as tight as she can. We're not going to make this one.

As we hit the threshold, I do the only thing I can think of. I lean over, punch the horn, and hold it down. We shoot out of the side street like a fifty-mile-an-hour banshee. Two cars swerve. Another hits his brakes. A fourth driver, in a black Acura, tries to slow down, but there's not enough time. His tires screech against the pavement, but he's still moving. Although Nora does her best to swerve out of his way, he nicks us right on the back tip of our bumper. It's just enough to make us veer out of control. And to put the Acura directly in front of the Secret Service Suburban. The Suburban pulls a sharp right and comes to a dead halt. We keep moving.

"It's okay!" Nora screams as she fights the steering wheel. "It's okay!" And in a two-second interval, I realize it's true. Everyone's safe and we're free to go. Nora lights up the car with a smile. As we motor up the block, I'm still remembering how to breathe.

Her chest is heaving as she catches her own breath. "Not bad, huh?" she finally asks.

"Not bad?" I ask, wiping my forehead. "You could've killed us—not to mention the other drivers and the—"

"But did you have fun?"

"It's not a question of fun. It was one of the stupidest stunts I've ever—"

"But did you have fun?" As she repeats the question, her voice grows warm. In the moonlight, her wild eyes shine. After seeing so many two-dimensional photos of her at public events in the papers, it's odd to see her just sitting there. I thought I knew how she smiled and how she moved. I wasn't even close. In person, her whole face changes—the way her cheeks pitch and slightly redden at the excitement—there's no way to describe it. It's not that I'm starstruck, it's just . . . I don't know how else to say it . . . she's looking at me. Just me. She slaps my leg. "No one was hurt, the Acura barely tapped us. At the very worst, we both scraped our bumpers. I mean, how many nights do you get to outrun the Secret Service and live to tell about it?"

"I do it every other Thursday. It's not that big a deal."

"Laugh all you want, but you have to admit it was a thrill."

I look over my shoulder. We're completely alone. And I have to admit, she's right.

It takes about ten minutes before I realize we're lost. In the span of a few blocks, the immaculate brownstones of Dupont Circle have faded into the run-down tenements on the outskirts of Adams Morgan. "We should've turned on 16th," I say.

"You have no idea what you're talking about."

"You're absolutely right; I'm two hundred percent clueless. And you want to know how I know that?" I pause for effect. "Because I trusted you to drive! I mean, what the hell was I thinking? You barely live here; you're never in a car; and when you are, it's usually in the backseat."

"What's that supposed to mean?"

Just as she asks the question, I realize what I've said. Three years ago, right after her father got elected, during Nora's sophomore year at Princeton, *Rolling Stone* ran a scathing profile of what they called her college "Drug and Love Life." According to the article, two different guys claimed that Nora went down on them in the backseats of their cars while she was on Special K. Another source said she was doing coke; a third said it was heroin. Either way, based on the article, some horny little Internet-freak used Nora's full name—Eleanor—and wrote a haiku poem entitled "Knee-Sore Eleanor." A few million forwarded e-mails later, Nora gained her most notorious sobriquet—and her father saw his favorability numbers fall. When the story ran, President Hartson called up the editor of *Rolling Stone* and asked him to leave his daughter alone. From then on, they did. Hartson's numbers went back up. All was well. But the joke was already out there. And obviously, from the look on Nora's face, the damage had already been done.

"I didn't mean anything," I insist, backing away from my unintended insult. "I just meant that your family gets the limo treatment. Motorcades. You know, other people drive you."

Suddenly, Nora laughs. She has a sexy, hearty voice, but her laugh is all little girl.

"What'd I say?"

"You're embarrassed," she answers, amused. "Your whole face is red."

I turn away. "I'm sorry . . ."

"No, it's okay. That's really sweet of you. And it's even sweeter that you blushed. For once, I know it's real. Thank you, Michael."

She said my name. For the first time tonight, she said my name. I turn back to her. "You're welcome. Now let's get out of here."

Turning around on 14th Street and still searching for the small strip of land known as Adams Morgan, home to Washington's most overrated bars and best ethnic restaurants, we find ourselves weaving our way back from the direction we came. Surrounded by nothing but deserted buildings and dark streets, I start worrying. No matter how tough she is, the First Daughter of the United States shouldn't be in a neighborhood like this.

When we reach the end of the block, though, we see our first indication of civilized life: Around the corner is a small crowd of people coming out of the only storefront in sight. It's a large brick building that looks like it's been converted into a two-story bar. In thick black letters, the word "Pendulum" is painted on a filthy white sign. A hip, midnight blue light surrounds the edges of the sign. Not at all my kind of place.

Nora pulls into a nearby parking spot and turns off the ignition.

"Here?" I ask. "The place is a rathole."

"No, it's not. People are well dressed." She points to a man wearing camel-colored slacks and a tight black T-shirt. Before I can protest, she adds, "Let's go—for once, we're anonymous." She pulls a black baseball hat from the shoulder strap of her purse and lowers the brim over her eyes. It's a terrible disguise, but she says it works. Never been stopped yet.

We pay ten bucks at the door, step inside, and take a quick look around. The place is packed with the typical D.C. Thursday night crowd—most still in their suits, ties undone; some already in their Calvin Klein V-necks. In the corner, two men are playing pool. By the bar, two men are ordering drinks. Next to them, two men are holding hands. That's when I realize where we are: Besides Nora, there's not a woman in this place. We're standing in the middle of a gay bar.

Behind me, I feel someone grab my ass. I don't even bother to turn around. "Oh, Nora, how I wish you were a man."

"I'm impressed," she says, stepping forward. "You don't even look uncomfortable."

"Why should I be uncomfortable?"

From the gleam in her eye, I can tell she's setting up another test. She needs to know if I can hang with the cool kids. "So it's okay if we stay?"

"Absolutely," I say with a grin. "I wouldn't have it any other way."

She stares me down with that sexy look. For the moment, I pass.

We squeeze up to the bar and order drinks. I get a beer; she gets a Jack and Ginger. Following her lead, we head to the far end of the L-shaped bar, where it runs perpendicular to the wall. In a move that's been honed by years

of being hounded and gawked at, Nora motions me into
the last seat and puts her back to the crowd. For her, it's
pure instinct. With her baseball cap covering her hair, there
isn't a chance she's going to be recognized. The way she's
set us up, the only one who can even see her is me. She
takes one last overview of the room, then, satisfied, goes
for her drink. "So have you always hugged your serious
side?"

"What do you mean? I'm not—"

"Don't apologize for it," she interrupts. "It's who you
are. I just want to know where it comes from. Family issues? Bitter divorce? Dad abandoned you and your m—?"

"Nobody *did* anything," I say. "What you see is me."
By the tone of my answer, she thinks it's an issue. She's
right. And it's not something she's getting on a first date.
Searching for a smooth segue, I try to steer us back to safer
subjects. "So tell me what you thought of Princeton. En-
joyable or Muffyville snob factory?"

"I didn't know you wanted to do an interview."

"Don't give me that. College tells you a lot about a person."

"College tells you jack squat—it's a rationalized decision based on nothing more than a vacuous campus visit
and a prefigured range of SAT scores. Besides, you're almost thirty," she says with a lick-it-up grin, "that's ancient
history for you. What've you done in between?"

"After law school? A quick clerkship, then off to a local
law firm. To be honest, though, it was just a way to fill
time between campaigns. Barth in the Senate, a few local
council guys—then three months as the Hartson Campaign's
Get-Out-the-Vote Chairman, Great State of Michigan." She
doesn't respond and I get the sense she's judging me.
Quickly, I add, "You know what a zoo it is to do it na-

tionally—if I wanted any real responsibility, it was better for me to stay in-state."

"Better for you or better for your ego?"

"All of us. The headquarters was only twenty minutes from my house."

She sees something in my answer. "So you wanted to be in Michigan?"

"Yeah. Why?"

"I don't know . . . smart guy like you . . . working in the Counsel's Office. Usually you guys run away from the hometowns."

"As a volunteer, it was a financial decision. Nothing more."

"And what about college and law school? Michigan for both, right?"

It's really incredible—when it comes to weaknesses, she knows exactly where to look. "School was a different story."

"Something with your parents?"

Once again, we've reached my limit. "Something personal. But it wasn't their fault."

"You always so forgiving?"

"You always so pushy?"

She rests an elbow on the bar, leans in close, and forces me back against the wall. "What you see is me," she says with a dark smile.

"Exactly," I tease back. "That's exactly my point." I hop off my stool and head toward her. In the Counsel's Office, it's the first rule they teach you: Never let them pin you down.

"Where you going?" she asks, blocking my way.

"Just to the restroom." I squeeze past her and everything between my chest and my thighs brushes against her. She grins. And doesn't give up an inch.

"Don't be too long," she purrs.

"Do I look that stupid?"

I return from the restroom just in time to see Nora taking a sip of my beer. I put a hand on the back of her shoulder. "You can order your own—they have plenty for everyone."

"I just needed it to take some aspirin," she explains, placing a small brown prescription vial back into her purse.

"Everything okay?"

"Just a headache." Pointing to the vial, she adds, "Want some?"

I shake my head.

"Suit yourself," she says with a grin. "But when you see this one, I think you're going to need it."

"What's that supposed to mean?"

As I take my seat against the wall, Nora leans in close. "When you were on your way to the restroom, did you happen to see any familiar faces walk in?"

I look over her shoulder and scan the bar. "I don't think so. Why?"

Her grin goes wide. Whatever's going on, she's enjoying herself. "Far left corner of the room. By the video screen. White button-down. Saggy khakis."

My eyes follow her instructions. There's the video screen. There's the . . . I don't believe it. Across the room, running his hand through his salt-and-pepper hair and trying to look as inconspicuous as possible, is Edgar Simon. White House Counsel. Lawyer to the President himself. My boss.

"Guess who just got the best office gossip?" Nora sings.

"This isn't funny."

"What's the big deal? So he's gay."

"That's not the point, Nora. He's married. To a woman. At his level, if this gets out, the press'll . . ."

Nora's smile falls away. "He's married? Are you sure?"

"For something like thirty years," I say nervously. "He's getting ready to send his first kid off to college." I lower my head to make sure he doesn't see me. "I just met his wife at that reception for AmeriCorps. Her name's Ellen. Or Elena. Something with an *E*."

"Dumb-ass, that's where you met *me*."

"Before you got there. Right when it started. Simon introduced me to her. They seemed really happy."

"And now he's here hoping for some extra tricks on the side. Man, when it comes to adulterers, my dad can pick 'em."

In the two weeks since we met, it's the fourth time Nora's made a reference to her father. And not just *her* father. *The* father. The father of the American people. The President of the United States. I have to admit, no matter how many times she says it, I don't think I'll ever get used to it.

Bent forward, with a sweaty hand grasping the edge of the bar, I'm frozen in position. Facing me, Nora has her back to Simon. "What's he doing now?" she asks.

Using her head to run interference, I refuse to look. If I can't see Simon, he can't see me.

"Tell me what he's doing," she insists.

"No way. He sees me, I'm meat. I won't get another assignment until I'm ninety."

"The way you're acting, that's not too far off." Before I can react, Nora grabs me by the collar and ducks her head down. As she holds me up, I get a good look at Simon.

"He's talking to someone," I blurt.

"Anyone we know?"

The stranger has curly black hair and is wearing a denim shirt. I shake my head. Never seen him before.

Nora can't help herself. She takes a quick peek and turns back around, just as the stranger hands Simon a small sheet of paper. "What was that?" Nora asks. "Are they exchanging numbers?"

"I can't tell. They're—" Just then, Simon looks my way. Right at me. Oh, shit. I drop my head before we make eye contact. Was I fast enough? With our foreheads touching, Nora and I look like we're searching for lost change under the bar.

Suddenly, a male voice says, "Can I help you?"

My heart sinks. I look up. It's just the bartender. "No, no," I stutter. "She just lost an earring."

When the bartender leaves, I turn back to Nora. She has an almost giddy look on her face. "Quick on your feet, macho man."

"What're you—"

Before I can finish, she says, "Where's he now?"

I raise my head and glance in his direction. The problem is, there's no one there. "I think he's gone."

"Gone?" Nora picks her head up. We're both scanning the bar. "There," she says. "By the door."

I turn to the door just in time to see Simon leave. I take another look around the bar. Pool table. Video screen. Along the wall by the restrooms. The guy in the denim shirt is gone too.

Nora responds like a lightning bolt. She grabs my hand and starts pulling. "Let's go."

"Where?"

"We should follow him."

"What? Are you nuts?"

She's still pulling. "C'mon, it'll be fun."

"Fun? Stalking your boss is fun? Getting caught is fun? Getting fired's f—"

"It'll be fun and you know it. Aren't you dying to know where he's going? And what was on the paper?"

"My guess is he got the address for a nearby motel,

where Simon and his denim-man can play Buy Me a Blowjob to their heart's content."

Nora laughs. "Buy Me a Blowjob?"

"I'm making a few assumptions—you know what I mean."

"Of course I know what you mean."

"Good. Then you also know there's nothing gained from a little gossip."

"Is that what you think? That I'm in it for the gossip? Michael, think about it for a second. Edgar Simon is *the* White House Counsel. Lawyer to my father. Now if he gets caught with his lasso out, who do you think's going to be publicly embarrassed? Besides Simon, who else do you think is going to take the black eye?"

Reference number five hits me where it hurts. Reelection's only two months away and Hartson's having a hard enough time as it is. Another black eye'll start the jockeying.

"What if Simon's not in it for the sex?" I ask. "What if he was meeting here for something else?"

Nora stares me down. Her let-me-drive eyes are working overtime. "That's the best reason of all to go."

I shake my head. She's not talking me into this.

"C'mon, Michael, what're you gonna do—sit around here and spend the rest of your life playing *what-if?*"

"Y'know what—after everything else that happened tonight, sitting here is more than enough."

"And that's all you want? That's your big goal in life? To have *enough?*"

She lets the logic sink in before she goes for the kill. "If you don't want to follow, I understand. But I have to go. So give me your keys and I'll be out of your way."

No question about it. She'll be gone. And I'll be here.

I pull the keys from my pocket. She opens her hand.

I once again shake my head and tell myself I won't regret it. "You really think I'm going to let you go alone?"

She shoots me a smile and darts for the door. Without pause, I follow. The moment we get outside, I see Simon's black Volvo pull out from a spot up the street. "There he goes," I say.

We run down the block in a mad dash for my Jeep. "Throw me the keys," she says.

"Not a chance," I reply. "This time, I drive."

CHAPTER 2

It takes a couple of blocks of speeding to regain sight of Simon's car and his "Friend of the Chesapeake" Virginia license plate. "Are you sure that's him?" Nora asks.

"It's definitely him." I drop back and put about a block between us. "I recognize the plates from West Exec."

Within a few minutes, Simon's woven his way through Adams Morgan and is heading up 16th Street. Still a block behind him, we hit Religion Row and pass the dozens of temples, mosques, and churches that dot the landscape.

"Should we get closer?" Nora asks.

"Not if we want to be inconspicuous."

She seems amused by my answer. "Now I know how Harry and Darren feel," she says, referring to her Secret Service agents.

"Speaking of which, do you think they put out an APB on you? I mean, don't they call this stuff in?"

"They'll call the night supervisor and the agent in charge of the House detail, but I figure we've got about two hours before they make it public."

"That long?" I ask, looking at my watch.

"Depends on the incident. If you were driving when we

took off, they'd probably treat it as a kidnapping, which is the primary threat for a First Family member. Beyond that, though, it also depends on the person. Chelsea Clinton got a half hour at the most. Patti Davis got days. I get about two hours. Then they go nuts."

I don't like the sound of that. "What do you mean, nuts? Is that when they send out the black helicopters to hunt us down?"

"There're already trying to hunt us down. In two hours, they'll put us on the police scanners. If that happens, we make the morning news. And every gossip columnist in the country will want to know your intentions."

"No—no way." Since we met, my encounters with Nora have been limited to a reception, a bill-signing ceremony, and the Deputy Counsel's birthday party—all of them White House staff events. At the first, we were introduced; at the second, we spoke; at the third, she asked me out. I think there're only ten people on this planet who would've refused the offer. I'm not one of them. But that doesn't mean I'm ready for the magnifying glass. As I've seen so many times before, the moment you hit that glare of publicity is the exact same moment they burn your ass.

I look back at my watch. It's almost a quarter to twelve. "So that means you have an hour and a half until you become the pumpkin."

"Actually, you're the one who becomes the pumpkin."

She's right about that one. They'll eat me alive.

"Still worried about your job?" she asks.

"No," I say, my eyes locked on Simon's car. "Just my boss."

Simon puts on his blinker, makes a left-hand turn, and weaves his way onto Rock Creek Parkway, whose wooded embankments and tree-shaded trails have favorite-path status among D.C. joggers and bike riders. At rush hour, Rock

Creek Parkway is swarming with commuters racing back to the suburbs. Right now, it's dead-empty—which means Simon can spot us easily.

"Shut off the lights," Nora says. I take her suggestion and lean forward, straining to see the now barely visible road. Right away, the darkness leaves an eerie pit in my stomach.

"I say we just forget it and—"

"Are you really that much of a coward?" Nora asks.

"This has nothing to do with cowardice. It just doesn't make any sense to play private eye."

"Michael, I told you before, this isn't a game to me— we're not playing anything."

"Sure we are. We're—"

"Stop the car!" she shouts. Up ahead, I see Simon's brake lights go on. "Stop the car! He's slowing down!"

Sure enough, Simon pulls off the right-hand side of the road and comes to a complete stop. We're about a hundred feet behind him, but the curve of the road keeps us out of his line of vision. If he looks in his rearview mirror, he'll see nothing but empty parkway.

"Shut the car off! If he hears us . . ." I turn off the ignition and am surprised by the utter silence. It's one of those moments that sound like you're underwater. Staring at Simon's car, we float there helplessly, waiting for something to happen. A car blows by in the opposite direction and snaps us back to the shore.

"Maybe he has a flat tire or—"

"Shhhhh!"

We both squint to see what's going on. He's not too far from a nearby lamppost, but it still takes a minute for our eyes to adjust to the dark.

"Was there anyone in the car with him?" I ask.

"He looked alone to me, but if the guy was lying across the seat . . ."

Nora's hypothesis is interrupted when Simon opens his door. Without even thinking about it, I hold my breath. Again, we're underwater. My eyes are locked on the little white light that I can see through the back window of his car. In silhouette, he fidgets with something in the passenger seat. Then he gets out of the car.

When you stand face-to-face with Edgar Simon, you can't miss how big he is. Not in height, but in presence. Like many White House higher-ups, his voice is charged with the confidence of success, but unlike his peers, who're always raging over the latest crisis, Simon exudes a calmness honed by years of advising a President. That unshakable composure runs from his ironing-board shoulders, to his always-strong handshake, to the perfect part in his perfectly shaded salt-and-pepper hair. A hundred feet in front of us, though, all of that is lost in silhouette.

Standing next to his car, he's holding a thin package that looks like a manila envelope. He looks down at it, then slams the door shut. When the door closes, the loss of the light makes it even harder to see. Simon turns toward the wooded area on the side of the road, steps over the metal guardrail, and heads up the embankment.

"A bathroom stop?" I ask.

"With a *package* in his hand? You think he's bringing reading material?"

I don't answer.

Nora's starting to get fidgety. She unhooks her seatbelt. "Maybe we should we go out and check on—"

I grab her by the arm. "I say we stay here."

She's ready to fight, but before she can, I see a shadow move out from the embankment. A figure steps back over the guardrail and into the light.

"Guess who's back?" I ask.

Nora immediately turns. "He doesn't have the envelope!" she blurts.

"Lower your voi—" I fall silent when Simon looks our way. Nora and I are frozen. It's a short glance and he quickly turns back to his car.

"Did he see us?" Nora whispers. There's a nervousness in her voice that turns my stomach.

"If he did, he didn't react," I whisper back.

Simon opens the door and gets back in his car. Thirty seconds later, he pumps the gas and peels out, leaving a cloud of dust somersaulting our way. He doesn't put his lights on until he's halfway up the road.

"Should we follow him?" I ask.

"I say we stay with the envelope."

"What do you think he has in there? Documents? Pictures?"

"Cash?"

"You think he's a spy?" I ask skeptically.

"I have no idea. Maybe he's leaking to the press."

"Actually, that wouldn't be so bad. For all we know, this is his drop-off."

"It's definitely a drop-off," Nora says. She checks over her shoulder to make sure we're alone. "What I want to know is what they're picking up." Before I can stop her, she's out the door.

I reach to grab her, but it's too late. She's gone—running up the road, headed for the embankment. "Nora, get back here!" She doesn't even pretend to care.

I start the car and pull up alongside her. Her pace is brisk. Determined.

She's going to hate me for this, but I don't have a choice. "Let's go, Nora. We're leaving."

"So leave."

I clench my teeth and realize the most obvious thing of all: She doesn't need me. Still, I give it another go. "For your own sake, get in the car." No response. "Please, Nora, it's not funny—whoever he dropped it for is probably watching us right now." Nothing. "C'mon, there's no reason to—"

She stops in her tracks and I slam on the brakes. Turning my way, she puts her hands on her hips. "If you want to leave, then leave. I need to know what's in the envelope." With that, she climbs over the guardrail and heads up the embankment.

Alone in the car, I watch her disappear. "See you later," I call out.

She doesn't answer.

I give her a few seconds to change her mind. She doesn't. Good, I finally say to myself. This'll be her lesson. Just because she's the First Daughter, she thinks she can— There it is again. That pain-in-the-ass title. That's who she is. No, I decide. Screw that. Forget the title and focus on the person. The problem, however, is it's impossible to separate the two. For better or worse, Nora Hartson *is* the President's daughter. She's also one of the most intriguing people I've met in a long time. And much as I hate to admit it, I actually like her.

"Dammit!" I shout, pounding the steering wheel. Where the hell is my spine?

I rip open the glove compartment, pull out a flashlight, and storm out of the car. Scrambling up the embankment, I find Nora wandering around in the dark. I shine the light in her face and the first thing I see is that grin. "You were worried about me, weren't you?"

"If I abandoned you, your monkeys would kill me."

She approaches me and pulls the flashlight from my hands. "The night's young, baby."

I glance down at my watch. "That's what I'm worried about."

Up the hill, I hear something move through the brush and quickly realize that Simon could've been meeting someone up there. Someone who's still here. Watching us. "Do you think . . ."

"Let's just find the envelope," Nora says, agreement in her voice.

Cautiously walking together, we zigzag up the embankment, which is overflowing with trees. I look up and see nothing but jagged darkness—the treetops hide everything from the sky to the parkway's lamps. All I can do is tell myself that we're alone. But I don't believe it.

"Shine it over here," I tell Nora, who's waving it in every direction. As the flashlight rips through the night, I realize we're going to have to be more systematic about this. "Start with the base of each tree, then work your way upward," I suggest.

"What if he stuffed it high in a tree?"

"You think Simon's the tree-climbing type?" She has to agree with that one. "And let's try to do this fast," I add. "Whoever he left it for—even if they're not here now, they're going to be here any minute." Nora turns the flashlight toward the base of the nearest tree and we're once again encased in underwater silence. As we move up the hill, my breathing gets heavier. I'm trying to look out for the envelope, but I can't stop checking over my shoulder. And while I don't believe in mental telepathy or other paranormal phenomena, I do believe in the human animal's uncanny and unexplainable ability to know when it's being watched. Racing to the top of the embankment, it's a feeling I can't shake. We're not alone.

"What's wrong with you?" Nora asks.

"I just want to get out of here. We can come back to-

morrow with the proper—" Suddenly, I see it. There it is.
My eyes go wide and Nora follows my gaze. Ten feet in
front of us, at the base of a tree with a Z carved into it, is
a single manila envelope.

"Son of a bitch," she says, rushing forward. Her reaction is instantaneous. Pick it up and rip it open.

"No!" I shout. "Don't touch . . ." I'm too late. She's got
it open.

Nora shines the flashlight down into the envelope. "I
don't believe it," she says.

"What? What's in there?"

She turns it upside down and the contents fall to the
ground. One. Two. Three. Four stacks of cash. Hundred
dollar bills.

"Money?"

"Lots of it."

I pick up a stack, remove the First of America billfold,
and start counting. So does Nora. "How much?" I ask when
she's done.

"Ten thousand."

"Me too," I say. "Times two more stacks is forty thousand." Noticing the crispness of the bills, I again flip
through the stack. "All consecutively numbered."

We nervously look at each other. We're sharing the same
thought.

"What should we do?" she finally asks. "Should we take
it?"

I'm about to answer when I see something move in the
large bush on my right. Nora shines the flashlight. No one's
there. Yet I can't shake the feeling that we're being watched.

I pull the envelope from Nora's hands and stuff the four
stacks of bills back inside.

"What're you doing?" she asks.

"Throw me the flashlight."

"Tell me why—"

"Now!" I shout. She gives in, tossing it to me. I shine the light on the envelope, looking to see if there's any writing on it. It's blank. There's a throbbing pain kicking at the back of my neck. My forehead's soaked. Feeling like I'm about to pass out, I quickly return the envelope to the base of the tree. The late summer heat isn't the only thing that's got me sweating.

"You okay?" Nora asks, reading my expression.

I don't answer. Instead, I reach up and pull some leaves from the tree. Putting the flashlight aside, I fold the leaves and scrub them against the edges of the envelope.

"Michael, you can't wipe off fingerprints. It doesn't work like that."

Ignoring her, I keep scrubbing.

She kneels next to me and puts a hand on my shoulder. Her touch is strong, and even in the midst of it all, I have to admit it feels good. "You're wasting your time," she adds.

Naturally, she's right. I toss the envelope back toward the tree. Behind us, a twig snaps and we both turn around. I don't see anyone, but I can feel a stranger's eyes on me.

"Let's get out of here," I say.

"But the people who're going to pick up the package . . ."

I take another glance around the darkness. "To be honest, Nora, I think they're already here."

Looking around, Nora knows something's wrong. It's too quiet. The hairs on my arm stand on edge. They could be hiding behind any tree. On our left, another twig snaps. I grab Nora by the hand and we start walking down the embankment. It doesn't take ten steps for our walk to turn into a jog. Then a run. When I almost trip on a wayward rock, I ask Nora to turn on the flashlight.

"I thought you had it," she says.

Simultaneously, we look over our shoulders. Behind us, at the top of the embankment, is the faint glow of the flashlight. Exactly where I left it.

"You start the car; I'll get the light," Nora says.

"No, I'll get the—"

Once again, though, she's too fast. Before I can stop her, she's headed back up the embankment. I'm about to yell something, but I'm worried we're not alone. Watching her run up the hill, I keep my eyes on her long, lithe arms. Within seconds, though, she fades into the darkness. She said I should get the car, but there's no way I'm leaving her. Slowly, I start heading up the embankment, walking just fast enough to make sure she's in sight. As she gets farther away, I pick up speed. My jog again quickly turns into a run. As long as I can see her, she'll be okay.

Next thing I know, I feel a sharp blow against my forehead. I fall backwards and hit the ground with an uneven thud. Feeling the dampness of the grass seep into the seat of my pants, I look for my attacker. As I prop myself up on an elbow, I feel a slick wetness on my forehead. I'm bleeding. Then I look up and see what put me down: a thick branch from a nearby oak tree. I'm tempted to laugh at my slapstick injury, but I quickly remember why I wasn't looking where I was going. Squinting toward the top of the embankment, I climb to my feet and search for Nora.

I don't see anything. The faint glow of the flashlight is in the same spot, but there's no one moving toward it. I look for shadows, search for silhouettes, and listen for the quiet crunching of broken sticks and long-dead leaves. No one's there. She's gone. I've lost the President's daughter.

My legs go weak as I try to fathom the consequences. Then, without warning, the light moves. Someone's up there. And like a knight with a luminescent lance, the person turns around and barrels straight at me. As the figure approaches, I feel the piercing glow of the light blinding me. I turn away and stumble through the black woods, hands out in front, feeling for trees. I can hear him hopping through bushes, gaining on me. If I drop to the ground, maybe I can trip him up. Suddenly, I slam into a thicket as strong as a wall. I turn toward my enemy as the glaring light hits me in the eyes.

"What the hell happened to your forehead?" Nora asks.

All I can muster is a nervous laugh. The trees still surround us. "I'm fine," I insist. I give her a reassuring nod and we head for my car.

"Maybe we should stay here and wait to see who picks it up."

"No," I say, holding her tightly by the hand. "We're leaving."

At full speed, we race out of the wooded area. When we emerge, I hurdle the guardrail and make a mad dash for my Jeep, which is up the road. If I were alone, I'd probably be there by now, but I refuse to let go of Nora. Slowing myself down, I swing her in front of me, just to make sure she's safe.

The first one to reach the car, she jumps in and slams the door shut. A few seconds later, I join her. Simultaneously, we punch the switches to lock the doors. When I hear that click of solitude, I take an overdue deep breath.

"Let's go, let's go!" she says as I start the car. She sounds scared, but from the gleam in her eyes, you'd think it was a thrill ride.

I hit the gas, turn the wheel, and tear out of there. A sharp U-turn causes the wheels to scream and sends us back toward the Carter Barron/16th Street exit. As I fly forward, my eyes are glued to the rearview mirror. Nora's staring at her sideview.

"No one's there," she says, sounding more wishful than confident. "We're okay."

I stare at the mirror, praying she's right. Hoping to tip the odds in our favor, I give the gas another push. As we turn back onto 16th Street, we're flying. Once again, D.C.'s rugged roads are tossing us around. This time, though, it doesn't matter. We're finally safe.

"How'd I do?" I ask Nora, who's turned around in her seat and staring out the back window.

"Not bad," she admits. "Harry and Darren would be proud."

I laugh to myself just as I hear the screech of tires behind us. I turn to Nora, who's still looking out the back window. Her face is awash in the headlights of the car that's now gaining on us. "Get us out of here," she shouts.

I take a quick survey of the area. We're in the run-down section of 16th Street, not far from Religion Row. There're plenty of streets to turn on, but I don't like the looks of the neighborhood. Too many dark corners and burned-out streetlights. The side streets are filthy. And worst of all, desolate.

I gun the engine and swerve into the left lane just to see if the car follows. When it does, my heart drops. They're a half a block behind and closing fast. "Is it possible they're Secret Service?"

"Not with those headlights. All my guys drive Suburbans."

I check their lights in the rearview mirror. They've got their brights on, so it's hard to see, but the shape and the height tell me it's definitely not a Suburban. "Get down," I say to Nora. Whoever they are, I'm not taking any chances.

"That's not Simon's car, is it?" she asks.

We get our answer in the form of red and blue swirling

lights that engulf our back window. *"Pull over,"* a deep voice blares from a bullhorn mounted to the roof.

I don't believe it. Cops. Smiling, I slap Nora's shoulder. "It's okay. They're cops."

As I pull over, I notice Nora isn't nearly as relieved. Unable to sit still and in full frenzy, she checks the side-view mirror, then looks over her shoulder, then back to the mirror. Her eyes are dancing in every direction as she anxiously claws her way out of her seatbelt.

"What's wrong?" I ask as we come to a stop.

She doesn't respond. Instead, she reaches down for her clunky black purse, which is on the floor in front of her. When she starts rummaging through it, a cold chill runs down my back. This isn't the time to hold back. "Do you have drugs?" I ask.

"No!" she insists. In my rearview mirror, I see a uniformed D.C. police officer approaching my side of the Jeep.

"Nora, don't lie to me. This is—" The police officer taps on my window. Just as I turn around, I hear my glove compartment slam shut.

I lower my window with a forced smile on my face. "Good evening, Officer. Did I do something wrong?" He holds a flashlight above his shoulder and shines it right at Nora. She's still wearing her baseball cap and doing her best to remain unrecognizable. She won't look the cop in the face.

"Is everything okay?" I ask, hoping to divert his attention.

The officer is a thick black man with a crooked nose that gives him the look of a former middleweight boxer. When he leans into the window, all I see are his huge hairless forearms. He uses his chin to motion toward the glove compartment. "What're you hiding there?" he asks Nora.

Damn. He saw her.

"Nothing," Nora whispers.

The cop studies her answer. "Please step out of the car," he says.

I jump in. "Can you tell me wh—"

"Step out of the car. Both of you."

I look at Nora and know we're in trouble. When we were in the woods, she was nervous. But now . . . now Nora has a look I've never seen before. Her eyes are wide and her lips are slightly open. She tries to tuck a stray piece of hair between her ear and the edge of the baseball cap, but her hands are shaking. My world comes to an instant halt.

"Let's go!" the officer barks. "Out of the car."

Nora slowly follows his instructions. As she walks around to the driver's side, the officer's partner approaches the three of us. He's a short black man with an arrogant cop stride. "Everything okay?" he asks.

"Not sure yet." The first cop turns back to me. "Let's see 'em spread."

"Spread? What'd I do?"

He grabs me by the back of the neck and whips me against the side of the Jeep. "Open up!"

I do as he says, but not without protest. "You've got no probable cause to—"

"You a lawyer?" he asks.

I shouldn't have picked this fight. "Yeah," I say hesitantly.

"Then sue me." As he pats me down, he jabs a sharp thumb into my ribs. "Should've told her to calm down," he says. "Now she's going to have to miss work tomorrow."

I don't believe it. He doesn't recognize her. Keeping her head as low as possible, Nora stands next to me and spreads her arms across the side of the Jeep. The second officer pats Nora down, but she's not paying much attention. Like me, she's too busy watching the first officer head for the glove compartment.

From where I'm standing, I see him open the passenger door. As he climbs inside, there's a jingle of handcuffs and keys. Then a quiet click near the dashboard. My mouth goes dry and it's getting harder to breathe. I look over at Nora, but she's decided to look away. Her eyes are glued to the ground. It's not going to be much longer.

"Oh, baby," the officer announces. His voice is filled with shove-it-in-your-face glee. He slams the door shut and strides around to our side of the car. As he approaches, he's holding one hand behind his back.

"What is it?" the second officer asks.

"See for yourself."

I look up, expecting to see Nora's brown prescription vial. Maybe even a stash of cocaine. Instead, the cop is holding a single stack of hundred dollar bills.

Son of a bitch. She took the money.

"Now either of you want to tell me what you're doing driving around with this kinda cash?"

Neither of us says a word.

I look at Nora, and she's paste white. Gone is the cocky and wild vitality that led us through the stop signs, out of the bar, and up the embankment. In its place is that look she's had since we got pulled out of the car. Fear. It's all over her face and it's still making her hands shake. She simply can't be caught with this money. Even if it's not against the law to have it, even if they can't arrest her, this isn't something that's going to be easy to explain. In this neighborhood. With this amount of cash. The drug stories alone will shred what's left of her reputation. *Rolling Stone* will be the least of her problems.

She turns to me and once again opens her soft side. Her

usually tough eyes are welled up with tears. She's begging for help. And like it or not, I'm the only one who can save her. With a few simple words, I can spare her all that pain and embarrassment. Then she and the President . . . I catch myself. No. No, it's not about that. It's like I said before. It's not for her father. Or her title. It's for her. Nora. Nora needs me.

"I asked you a question," the officer says as he waves the pile of cash. "Whose is this?"

I take one last look at Nora. That's all I need. Shoving confidence back into my voice, I turn to the officer and say two words: "It's mine."

CHAPTER 3

Like a judge with a gavel, the officer slowly taps the wad of money in his right hand against the open palm of his left. "Where'd you get it?" he asks, annoyed.

"Excuse me?" I reply. Time to stall.

"Don't yank my chain, boy. Where's someone like you get ten grand in cash?"

"Someone like me? What's that supposed to mean?"

He kicks the rusty bumper on the back of my Jeep. "No offense, but you're not exactly traveling in style."

I shake my head. "You don't know anything about me."

He smirks at my response and knows he's hit a sore spot. "You can't hide who you are—it's written all over your face. And your forehead."

Self-consciously, I touch the cut on my head. The blood's starting to dry. I'm tempted to fight back, but instead let it pass. "Why don't you give me my speeding ticket and I'll be out of your way."

"Listen, Smallville, I don't need to hear your attitude."

"And I don't need to hear your insults. So unless you have some reasonable suspicion of a crime taking place, you have no right to harass me."

"You have no idea what you're—"

"Actually, I have a really good idea. Far more than you're giving me credit for. And since there's no law against carrying money, I'd appreciate it if you'd give me my stuff and write up my ticket. Otherwise, you're risking a harassment suit and a letter to your sergeant that'll be a bitch to explain when you're up for promotion."

Out of the corner of my eye, I see Nora smile. The cop just stands there. The way he scratches his cheek, I can tell he's plenty pissed off. "Vate, do me a favor?" he eventually says to his partner. "They're doing a drug sweep on 14th and M. See if they've broadcasted any lookouts yet. Maybe we'll get lucky."

"It's not like that," I tell him.

He looks at me skeptically. "Let me tell you something, Smallville—pretty-boy, clean-cut white boys like you only come to this neighborhood for two reasons: drugs and whores. Now let's see that license and registration." I hand them over and he turns back to his partner. "Any word yet, Vate?"

"Nothing."

The cop walks away from me and heads back to his car. Five minutes go by and I climb into the driver's seat of my Jeep. Nora's next to me, but she's brutally quiet. She looks my way and offers a faint smile. I try to smile back, but she turns away. I could kill her for taking that cash. Why the hell would she be so stupid? I mean, what would she even use it for? My mind jumps back to her so-called aspirin, but I'm not ready to believe the worst. Not yet.

Staring vacantly out the window, she's resting her chin in the palm of her hand. The way her shoulders sag, I realize the eyes of the world are always on her. It never lets up. Eventually, the cop returns with a pink slip that's marked "Confirmation of Receipt."

"Where's my money?" I ask.

"As long as it's clean, you'll get every cent of it back." Reading my confused expression, he adds, "If our boys on the street are unavailable to make an ID, we can legally hold your cash as the likely proceeds of a criminal act." He's not smiling, but I can tell he's loving every minute of this. "Now does that check out with you, Mr. Attorney-at-Large, or do you want to speak to my sergeant yourself?"

I shake my head, calculating the consequences in my head. "When do I get it back?"

"Give us a call next week." He knows we're not selling drugs; he's just doing this to bust my chops. Leaning in toward the window, he adds, "And just so we're clear . . ." He motions to Nora, who's still sitting next to me. "I'm not blind, boy. I just don't need the headache that comes along with this."

Unnerved by the confidence in his voice, I shrink down in my seat. He knew who she was all along.

"And one last thing . . ." He reaches in the window and slaps a piece of paper against my chest. "Here's your speeding ticket."

Ten minutes later, Nora and I have returned to downtown D.C. and are heading straight for the White House. The adrenaline bath with every spigot open is now finally over. The cut on my forehead hurts and my stomach's churning, but all I really feel is numb. Numb and out of control. My eyes are locked on the road, while my thumbs are shaking as they tap against the top of the steering wheel. The casual repetition is a vain attempt to fight fear, but it's not fooling anyone. Including me. Being nailed with the cash, I'm not only known by the cops—I'm officially, on paper, tied to that money and whatever it was paying for.

Neither of us has said a word since the cops left. Watching me, Nora sees the pace of my thumb-tapping quickly increase. Finally, she breaks the silence. "You doing okay?" she asks.

All I do is nod.

"I appreciate what you did for me back there," she offers.

My eyes stay glued to the road. "It's okay," I say coldly.

"I'm serious."

"I told you, it's okay. It's not that big a—"

"It is a big deal. It really is—that's not something that happens to me every day."

"I would hope not," I blurt angrily.

She pauses for a moment, sensing I'm about to boil. "You know what I mean, Michael. The way you acted . . . it wasn't just for you. You did it for—" She once again stops—this doesn't come naturally for her. "Thank you, Michael. It meant a lot to me."

An hour ago, I would've done anything to hear those words. Right now, though, I couldn't care less.

"Say what you're thinking," she says.

I brake to a sharp stop at a red light. Turning to my right, I take a long, hard look at her. "What do you think I'm thinking? Why the hell'd you take the money?"

She crosses her arms and lets out that little girl laugh.

"You think it's a joke?" I shout.

"Not at all," she says, suddenly serious. "Not after what you did."

I'm not in the mood for compliments. "Just tell me why you took it."

"Honestly? I'm not sure. I ran up, grabbed the flashlight, and saw the envelope. Part of me thought we should take it as evidence, so I went for it. I thought it'd be an easy way to prove Simon was there—but after the first ten grand, I got scared and ran."

It's not a bad explanation, but it comes too easily. For Nora, it's too rational. "So all you wanted was some proof?"

"I'm telling you—that was it."

I keep staring at her.

"What? You don't believe me?"

"Are you kidding? Give me one good reason why I—"

"Michael, I swear to you, if I could take it back I would. There's no easier way to say it." Her voice cracks, catching me by surprise. Right there, her guard drops—and the gnawing feeling inside my chest subsides. "I'm sorry," she cries, leaning in next to me. "I'm so sorry I put you in that position. I never . . . I should've just left it there and walked away."

In the back of my brain, I still picture that brown vial of aspirin . . . but in front of my eyes—all I see is Nora. The look on her face . . . the way her thin eyebrows rise and wilt as she apologizes . . . she's as terrified as I am. Not just for herself. But for me. Glancing down, I notice her hand tightly clutching my own. From there, the words come out of my mouth almost instantly. "It was an impulse. You couldn't have known."

"You still didn't have to do it," she points out.

I nod. She's right.

As we once again start moving toward Pennsylvania Avenue, I have a perfect view of the White House. When I make a left on H Street, it disappears. One sudden move and it's gone. That's all it takes. For both of us.

"Maybe we should . . ."

"We'll take care of it first thing tomorrow," Nora promises, already two steps ahead. "Whatever he's up to, we'll figure it out." Despite her confidence, I can't stop thinking about Simon. But for Nora, as soon as she sees her big white mansion, she's back to her old self. Two people. One body. As I make a sharp right turn, she adds, "Now pull over."

I stop the car on 15th Street, around the corner from the Southeast Gate. At this hour, all of downtown is dead. There's no one in sight.

"Don't you want me to pull up to the gate?"

"No, no—here. I have to get out here."

"Are you sure?"

At first, all she does is nod. "It's just around the corner. And this way I save you from a confrontation with the Service." She looks down at her watch. "I'm in under two hours, but that doesn't mean I'm not going to get my head ripped off."

"That's why I always leave my bodyguards at home," I say, trying to sound half as calm as my date. It's all I can do to keep up.

"Yeah, that's why I picked you," she laughs. "You know how it really is." She's about to say something else, but she stops herself.

"Everything okay?"

Moving closer, she again puts her hand on mine. "People don't do nice things for me, Michael. Not unless they want something. Tonight, you proved that wrong."

"Nora . . ."

"You don't have to say it. Just promise me you'll let me make it up to you."

"You don't have to . . ."

She runs her short nails up my arm. "Actually, I do."

I see that look in her eyes. It's the same one she gave me in the bar. "Nora, no offense, but this isn't the time or the place to—" She wraps a hand around the back of my head and pulls me toward her. Before I can argue, she grips my hair in a tight fist and slides her tongue in my mouth.

There are probably ten heterosexual men in this world who would pull away from this kiss. Again, I'm not one of them. Her smell . . . her taste . . . they instantly overwhelm. I reach up to touch her cheek, but she lets me go.

"Doesn't taste like pumpkin to me," she says.

"That's because I have five more minutes."

Well aware of the time, she sneaks out a grin. "So you're ready to move past the foreplay?"

I look out the front window, then back at Nora. "Here?" I ask nervously.

She leans forward and snakes her hand along the inside of my thigh. Still going, she brushes up the front of my pants. Just like *Rolling Stone*. She's going to do it right here. But as our lips are about to touch, she stops. "Don't believe everything you read, handsome. That stuff'll rot your brain." She pulls her hand away and gives me two light slaps on the cheek. My mouth's still agape as she opens the door.

"What're you—"

She hops out, turns around, and blows me a kiss. "Later, Cookie Puss."

The door slams shut in my face. Out the front window, I watch her run up the block. I put on my brights. The entire time, my eyes stay glued to the curve of her neck. Eventually, she turns the corner and disappears. I reach into my pants and rearrange myself. It's going to be a long ride home.

My alarm screams through the bedroom at five-forty-five the following morning. In college, I used to hit my snooze bar at least six times before I got out of bed. In law school, that number shrank by half. Throughout my first few years of government work, I was still able to cling to a single nine-minute pause, but when I reached the White

House, I lost that too. Now, I'm up at the first buzzer and staggering to the shower. I didn't get home until almost one-thirty, and the way my head's throbbing, the four hours of sleep obviously weren't enough to make me forget about Simon.

It doesn't take long for me to complete my shower/ shave/hair and toothbrush rituals, and I'm proud to say it's been twenty-seven days without hair gel. That's not true, I realize, still blinking myself awake. I used some last night before going out with Nora. Damn. Here we go: hair gel boycott—day one.

I open the door to my apartment and find four newspapers waiting for me: the *Washington Post, Washington Herald, New York Times,* and *Wall Street Journal.* With an anxious spot check, I make sure none of them have front-page stories on White House lawyers and newfound cash. So far, so good. Bringing them inside, I scan more headlines and dial Trey's work number.

In ninety minutes, the President's Senior Staff will have their daily seven-thirty meeting in the Roosevelt Room of the White House. There, the Chief of Staff and the President's closest advisors will discuss a variety of issues that will inevitably become the hot topics of the day—and key issues for the reelection. School uniforms, gun control, whatever's the issue of the moment and whatever's going to bring in votes. In my two years in the Counsel's Office, I've never once been invited to the early Senior Staff meeting. But that doesn't mean I won't know what they're talking about.

"Who needs lovin'?" Trey says, answering the phone.

"Hit me with it," I reply, staring down at the front page of the *Washington Post.*

He doesn't waste any time. "A1, the China story. A2, Chicago welfare. A2, Dem race in Tennessee. A4, Hartson versus Bartlett. A5, Hartson–Bartlett. A6, Hartson–Bartlett. A15, World in Brief: Belfast, Tel Aviv, and Seoul. A17, Federal Page. Editorials—look at Watkins and Lisa Brooks. The Brooks editorial on the census is the one to watch. Wesley's already called her on it."

Wesley Dodds is the President's Chief of Staff. By *her*, Trey means the First Lady. Susan Hartson. Trey's boss. And one of Wesley's closest confidants. If the two of them are already talking about it, it's on today's agenda and on tonight's news.

"What about numbers?" I ask.

"Same as yesterday. Hartson's up by a dozen points, but it's not a solid dozen. I'm telling you, Michael, I can feel it slipping."

"I don't understand—how can we possibly be—"

"Check out the front page of the *Times*."

I flip through the pile and pull it out. There, in full color, is a picture of E. Thomas Bartlett—the opposing side's candidate for President of the United States—sitting in the middle of a semicircle while addressing an enraptured group of senior citizens. They look so happy, you'd think he was FDR himself.

"You gotta be kidding me," I moan.

"Believe me, I've already heard it." In a world where, every day, the number of people who actually read their newspaper is shrinking, the front photo is the *Cliffs Notes* to the news. You get that and the day's yours. "And y'know what the worst part is?" Trey asks. "He hates old people. I heard him say so. *I, Tom Bartlett, hate old people*. Just like that. He said it." Trey pauses. "I think he hates babies too. Innocent babies."

Trey spends the next five minutes selecting the rest of my morning reading. As he tells me each page, I flip to it and draw a big red star next to the headline. In almost

every story, I look for some tie to Simon. It never comes—
but when we're done, four full newspapers are ready for
reading. It's our daily ritual and was inspired by a former
senior staffer who used to have his assistant read the hot
articles to him via cell phone while he drove to work. I
don't have an assistant. And I don't need a cell phone. All
I need is one good friend in the right place.

"So how'd your date go last night?" Trey asks.

"What makes you think I had a date?" I bluff.

"Who do you think you're dealing with here? I see, I
hear, I talk, I move, I shake, I—"

"Pester, gossip, and eavesdrop. I know your tricks."

"Tricks?" he laughs. "If you prick us, do we not bleed?"

"Don't cry to me, Argentina. Do you promise to keep
it to yourself?"

"For you? What do you think? The only reason I know
about it in the first place is because Nora came in here to
make sure it was okay."

"And what'd the First Lady say?"

"Don't know. That's when they closed the door. Son of
a bitch is thick too. I had my ear against it the entire time.
Nothing but mumbling."

"Did anyone else hear?" I ask nervously as I rip a corner off the edge of the newspaper.

"No, it was late and she was using the conference room,
so I was the only one here. Now how'd it go?"

"It was fine . . . it was great. She's really great."

Trey pauses. "What're you not telling me?"

The man is good. Too good.

"Let me guess," he adds. "Early in the night, she pea-
cocked around acting like a bad-ass, and you, like the rest
of America—including me—found yourself slightly turned
on by the thrill of First Family sexual domination. So there
you are . . . she's huffing and puffing, and you're hoping

she'll blow your house down—but just as you hit the magical moment, just as you're about to sign on the skimpily dotted line, you get a whiff of the innocent girl inside— and right there, you back off, determined to save her from her own wild ways."

I pause a second too long. "I don't know what you're—"

"That's it!" Trey cries. "Always raring to play protector. It's the same thing with that old pro bono client you had during the campaign—the more he lied to you and led you along, the more you were determined he needed your help. You do it every time you get the bird-with-a-broken-wing face. Forever ready to save the world . . . except with Nora, swinging to the rescue makes you feel like a rock star . . ."

"Who says I want to be a rock star?"

"You work in the White House, Michael—everyone wants to be a rock star. It's the only reason we take the low pay and the abusive hours . . ."

"Oh, so now you're going to tell me you'd do this job for just anyone? That Hartson and the issues are all bullshit? That all we're here for are the bragging rights?"

Trey takes a long, silent moment to answer. Idealism dies hard—especially when the President's involved. As it is, we spend every day changing lives. Sometimes we get a chance to make them better. Corny as it sounds, both of us know it's a dream job. Eventually, Trey adds, "All I'm saying is, even if you liked her, you wouldn't have asked her out if it didn't give you some sort of inside track to Daddy."

"You really think I'm that conniving?"

"You really think I'm that naive? She's the honcho's kid. One leads right to the other. Whatever you told yourself, the political lizard in you can't ignore it. But take it from me—just because you're dating the President's daughter, doesn't mean you're the First Counsel."

I don't like the way he says that, but I can't help thinking about why Nora and I went out in the first place. She's beautiful and thrillingly wild. It wasn't just about a career move. At least, I pray I'm better than that.

"So are you gonna tell me what happ—"

"Can we please talk about it later?" I interrupt, hoping it'll go away. "Now you got any other predictions for the morning?"

"Take my word on the census. It's gonna be big. Bigger than Sir Elton at Wembley, at the Garden, even live in Australia."

I roll my eyes at the only black person in existence who's obsessed with Elton John. "Anything else, Levon?"

"Census. That's all it's going to be today. Learn how to spell it. Cen-sus."

I hang up the phone and read the census story first. When it comes to the politics of politics, Trey's never wrong. Even among political animals—including myself—there's no one better. For four years, even before I saved his ass on the campaign, he's been the First Lady's favorite; so even though he's only a Deputy Press Secretary in title, it doesn't go into her office without first going through his fingers. And believe me, they're great fingers to know.

I blow through the *Post* while shoveling my way through a quick bowl of Lucky Charms. After last night, I could use them. When the cereal's gone, I go through the *Times* and the *Journal*, then I'm ready to go. With the last paper under my arm, I leave my one-bedroom apartment without making my bed. With the loss of my snooze bar and hair gel, I'm slowly acknowledging that, at twenty-nine years old, adulthood is upon me. The messy bed is simply a final act of denial. And one I won't be giving up soon.

It takes me three stops on the Metro to get from Cleveland Park to Farragut North, the closest station to the White House. On the ride, I knock off half of the *Herald*. I can usually get through all of it, but Simon's escapades make for an easy distraction. If he saw us, it's over. I'll be buried by lunch. Looking down, I see an inky handprint where my fingers grasp the paper.

The train pulls in and it's almost eight o'clock. When I'm done climbing the escalator with the rest of the city's suit-and-tie crowd, I'm hit in the face with a wave of D.C. heat. The remnant summer air is like licking grease, and the intensity of the bright sun is disorienting. But it's not enough to make me forget where I work.

At the Pennsylvania Avenue entrance of the Old Executive Office Building, I force myself up the sharp granite stairs and pull my ID from my suit pocket. The whole area looks different than last night. Not as dark.

The long line of co-workers who're trailing through the lobby and waiting to pass through security makes me keenly aware of one thing: Anyone who says they work in the White House is a liar. And that's the truth. In reality, there are only a hundred and two people who work in the West Wing, where the Oval Office is. All of them are bigshots. The President and his top assistants. Grade-A prime meat.

The rest of us, indeed, just about everyone who *says* they work in the White House, actually works in the Old Executive Office Building, the ornate seven-story behemoth located right next door. Sure, the OEOB houses the majority of the people who work in the Office of the President, and sure, it's enclosed by the same black steel bars that surround the White House. But make no mistake—it's not the White House. Of course, that doesn't stop every single person in there from telling their friends and family that they work in the White House. Myself included.

As the line shortens, I wedge my way in the front door. Inside, under the two-story high ceiling, two uniformed Secret Service officers sit at an elevated welcoming desk and clear visitors into the complex. I try not to let my eye contact linger, but I can't help staring them down. Did they hear about last night? Without a word, one of them turns to me and nods. I freeze, then quickly relax. Checking the rest of the line, he does the same to the guy behind me. Just a friendly hello, I decide.

Those of us with IDs are waiting for the turnstiles. Once there, I put my briefcase on the X-ray conveyor and press my ID against an electronic eye. Below the eye is a keypad that looks like the keypad on a telephone, but without any numbers. Within seconds, my ID registers, the beep sounds, and ten red numbers light up inside the buttons. Every time someone checks in, the numbers appear in a different order, so if someone's watching me, they can't decipher my PIN code. It's the first line of security to enter the OEOB, and easily the most effective.

After entering my code, I walk through the X-ray machine, which, as always, goes off. "Belt," I say to the uniformed Secret Service officer.

He runs his handheld metal detector over my belt and confirms my explanation. Every day we do this, and every day he checks. He usually doesn't give me a second look; today, his gaze hovers for a few seconds too long. "Everything okay?" I ask.

"Yeah . . . sure."

I don't like the sound of that. Does he know? Did Nora's crew put the word out?

No, not these guys. Dressed in their white button-down

security guard uniforms, the Secret Service agents at the front door of the OEOB are different from the plainclothes agents who protect Nora and the First Family. In the hierarchy of the agents, the two worlds rarely mix. I keep telling myself that as I grab my briefcase from the conveyor belt and head toward my office.

Just as I open the door to Room 170, I see Pam running straight at me. "Turn around—we're going early," she shouts, her thin blond hair wisping behind her.

"When did they—"

"Just now." She grabs me by the arm and spins me around. "Senior Staff went early, so Simon bumped us up. Apparently, he's got somewhere to be." Before I can get a word out, she adds, "Now what happened to your forehead?"

"Nothing," I say, looking at my watch. "What time's it called for?"

"Three minutes ago," she answers.

Simultaneously, we both race up the hallway. Lucky for us, we have first-floor offices—which means we also have the shortest walk to the West Wing. And the Oval. To an outsider, it might not seem like much of a perk, but to those of us in the OEOB, it matters. Proximity is all.

As the heels of our shoes slam against the black and white checkerboard marble floor, I see the West Exec exit straight ahead. Pulling open one of the double doors, we step outside and cross the closed-off street between the OEOB and the White House. On the other side of the narrow road, we head for the awning that leads to the West Wing and make our way through two more sets of doors. Ahead of us, a uniformed Secret Service officer with buzzed black hair sits at a table and checks the IDs that hang around our necks. If our IDs had an orange background, he'd know we only have access to the OEOB and he'd have to stop us. A blue background means we can go almost anywhere, including the West Wing.

"Hey, Phil," I say, instinctively slowing down. This is the real test—if word's out, I'm not getting in.

Phil takes one look at my blue background and smiles. "What's the rush?"

"Big meetings, big meetings," I reply calmly. If he knew, he wouldn't be smiling.

"Someone's got to save the world," he says with a nod. "Have a good one now." At this point, his job is done. Once we're past him, he's supposed to let us go. Instead, he pays us the highest compliment. As we turn toward the elevator, he hits a button below his desk and the elevator door on my left opens. When we step inside, he pushes something else and the button for the second floor lights up. He doesn't do that for just anyone—only for the people he likes. Which means he finally knows who I am. "Thanks!" I shout as the doors close. As I collapse against the back of the elevator, I have to smile. Whatever Simon saw, it's clear he's kept his mouth shut. Or better yet, maybe he never knew we were there.

Reading the joy on my face, Pam says, "You love it when Phil does that, don't you?"

"Who wouldn't?" I play along.

"I don't know . . . people with well-adjusted priorities?"

"You're just jealous because he doesn't open it for you."

"Jealous?" Pam laughs. "He's a doorman with a gun—you think he has any bearing on your place in the food chain?"

"If he does, I know where I'm going: onward and upward, honey." I throw in the "honey" just to push Pam's buttons. She's too smart to fall for it.

"Speaking of fruitless pandering to the top, how'd your date go last night?"

That's the true beauty of Pam. Guerrilla honesty. Glancing at the tiny video camera in the corner, I reply, "I'll tell you later."

She looks up and falls silent. A second later, the elevator doors open.

The second floor of the West Wing houses some of the best high-powered offices, including the First Lady's personal office and the one immediately on my right—the last place I want to be right now: our destination—the office of Edgar Simon, Counsel to the President.

CHAPTER 4

Racing through the already-open double doors and the waiting area where Simon's assistant sits, Pam and I make a sharp right into Simon's office. Hoping to sneak in quietly, I check to see if . . . Damn—the gang's already waiting. Crowded around a walnut conference table that looks more like an antique dining room set, six associates sit with their pens and legal pads primed. At one end of the table, in his favorite wingback chair, is Lawrence Lamb, Simon's Deputy Counsel. At the other end is an empty seat. Neither of us takes it. That's Simon's.

As Counsel, Simon advises the President on all legal matters arising in the White House. Can we require blood tests to nail deadbeat dads? Is it okay to limit cigarette companies' right to advertise in youth-oriented magazines? Does the President have to pay for his seat on Air Force One if he's using it to fly to a fund-raiser? From inspecting new legislation to researching new judicial nominees, the Counsel and the seventeen associates who work for him, including Pam and myself, are the law firm for the presidency. Sure, most of our work's reactive: In the West Wing, the Senior Staff decides *what* ideas the President should pursue, then we get called in to do the *how* and *if*. But as any lawyer knows, there's plenty of power in *how*s and *if*s.

In the corner of the dark-wood-paneled room, hunkered down on the all-powerful couch, the Vice President's Counsel is whispering to the Counsel for the Office of Administration, and the Legal Advisor for the National Security Counsel is whispering to the Deputy Legal Counsel for OMB. Bigshots talking to bigshots. In the White House, some things never change. Squeezing our way toward the back of the room, Pam and I stand with the rest of the seatless associates and wait for Simon to arrive. Within a few minutes, he walks in and takes his seat at the head of the table.

My eyes shoot to the floor as fast as they can.

"What's wrong?" Pam asks me.

"Nothing." My head's still down, but I steal a quick peek at Simon. All I want to know is whether he saw us last night. I assume it'll show on his face. To my surprise, it doesn't. If he's hiding something, you wouldn't know it. His salt-and-pepper hair is as perfectly combed as it was on Rock Creek Parkway. He doesn't look tired; his shoulders stand wide. As far as I can tell, he hasn't even glanced at me.

"Are you sure you're okay?" Pam persists.

"Yeah," I answer. I slowly pick my head up. That's when he does the most incredible thing of all. He looks right at me and smiles.

"Is everything okay, Michael?" he asks.

The entire room turns and waits for my answer. "Y-Yeah," I stammer. "Just waiting to get started."

"Good, then let's get right to it." As Simon makes a few general announcements, I try my best to wipe the bewilderment from my face. If I hadn't looked him straight in the eyes, I wouldn't believe it. He didn't even take a second glance at the cut on my forehead. Whatever happened last night, Simon doesn't know I was there.

"There's one last thing I want to comment on and then we can get to new business," Simon explains. "In this morning's *Herald*, an article made reference to a birthday party we threw for our favorite assistant to the President." All eyes shoot to Lawrence Lamb, who refuses to acknowledge even the slightest bit of attention. "The article went on to mention that the Vice President was noticeably absent from the invite list, and that the crowd was buzzing with rumors of why he wasn't there. Now, in case you've already forgotten, besides the President and the First Family, the only other people in that room were a handful of senior staffers and approximately fourteen representatives from this office." He rests his hands flat on the desk and lets the silence drive home his point.

Without question, he has us. I may never look at him the same way again, but when he turns it on, Edgar Simon is an incredible lawyer. A master of saying it without saying it, he takes a quick scan of everyone in the room. "Whoever it was—it has to stop. They're not asking those questions to make us look good, and this close to reelection, you should all be smarter than that. Am I making myself clear?"

Slowly, a grumble of acquiescence runs through the room. No one likes to be blamed for leaks. I stare at Simon knowing it's the least of his problems.

"Great, then let's put it behind us and move on. Time for some new business. Around the room, starting with Zane."

Looking up from his legal pad, Julian Zane smirks wide. It's the third meeting in a row that he's been called on first. Pathetic. As if any of us is even counting.

"Still haggling with SEC reform," Julian says in a self-important tone that slaps us all across the face. "I'm meeting with the Speaker's counsel today to hit a few of the issues—he wants it so bad, he's skipping recess. After that, I think I'll be ready to present the decision memo."

I cringe as Julian blurts his last few syllables. The decision memo is our office's official policy recommendation on an issue. And while we do the research and writing for it, the finished product is usually presented to the President by Simon. Every once in a while, we get to do the presentation too. *"Mr. President, here's what we're looking at . . ."* It's the ultimate White House carrot—and something I've been waiting two years for.

Last week, Simon announced that Julian was presenting. It's no longer news. Still, Julian can't help but mention it.

Shading his eyes as he checks his schedule, Simon reveals the same silhouette I saw in his car. I try to bury it, but I can't. All I see is that forty grand—ten of which is now linked to me.

Simon shoots me a look, and a hiccup of bile stabs up from my stomach. If he does know, he's playing games. And if he doesn't . . . I don't care if he doesn't. As soon as we're out of here, I'm calling in some favors.

With a quick nod, we move to the person on Julian's right. Daniel L. Serota. A shared smile engulfs the rest of the room. Here comes Danny L.

Everyone hired by the Counsel's Office brings their own personal strength to the office. Some of us are smart, some are politically connected, some are good at dealing with the press, and some are good at dealing with pressure.

Danny L? He's good at dealing with large documents.

He scratches the front of his glasses with his fingernails, trying to remove a smudge. As always, his dark hair is out of control. "The Israelis had it right. I went through every MEMCON we have on file," he explains, referring to the memoranda of conversations, which are taken by aides when the President talks to a head of state. "The President and the Prime Minister never even speculated about how the hardware got there. And they certainly never mentioned U.N. interference."

"And you got through every MEMCON that was in Records Management?" Simon asks.

"Yeah. Why?"

"There were over fifteen thousand pages in there."

Danny L. doesn't skip a beat. "So?"

Simon shakes his head, while Pam leans over to pat Danny L. on the back. "You're my hero," she tells him. "You really are."

As the laughter dies down, I continue to fight my panic. Simon's enjoying himself too much. That doesn't bode well for what he was doing in the woods. At first, I liked to think he was a victim. Now I'm not so sure.

My mind churns through the possibilities as Pam takes her turn. The associate in charge of background checks for judicial appointments, Pam knows all the dirt about our country's future judges. "We have about three that should be ready for announcement by the end of the week," she explains, "including Stone for the Ninth Circuit."

"What about Gimbel?" Simon asks.

"On the D.C. Circuit? He's one of the three. I'm waiting for some final paperw—"

"So everything checks out with him? No problems?" Simon interrupts in a skeptical tone.

Something's wrong. He's setting Pam up.

"As far as I know, there're no problems," Pam says hesitantly. "Why?"

"Because at the Senior Staff meeting this morning, someone told me there are rumors floating around that Gimbel had an illegitimate child with one of his old secretaries. Apparently, he's been sending them hush money for years."

The consequences quickly sink in. As the room falls silent, all eyes turn toward Pam. Simon's going to hammer her on this one. "We've got an election that's two months away," he begins, his tone unnervingly composed, "and a President who just signed major legislation against deadbeat dads. So what do we do for an encore? We tell the world that Hartson's current judicial candidate has intimate knowledge of our newest law." Across the room, I see Julian and a few others laugh. "Don't even snicker," Simon warns. "In all the time I've been here, I can't remember the last time I've seen all three branches of government collide so embarrassingly."

"I'm sorry," Pam says. "He never mentioned anything abou—"

"Of course he didn't mention it—that's why it's called a background check." Simon's voice remains calm, but he's losing his patience. He must've taken plenty of heat in Senior Staff to be this worked up—and with Bartlett's campaign slowly closing in, all the bigshots are on edge. "Isn't that your job, Ms. Cooper? Isn't that the point?"

"Take it easy, Edgar," a female voice interrupts. I turn to my right and see Caroline Penzler wagging a finger from the couch. Dressed in a cheap wool blazer despite the warm weather, the heavyset Caroline is Pam's supervisor on nominations. She's also one of the few people in the room who's not afraid of Simon. "If Gimbel kept it quiet and there's no paper trail, it's almost impossible for us to know."

Appreciating the save, Pam nods a silent thank-you to her mentor.

Still, Simon's unimpressed. "She didn't ask the right

questions," he blasts at Caroline. "That's the only reason
it went through your legs."

Caroline shoots an angry look at Simon. There's a long
history between these two. When Hartson first got elected,
they were both up for the Counsel top spot. Caroline was
a friend of the First Lady. She lobbied hard, but Simon
won. And the white boys ruled. "Maybe you're not appreciating the process," Caroline says. "There's a difference
between asking the hard questions and asking every question under the sun."

"In an election year, there's no difference. You know
how opinions run—every little detail gets magnified. Which
means every question's an important question!"

"I know how to do my job!" Caroline explodes.

"That's clearly up for debate," Simon growls back.

Refusing to let Caroline take the fall, Pam jumps back
in. "Sir, I appreciate what you're saying, but I've been calling him for days. He keeps saying he's—"

"I don't want to hear it. If Gimbel doesn't have the time,
he doesn't have the nomination. Besides, he's a friend of
the President. For that reason alone, he'll sit for the questions."

"I tried, but he—"

"He's a friend of the President. He understands."

Before Pam can respond, someone else says, "That's not
true." At the other end of the table, Deputy Counsel
Lawrence Lamb continues, "He's not a friend of the President." A tall, thick man with crystal blue eyes and a long
neck that cranes slightly lower from years of hunching over
to talk to people, Lawrence Lamb has known President
Hartson since their high school days in Florida. As a result, Lamb is one of the President's closest friends and most
trusted advisors. Which means he has what every one of
us wants: the President's ear. And if you have the ear, you

have power. So when Lamb tells us that Gimbel isn't a friend of the President, we know the argument's over.

"I thought they went to law school together," Simon persists, trying not to lose face.

"That doesn't mean he's a friend," Lamb says. "Trust me on this one, Edgar."

Simon nods. It's over.

"I'll ask him about the rumors and the child," Pam finally adds, breaking the silence of the room. "Sorry I missed it."

"Thank you," Simon replies. Determined to move on, he turns to me and signals that it's my turn to present.

Lowering my legal pad, I step forward and tell myself that nothing's changed. Whatever I saw last night, this is still my moment. "Been working on Justice's wiretap issue. When it comes right down to it, they want something called roving wiretap authority. Currently, if Justice or the FBI wants to wiretap someone, they can't just say, 'Jimmy "The Fist" Machismo is a lowlife, so give us the wiretaps and we'll set him up.' Instead, they have to list the exact places where suspicious activity is taking place. If they change the rule and get roving authority, they can be far less specific in their requests and they can put the taps wherever they want."

Simon runs his fingers along his beard, carefully weighing the issue. "It's got great tough-on-crime potential."

"I'm sure it does," I reply. "But it throws civil liberties out the window."

"Oh, c'mon," Julian interrupts. "Put away the tear towel. This should be a no-brainer—endorsed by Justice, endorsed by the FBI, hated by criminals—this issue's bulletproof."

"Nothing's bulletproof," I shoot back. "And when the *New York Times* throws this on the front page and says Hartson's now got the right to eavesdrop in your home, without reasonable suspicion, everyone from the liberal media to the conspiracy conservatives is going to be tearing hair. Just what Bartlett needs. It's not an issue for an election year, and more important, it's not right."

"It's not right?" Julian laughs.

Pompous political ass. "That's my opinion. You have a problem with that?"

"Back to your corners," Simon intercedes, waving us apart. "Michael, we'll talk about it later. Anything else?"

"Just one. On Tuesday, I got the OMB memo on the new Medicaid overhaul. Apparently, in one of their long-term-care programs, HHS wants to deny benefits to people with criminal records."

"Another reelection tough-on-crime scheme. It's amazing how creative we can be when our jobs are on the line."

I search his eyes, wondering what he means by that. Cautiously, I add, "The problem is, I think it conflicts with the President's Welfare to Work Program and his rehabilitation stance in the Crime Bill. HHS may think it's a great way to save cash, but you can't have it both ways."

Simon takes a second to think about it. The longer he's silent, the more he agrees. "Write it up," he finally says. "I think you may have someth—"

"Here you go," I interrupt as I pull a two-page memo from my briefcase. "They're about to go out with it, so I made it a priority."

"Thanks," he says as I pass the memo forward. I nod, and Simon casually turns back to the group. He's accustomed to overachievers.

When we finish going around the room, Simon moves to new business. Watching him, I'm truly amazed—through it all, he looks and sounds even calmer than when he started. "Not much to report," he begins in his always steady tone.

"They want us to take another look at this thing with the census—"

My hand shoots up first.

"All yours, Michael. They want to revisit the outcome differences between counting noses one by one and doing a statistical analysis."

"Actually, there was an editorial in the—"

"I saw it," he interrupts. "That's why they're begging for facts. Nothing elaborate, but I want to give them an answer by tomorrow." Simon takes one last survey of the room. "Any questions?" Not a hand goes up. "Good. I'm available if you need me." Standing from his seat, Simon adjourns the meeting.

Immediately, half of the associates head for the door, including Pam and me. The other half stay and form a line to talk to Simon. For them, it's simply the final act in the ego play—their projects are so top secret, they can't possibly be talked about in front of the rest of us.

As I head for the door, I see Julian staking out a spot in the line. "What's the matter?" I ask him. "You don't like sharing with the rest of the class?"

"It's amazing, Garrick, you always know exactly what's going on. That's why he puts you on the big, sexy issues like the census. Oooooh, baby, that sucker's gold. Actuaries, here I come."

I pretend to laugh along with his joke. "Y'know, I've always had a theory about you, Julian. In fourth grade, when you used to have show-and-tell, you always tried to bring yourself, didn't you?"

"You think that's funny, Garrick?"

"Actually, I think it's real funny."

"Me too," Pam says. "Not hysterical, but funny."

Realizing he'll never survive a confrontation against the two of us, Julian goes nuclear. "Both of you can eat shit."

"Sharp comeback."

"Well done."

He storms around us to get back in line, and Pam and I head for the door. As we leave, I glance over my shoulder and catch Simon quickly turning away. Was he looking at us? No, don't read into it. If he knew, I'd know. I'd have to.

Avoiding the line at the elevator, we take the stairs and make our way back to the OEOB. As soon as we're alone, I see Pam's mood change. Staring straight down as we walk, she won't say a word.

"Don't beat yourself up over this," I tell her. "Gimbel didn't disclose it—you couldn't have known."

"I don't care what he told me; it's my job to know. I've got no business being here otherwise. I mean, as it is, I can barely figure out what I'm even doing anymore."

Here she goes—the yin to her own yang—toughness turned in on itself. Unlike Nora, when Pam's faced with criticism, her first reaction is to rip herself apart. It's a classic successful person's defense mechanism—and the easiest way for her to lower expectations.

"C'mon, Pam, you know you belong here."

"Not according to Simon."

"But even Caroline said—"

"Forget the rationalizing. It never works. I want to take some time to be mad at myself. If you want to cheer me up, change the subject."

Aaaand we're back—guerrilla honesty. "Okay, how's about some office gossip: Who do you think leaked the birthday party?"

"No one leaked it," she says as we return to the sterile hallways of the OEOB. "He just used it to make a point."

"But the *Herald*—"

"Open your eyes, boy. It was a party for Lawrence Lamb,

First Friend. Once word got out about that, the whole complex came running. No one misses a social function with the President. Or with Nora."

I stop right in front of Room 170. Our office. "You think that's why I went?"

"You telling me otherwise?"

"Maybe."

Pam laughs. "You can't even lie, can you? Even that's too much."

"What're you talking about?"

"I'm talking about your unfailing predisposition to always be the Boy Scout."

"Oh, and you're so hyper-cool?"

"Life of a city girl," she says, proudly brushing some invisible lint from her shoulder.

"Pam, you're from Ohio."

"But I lived in—"

"Don't tell me about New York. That was law school— you spent half the time in your room, and the rest in the library. Besides, three years does not hyper-cool make."

"It makes sure I'm not a Boy Scout."

"Will you stop already with that?" Before I can finish, my beeper goes off. I look down at the digital screen, but don't recognize the phone number. I unclip it from my belt and read the message: "Call me. Nora."

My eyes show no reaction. My voice is super-smooth. "I have to take this one," I tell Pam.

"What's she want?"

I refuse to answer.

She's laughing again. "Do you sell cookies also, or is that just a Girl Scout thing?"

"Kiss my ass, homegrown."

"Not on the very best day of your life," she says as I head for the door.

I pull open the heavy oak door of our office and step into the anteroom that leads to three other offices. Three doors: one on the right, one in the middle, one on the left. I've nicknamed it the Lady or the Tiger Room, but no one ever gets the reference. Barely big enough to hold the small desk, copier, and coffee machine we've stuffed into it, the anteroom is still good for a final moment of decompression.

"Okay, fine," Pam says, moving toward the door on the right. "If it makes you feel any better, you can put me down for two boxes of the thin mints."

I have to admit the last one's funny, but there's no way I'm giving her the satisfaction. Without turning around, I storm into the room on the left. As I slam the door behind me, I hear Pam call out, "Send her my love."

By OEOB standards, my office is a good one. It's not huge, but it does have two windows. And one of the building's hundreds of fireplaces. Naturally, the fireplaces don't work, but that doesn't mean having one isn't a notch on the brag belt. Aside from that, it's typical White House: old desk that you hope once belonged to someone famous, desk lamp that was bought during the Bush administration, chair that was bought during the Clinton administration, and a vinyl sofa that looks like it was bought during the Truman administration. The rest of the office makes it mine: flameproof file cabinets and an industrial safe, courtesy of the Counsel's Office; over the fireplace, a court artist's rendition of me sitting in the moot court finals, courtesy of Michigan Law School; and on the wall above my desk, the White House standard, courtesy of my ego: a signed picture of me and President Hartson after one of his radio addresses, thanking me for my service.

Throwing my briefcase on the sofa, I head for my desk. A digital screen attached to my phone says that I have twenty-two new calls. As I scroll through the call log, I can see the names and phone numbers of all the people who called. Nothing that can't wait. Anxious to get back to Nora, I take a quick glance at the toaster, a small electronic device that bears an uncanny resemblance to its namesake and was left here by the office's previous occupant. A small screen displays the following in digital green letters:

POTUS: OVAL OFFICE
FLOTUS: OEOB
VPOTUS: WEST WING
NORA: SECOND FLOOR RESIDENCE
CHRISTOPHER: MILTON ACADEMY

There they are—The Big Five. The President, the VP, and the First Family. The principals. Like Big Brother, I instinctively check all of their locations. Updated by the Secret Service as each principal moves, the toaster is there in case of emergency. I've never once heard of anyone using it, but that doesn't mean it's not everyone's favorite toy. The thing is, I'm not concerned with the President of the United States, or the First Lady, or the VP. What I'm really looking at is Nora. I pick up the phone and dial her number.

She answers on the first ring. "Sleep okay last night?"

Clearly, she's got the same caller ID we do. "Somewhat. Why?"

"No reason—I just wanted to make sure you were okay. Again, I'm really sorry I put you in that position."

Sad as it is to admit, I love hearing the concern in her voice. "I appreciate the thought." Turning toward the toaster, I add, "Where am I calling you anyway?"

"You tell me—you're the one staring at the toaster."

I smile to myself. "No, I'm not."

"I told you last night—you're a bad liar, Michael."

"Is that why you were so intent on washing my mouth out?"

"If you're talking about my tongue down your throat, that was just to give you something exciting to think about."

"And that's your idea of excitement?"

"No, excitement would be if that little contraption you're staring at showed you exactly what I'm doing with my hands."

The woman's ruthless. "So this thing really works?"

"Don't know. They only give them to staff."

"So that's it, huh? Now I'm just staff?"

"You know what I mean. I usually . . . the way it works . . . I've never had the chance to watch myself," she stutters.

I can't believe it—she's actually embarrassed. "It's okay," I tell her. "I'm only joking."

"No, I know . . . I just . . . I don't want you to think I'm some spoiled snob."

I pause, lost in the almost scientific curiosity of what she finds important. "Well get it out of your head," I eventually say. "If I thought you were a snob, I wouldn't have gone out with you in the first place."

"That's not true," she teases. She's right. But the playfulness in her tone tells me she admires the attempt. Being Nora, her recovery's immediate. "So where does it say I am?" she adds, turning my attention back to the toaster.

"Second Floor Residence."

"And what does that tell you?"

"I have no idea—I've never been up there."

"You've never been up here? You should come."

"Then you should invite me." I'm proud of myself for that one. The invitation should be just around the corner.

"We'll see," she says.

"Oh, so now I haven't passed that test yet? What do I have to do? Act interested? Show a steady follow-up? Go to some group dinner and get checked out by your girl-friends?"

"Huh?"

"Don't act all coy—I know how it is with women—everything's a group decision these days."

"Not with me."

"And you expect me to believe that?" I ask with a laugh. "C'mon, Nora, you have friends, don't you?"

For the first time, she doesn't answer. There's nothing but dead air. My smile sags to a flat line. "I . . . I didn't mean . . ."

"Of course I have friends," she finally stammers. "Meanwhile, have you seen Simon yet?"

I'm tempted to go back, but this is more important. "At the meeting this morning. He walked in and the whole world hit slow motion. The thing is, watching his reaction, I don't think he saw us. I would've seen it in his eyes."

"Suddenly you're the arbiter of truth?"

"Mark my words, he didn't know we were there."

"So have you decided what you're going to do?"

"What's to decide? I have to report him."

She thinks about this for a second. "Just be careful abou—"

"Don't worry, I'm not going to tell anyone you were there."

"That's not what I was worried about," she shoots back, annoyed. "I was going to say, be careful who you go to with this. Considering the time period, and the person in-volved, this thing's going to *Hindenburg*."

"You think I should wait until after the election?"

There's a long pause on the other line. It's still her father.

Finally, she says, "I can't answer that. I'm too close." I can hear it in her voice. It's only a twelve-point lead. She knows what could happen. "Is there a way to keep it out of the press?" she asks.

"Believe me, there's no way I'm throwing this to the press. They'd eat us alive by lunch."

"Then who do you go to?"

"I'm not sure, but I think it should be someone in here."

"If you want, you can tell my dad."

There it is again. Her dad. Every time she says it, it seems that much more ridiculous. "Too big," I say. "Before it goes to him, I want someone to do a little bit more research."

"Just to make sure we're right?"

"That's what I'm worried about. The moment this gets out, we're going to wreck Simon's career. And that's not something I take lightly. In here, once the finger's pointed at you, you're gone."

Nora's been on the receiving end for too long. She knows I'm right. "Is there someone you have in mind?"

"Caroline Penzler. She's in charge of ethics for the White House."

"Can you trust her?"

I pick up a nearby pencil and tap the eraser against my desk. "I'm not sure—but I know exactly who to ask."

CHAPTER 5

Leaving my office, I cross through the anteroom and head straight for Pam's. The door is always open, but I still give her a courtesy knock. "Anyone home?"

By the time she says "Come in," I'm already standing across from her desk. The setup of her office is a mirror image of mine, right down to the nonworking fireplace. As always, the differences are on the walls, where Pam has replaced my ego items with two personal effects: over her couch, a blown-up photograph of the President when he spoke at the Rock and Roll Hall of Fame in Cleveland, her hometown; and over her desk, an enormous American flag, which was a gift from her mother when Pam first got the job. Typical Pam, I think to myself. Apple pie at heart.

Facing the computer table that runs perpendicular to her desk, Pam is typing furiously with her back to me. As is her usual work mode, her thin blond hair is pulled back in a tight twist held by a red clip. "What's up?" she asks without turning around.

"I've got a question for you."

She flips through a pile of papers, looking for something in particular. When she finds it, she says, "I'm listening."

"Do you trust Caroline?"

Pam immediately stops typing and turns my way. Raising an eyebrow, she asks, "What's wrong? Is it Nora?"

"No, it's not Nora. It has nothing to do with Nora. I just have a question about this issue I'm working on."

"And you expect me to believe that?"

I'm too smart to argue with her. "Just tell me about Caroline."

Biting the inside of her cheek, she studies me carefully.

"Please," I add. "It's important."

She shakes her head and I know I'm in. "What do you want to know?"

"Is she loyal?"

"The First Lady thinks so."

I nod at the reference. A longtime friend of the First Lady, Caroline met Mrs. Hartson at the National Parkinson's Foundation in Miami, where Mrs. Hartson mentored and encouraged her to take night classes at the University of Miami Law School. From there, the First Lady brought her to the Children's Legal Defense Fund, then to the campaign, and finally, to the White House. Long battles forge the strongest bonds. I just want to know, *how strong?* "So if I tell her something vitally important, can I trust her to keep a secret?"

"Help me out with what you mean by *vitally*."

I sit in the chair in front of her desk. "It's big."

"Front-page big or cover-of-*Newsweek* big?"

"*Newsweek*."

Pam doesn't flinch. "Caroline's in charge of screening all the bigshots: Cabinet members, ambassadors, the Surgeon General—she opens their closets and makes sure we can live with their skeletons."

"So you think she's loyal?"

"She's got dirt on just about every hotshot in the executive branch. That's why the First Lady put her here. If she's not loyal, we're dead."

Falling silent, I lean forward and rest my elbows against my knees. It's true. Before anyone's nominated, they go through at least one confession session with Caroline. She knows the worst about everyone: who drinks, who's done drugs, who's had an abortion, and who's hiding a summer home from their wife. Everyone has secrets. Myself included. Which means if you expect to get anything done, you can't disqualify everyone. "So I shouldn't worry?" I ask.

Pam stands up and crosses around to the other side of her desk. Sitting in the seat next to me, she looks me straight in the eye. "Are you in trouble?"

"No, not at all."

"It's Nora, isn't it? What'd she do?"

"Nothing," I say, pulling back a little. "I can handle it."

"I'm sure you can. You always can. But if you need any help at all . . ."

"I know—you'll be there."

"With bells on, my friend. And maybe even a tambourine."

"Honestly, Pam, that means more than you know." Realizing that the longer I sit here, the more she's going to pry, I stand from my seat and head for the door. I know I shouldn't say another word, but I can't help myself. "So you really think she's okay?"

"Don't worry about Caroline," Pam says. "She'll take care of you."

I'm about to head over to Caroline's when I hear the phone in my office ring. Running inside, I check the dig-

ital screen to see who it is. It's the number from before.
Nora. "Hello?" I say, picking it up.

"Michael?" She sounds different. Almost out of breath.

"Are you okay?" I ask.

"Have you spoken to her yet?"

"Caroline? No, why?"

"You're not going to tell her I was there, are you? I
mean, I don't think you should . . ."

"Nora, I already told you I wouldn't—"

"And the money—you're not going to say I took the
money, right?" Her voice is racing with panic.

"Of course not."

"Good. Good." Already, she's calming down. "That's all
I wanted to know." I hear her take a deep breath. "I'm
sorry—I didn't mean to freak like that—I just started getting a little nervous."

"Whatever you say," I tell her, still confused by the outburst. I hate hearing that crack in her voice—all that confidence crushed to nothing. It's like seeing your dad cry;
all you want to do is stop it. And in this case, I can. "You
don't have to worry," I add. "I've got it all taken care of."

Walking down the hall to Caroline's office is easy. So
is knocking on her office door. Stepping inside is a piece
of cake, and hearing the door slam behind me is an ice
cream sundae. But when I see Caroline, sitting at her desk
with her jet black dyed hair spreading on the shoulders of
her black wool blazer, everything that I've been holding
together—all of it—suddenly falls apart. My fear has a
face. And before I can even say hello, the back of my neck
floods with sweat.

"Take a seat, take a seat," she offers as I almost collapse in front of her desk. Accepting the invitation, I lower
myself into one of her two chairs. Without saying a word,

I watch her pour four sugar packets into an empty mug. One by one, she rips each one open. In the left corner of the room, the coffee's almost done brewing. Now I know where she gets her energy. "How's everything going?" she asks.

"Busy," I reply. "Really busy." Over Caroline's shoulder, I see her version of the ego wall: forty individual frames filled with thank-you notes written by some of Washington's most powerful players. Secretary of State. Secretary of Defense. Ambassador to the Vatican. Attorney General. They're all up there, and they were all cleared by Caroline.

"Which one's your favorite?" I ask, hoping to slow things down.

"Hard to say. It's like asking which of your children is your favorite."

"The first one," I say. "Unless they move away and never call. Then it's the one who lives closest."

In her line of work, Caroline spends every day having uncomfortable conversations with people. As a result, she's seen just about every different manifestation of nervousness that exists. And from the sour look on her face, making jokes ranks near the bottom of her list. "Is there something I can help you with, Michael?"

My eyes stay locked on her desk, which is submerged under stacks of paper, file folders, and two presidential seal ashtrays. There's a portable air filter in the corner of the room, but the place still reeks of stale cigarettes, which, besides collecting thank-you notes, are Caroline's most obvious habit. To help me along, she takes off her glasses and offers a semiwarm glance. She's trying to inspire faith and imply that I can trust her. But as I pick my head up, all I can think is that it's the first time in two years that I've really looked at her. Without her glasses, her almond-shaped hazel eyes seem less intimidating. And although her furrowed brow and thin lips keep her appearance professional, she honestly looks worried about me. Not worried like Pam, but, for a woman in her late forties who's still mostly a stranger, truly concerned.

"Do you need a drink of water?" she asks.

I shake my head. No more stalling.

"Is this a Counsel's Office question or an ethics issue?" she asks.

"Both," I say. This is the hard part. My mind's racing— searching for the perfect words. Yet no matter how much I mentally practiced on the way over, there's nothing like removing the net and doing it for real. As I'm about to step out on the tightrope, I run through the story one last time, hoping to stumble onto a lawful reason for the White House Counsel to be dropping money in the woods. Nothing I come up with is good. "It's about Simon," I finally say.

"Stop right there," she commands. Reaching into the top drawer of her desk, she pulls out a small cassette recorder and a single blank tape. She knew that tone as soon as she heard it. This is serious.

"I don't think that's necess—"

"Don't be nervous—it's just for your protection." She grabs a pen and writes my name on the cassette. When it's in the recorder, I can see the words "Michael Garrick" through the tiny piece of glass. Hitting Record, she slaps the recorder against her desk, right in front of me.

She knows what I'm thinking, but she's been through it before. "Michael, if this is important, you should have the proper documentation. Now why don't you start from the beginning."

I close my eyes and pretend there's still a net. "It all happened last night," I begin.

"Last night being Thursday the third," she verifies.

I nod. She points to her lips. "I mean, that's correct," I quickly say. "Anyway, I was driving along 16th Street when I saw—"

"Before we get there, was anyone with you?"

"That's not the important part—"

"Just answer the question."

I respond as quickly as I can. "No. I was alone."

"So no one was with you?"

I don't like the way she asks that. Something isn't right. Once again, I feel the back of my neck hot with sweat. "No one was with me," I insist.

She doesn't seem convinced.

I reach forward and stop the tape. "Is there a problem?"

"Not at all." She attempts to restart the tape, but my hand is over the recorder.

"I'm not doing this on tape," I tell her. "Not yet."

"Calm down, Michael." Sitting back, she lets me have my way. The recorder stays off. "I know it's hard. Just tell your story."

She's right. This isn't the time to lose it. For the second time, I find calm in a deep breath and take solace in the fact that it's no longer being recorded. "So I'm driving down 16th Street, when I suddenly see a familiar car in front of me. When I take a closer look at it, I realize it belongs to Simon."

"Edgar Simon—Counsel to the President."

"Exactly. Now, for whatever reason—maybe it's the time of night, maybe it's where we are—as soon as I see him, something doesn't seem kosher. So I drop back and start to follow." Detail by detail, I tell her the rest of the story. How Simon pulled over on Rock Creek Parkway. How he got out of his car carrying a manila envelope. How he climbed over the guardrail and disappeared up the embankment. And most important, once he was gone, what I found in the envelope. The only thing I leave out is Nora. And the cops. "When I saw the money, I thought I was going to have a heart attack. You have to imagine it: It's past midnight, it's pitch black, and there I am holding my boss's forty-thousand-dollar payoff. On top of all that, I could swear someone was watching me. It was like they were right over my shoulder. I'm telling you, it was one of the scariest moments of my entire life. But before I went and blew the whistle, I thought I should talk to someone first. That's why I came to you."

I wait for a reaction, but she doesn't give one. Eventually, she asks, "Are you done?"

I nod. "Yeah."

She leans across the desk and picks up the cassette recorder. Her thumb flicks back and forth against the pause button. Nervous habit.

"So?" I ask. "What d'you think?"

Putting on her glasses, she doesn't look amused. "It's an interesting story, Michael. The only problem is, fifteen minutes ago, Edgar Simon was in this office telling me the exact same story about you. In his version, though, you were the one with the money." She crosses her arms and sits back in her chair. "Now do you want to start over?"

CHAPTER 6

Why would he say that?" I ask, panicking.

"Michael, I don't know what kind of trouble you're in, but there's—"

"I'm not in any trouble," I insist. My mouth goes dry and nausea washes over me. I can feel it in my stomach. It's all about to collapse. "I-I don't know what you're talking about. I swear . . . it was him. We saw him carrying the—"

"Who's *we?*"

"Huh?"

"*We*. You just said *we*. Who else was with you, Michael?"

I sit up straight in my seat. "No one was with me. I swear, I was all alone."

Silence envelops the room and I can feel the weight of her judgment. "You really have balls, y'know that? When Simon came in here, he told me to take it easy on you. He figured you had problems. And what do you do? You lie to my face and blame it on him! On *him* of all people!"

"Wait a minute . . . you think I'm making this up?"

"I'm not answering that question." She brushes her hand

against a stack of red file folders. "I've already seen the answer."

In the world of vetting and background checks, a red folder means an FBI file. Instinctively, I check the name on the tab of the top file. Michael Garrick.

My fists tighten. "You pulled my file?"

"Why don't you tell me about your work on the new Medicaid overhaul—preserving Medicaid for criminals? It looks like a real crusade for you."

There's a tone in her voice that stabs like a stick in the eye. "I don't know what you're talking about."

"Don't insult me, Michael. We've been through this once before. I know all about him. Still a real proud poppa, huh?"

I shoot out of my seat, barely able to control myself. She's pushing the wrong buttons. "Leave him alone," I growl. "He has nothing to do with this."

"Really? It looks like a clear conflict of interest to me."

"The only reason I'm on that issue is because Simon put the reference memo on my desk."

"So you never thought about the fact that your father benefits from the program?"

"He doesn't get the money; it goes straight to his facility!"

"He benefits, Michael! You can rationalize all you want, but you know it's true. He's your father, he's a criminal, and if the program gets overhauled, he'll lose his benefits."

"He's not a criminal!"

"The moment you got this issue, you should've recused yourself. That's what the Standards of Conduct require and that's what you neglected to do! It's just like last time!"

"That was different!"

"The only thing different was that I gave you the benefit of the doubt. Now I know better."

"So now you think I'm lying about Simon and the money?"

"You know what they say: Like father, like son."

"Don't you dare say that! You know nothing about him!"

"Is that what the money was for? Some sort of payout to keep him safe?"

"I wasn't the one with the money . . ."

"I don't believe you, Michael."

"Simon was the one who—"

"I said, I don't believe you."

"Why the hell won't you listen?" I shout as my voice booms through the room.

Her answer is simple. "Because I know you're lying."

That's it. I need help. I turn around and head for the door.

"Where do you think you're going?"

I don't say a word.

"Don't walk away from me!" she shouts.

I stop and turn around. "Does that mean you're going to hear my side of the story?"

Locking her hands together, she drops them on her desk. "I think I've already heard everything I need."

I reach for the door and pull it open.

"If you walk out of here, Michael, I promise you, you'll regret it!"

It doesn't slow me down.

"Get back here! Now!"

I step into the hallway and my world goes red. "Drop dead," I say without turning around.

Ten minutes later, I'm sitting in my office, staring at the small television that rests on the ledge by the window. Every office in the OEOB is wired for cable, but I keep the set locked on channel twenty-five—where the menu for the White House Mess runs endlessly throughout the day.

Soup of the day: French onion.

Yogurt of the day: Oreo.

Sandwich selections: Turkey, roast beef, tuna salad.

One by one, they scroll up the screen; boring white letters against a royal blue background. Right now, it's about all I can handle.

By the third rerun of the Yogurt of the day, I've come up with thirteen unarguable reasons to rip Caroline's head off. From setting me up, to taking those potshots at my dad—what the hell is wrong with her? She knew what she was doing from the moment I walked in there. Slowly, surely, though, adrenaline fades into a quiet calm. And with that calm comes the realization that unless we have another conversation, Caroline's going to take Simon's version of the story and bury me with it.

For the fourth time in ten minutes, I check the toaster and dial Nora's number. It says she's in the Residence, but no one picks up. I hang up and dial another two extensions. Trey and Pam are just as hard to find. I beeped both of them as soon as I got back, but neither has checked in.

I scan the digital call log one last time, just to make sure they didn't call while I was on the line. Nothing. No one's there. No one but me. That's what it comes down to. A world of one.

Inside the White House, the heat, vent, and cooling systems keep the air pressure of the mansion higher than normal for one simple reason: If someone attacks with a bio weapon or nerve gas, the poison-filled air will be forced outward, away from the President. Of course, the joke among the staff is that this *by definition* makes the White House the most high-pressured place to work. Right now, sitting in my office, it's got nothing to do with air systems.

Feeling self-preservation surpass anger, I get up and head for the anteroom. As I open the door, I hear someone by the coffeemaker. If I'm lucky, it'll be Pam. Instead, it's Julian.

"Tastes like someone pissed in this," he says, shoving his coffee mug toward my face.

"Well, it wasn't me."

"I'm not blaming you, Garrick—I'm making a point. Our coffee sucks."

This isn't the time to fight. "Sorry to hear that."

"What's wrong with you? You look like crap."

"Nothing, just some stuff I'm working on."

"Like what? Sucking up to more criminals? You were two for two this morning."

I step past him and open the door. Although we tend to disagree on just about everything, I have to admit that our third officemate isn't a bad person—he's just a bit too intense for the general populace. "Enjoy the coffee, Julian."

Walking back to Caroline's office, I find the massive hallway longer than ever. When I first started working here, I remember being so impressed with how big everything seemed. Over time, it all became both manageable and comfortable. Today, I'm right back where I started.

Reaching Caroline's office, I grab the doorknob without knocking. "Caroline, before you go nuts, let me expl—"

I come to a trainwrecking halt.

In front of me, Caroline is sunk low in her highback chair. Her head sags forward like an abandoned marionette's, and one arm is dangling over the armrest. She's not moving. "Caroline?" I ask, moving closer.

No answer. Oh, God.

In her lap, her other hand is holding on to an empty

coffee mug that has the words "I Got Your State of the Union Right Here" written on it. Turned on its side and resting on her thigh, the mug is empty. "Caroline, are you okay?" I ask. That's when I notice the slow dripping sound. It catches me by surprise and reminds me of the leaky faucet in my apartment. Following the sound, I realize it's running from the chair to the floor. Caroline's sitting in a puddle of coffee.

Instinctively, I reach out and touch her shoulder. Her head flops back and hits the edge of the chair with a sickly thud. The vacancy in Caroline's wide-open hazel eyes violently rips through me. One eye stares straight forward; the other slumps cockeyed to the side.

Around me, the room starts to spin. My throat contracts and it's suddenly impossible to breathe. Staggering backwards, I crash into the wall, knocking a framed thank-you note to the floor. Her life's work shatters. I open my mouth, but I can barely hear what comes out. "Someone . . ." I cry, gasping for air. "Please . . . someone help."

CHAPTER 7

A uniformed Secret Service officer with a nasty hooked jaw helps me to my feet. "Are you okay? Are you okay? Can you hear me?" he asks, shouting the questions until I nod yes. The phone and its wires are tangled around my ankles—from when I pulled the console off the desk. It was all I could think of, the only way to get help. He kicks the phone aside and helps me to the couch in the corner. I look back at Caroline, whose eyes are still wide open. For the rest of my life, she'll be frozen in that position.

The next fifteen minutes are a haze of investigative efficiency. Before I know what's happening, the room is filled with an assortment of investigators and other law enforcement officials: two more uniformed officers, two Secret Service suits, a five-person FBI Crime Scene Unit, and a member of the Emergency Response Team holding an Uzi by the door. After some brief posturing over jurisdiction, the Secret Service let the FBI get to work. A tall man in a dark blue FBI polo shirt takes photos of the office, while a short Asian woman and two other men in light blue shirts pick the place apart. A fifth man with a Virginia twang in his voice is the one giving orders.

"You, boys," he says to the uniformed Secret Service.
"You'd be a far bigger help if you waited outside." Before
they even move, he adds, "Thanks for your time now." He
turns to the Secret Service suits and gives them a quick
once-over. They can stay. Then he comes over to me.

"Michael Garrick," he says, reading from my ID. "You
okay there, Michael? You able to talk?"

I nod, staring at the carpet. Across the room, the photographer is taking pictures of Caroline's body. When the
first flash goes off, it seems so normal—photographers are
at almost every White House event. But when I see her
head sagging and twisting to the side, and the awkward
way her mouth gapes open, I realize it's not Caroline anymore. She's gone. Now it's just a body; a slowly stiffen-
ing shell posed for a macabre photo shoot.

The agent with the Virginia twang lifts my chin, and
his latex gloves scrape against the remnants of my morning shave. Before I can say a word, he looks me in the
eyes. "You sure you're okay? We can always do this later,
but . . ."

"No, I understand—I can do it now."

He puts a strong hand on my shoulder. "I appreciate you
helping us out, Michael." Unlike the FBI polo crew, he's
wearing a gray suit with a small stain on his right lapel.
His tie is pulled tight, but the top button on his stark white
shirt is open. The effect is the most subtle hint of casual-
ness in his otherwise professional demeanor. "Quite a day,
huh, Michael?" It's the third time since we've met that he's
said my name, which I have to admit sets off my radar.
As my old crim law professor once explained, name repetition is the first trick negotiators use to establish an initial level of intimacy. The second trick is physical contact.
I look down at his hand on my shoulder.

He pulls it away, removes his glove, and offers up a

handshake. "Michael, I'm Randall Adenauer, Special Agent in Charge of the FBI's Violent Crimes Unit."

His title catches me off guard. "You think she was murdered?"

"That's getting a little ahead of ourselves, don't you think?" he asks with a laugh that's even more forced than the way he buttons his shirt. "Far as we can tell right now, it looks like a simple heart attack—autopsy'll tell for sure. Now, you're the one who found her, aren't you?"

I nod.

"How long before you called it in?"

"Soon as I realized she was dead."

"And when you found her, she was exactly like that? Nothing moved?"

"Her head was down when I walked in. But when I shook her and saw her eyes—the way they are now—the way she looks back at you. That's when I crashed into the wall."

"So you knocked the picture over?"

"I'm pretty sure. I didn't expect to see her like—"

"I'm not blaming you, Michael."

He's right, I tell myself. There's no reason to get defensive.

"And the phone on the floor . . . ?" he asks.

"The whole room was spinning—I sat down to catch my breath. In a panic, I pulled it off the desk to call for help."

As I explain what happened, I realize he's not writing anything down. He just sort of stares my way, his sharp blue eyes barely focused on me. The way he's watching— if I didn't know better, I'd think he was reading cartoon word balloons just above my head. No matter how hard I try to get his attention, our eyes never meet. Finally, from his pants pocket, he pulls out a roll of butterscotch Life Savers and offers me one.

I shake my head.

"Suit yourself." He puts the top of the pack in his mouth and bites one off. "I'm telling you, I think I'm addicted to these things. I'm up to a pack a day."

"Better than smoking," I say, motioning to one of the many ashtrays in Caroline's office.

He nods and looks back at the word balloons. The small talk's over. "So when you found her, what were you coming to see her about?"

Over his shoulder, I spot the small stack of red file folders that are still on Caroline's desk. "Just some work-related stuff."

"Any of it personal?"

"Not really. Why?"

He looks down at the pack of Life Savers he's holding and pretends to be nonchalant. "Just trying to figure out why she had your file."

Adenauer is no dummy. He set me up for that one.

"Now you want to tell me what's really going on?" he asks.

"I swear to you, it was nothing. We were just going over a conflict of interest. She's the ethics officer; that's what she works on. I'm sure she pulled my file to check things out." Unsure if he's buying it, I point to Caroline's desk. "Look for yourself—she's got other files besides mine."

Before he can answer, the Asian agent in the light blue shirt approaches us. "Chief, did the uniformed guys leave you the combination to the—"

"Here you go," Adenauer says. He reaches into his jacket pocket and hands her a yellow sheet of paper.

Taking the combination, she starts working on the safe behind Caroline's desk.

When the distraction's over, Adenauer turns my way and stares me down. I lean back on the couch, trying to look unconcerned. Behind the desk, there's a loud thunk. The woman opens the safe.

"Michael, I understand why you want to be as far away from this as possible—I know how it works here. But I'm not accusing you of anything. I'm just trying to figure out what happened."

"I already told you everything I know."

"Chief, you better take a look at this," the Asian woman says from behind the desk.

Adenauer gets up and heads for the safe. The woman pulls out a manila envelope. She turns it upside down and the contents tumble onto the desk. One. Two. Three stacks of cash. Hundred dollar bills. Each stack wrapped in a First of America billfold.

I do everything in my power to look surprised, and to my credit, I think I actually get away with it. But deep down, as I stare at the three piles of cash that Nora left behind, I know this is just the beginning.

CHAPTER 8

Two hours of questioning later, I'm walking back to my office with a ruthless migraine and a throbbing pain at the base of my neck. I still can't believe Caroline had the money. Why would she . . . I mean, if she's got that . . . does that mean she was also in the woods? Or did she just pick it up later? Is that why she went after Simon at the morning meeting—because it was ten grand short? My mind tumbles through explanations, searching for the corner pieces of the puzzle. I can barely find an edge.

Around me, the hallways are almost completely empty, and as I pass every door, I can hear the faint echoes of dozens of televisions. Usually, the televisions in the OEOB run with the sound off. With news like this, everyone's listening.

The reaction is typical White House. As a former Clinton advisor explained to me years ago, the power structure of the White House is similar to a game of soccer played by ten-year-olds. You can assign everyone to a position, and you can demand that everyone stay where they're supposed to be, but the moment the game starts, every person on the field abandons their post and runs for the ball.

Case in point: the empty halls of the OEOB. Even before I check in with Trey, I know what's going on. The President is demanding information, which means the Chief of Staff is demanding information, which means the top advisors are demanding information, which means the press is demanding information. From there, everyone else is searching—calling one another and every other connection they can think of—trying to be the first one to reel in the answers. In a hierarchy where most of us are paid similar government salaries, the currency of choice is access and influence. Information is the key to both.

Every other crisis is put on hold as the kids desperately chase the ball. Under any other set of circumstances, I'd be right along with them. Today, though, as I return to my office, I can't help but think that the ball is me.

Closing the door behind myself, I turn on the squawk box, then head straight for the TV, where every network with a press pass is live from the White House. To double-check, I glance out the window and see the line of reporters doing stand-ups on the northwest corner of the lawn.

Panicking, I pick up the phone and dial Nora's number. The toaster says she's still in the Residence, but again, there's no answer. I need to know what's going on. I need Trey.

"Michael, this isn't exactly a good time," he says as he answers the phone. In the background, I hear what sounds like a roomful of people and the nonstop ringing of phones. It's a bad day to be a press secretary.

"Just tell me what's happening," I plead. "What do you have?"

"Rumors are it's a heart attack, though the FBI isn't putting anything out there until two. The first officer on the scene gave us most of it—says there were no external wounds and nothing suspicious." As Trey continues his explanation, his phone doesn't stop ringing. "You should see this guy—typical uniform division—begging for attention, then pretending he doesn't want to talk."

"So I'm not the ball?"

"Why would you be the ball?"

"Because I was the one who found her."

"So that's confirmed? We heard a rumor, but I figured you'd call me if— Jami, listen to this: I got the . . ."

"Trey, shut up!" I shout as loud as I can.

". . . the best gossip about Martin Van Buren. Did you know they used to make fun of him for wearing corsets? Isn't that great? I can't get enough of that guy—corset-wearing little Democrat. Cute as a button, he was. And let me tell you, that Panic of 1837 was all media hype—I don't believe a word of—"

"Did she walk away yet?" I interrupt.

"Yeah," he says. "Now tell me what's going on."

"It's not that big a deal."

"Not that big a deal? Do you know how many calls I've gotten on this thing just since we've been talking?"

"Fourteen," I say flatly. "I've been counting."

There's a pause on the other end. Trey knows me too well. "Maybe we should talk about it later."

"Yeah. I think that's best." Staring out the window, I look back at the line of reporters on the lawn. "Think you can keep me out of this?"

"Michael, I can get you information, but I can't work miracles. It all depends on what the FBI comes back with."

"But can't you—"

"Listen, the way this uniformed guy is talking, most people think he found her. For anyone else who asks, your name is officially changed to 'a fellow White House staffer.' That should save you from at least a thousand constituent letters."

"Thank you, Trey."

"I do my best," he says as the door to my office opens. Pam sticks her head in.

"Listen, I better go. I'll talk to you later."

I hang up the phone and Pam hesitantly asks, "Is now a good time, because . . ."

"Don't worry—c'mon in."

As she steps inside, I notice the sluggishness in her walk. Usually bouncy with a tireless stride, she's moving in slow motion, her shoulders sagging at her side. "Can you believe it?" she asks, collapsing in the seat in front of my desk. Her eyes are tired. And red. She's been crying.

"Are you okay?" I ask.

The single question causes a relapse in emotion that wells up her eyes with tears. Clenching her jaw, Pam fights it back down. She's not the type to cry in public. I reach into my desk and look for a tissue. All I have are some old presidential seal napkins. I hand them over, but she shakes her head.

"Are you sure you're okay?"

"She hired me, y'know." Clearing her throat, she adds, "When I came through for interviews, Caroline was the only person who liked me. Simon, Lamb, all the rest, they didn't think I was tough enough. Simon wrote the word 'Whitebread' on my interview sheet."

"No, he didn't."

"Sure did. Caroline showed it to me," Pam says with a laugh. "But since I was going to be working for her, she was able to pull me through. First day I started, she handed me Simon's evaluation and told me to keep it. Said one day, I was going to shove the whole sheet down his throat."

"Did you keep the sheet?"

Pam continues to laugh.

"What?"

A wicked smile takes her cheeks. "Remember that victory party we had when Simon gave his congressional testimony on alcohol advertising?"

I nod.

"And remember the victory cake we served—the one Caroline said we made from scratch?"

"Oh, no."

"Oh, yes," Pam adds with a wide smile. "On my hundred and fifty-second day here, Edgar Simon ate his words."

I laugh along with her. "Are you telling me you put your old evaluation in the cake?"

"I admit nothing."

"How's that even possible? Wouldn't he taste it?"

"What do you mean *he?* Trust me, I watched the whole thing—you ate quite a nice piece yourself."

"And you didn't stop me?"

"I didn't like you as much back then."

"But how'd you—"

"We wet the sheet, ripped it into small pieces, and threw it in the blender. That sucker puréed in no time. Best cooking lesson I ever took. Caroline was a mad genius. And when it came to Simon—she hated that bastard."

"Right up until the hour before she di—" I catch myself. "I'm sorry—I didn't mean . . ."

"It's okay," she says. Without another word, the two of us spend the next minute in complete, stark silence; an impromptu memorial for one of our own. To be honest, it's not until that moment that I realize what I'd left out. Through the two hours of questioning, and the worrying, and the angling to protect myself, I forgot one key thing: I forgot to mourn. My legs go numb and my heart sinks. Caroline Penzler died today. And whatever I thought of her, this is the first moment it's actually hit me. The short silence doesn't make her a saint, but the realization does me a world of good.

As soon as Pam looks up, she sees the change in my expression. "You okay?"

"Y-Yeah . . . I just can't believe it."

Pam agrees and shrinks back in her seat. "How'd she look?"

"What do you mean?"

"The body. Weren't you the one who found the body?"

I nod, unable to answer. "Who told you?"

"Debi in Public Liaison heard it from her boss, who has a friend who has the office right across from—"

"I got it," I interrupt. This isn't going to be easy.

"Can I ask you a separate question?" Pam adds. From the tone in her voice, I know where she's going with this. "Last night—whatever you got into—is that why Caroline died?"

"I don't know what you're talking about."

"Don't do that to me, Michael. You said it was cover-of-*Newsweek* big. That's what you went to see her about, isn't it?"

I don't answer.

"It was about Nora, wasn't it?"

Still, nothing.

"If Caroline was killed for some—"

"She wasn't killed! It was a heart attack!"

Pam watches me carefully. "You really believe that?"

"I actually do."

When we first got assigned to the same office, Pam described herself as the person in fifth grade who got left behind when her friends got popular. It was a self-effacing icebreaker, but I have to say, even then, I never believed it. She's way too savvy for that—she wouldn't be here if she wasn't. So even if she loves to play the underdog and put herself down—even if she constantly feels the need to lower expectations—I, until today, have always thought she was a guru of interpersonal dynamics.

"So the little psycho's really worth that much to you?" she asks.

"You may have a hard time believing this, but Nora's a good person."

"If she's so good, where's she now?"

I look over at the toaster. Nothing's changed. In green digital letters are the same three words: SECOND FLOOR RESIDENCE.

Running up the hallway of the OEOB, I know that the only way to find out what's going on is face-to-face and in person. At full speed, with an empty interoffice mailer clutched in an anxious fist, I blow through the West Exec exit, cross the corridor between the buildings, and head for the West Wing of the White House. Passing through the doors under the sharp white awning, I wave a quick hello to Phil.

"Going up?" he asks, calling the elevator for me.

I shake my head.

"Crazy news, huh?"

"No question about it," I say as I rush past him. Climbing the short flight of stairs on my left, I slow my pace to a brisk walk. You don't run this close to the Oval. Not unless you want to be tackled or shot. I take a quick peek at Hartson's secretary's office to see how things are going. As always, the Oval and everything else near the President is lightning hot. It's charged with an energy that's impossible to describe. It's not panic—there's no panicking when you're near the President. It's simply a wave of energy that's conspicuously and unapologetically alive. Like Nora.

Staying on course, I push forward. Ahead of me, I see

another two uniformed officers and the lower press office, where four original Norman Rockwells line the wall that leads to the West Colonnade. Shoving open the doors, I step outside, fly past each of the spectacular white columns that line the Rose Garden, and reenter the mansion of the White House in the Ground Floor Corridor.

Straight ahead, across the wave of lush, pale red carpet, there're four cherry-wood foldable dividers blocking the back half of the corridor. Public tours are on the other side. Every year thousands of tourists are led through the Ground Floor and the State Floor, the first two floors of the White House. They see the Vermeil Room, the China Room, the Blue Room, the Red Room, the Green Room, the Fill-in-the-Blank Room. But they don't see where the President and the First Family actually live—where they sleep, where they entertain, and where they spend their time—the top two floors of the White House. The Residence.

Up the hallway, through the second door on my left, is the entryway that houses an elevator and a set of stairs. Both lead up to the Residence. The only thing in my way is the Secret Service: one uniformed officer on this floor; two on the floor above. No need to lose it, I tell myself. It's just like anything else in life—a purposeful walk gets you inside. With an even, deliberate pace, I hold out the interoffice mailer and make my way up the hallway, to-ward the first officer. He's leaning against the wall and ap-pears to be staring at his own shoes. Keep your head down—just keep your head down. I'm only ten feet from the door. Five feet from the door. Three feet from the—Suddenly he looks up. I don't stop. I shoot him a friendly nod as he eyes my ID. Blue pass goes just about anywhere. And presidential interoffice mail goes straight upstairs to the Usher's Office. "Have a good one," I add, for authen-ticity's sake. He looks back at his shoes without a sound.

Confidence is once again the ultimate hall pass. I head for the stairs. Only one more floor to go.

Although I'm tempted to celebrate, I know that the Ground Floor officer is just there to make sure people don't wander in off the tour. The real checkpoint for the Residence is on the next landing. As I make my way up, I quickly spot two uniformed Secret Service officers waiting for me. Standing across from the elevator, these two aren't looking at their shoes. I avoid eye contact and maintain the purposeful pace.

"Can I help you?" the taller of the two officers asks.

Keep walking—they'll buy it, I tell myself. "How you doing?" I say, trying to sound like I'm here all the time. "She's expecting me."

The other officer steps in front of me and blocks my path to the next flight of stairs. "Who's expecting you?"

"Nora," I reply, showing them the mailer. I step to my right and act like I planned to take the elevator the rest of the way. When I push the call button, a rasping buzzer screams through the small entryway.

I turn around and both officers are looking at me.

"You can leave the mail with the usher," the taller one says.

"She asked that it be hand-delivered," I offer.

Neither of them is impressed. After reading my name from my ID, the taller officer steps into the Usher's Office, which is right next to the stairs, and picks up the telephone. "I have a Michael Garrick down here." He listens for a second. "No. Yeah. I'll tell him. Thanks." He hangs up the phone and looks back at me. "She's not up there."

"What? That's impossible. When did she leave?"

"They said it was in the last ten minutes. If she takes the elevator down, we don't see her."

"Don't they update her movements on your radio?"

"Not until she leaves the building."

I stare him down. There's nothing left to say. "Tell her I came by," I add, heading back down the stairs.

As I make my way down, I see someone heading up. The staircase isn't a wide one, so we brush shoulders, and I get my first good look at him. He's wearing khakis and a navy blue polo. But it's the earpiece he's wearing that gives him away. Secret Service. One of Nora's agents. Harry. His name's Harry. He's part of her personal detail. And the only time he leaves her side is when she's upstairs in the Residence.

I turn around and follow him upstairs. As soon as the uniformed officers see me, they know I know.

"You were lying to me?" I ask the taller officer.

"Listen, son, this isn't—"

"Why'd you lie?"

"Take it easy," Harry says.

Within seconds, I see a plainclothes agent running up the stairs, from the Ground Floor. A second in a dark suit steps in and blocks the entrance to the hallway.

How the hell did they react so quickly? I look over my shoulder and get the answer. In the air conditioner vent by the doorway is a tiny penlight camera pointed straight at me.

Harry puts a hand on my shoulder. "Take my word for it," he says. "You can't win."

He's right about that one. I pull away from him and head back toward the stairs. Looking at Harry, I add, "Tell her we have to talk."

He nods, but doesn't say a word.

Storming down the stairs, I brush past the agent who's blocking my way. "Have a nice day," he says as I leave.

*   *   *

On my way back to the OEOB, I realize I'm squeezing both hands into tight fists. Opening them up, I stretch out my fingers, trying to shake off Nora's dismissal. Yet with release comes panic. It's not that bad, I tell myself. She'll come through. She's just being careful now. Besides, all I did was find the body and yell a bit. It's not like I'm a suspect. No one even knows about the money. Except for Nora. And the D.C. police. And Caroline. And anyone else she told about the . . . Damn, the rumors could already be out there. And when they realize the bills are consecutive . . .

My thoughts are interrupted by the vibrations of my beeper. I pull it from my pocket and check the message. That's when I'm reminded of the one other person who knows about the money. The message says it all: "Would like to speak to you. In person. E.S."

E.S. Edgar Simon.

CHAPTER 9

Sitting in the waiting room outside Simon's office, my only distraction is Judy's typing. Simon's personal assistant, Judy Stohr, is a chubby little woman with dyed red hair. Divorced the year Hartson decided to run for President, she gave up on men, moved from New Jersey to Hartson's home state of Florida, and joined the campaign. A walking encyclopedia for every day that's passed since then, Judy loves her new life. But as the always attentive mother of two college-age kids, she'll never be able to change who she is.

"What's wrong? You look sick."

"I'm fine," I tell her.

"Don't tell me 'fine.' You're not fine."

"Judy, I promise you, there's nothing wrong." As she stares me down, I add, "I'm sad about Caroline."

"Ucch, it's terrible. On my worst enemy, I wouldn't wish such—"

"Does he have anyone in there?" I interrupt, pointing to Simon's closed door.

"No, he's just been making calls. He's the one who told

the President. And Caroline's family. Now he's talking to
the major papers . . ."

"Why?" I ask nervously.

"His office; his territory. He's the point man on this.
Press wants reaction from her boss."

That makes sense. Nothing out of the ordinary. "Any
other news?"

Judy leans back in her chair, enjoying her moment as
the most informed. "It's a heart attack. FBI's still going
through the office, but they know what's going on—Caroline smoked more than my Aunt Sally and drank six cups
of coffee a day. No offense, but what'd she expect?"

I shrug, unsure of how to respond.

In my silence, Judy sees something in my eyes. "You
want to tell me what's really upsetting you, Michael?"

"It's nothing. Everything's fine."

"You're not still intimidated by these guys, are you? You
shouldn't be—you're better than 'em all. That's truth talking to you: You're a real person. That's why people like
you."

During my third week on the job, I mistakenly sent a
letter to the head of the House Judiciary Committee that
began *"Dear Congressman"* as opposed to *"Dear Mr.
Chairman."* This being egoville, the Chairman's staff left
a snide remark about it on Simon's voice-mail, and after
a quick lashing by Simon, I made the mistake of telling
Judy how intimidating it was being a state school boy in
the White House's Ivy League world. Since then, I've realized I could hold my own. For me, it's no longer an issue.
For Judy, it's always my problem.

"The more you succeed, the more they get scared," she
explains. "You're a threat to the old boy network—rock-
solid proof that it doesn't matter where you went to school
or who your parents—"

"I get the point," I say with a snap.

Judy gives me a second to cool down. "You're still not over it, are you?"

"I promise you, I'm fine. I just need to speak to Simon."

Before last night, Edgar Simon was a great guy. Born and raised in Chapel Hill, North Carolina, he had less swagger than the East Coast power brokers and Beltway insiders who'd previously held the White House Counsel position. As a double-Harvard graduate, he wasn't lacking in gray matter. But I never focus on résumés. What impressed me most about Simon was his personal life.

A few months after I was hired, the press began to suspect that President Hartson was hiding the fact that he had prostate cancer. When the *New York Times* suggested that Hartson had a legal responsibility to share his medical records with the public, Simon stepped into his first major crisis. Forty-eight hours later, he found out that his twelve-year-old son was diagnosed with neurofibromatosis, a genetic disorder of the nervous system that's potentially disabling for children.

After a three-day, no-sleep, rip-your-hair-out research marathon dedicated to the legal issues surrounding presidential medical privacy, Simon handed two things to the President: a briefing book on the crisis and his own resignation. Simon made it clear—his son came first.

Needless to say, the press ate it like popcorn. *Parenting* magazine crowned him Father of the Year. Then, one month later, when the initial crisis had passed, Simon returned to his position as Counsel. He said the President twisted his arm. Others said Simon couldn't stand being away from power. Either way, it didn't matter. At the height of his career, Edgar Simon walked away from it all. For his son. I'd always respect him for that.

Stepping into his office, I try to picture the Edgar Simon I used to know—the Father of the Year. All I see, though, is the man from last night—the viper with the forty-thousand-dollar secret.

Sitting at his desk, he looks up at me with the same mischievous smile he gave me this morning. But unlike our earlier encounter, I now know that he saw us last night. And I know what he told Caroline—whatever their disagreements were, he put the finger on me. Still, there's not a hint of anger on his face. In fact, the way his dark eyebrows are raised, he actually looks concerned.

"How're you doing?" he asks as I sit down in front of his desk.

"Okay."

"I'm sorry you had to find her like that."

I stare at the floor. "Me too."

There's a long pause in the air—one of those forced pauses where you know bad news is standing on your nose, waiting to springboard into your chest. Eventually, I lift my head.

Simon says it as soon as our eyes meet. "Michael, I think it'd be best if you went home."

"What?"

"Don't get upset—it's for your own protection."

I can barely contain myself; I'm not letting him pin this on me. "You're sending me home? How's that for my protection?"

Simon doesn't like being challenged. His tone is slow and deliberate. "People heard you yell at her. Then you found the body. The last thing we—"

"What are you saying?" I ask, jumping out of my seat.

"Michael, listen to me. The campaign guys are breathing fire all over us—this a dangerous game. If you put forth the wrong impression, you'll raise every voting eyebrow in the country."

"But I didn't—"

"I'm not accusing you of anything. I'm simply suggesting that you go home and take a breath. You've been through a great deal this morning, and you can use the time off."

"I don't need the—"

"It's not up for discussion. Go home."

Biting my lower lip, I return to my seat, unsure of what to say. If I bring up last night, he'll bury me with it—handing me to the press with a bird-in-his-teeth grin. Better to stay quiet and see where he goes. A little détente goes a long way; especially if it keeps me by his side. And behind his back.

Still, I can't help myself. There're too many unknowns. What if I have it backwards? Maybe it's about more than last night. Simon doesn't seem suspicious or accusatory, but that doesn't make me feel any less defensive. "Do you even know why Caroline and I were fighting?" I blurt, struggling to keep things honest. Before he can respond, I add, "She thought my dad's criminal record conflicted with my work on the Medicaid—"

"Now's not the time, Michael."

"But don't you think the FBI—"

Simon doesn't give me a chance to finish. "Do you know why this office is paneled?" he asks.

"Excuse me?"

"The office," he says, pointing to the walnut paneling that covers the surrounding four walls. "Do you have any idea why it's paneled?"

I shake my head, confused.

"Back in the Nixon administration, this office used to belong to Budget Director Roy Ash. The office down the

hallway belonged to John Erlichman. Both were great corner offices. The only difference was, Erlichman's office
was paneled and this one wasn't. This being the White
House, Ash felt that that must've meant something. He
thought everyone was watching and judging. So, being the
wealthy sort he was, Ash used his own money and paneled this office. Now they were equals."

"I'm sorry, I don't understand."

"The point is, Michael, don't spend your time defend-
ing yourself. Ash had it right. Everyone is watching. And
right now, all they see is a woman who had a heart attack.
If you start apologizing, they're going to start thinking otherwise."

I sit up straight in my seat. "What's that supposed to
mean?"

"Nothing at all," he says cheerfully. "I'm just looking
out for you. That scab on your forehead'll be gone by tomorrow. Take it from me—you don't need another one."

"I didn't do anything wrong," I insist.

"No one says you did. It was a heart attack. We both
know that." He presses his pointer fingers against each
other and brings them to his lips. With a silent grin, he
sends home the threat. Go home and keep quiet, or stay
here and pay the price. "By the way, Michael, don't pick
any more fights with the Secret Service. I don't want to
hear from them again."

Over Simon's shoulder, my eyes wander to his ego wall.
In a silver frame is a copy of last year's crime bill and one
of four pens the President used to sign it. There's a photo
of Hartson and Simon fishing on a boat in Key West. And
one of Simon advising Hartson in the Oval. There's a personal note handwritten by Hartson, welcoming Simon back
to the job. And there's a great shot of the two men standing in the aisle on Air Force One: Simon's laughing and

the President's holding up a bumper sticker that says: "My Lawyer Can Beat Up Your Lawyer."

"Believe me, it's for the best," he says. "Take the rest of the day to relax."

He's a ruthless son of a bitch, I think to myself as I climb out of my seat. The prototypical White House attorney, he's managed to say nothing, and yet still make his point perfectly clear. As of right now, the safest thing to do is stay quiet. It's not something I'm happy with, but as I saw in Caroline's office this morning, the alternative has its consequences. Heading toward the door, I do the only thing I can think of. I nod and go along with it. For now.

As soon as I get back to my apartment, I go straight for the only piece of furniture that I brought with me from Michigan: a makeshift desk that was created by resting an oversized piece of oak on top of two short black file cabinets. As beat up and ugly as it looks, is as comfortable as it makes me feel.

The rest of my furniture is rented along with the apartment. The black pullout sofa, the black Formica coffee table, the oversized leather easy chair, the small rectangular kitchen table, even the queen-size bed on the black-lacquered platform—none of it's mine. But when the renting agent showed me the furnished apartment, it felt like home, with enough black furniture to keep any bachelor feeling manly. To make it complete, I added a TV and a tall black bookshelf. Certainly, using someone else's stuff is a little impersonal, but when I first got to the city, I didn't want to buy any furniture until I was sure I was going to be able to hack it. That was two years ago.

Like my office at work, the walls are what make the place mine. Over the couch are two red, white, and blue campaign posters with the worst slogans I could find. One is from a 1982 congressional race in Maine and says: "Charles Rust—Rhymes With Trust." The other is from a 1996 race in Oregon that brings lack of creativity to a new low: "Buddy Eldon—American. Patriot. American."

Pulling up my chair to the desk, I flip up the lid of my laptop and prepare to get some work done. When my mom left, when my dad got sent away, it was always my first instinct: Bury it all in work. But for the first time in a long while, it's not making me feel any better.

I spend twenty minutes on Lexis before I realize that my census research is going nowhere. Regardless of how hard I try to concentrate, my mind keeps drifting back to the past few hours. To Caroline. And Simon. And Nora. I'm tempted to call her again, but I quickly decide against it. Internal calls made in the White House can't be documented. Ones that originate from my home can. This is no time to take chances.

Instead, I pull out my wallet, remove my SecurID, and call the office. The size of a credit card, the SecurID resembles a tiny calculator without the numbered buttons. Utilizing a continuous-loop encryption program and a small liquid crystal display, SecurID gives you a six-digit code that changes every sixty seconds. It's the only way to check your voice-mail from an outside line, and by constantly changing its numerical code, it ensures that no one can guess your password and listen to your messages.

Entering the SecurID code at the voice-prompt, I find out I have three messages. One from Pam, asking where I am. One from Trey, asking how I'm doing. And one forwarded from Deputy Counsel Lawrence Lamb's assistant, announcing that the afternoon meeting with the Commerce Secretary is canceled. Nothing from Nora. I don't like being abandoned like that.

I was eight years old the first time my mother left for her clinical trials. She was gone for three days, and my dad and I had no idea where she went. Since she was a nurse, it was easy to check the hospital, but they didn't know where she was either. Or at least they weren't saying. The leftovers lasted for two days, but we eventually reached the point where we needed some food. Because of my mom's job, we weren't poor, but my dad was in no shape to go shopping. When I volunteered to go for us, he stuffed a fistful of bills in my hand and told me to buy whatever I wanted. Beaming with the pride of newfound wealth, I marched down to the supermarket and stocked up the cart. Skippy instead of the generic peanut butter; Coca-Cola instead of the drab store brand; for once, we were going to live in style. It took me close to two hours to make my selections, filling the cart almost to the top.

One by one, the cashier rang up each item while I flipped through a *TV Guide*. I was Dad; all I was missing was the pipe and the smoking jacket. But when I went to pay—when I pulled the wad of crumpled-up cash from my pocket—I was told that three dollars wasn't going to cover it. After a scolding by an assistant manager, they told me to put every item back where I found it. I did. Every item but one. I kept the peanut butter. We had to start somewhere.

Two hours later, I'm sitting in front of the TV, mentally walking through every reason that Simon would want Caroline dead. To be honest, it's not that difficult. In her position, Caroline knew the dirt on everyone—that's how she found out about my dad—so the most obvious answer is that she found something on Simon. Maybe it was something he wanted kept quiet. Maybe that's why he was dropping the money. Maybe he was being blackmailed by her.

That'd certainly explain how it wound up in Caroline's safe. I mean, why else would it be there? If that's the case, though, it should be pretty obvious that Caroline didn't die of a simple heart attack. The problem is, if it looks like foul play, my life is over.

Panicking, I pick up the phone and start dialing. I need to know what's going on, but neither Trey nor Pam is there. There are others I can call, but I'm not going to risk looking suspicious. If they find out Simon sent me home, there'll be a new rumor buzzing through the halls. I hang up the phone and stare at the TV. It's been three hours since I left the office, and I'm already locked out.

Flipping through every news program I can find, I'm searching for what is arguably the most important reaction to the crisis: the official White House press conference. I look down at my watch, and notice it's almost five-thirty. It's got to happen soon. The press office is focused around the six o'clock news cycle, and they're too smart to let the evening news run with this on their own.

True to form, the announcement comes at exactly five-thirty. I hold my breath as Press Secretary Emmy Goldfarb does a quick rundown of the facts: Early this morning, Caroline Penzler was found dead in her office of a heart attack caused by coronary artery disease. As she says the words, I once again start breathing. Keeping the explanation short and sweet, Goldfarb turns it over to Dr. Leon Welp, a heart specialist from Georgetown Medical Center, who explains that Caroline had a hysterectomy a few years ago, which made her prematurely experience menopause. Combine the drop in estrogen with heavy smoking, and you've got a quick recipe for a heart attack.

Before anyone can ask a question, the President himself comes out to do the regrets. Its a masterstroke by the Press Office. Forget the hows and whys, let's get to the emotion.

I can practically taste the subtext: Our leader. A man who takes care of his own.

I hate election years.

As the President grasps the podium in two tight fists, I can't help but see the resemblance to Nora. The black hair. The piercing eyes. The reckless jaw. Always in control. Before he opens his mouth, we all know what's going to come out: "It's a dark day; she'll be sorely missed; our prayers go out to her family." Nothing suspicious; nothing to worry about. He tops it all off with a quick brush of his eye—he's not crying, but it's just enough to make us think that if he had a moment to himself, he might.

From Goldfarb, to the doctor, to the President, they all do their specialty. All I notice is that there's no mention of an investigation. Of course, the family has requested an autopsy, but Goldfarb spins it as a hope to help others with similar ailments. Brilliant touch. Just to be safe, though, the autopsy's set for Sunday, which means it won't be the topic of the weekend talk shows, and if the results show it's a murder, it'll be too late for the major magazines to make it a cover story. For at least two days, I'm safe. I try to tell myself that it may be over—that it'll all go away—but like Nora said, I'm a terrible liar.

Dinnertime comes and goes, and I still don't move from the couch. My stomach is screaming, but I can't stop flipping through channels. I have to be sure. I need to know no one is using those words: Suspicion. Foul Play. Murder.

The thing is, there's no mention of it anywhere. Whatever Adenauer and the FBI have found, they're keeping it to themselves. Relieved, I lean my head back on my rent-a-couch and finally accept that it's going to be a quiet night.

There's a loud knock on my door.

"Who is it?" I ask.

There's no answer. They just bang harder.

"Who is it?" I repeat, raising my voice.

Nothing.

I move quickly from the couch and head toward the door. Along the way, I pick up an umbrella that's hanging on the knob of the coat closet. It's a pathetically bad weapon, but it's the best I've got. Slowly, I bring my eye to the peephole and get a look at my imagined enemy. Pam.

Undoing the locks, I pull open the door. She's holding her briefcase in one hand and a blue plastic shopping bag in the other. Her eyes go right to the umbrella. "Nervous much?"

"I didn't know who it was."

"So that's what you grab? You've got a kitchen full of steak knives and you grab an umbrella? What're you going to do? Keep-me-dry to death?" She shoots me a warm smile and holds up the blue bag. "Now, c'mon, how about inviting me in? I brought Thai food."

I move out of her way and she steps inside. "And you call *me* the Boy Scout?" I ask.

"Just hold this," she adds, handing me her briefcase and heading for the kitchen. Before I can react, she's rummaging through cabinets and drawers, collecting plates and silverware. When she has what she needs, she moves to the small dining area outside the kitchen and unloads three cartons of Thai food from the blue bag. Dinner is served.

Confused, I'm still standing by the door. "Pam, can I ask you a question?"

"As long as you make it quick. I'm starving."

"What're you doing here?"

She looks up from the Pad Thai and her expression changes. "Here?" she asks. Her voice is hurt, almost pained. "I was worried about you."

Her answer catches me off guard. It's almost too honest. I take a step toward the dining room table and return her smile. She really is a good friend. And we can both use the company. "I appreciate what you're doing."

"You should've called me earlier."

"I tried all afternoon, but you weren't there."

"That's because the FBI was questioning me for two hours. We do share an office, y'know."

Right there, I lose my appetite. "What'd you say to them?"

"I answered their questions. They asked me what Caroline was working on, and I told them everything I knew."

"Did you tell them about me and Nora?"

"There's nothing to tell," she says with a grin. "I don't know anything, Mr. Agent. I just remember him leaving the office."

As I said, she's a good friend. "Did they ask you a lot of questions about me?"

"They're suspicious, but I don't think they have a clue. They just told me to take the rest of the night off. Now do you want to tell me what's really going on?"

I'm tempted, but decide against it.

"I know you're in trouble, Michael. I can see it in your face."

I keep my eyes focused on the Pad Thai. There's no reason to get her involved.

"No matter what you're thinking, you can't do this one alone. I mean, Nora's already hung you out to dry, hasn't she? Nothing's going to change that. The only question now is whether you're going to be too stubborn to ask for help." She reaches over and puts a hand on my shoulder. "I'd never betray your loyalty, Michael. If I wanted to see you drown, I would've done it already."

"Done what?"

"Told them what I think."

"Which is?"

"I think you and Nora ran into something you weren't supposed to. And whatever it was, it's got you thinking there's more to Caroline's heart attack than what they put in the press release."

I don't respond.

"You think someone killed her, don't you?"

All I can do is stay with the Pad Thai.

"We can get out of this, Michael," she promises. "Just tell me who it was. What'd you see? You don't have to keep it all to yoursel—"

"Simon," I whisper.

"What?"

"It's Simon," I repeat. "I know it sounds nuts, but that's who we saw last night." Once the gates open, it doesn't take long for me to tell her the whole story. Losing the Secret Service. Finding the bar. Trailing Simon. Getting caught with the money. By the time I'm done, I have to admit I feel the weight lift. There's nothing worse than being alone.

Slowly wiping her mouth with a napkin, Pam's still processing the information. "You think he *murdered* her?"

"I don't know what to think. I've barely had a second to catch my breath."

She shakes her head at me. "You're in trouble, Michael. This is Simon we're talking about." She says something else, but I don't hear it. All I notice is that 'we' has once again become 'me.'

My fork slips from my hand and crashes against my plate. Jolted by the noise, I'm back where I started. "So you're not going to help?"

"N-no, of course not," she stutters, looking down. "I'll definitely help."

Biting the inside of my lip, all I want to do is accept the offer. But the more I watch her pick at her food . . .

I'm not getting her into this—especially when I'm still strug-gling with how to get out. "I appreciate the ear, but—"

"It's okay, Michael, I know what I'm doing."

"No, you—"

"I do," she interrupts, growing more confident. "I didn't come here to let you fly alone." Pausing a moment, she adds, "We'll get you out of this."

On my face, I show her a smile, but deep down, I'm praying she's right. "I was thinking of pulling Simon's and Caroline's FBI files. Maybe that'll tell us why he—"

"Forget about their files," she says. "I think we should go straight to the FBI and—"

"No!" I blurt, catching us both by surprise. "I'm sorry . . . I just . . . I've already seen the results of that one. I open my mouth and Simon opens his."

"But if you tell them—"

"Who do you think they're going to believe—the Coun-sel to the President or the young associate who got nabbed with ten grand in his glove compartment? Besides, the mo-ment I start singing, I wreck my life. The vultures and their news vans'll be sniffing through every piece of dirty laun-dry they can find."

"You're worried about your dad?"

"Wouldn't you be?"

She doesn't answer. Clearing her plate from the table, she replies, "I still don't think you can just sit on this and hope it goes away."

"I'm not sitting on it—I just . . . you should've heard Simon today. Quiet's going to be what keeps me around . . ." I pause as it once again knocks the wind out of me. "That's all I have, Pam. Stay quiet and start searching. Anything else is just throwing myself to the wolves." Letting the logic make the point, I add, "Also, let's not forget the back-drop here: A scandal like this is a wrecking ball for the reelection. I guarantee that's why the FBI is keeping things so hush-hush."

Her silence lets me know I'm right. I pick up my own plate and follow her to the kitchen. Pam's pouring half of her food into the garbage disposal. Another lost appetite.

Without turning around, Pam asks, "What about Nora?"

I take a nervous sip of water. "What about her?"

"What's she going to do to help you? I mean, if she wasn't such a freakshow, you wouldn't be in this mess."

"It's not all her fault. Her life isn't as easy as you think."

"Not as easy?" Pam asks, facing me. She gives me a long, steady look, then quickly rolls her eyes. "Oh, *no*," she groans. "You're going to try and save her now, aren't you . . . ?"

"It's not that I want to save her . . ."

"You just *have to*, right? That's the way it always is."

"What're you talking about?"

"I know why you do it, Michael; I even admire why you do it . . . but just because you couldn't help your dad . . ."

"This has nothing to do with my dad!"

She lets the outburst go, knowing it'll calm me down. In the silence, I take a breath. Sure, I grew up being protective of my father, but that doesn't mean I'm protective of everyone. And with Nora, it's . . . it's different.

"It's a wonderful instinct, Michael, but this isn't like what you did with Trey. Nora's not going to be as easy to cover up."

"What're you talking about?"

"You don't have to play dumb—Trey told me how the two of you met: about how he came into your office looking for help."

"He didn't need help; he just wanted some advice."

"C'mon, now—he was caught painting devil beards and

monocles on Dellinger's campaign posters, then got arrested for destruction of property. He was terrified to bring it to his boss . . ."

"He wasn't arrested," I clarify. "All it was was a citation. The whole thing was just harmless fun, and more important, it was on his own time—it wasn't like he was acting for the campaign."

"Still, when he came in, you barely knew him; he was just a face from around headquarters . . . which means you certainly didn't have to call in any favors from your law school buddies at the DA's Office."

"I didn't do anything illegal . . ."

"I'm not saying you did, but you didn't have to run to his rescue either."

I shake my head. She doesn't understand. "Pam, don't make more of it than it is. Trey needed help, and he found me."

"No," she blurts, her voice rising. "He found you because he needed help." Watching me carefully, she adds, "For better or worse, we all have our reputations here."

"So what does that have to do with Nora?"

"Just what I said: helping Trey, and your dad, and your friends, and everyone else who needs a rescue, doesn't mean you can pull it off with Nora. Not to mention the fact that if you're not careful, she'll let you take the fall alone."

I think back to last night and the way Nora's voice cracked as she apologized. The way she said it . . . her chin quivering . . . she'd never let me fall alone. "If she's staying quiet now, it's gotta be for a reason."

"For a reason?" Pam asks. I can read it in the creases of her forehead. She thinks I'm starstruck. "Now you're being plain stupid."

"I'm sorry—that's how I see it."

"Well, regardless of how blind you want to be, you still need her help. She's the only one who can corroborate your story about Simon."

I nod, trying not to dwell on why she wouldn't see me today. "When everything calms down, I bet she comes through."

"Why do I have such a hard time believing that?"

"Because you don't like her."

"I could care less about her—I'm just worried about you."

"Don't worry, she's not going to let us down."

"I hope you're right," Pam says. "Because if she does, you're going to be free-falling without a parachute. And before you can blink, you're going to taste every second of that impact."

For financial reasons, Saturday morning means only two of my four newspapers are sitting outside my door. Even as a lawyer, government salaries only go so far. Regardless, the ritual's pretty much the same. Pulling the papers inside, I stare down at Bartlett's second consecutive day in the front photo—a beaming shot of him and his wife at their son's soccer game. Flipping the paper over, I scour the *Post*'s below-the-fold, front-page story on Caroline's death and search for my name. It's not there. Not yet.

Instead, I get a recap of her death, followed by a quick sketch of what a good friend Caroline was to the First Lady. According to the quote under the old photo of the two friends, the relationship changed Caroline's life. Looking at the picture, I can see why. Caroline's the law student, all wide-eyed and passionate in her cheap blouse and wrinkled skirt; Mrs. Hartson is her supervisor—the sparkling director of Parkinson's fund-raising in her white Miami power suit. A friendship ended by a heart attack. Please let it just be a heart attack.

On the Saturday morning drive downtown, as I approach the White House, Pennsylvania Avenue is packed with joggers and bicyclists trying to leave the work week behind. Behind them, the sun is gleaming off the mansion's ivory columns. It's the kind of sight that makes you want to spend the whole day outside. That is, unless you can't get your mind off work.

I pull up to the first checkpoint before the Southwest Appointment Gate and flash my ID to a uniformed Secret Service officer. He glances at my photo and offers me a subtle smirk. In his right hand, he's holding what looks like a pool cue with a round unbreakable mirror attached to the end of it. Without a word, he runs the mirror below the car. No bombs, no surprise guests. Knowing the rest of the ritual, I pop my rear hatch. The first officer rummages through the back of my Jeep, as I notice a second officer standing on the side with a way-too-alert German shepherd. When my car's finally parked, they'll send the dog sniffing on an hourly basis. Right now, they wave me in.

I find an open spot on State Place, right outside the steel bars of the gate. At my level, that's the best parking I can get. Outside the gate. Still, at least I have a parking pass.

Traveling the rest of the way on foot, I cross inside the gate, swipe my badge at the turnstile, and wait for the lock to click. I walk past two more guards, neither of whom gives me a second look. As I glance over my shoulder, however, I notice the officer with the mirror on the other side of the gate. Through the bars, he's staring straight at me. Smirk still on his face.

Picking up speed, I head up the sidewalk, with the OEOB

on my left and the West Wing on my right. The corridor between the two is lined with Mercedes, Jaguars, Saabs, and just enough beat-up Saturns to stave off elitist guilt. The most prestigious parking lot in the city. All of it inside the gate. An island unto itself, West Exec parking is also where the hierarchy of White House command is laid out for the world to see: the closer your spot to the entrance of the West Wing, the higher your rank. Chief of Staff is closer than the Deputy Chief of Staff, who's closer than the Domestic Policy Advisor, who's closer than me. And even though I don't usually drive to work, that doesn't mean I don't want to be inside the gate.

Getting closer to the front, I can't help myself. I pretend to hear someone calling my name and again look over my shoulder. The guard's still there. Our eyes lock and he whispers something into his walkie-talkie. What the hell is . . . Forget it. He's just trying to scare me. Who could he be speaking to anyway?

I turn back to the parking lot and see a black Volvo in Spot Twenty-six. Simon's somewhere in the building. At the end of the row, there's an old gray Honda in Spot Ninety-four. It belongs to Trey, whose boss lets him use her spot on weekends. Midway between the two, I notice there's a brand-new red car parked in Spot Forty-one. Caroline's been dead less than twenty-four hours, and someone's already taken her parking space.

As I approach the side entrance of the OEOB, I take one last glance at the guard outside the gate. For the first time since I arrived, he's gone—back to sliding his mirror under the belly of arriving cars. Still, it's just like the night on the embankment—not only is my neck soaked—I can't shake the feeling that I'm being watched.

Without even thinking, I look up at the dozens of gray windows on this end of the enormous building. Every one of them appears to be empty, but they're all somehow staring down at me like square magnifying lenses. My eyes flick across the panes of glass, searching for a friendly face. No one's there.

Inside the building, it doesn't take me long to reach the anteroom that leads to my office. Opening the door, though, I'm surprised to see that the lights are already on. I didn't see Julian's car on State Place, and Pam told me she was going to be working from home. The office should be dark. Putting the blame on a careless cleaning crew, I snake my arm behind the tallest of our file cabinets to flip off the silent alarm. But as I braille my way along the plaster, I don't like what I find. The alarm's already been turned off.

"Pam?" I call out. "Julian? Are you there?" No one answers.

Under Pam's door, I notice that the light is on. "Pam, are you there?" Just as I turn toward her office, I notice that the three stackable plastic file-trays that serve as our mailboxes are all full. Next to the table, the coffeemaker is off. I'm about to open her door when I freeze. I know my friend. Whoever's in there, it's not Pam.

I rush toward my office, push the door open, and dart inside. Spinning around, I grab the deadbolt and lock it. That's when it hits me. I shouldn't have been able to open my door. It's supposed to be locked.

Behind me, something moves by the sofa. Then by my desk. A creak of vinyl. A pencil rolling down a keyboard. They're not in Pam's office. They're in mine.

I turn around, struggling to catch my breath. It's too late. There are two men waiting for me. Both of them head my way. I turn back to the door, but it's locked. My hands are shaking as I lunge for the deadbolt.

A fist comes down and pounds me in the knuckles. My

hands still don't leave the deadbolt. Clutching. Clawing. Anything to get out.

Over my shoulder, a fat, meaty hand covers my mouth. I try to scream, but his grip's too tight. The tips of his fingers dig into my jaw, his nails scratching my cheek.

"Don't fight it," he warns. "This'll only take a second."

CHAPTER 10

W here the hell are we going?" I ask as we head up the hallway. On Saturday, the place is near-empty. The two men are holding me tightly by the back of my arms and forcing me toward the West Exec exit.

"Stop complaining," the one on my right says. He's a tall black man with a neck as thick as my thigh. From his posture and build, I'm assuming Secret Service, but he's not dressed the part—too casual, not enough polish. And there's no microphone in his ear. More important, they didn't identify themselves—which means these guys aren't who I thought they were.

Skittishly, I try to jerk my arm free. Annoyed, he squeezes even harder and jabs two fingers into my biceps. It hurts like a son of a bitch, but I refuse to give him the satisfaction of crying out. Instead, I bite down as hard as I can. He keeps digging, and I feel my face flush red. I can't keep it up much longer. My shoulder starts to go numb. From the smug grin on his face, he's definitely enjoying himself. His pleasure; my pain. "Ow!" I shout as he eventually lets go. "What the hell is wrong with you?"

He doesn't respond. He just pushes the door open and

forces me out into West Exec parking. Trying not to panic, I tell myself that nothing bad can happen as long as we're in the West Wing—security's too high. Before I can relax, though, a sharp tug to the left lets me know that the West Wing isn't on the itinerary. Crossing toward the north side of the White House, we head past the briefing room and toward the tradesmen's entrance, where most of the mansion's deliveries are made. My eyes are focused on the large yellow van that's straight ahead. There should be workmen around, but I don't see any. We get closer to the van. The back doors are wide open. I stop walking and start backtracking. My arms thrash to break free. I'm not letting them put me in there.

My escorts tighten their grip and drag me forward. My shoes scrape hopelessly against the concrete. My arms are held in place. As hard as I fight, it's no use. They're too strong. "Almost there," one of them warns. With one last tug, we're right behind the van. It's empty inside. I'm about to scream. And just like that, they shove me to the right and we're past it. I look over my shoulder and the van fades behind me. Then I look back and realize our real destination. The tradesmen's entrance. I'm not sure which is worse.

Inside the building, they throw a knowing nod to the uniformed officer who guards the door. When he lets us pass, it becomes clear that these guys are doing someone a favor. Only Lamb and Simon have that kind of power.

The hallway is cluttered with dozens of empty crates and boxes. The smell of fresh flowers from the White House florist fills the air.

We make a sharp left and head down another long hall. My heart's pounding against my chest. I've never been down here before. The white guy pulls out a janitor-size set of keys. He turns the lock and pulls the door open.

The area's too secluded. "Tell me what's—"

"Don't worry—you'll be safe." He reaches for my arm, but I quickly pull away. This isn't a place to meet Simon or Lamb.

"I'm not going in there!"

The first guy grabs me by the back of the neck. I lash out at him, but I don't have a chance. They twist my arms behind my back and, with a quick shove, force me inside. Stumbling to the ground, I nearly fall on my face. As I crash-land on my knees and the palms of my hands, I finally check my surroundings. It's a long, incredibly narrow room. In front of me is a long polished wooden floor. At the far end are ten striped pins. To my right, I hear the hum of the automatic ball return. What am I doing in a bowling alley?

"Up for a game, sport?" a familiar voice asks.

I turn to the spectator seats behind the scorekeeper's table. Nora stands up and walks toward me. Reaching down and extending a hand, she's hoping to help me to my feet. I refuse the offer.

"What the hell is wrong with you?" I ask.

"I wanted to speak to you."

"So that's what you do? You send the Planet of the Apes to manhandle me?" I struggle to my feet and brush myself off.

"I told them not to say anything—you never know who's listening."

"Or who's not listening. I must've called you twenty times; you never once returned my calls."

She goes back to her original seat and motions for me to join her. It's her way of avoiding the question.

"No, thanks," I tell her. "Now why'd you have the Service lie when I came by to see you?"

"Please don't be mad, Michael. I was abou—"

"Why'd you lie?" I shout, my voice echoing through the narrow room.

Realizing I need to vent, she lets it pass. It's been a tough two days. For both of us. Truthfully, though, I don't care. It's my ass they're going to pin it on, not hers.

Eventually, she picks her head up. "I didn't have a choice."

"Oh, suddenly you're sapped of your free will?"

"You know what I'm talking about. It's not that easy."

"Actually, it's really easy—all you have to do is pick up the phone and dial my extension. Near as I can tell, that's the least you can do."

"So now it's all my fault?"

"You *are* the one who took the money."

She gives me a steady, cold look. "And you're the last person who saw her alive."

I don't like that tone in her voice. "What're you saying?"

"Nothing," she purrs, suddenly unconcerned.

"Don't give me that—you just . . ." My voice cracks. "Are you threatening me, Nora?"

She tosses me a dark grin. Her voice is ice smooth. "Say a word to anyone, Michael, and I'll slaughter you with this." As the words leave her lips, I feel my heart in my throat. I swear, I can't breathe.

"That's what you get for being a nice guy," she adds, refusing to let up. "Sucks to be you, huh?"

Oh, God. It's just like Pam said . . .

Nora breaks into a smile. And starts laughing. Pointing at me and laughing. The whole room is filled with her playful cackle.

A joke. It was just a joke.

"C'mon, Michael, you really think I'd desert you?" she asks, still plenty amused.

The blood flushes back to my face. I look at her with disbelief. Two people—one body. "That wasn't funny, Nora."

"Then don't point fingers. It's no way to make friends."

"I wasn't pointing fingers . . . I just . . . I don't like being left out to dangle."

She turns away and shakes her head. Her whole body suddenly looks deflated. "I couldn't do that to you, Michael. Even if I wanted to. Not after you . . ." She stops, searching for words. "What you did for me . . . I owe you way more than that."

I can practically feel the pendulum swing back. "Does that mean you're going to help?"

She looks back, almost surprised by the question. "C'mon now, after all this, you really think I wouldn't be there for you?"

"It's not just about being there—if things go bad, I may need you to corroborate my side of the story."

Lowering her gaze, she studies the empty scorekeeper's sheet in front of her.

"What?" I ask. "Say it."

Again, all she does is stare down at the sheet.

I can't believe it. "So that's the way it goes, huh? Now I'm suddenly back on my own?"

"No, not at all," she shoots back. "I told you I'd never do that—it's just that—" She cuts herself off, but finally turns my way. "Don't you get it, Michael? If I get involved, all it does is get worse."

"What're you talking about?"

"Do you even realize what would happen if they found out we were dating?"

Did she just say we were dating?

"They'd kill you, Michael. They'd put your picture on the front page, talk to every teacher and enemy you ever had, and eat you alive—all to see if you're good enough for me. You saw how they tore through my last boyfriend. After three weeks of having reporters stalk him, he called me up, told me he was nursing an ulcer, and broke it off."

I know this is no time to get distracted, but I can't help but smile. "So now I'm your boyfriend?"

"Stay on subject here. Even if I jump in and take the beating myself, they're still going to tear you down with me."

I stop mid-step, a few feet from the scoreboard. "How do you know? Did someone say that to you?"

"They don't have to say it—you know how it works."

Much as I hate to admit it, she's right about that one. Every time a bigshot falls, everyone near the epicenter goes down with them. Even if I'm innocent, the public needs to think we've cleaned house.

I close my eyes and shade them with my hand, hoping to get some distance. For the past two days, there was always at least one clear way out—sacrifice Nora and save myself. But once again, with Nora, it's never that simple. Even if I give her up, they'll still hang me out to dry. "Damn!"

My shout rumbles down the lane, but Nora never looks up. With her head bent over, and the way she stuffs her hands behind her knees, she once again becomes that little girl. It's not easy for her either. She knows she's put me in this one. That's the penlight at the end of the tunnel—she's not just worried about herself—she's worried about me. "Michael, I swear to you, if I thought it'd be like this, I never would've—"

"You don't have to say it, Nora."

"No. I do. Whatever else happens, I got you into this, and I'll get you out."

She says the words forcefully, but I can still hear her fear. Her eyes are locked on the floor of the bowling alley. *Her* bowling alley. She's got a lot more to lose. "You sure you want to risk this, Nora?"

Slowly, she looks up at me. She's been debating this one since I dropped her off the other night. Her hands are still stuffed nervously behind her knees. But the answer comes as quickly as her grin. "Yeah," she nods. "No question."

My mind is racing with all the reasons Pam and Trey gave me to walk away. And all their Freud-babble explanations for why I'd stay: my need to protect, my need to help my dad, my need to somehow get the inside track to the President . . . But as I stand here—as I watch Nora—there's only one real thing that makes sense. Unlike before, it's not about the stupid things like the way she looks at me and the way she says my name. It's not about how much she needs me, or even who she is. In the end, as I take it all in, it's about what Nora Hartson is willing to give up—for me—to make things right.

"I'll get you out," she repeats confidently. "I'll get you—"

"We," I interrupt. *"We* got in. *We'll* get out." I take the seat next to her and put a hand on her shoulder. It's the same thing with my dad—sometimes the only way to problem-solve is to look past *how we got here*. And while I don't necessarily like it . . . with my family . . . it's the only way I know how to live.

Once again, she picks her head up. A soft smile lights her cheeks. "Just so you know, I hate romantics."

"Me too. Hate 'em with a passion," I shoot back. She's got the comeback ready, but I don't give her a chance. The only way out of the box is to figure out what really happened. "Now what about your bodyguards? Did you tell them what's going on?"

"These guys? They just work the weekends. I told them we went on a date and you pissed me off. They figure this is make-up time. Why? Did you tell your girlfriend Pam?"

"How do you know about Pam?"

"I checked you out, Garrick. I don't date every slob in the building."

"She's not my girlfriend," I add.

"That's not what she thinks, Romeo." She gets up from her seat, heads for the alley, and throws an imaginary bowling ball down the lane. "You know Nixon used to come down here and bowl ten games back-to-back? Is that psychoville, or what?"

As she asks the question, I can't help but notice how quickly her mood's changed. Within seconds, she's a different person. And once again I'm reminded that I've never met anyone who can make me feel so old and so young at the same time.

"So did you tell Pam, or what?"

"Yeah," I say hesitantly. "I didn't have anyone else to talk to, so I—"

"Don't apologize. Chris said I should've got to you sooner."

"You told your brother?"

"He's family—and one of the few who can handle it." She throws another imaginary ball down the lane.

Pointing to the rack of bowling balls, I say, "Y'know, the real ones are right behind you."

She looks at me with those pick-you-apart eyes. "I hate bowling," she says, matter-of-factly. "Now tell me what happened when you went to see her."

"Caroline?"

"No, the other dead woman with thirty grand in her safe. Of course, Caroline."

I quickly relay all the important details.

"So Simon narked on *you?*" she asks when I'm done. "Forget Washington-ruthless; this guy's film-industry."

"That's the least of it. Let's not forget he might've killed her."

"You don't think it was a heart attack?"

"I guess it could've been . . . but . . . with everything from the bar, it seems like a hell of a coincidence."

"Maybe," she begins. "But you'd be surprised why things happen—especially around here."

I'm not sure what she means by that, and she's not giving me a chance to ask.

"Assuming it was Simon," she continues, "why do you think he did it?"

"It's got to have something to do with that money."

"You still convinced he's selling secrets?"

"I don't know. When you sell secrets, you drop off information. He had nothing but cash—the same cash that was in Caroline's safe."

"So you think he was being blackmailed?"

"Married man in a gay bar? You saw his expression in there. He didn't look like he was in control—he was scared. If you wanted control, you talked to Caroline."

"I see where you're going. Caroline's the blackmailer, and Simon killed her to stay quiet."

"She's the only one with access to all that personal information. And she relished it. You should've seen how she came after me." Staring at the end of the alley, I have a lateral view that allows me to see all ten pins. "There's just this one thing that doesn't make sense: If Caroline was doing the blackmailing, why didn't Simon take back his money when he killed her?"

Once again, Nora finds that dark grin. She shakes her head like I'm missing something. "Maybe he didn't know the safe's combination. Maybe he didn't want to get caught with it. For all we know, maybe it really was a heart attack. Or best of all, with his fake story, maybe it's the best way to put the blame on you. If he saw us the other night, he certainly could've seen the cops. Now the whole plot changes. The ten thousand the cops confiscated was only a quarter of it. The rest you gave to Caroline as hush money. The consecutive numbers on the bills prove it. *You're* the one who was being blackmailed. *You're* the one who has the money. *You're* the one who killed her."

The money. It always comes back to the money. In the safe. In my glove compartment. In my name. Consecutively marked, it's all tied to me. She's hit it on the head. The money with the D.C. police is a time bomb. And as soon as someone finds out about it, it's going to explode. Even if it was a heart attack—with that kind of cash in my possession . . . in that neighborhood—just raising the specter of drugs, my job's history. They'll cut me loose simply to avoid the front-page story. And if the autopsy shows it's a murder . . . Oh, God. I rub the back of my neck, doing my best to stall. What I'm about to say is going to set her off, but it has to be done. "Nora, if this starts snowballing, it's going to work its way to the top."

Across the narrow room, she leans against the rack of bowling balls and stares directly at me. She knows it's true. I can see it in her dancing eyes. She's terrified. "They're going to try to kill him with it, aren't they?"

There he is again. Her father. However it plays out, a scandal like this takes a mean toll. Especially with Bartlett nipping at the lead.

"All we need is some time," she says, vigorously rubbing her nose. "It can still work out okay."

The more she talks, the more her voice picks up speed. It reminds me of the speech she gave at the party's national convention when her father was nominated all those years ago. Initially, they asked her brother, Chris, to speak, thinking that America would rally around a young man standing up for his dad. But after a few private run-throughs, where Chris stumbled over words and looked generally panicked, Nora asked if she could step in. The campaign played it as the firstborn child coming to the forefront, while our opponents played it as another bossy Hartson vying for control.

When it was all over, Nora, like any other eighteen-year-old speaking to a group of a hundred and ten million people, was criticized for being jittery and unpolished. That's what you get for trying to steal the spotlight, a few critics blasted. But as I watch her now, anxiously rocking back and forth at the mere mention of her father's pain, I think it was less a power play and more a protective one. When she got up there, Chris didn't have to. And when the beating gets particularly hard, we all take care of our own.

"For all we know—it's just a heart attack," she stutters. "Maybe Simon'll even stay quiet."

What am I supposed to say? *No, your father's life is definitely going to get wrecked—especially if I scream the truth?* In the span of a few unstrung seconds, my options quickly narrow: I open my mouth, her dad takes it in the knees, and since I'm at the epicenter, we all go down. If I keep my mouth shut, I buy some time to sniff around, but I risk going down alone. Once again, I look over at the pins at the end of the alley. I can't help but feel like the lead pin in the triangle. The one that always gets creamed by the ball.

"Maybe you should talk to him," I suggest. "Just so he knows who to trust. I mean, even if it was a heart attack, Simon was being blackmailed for something—and unless we figure it out, he's going to keep hanging the noose around me."

Nora looks at me, but doesn't say a word.

"So you'll talk to him?"

She pauses. "I can't."

"What do you mean *you can't?*"

"I'm telling you, he can't be bothered with this stuff. He won't . . . he won't understand. He's not your average dad." Right there, I stop arguing. I know that frustration in her voice. And I know that world—an orphan with a living parent.

"Is there anyone else you can—?"

"I already told my Uncle Larry."

"Who?"

"Larry. Larry Lamb."

"Of course," I say, trying to be nonchalant. She's not going to call him Lawrence. She's known him since birth— I read the *People* magazine cover story—she and her brother spent summers at his farm in Connecticut. There was a picture of Nora and Christopher in mid-scream on a swing set, and another one of them hiding under the covers of Lamb's four-poster bed. I sink down in my seat and gather my thoughts. *He's* the shadow of the President; *she* calls him Uncle Larry. It sounds almost silly when you think about it. But that's who she is. Still acting unimpressed, I eventually ask, "What'd he say?"

"Exactly what you'd expect. *'Thank you. I'm glad you told me. It was ruled a heart attack, but I'll look into it.'* He's got his eyes on reelection—there's no way he's pulling the plug now. When everything dies down, they'll do the official investigation."

"So where does that leave us?" I ask.

"It leaves us as the only two people who care about protecting your butt. As it is, Simon seems happy to keep it quiet—but that's not much of a solution."

I nod. Détente won't work forever. Sooner or later, the more powerful side realizes its advantage. And the other side dies. "I just wish we had some more information. If Caroline was doing this, it probably wasn't just to Simon. She had all our secrets—she could've been doing this to—"

"Actually, that reminds me . . ." Nora walks over to the scorekeeper's seat, picks up her black leather purse, and pulls out a folded-up sheet of paper.

"What's this?" I ask as she hands it to me.

"It came in when I was talking to Uncle Larry. They're the names on two of the FBI files that were found in Caroline's office."

Rick Ferguson and Gary Seward. One's up for a presidential appointment at Treasury, the other just started at Commerce. "I don't understand," I say. "Why only two?"

"Apparently, she had tons of files all over her office—and not just for presidential appointments. Some were judicial, some were from the Counsel's Office . . ."

"She had mine. I saw it."

"The FBI's rechecking each one."

"So they released a full list of the names?"

"Not until they're done. According to the memo, they don't want to tip anyone off. Instead, for security purposes, we get them as they clear them—one or two at a time."

"And how'd you get these?" I ask, holding up the sheet of paper.

"I told you, Uncle Larry."

"He gave them to you?"

"Actually, he walked out to talk to his secretary, and I copied the names on some scrap paper."

"You stole them?"

"Do you want them or not?"

"Of course I want them. I just don't want you stealing them from Lawrence Lamb."

"He doesn't care. The man's my godfather—he took the training wheels off my bike; he's not gonna care if I sneak a peek at a file. At least this way, we're not sitting in the dark."

It's no consolation. "So that means the FBI's looking at my file."

"Relax, Michael. I'm sure they'll clear you."

Trying to believe that, I stare down at the list. Nora's

handwriting has a circular bubble-quality to it. Like a third-grade girl who's just learning to write in cursive. Rick Ferguson. Gary Seward. Two people who've been declared innocent by the FBI. I try to remember how many files I saw in Caroline's office. There were at least five or six under mine—and probably more in the drawers. Looks like the FBI is also thinking blackmail. Turning back to Nora, I ask, "Why'd you wait until now to give these to me?"

"I don't know. I guess I forgot," she says with a shrug. "Listen, I gotta run. Some Prime Minister's bringing his family by for a photo-op."

"Are you going to see your uncle there?"

"The only person I'm going to see is the Prime Minister's son. Handsome lad, y'know."

I'm not sure if she's trying to change the subject or make me jealous. Either way, it's worked. "So that's who you're dumping me for?"

"Hey, if you get your own country, they'll try to get me to kiss your ass as well. In the meantime, though, I'm puckering elsewhere—these guys'll freak if I'm late."

"I'm sure they will. Foreign markets'll tumble; honor'll be lost. It goes hand in hand with tardiness: international incident."

"You like to hear yourself talk, don't you?"

"Even more than you like photo-ops with foreign strangers. But that's just another day in the life, huh?"

"Ever since the last hour of sixth grade."

"I don't understand."

"That's the day my dad decided. Running for Governor; or at least, that's the day he told me. I still remember waiting for the last bell to ring—and then tearing out of the classroom and flying toward the bike rack with Melissa Persily. I was supposed to sleep over her house that night. She was one of those cool kids who lived close enough to bike to school—so the bike rack itself was a big deal. She had her own combination lock and this beat-up black ten-speed that used to be her brother's . . ." Nora's voice is racing as she looks up. "Man, it was tomboy heav—" The second our eyes connect, she cuts herself off. Like before, her gaze goes straight to the floor.

"What?" I ask.

"No . . . nothing . . ."

"What d'you mean *nothing?* What happened? You're at the bike rack . . . you're going to the sleepover . . ."

"It's really nothing," she insists, stepping backwards. "Listen, I really should go."

"Nora, it's just a childhood story. What're you so scared—"

"I'm not scared," she insists.

That's when I see the lie.

For the past two months, Nora's spent every day in full election mode—from three-hundred-person luncheons with big donors, to sitting next to her mom at satellite-televised rallies, to, if she's in a real good mood and they can get her to cooperate, giving interviews on why college kids should mobilize and vote—she's been the youngest and most reluctant master of the grip-and-grin. That's what she's known since sixth grade. But today . . . today she got caught up in a real moment; she was even enjoying it. And it scared the hell out of her.

"Nora," I call out as she heads for the door. "Just so you know, I'd never tell anyone."

She stops where she is and slowly turns around. "I know," she says, nodding me a thank-you. "But I really have to go—you know the game—sitting Presidents have to look strong on foreign policy."

I think back to Bartlett in the front photo.

Nora's almost out the door. Then, just as she's about to

leave, she turns my way and takes a deep breath. Her voice is a hushed reluctance. "When we got to the bike rack, my mom was sitting there, waiting for me. She took me home, my dad told me he was running for Governor, and that was it. No sleepover at Melissa Persily's—I'm the only one who missed it. The next year, Melissa started calling me 'It.' As in, 'There *It* is,' and 'Don't let *It* come near me.' It was stupid, but the class sided with her. That was junior high." Without another word, Nora regrabs the doorknob. The Prime Minister's son awaits.

"Don't you ever get sick of it?" I ask.

Once again, it's a chance to open up. She offers a weak smile. "No."

It doesn't take much to see through her answer. But instinct still made her say *no*. On some level, she doesn't trust me with everything just yet. I'll get there eventually. She said it herself. Whatever else is going on, I'm *dating* the First Daughter of the United States.

I walk into Trey's office sporting a Cheshire cat grin. Ten minutes later, he's yelling at me.

"Stupid, Michael. Stupid, stupid, stupid!"

"Why're you getting so nuts?"

"Who else have you told about this? How many?"

"Just you," I answer.

"Don't lie to me."

He knows me too well. "I told Pam. Just you and Pam. That's it. I swear."

Trey runs the palm of his hand from the light brown skin of his forehead to the back of his shortly buzzed afro. His small hand moves slowly across his head—I've seen it before—he calls it "the rub." A quick rub is like an embarrassed little laugh or snicker, used when a dignitary trips or falls in the middle of a photo-op. The speed slows down as the consequences grow, and the slower the rub, the more he's upset. When *Time* ran an unflattering profile of the First Lady, the rub was slow. When the President was rumored to have cancer, it was even slower. Five minutes ago, I told him what happened with Nora and Caroline. I check his hand to clock the speed. Molasses.

"It's only two people. Why're you making such a big deal?"

"Let me make this as clear as possible: I love the fact that you're moving up in the world, and I love the fact that you trust me with all your secrets. I even love the fact Nora wants to climb in your pants—believe me, we're going to be getting back to that one—but when it comes to something this big, you should keep your mouth shut."

"So I shouldn't have told you?"

"You shouldn't have told me and you shouldn't have told Pam." He pauses a moment. "Okay, you should've told me. But that's it."

"Pam would never say anything."

"How do you know that? Has she trusted you with any of her stuff?"

I know what he's driving at when he asks that question. He may only be a twenty-six-year-old staffer, but when it comes to figuring out where to step, Trey knows where all the land mines are.

"I'm telling you," he says, "if Pam doesn't share it with you, you shouldn't share it with her."

"See, now you're being too political. Not everything in life is tit for tat."

"This is the White House, Michael. It's always tit for tat."

"I don't care. You're wrong about Pam. She doesn't have anything to gain."

"Please, boychick, you know she loves you."

"So? I love her too."

"No, not like that, Magoo. She doesn't just love you."
He puts his hand over his heart like he's doing the Pledge
of Allegiance, then quickly starts drumming against his chest.
"She *wuuuvs* you," he croons, rolling his eyes. "I'm talking
the pretty pink dreams: teddy bears . . . ice-cream shakes . . .
happy floating rainbows . . ."

"Get over yourself, Trey. You couldn't be further from
reality."

"Don't mock me, boy. It's just like what the President
does with Lawrence Lamb."

"What do you mean?"

Instinctively, Trey leans back in his chair and cranes his
neck to check the rest of the reception area. He shares an
office with two other people. Both of his officemates' desks
are by a window, sectioned off by a few filing cabinets.
Trey's is by the door. He likes to see who's coming and
going. Neither of his co-workers is in today, but Trey can't
help himself. It's the first rule of politics. Know who's listening. When he's satisfied we're alone, he says, "Look at
their relationship. Lamb sits in on all your meetings, he's in
on all the final decisions, his title's even Deputy Counsel,
but when it comes to actual legal work, he's nowhere to be
found. Now why do you think that is?"

"He's a lazy, toothless bastard?"

"I'm serious. Lamb's there to keep an eye on you and
the rest of your office."

"That's not—"

"C'mon, Michael, if you were President, who would you
rather have watching your back: a group of strangers from
your staff, or a friend you've had for thirty years? Lamb
knows all the personal stuff—that's why he's trusted. The
same goes for us; it's been almost four years since I first
spoke to you on the campaign, but this place moves in dog
years. Yet with Pam . . ."

"I appreciate the concern, but she'd never say anything. She's from Ohio."

"Ulysses S. Grant was from Ohio and he had the most corrupt administration in history. It's all an act—those Midwesterners are ruthless."

"I'm from Michigan, Trey."

"Except for the ones from Michigan. Love those people."

Shaking my head, I say, "You're just mad because I told Pam first."

He can't help but leak a smile. "I want you to know, I'm the one who kept your name out of the papers. I didn't tell anyone you found the body."

"And I appreciate that. But right now, I want to talk about Nora. Tell me what you know."

"What's to know? She's the First Daughter. She's got her own fan club. She doesn't answer her own mail. And she's severely yummy. She's also a little bit of a headcase, but, now that I think about it, that actually turns me on."

He's making too many jokes. Something's wrong. "Say what you're thinking, Trey."

He runs his hands down the length of his cheap maroon-striped tie. With his scuffed tasseled loafers, knockoff John Lennon glasses, and his stiff navy jacket with the gold button covertly safety-pinned in place, he's a few dollars short of the model young prep. It's amazing, really. He's got less money than anyone on staff, and he's still the only one wearing a suit on Saturday.

"I told you before, Michael: You're in trouble. These people aren't lightweights."

"But what do you think about Nora?"

"I think you better be careful. I don't know her personally, but I see her when she comes in to find her mom. In and out: always quick; sometimes upset; and never a word to anyone."

"That doesn't mean—"

"I'm not talking about courtesy—I'm talking about the underneath. She may let you touch her cookies, and she may be a braggable girlfriend, but you know the rumors—X, Special K, maybe some cocaine . . ."

"Who said she's doing coke?"

"No one. At least not yet. That's why we call it a rumor, my friend. It's too big to print without a source."

I stay silent.

"You don't know her, Michael. You may've watched her throw Frisbees with her dog on the South Lawn, and you may've seen her go off to her first sociology class at college, but that's not her life. Those're just press clippings and fluff for the nightlies. The rest of the picture is hidden. And the picture's huge."

"So you're saying I should just abandon her?"

"Abandon her?" he laughs. "After all you've done . . . no one could accuse you of that. Not even Nora."

He's right. But it doesn't make it any easier. When I don't respond, he adds, "It's really starting to get to you, isn't it?"

"I just don't like how everyone automatically paints the target on her."

"On *her?* What abou—" He catches himself. And sees the look on my face. "Oh, jeez, Michael, don't tell me you're . . . Oh, you are, aren't you? This isn't just about protecting her . . . you're actually starting to like her now, aren't you?"

"No," I shoot back. "Now you're reading too much into it."

"Really?" he challenges. "Then answer me this: Sexually speaking, when you went out that first night, what actually happened?"

"I don't understand."

"You want me to ask in Latin? The two of you went on a date. Before you left, you swore you'd give me every last detail. In fact, I think the quote was, *'I'm gonna check out the underwear on the First Daughter.'* You were all primed for the locker room debriefing—so let's hear it. What actually happened? How'd she kiss? Throw me some play-by-play."

Once again, I'm silent.

"Don't hold back," Trey adds. "Was she good or tongue-sloppy?"

My mind is flooded with images of her in my arms . . . and the way she slid her hand across my thigh . . . Oh, man, Trey would die if he heard tha— I stop myself and look down at the muted blue industrial carpet.

"So?" Trey asks. "Tell me what happened."

I'm sure every guy who's ever dated her has been put in this position. My answer comes in a whisper. "No."

"What?"

"No," I repeat. "It's no one's business. Not even yours."

Rolling his eyes and crossing his arms against his chest, Trey leans back in his seat. "Just because you've seen her on the TV in your living room, doesn't mean she's been there, Michael. Besides, even if the whisperings are wrong, first and foremost, she's Hartson's daughter."

"What's that supposed to mean?"

"It means she's got politics in her blood. So if the two of you get pinned against the wall, well . . . she'll be the one slithering away."

CHAPTER 11

The first thing I do when I get home is open the tiny metal mailbox for apartment 708, collect my newest pile of mail, and head over to the front desk. "Anything down there?" I ask Fidel, who's been the building's doorman since before I moved in.

He looks below the counter, where they keep the packages.

"Can you also check for Sidney?" I add.

He stands up holding a cardboard box with a FedEx sticker on it and slaps it on the counter. It rattles like a Spanish maraca. "Nothing for you; pills for Sidney," Fidel says, flashing his wide smile.

With my briefcase in one hand and mail in the other, I wedge the package under my armpit, slide it off the desk, and head for the elevator. "Have a good night, Fidel."

Angling the corner of the oversized box to press the elevator button marked 7, I stare at the name on the package. Sidney Gottesman. Apartment 709. Celebrating his ninety-sixth birthday in October, Sidney's been my neighbor for the past two years. And bedridden for two months.

When I first moved in, on a Superbowl Sunday, he was

nice enough to invite me over to watch the game—he was asleep by the second quarter. When his doctors amputated his right leg because of diabetes complications, I did my best to return Sidney's favor. In his wheelchair, he can handle the mail—he just hates taking packages.

Balancing the package in one arm and my briefcase in the other, I knock on his door. "Sidney! It's me!" He doesn't answer. He never answers.

Knowing the routine, I leave the box on his rubber doormat and cross the hall to my apartment. As I turn, the hallway's quiet. More quiet than when I arrived. The building's air-conditioning hums. The dryer in the laundry room tumbles. Behind me, I hear the clunky arrival of the elevator. I spin around to see who's there, but no one gets out. The door slides shut. The hallway's still silent.

Searching for my keys, I reach into my right pocket, then my left. They're not there. Damn. Don't tell me I . . . Did I leave them downstairs with the . . . No—here—in my hand. Wasting no time, I shove the key into my front door and twist the lock. "Looking for a new job?" a man's voice asks from down the hall.

Startled, I turn to my right and see Joel Westman, my next-door neighbor, coming out of his apartment. "Excuse me?" I ask.

"Some guy knocked on my door this afternoon and asked me a few quick questions about you. Last time that happened, it was the FBI."

My briefcase slips from my hand and falls to the floor. As it hits, the locks pop open, releasing my papers all along the front of my door.

"You okay there?" Joel asks.

"Y-Yeah. Of course," I say, struggling to sweep the papers back into place. When I started at the White House, the FBI talked to my neighbors as part of the background check. Whatever they're up to, it's faster than I expected.

"So you're not looking for a new job?"

"No," I say with a forced laugh. "They're probably just updating their files." As Joel heads up the hall, I add, "What'd they ask anyway?"

"It was just one guy this time. Late twenties. Boston accent. Heavy on the gold chains."

I look up at Joel, but stifle my reaction. Since when does the FBI wear gold chains?

"I know, kinda weird, but . . . hey, whatever keeps the nation safe," Joel continues. "Don't sweat it, though—he didn't ask anything special: what I knew about you; when you were home; what kind of hours you kept. Similar to last time." Joel starts to read the nervousness on my face. "Was I not supposed to say anything?"

"No, no, not at all. They do this every couple of years. Nothing to worry about."

As Joel heads toward the elevator, I'm left trying to figure out who he was talking to. A minute ago, I was panicked by the FBI. Now I'm praying for them.

Opening the door to my apartment, I notice a sheet of paper folded in half. Someone slipped it under the door while I was gone. Inside is a three-word message: "We Should Talk." It's signed "P. Vaughn."

P. Vaughn, P. Vaughn, P. Vaughn. I roll the name through my subconscious, but nothing comes up. Behind me, the front door to my apartment slams shut. I jump from the bang. Although the sun hasn't set, the apartment feels dark. As quickly as possible, I turn on the lights in the hallway, the kitchen, and the living room. Something still feels wrong.

In the kitchen, I hear the measured pings of the leaky faucet. Two days ago, it was a sound I had long since internalized. Today, all it does is remind me of finding Caroline. The puddle of coffee that ran to the floor. One eye straight, one eye cockeyed.

I pull a sponge from the counter and stuff it in the drain. It doesn't stop the leaking, but it muffles the sound. Now all I notice is the muted humming of the central air-conditioning. Desperate for silence, I head toward the living room and shut it off. It fades with an awkward cough.

I look around the apartment, studying its details. My desk. The rented furniture. The posters. It all looks the same, but something's different. For no reason whatsoever, my eyes focus on the black leather couch. The two beige throw-pillows are exactly where I left them. The middle cushion still bears the imprint from where I watched TV last night. A single bead of sweat runs down the back of my neck. Without the air conditioner, the room is stifling. I look back at the name in the note. P. Vaughn. P. Vaughn. The faucet's still dripping.

I step out of my shoes and take off my shirt. Best thing to do is lose myself in a shower. Clean up. Start over. But as I head to the bathroom, I notice, right by the edge of the couch, the pen that's sitting on the floor. Not just any pen—my red-white-and-blue-striped White House pen. With a tiny presidential seal and the words "The White House" emblazed in gold letters, the pen was a gift during my first week at work. Everyone has one, but that doesn't mean I don't treasure it—which is exactly why I wouldn't leave it on the floor. Once again looking around, I don't see anything out of place. It could've just fallen from the coffee table. But as I reach down to pick it up, I hear a noise from the hall closet.

It's not anything loud—just a quiet click. Like the flick of two fingers. Or someone shifting their weight. I spin around, watching for movement. Nothing happens. I put on my shirt and stuff my pen in my pocket, as if that's going to help. Still nothing. The apartment is so quiet, I notice the sound of my own breathing.

Slowly, I move toward the closet door. It's barely ajar. I feel the adrenaline rushing. There's only one way to deal with this. Time to stop being a victim. Before I can talk myself out of it, I race at the door, ramming it shoulder first. The door slams shut and I grab the handle with everything in me.

"Who the hell are you?" I scream in my most intimidating voice.

With my weight against the door, I'm braced for impact. But no one fights back. "Answer me," I warn.

Once again, the apartment's silent.

Looking over my shoulder, I peer into the kitchen. A wooden block full of knives is on the counter. "I'm opening the door, and I have a knife!"

Silence.

"This is it—come out slowly! On three! One . . . two . . ." I pull open the door and race for the kitchen. By the time I turn around, there's a six-inch steak knife in my hand. The only thing I see, though, is a closetful of coats.

Wielding the knife in front of me, I take a step toward the closet. "Hello?" In a teen slasher pic, this is the moment when the killer jumps out. It doesn't stop me.

Slowly, I pick my way through the rack of coats. When I'm done, though, I realize the truth: No one's there.

My shirt now pressed with sweat against my chest, I return the knife to the kitchen and turn the air-conditioning back on. Just as the hum returns, I hit the play button on the answering machine. Time to get rid of the silence.

"You have one message," the machine tells me in its mechanical voice. "Saturday, one-fifty-seven P.M."

A second passes before a man's voice begins, "Michael,

this is Randall Adenauer with the FBI. We have an appointment on Tuesday, but I'd like to send some officers over tomorr—" He stops, distracted. "Then tell them I'll call him back!" he shouts, sounding like he's covering the receiver. Turning back to the phone, he adds, "I apologize, Michael. Please give me a call."

Pulling the White House pen from my pocket, I jot down his number and breathe a quick sigh of relief. He sent them over—that's who it was—gold chains or not, that must've been who Joel was talking to. FBI Agent Vaughn. I hit Erase on the answering machine and walk back to my bedroom. When I reach my nightstand, I stop dead in my tracks. There it is, on top of yesterday's crossword puzzle—a red-white-and-blue-striped pen with the words "The White House" emblazed on it. I look down at the pen in my hand. Then back at the one on my nightstand. Rewinding twenty-four hours, I think about Pam's visit with the Thai food. It could easily be Pam's, I tell myself. Please let it be Pam's.

Early Monday morning, on Labor Day, I'm sitting in the back row of a passenger van, still trying to convince myself that an FBI agent would communicate by sliding a note under my door. P. Vaughn. Peter Vaughn? Phillip Vaughn? Who the hell is this guy?

Driven by a sergeant in a gray sportcoat and a thin black tie, the van thunders down the highway, following the two identical vans in front of it. Sitting next to me is Pam, who hasn't said a word since our six A.M. pickup in West Exec parking. The remaining eleven passengers are following her lead. It's a minor miracle, really: thirteen White House lawyers packed in a van and no one's bragging, much less talking. But it's not just the early hour that's keeping everyone quiet. It's our destination. Today we bury one of our own.

Twenty minutes later, at Andrews Air Force Base, we check in with a uniformed guard at the gatehouse. At barely half past six, the sky's still dark, but everyone's wide awake. We're almost there. It's my first time on a military base, so I expect to see platoons of young men marching and jogging in step. Instead, as we weave across the winding paved road, all I can make out are a few low-lying buildings that I assume are barracks and a wide-open parking lot with tons of cars and a few scattered military jeeps. At the far end of the road, the van finally stops at the Distinguished Visitors Lounge, a mundane one-story brick building that evokes all the creativity of a 1950s sneeze.

Once inside, just about everyone strolls up to the wide glass window that overlooks the runway. They're trying to look nonchalant, but they're too anxious to pull it off. You can see it in the way they move. Like a kid sneaking an early peek at his birthday presents. What's the big deal? I ask myself. For the answer, I head straight for the window, prepared to be unimpressed. Then I see it. The words "United States of America" are printed in enormous black letters across its blue and white body, and a huge American flag is painted on its tail. It's the biggest plane I've ever seen. And we're riding it to Minnesota for Caroline's funeral: Air Force One.

"Have you seen it?" I ask Pam, who's sitting alone on a bench in the corner of the room.

"No, I . . ."

"Go to the window. Trust me, you won't be disappointed. It's like a pregnant 747."

"Michael . . ."

"I know—I sound like a tourist—but that's not always

such a bad thing. Sometimes you have to pull out the camera, put on the Hard Rock T-shirt, and let it all hang—"

"We're not tourists," she growls, her frozen glare stabbing me in the chest. "We're going to a funeral." As usual, she's right.

I step back to stop myself. Head to toe, I feel about two feet tall. "I'm sorry. I didn't mean to—"

"Don't worry about it," she says, refusing to face me. "Just tell me when it's time to go."

At a quarter to seven, they lead us out to the plane, where we line up single file. Dark suit, leather briefcase. Dark suit, leather briefcase. Dark suit, leather briefcase. One behind the other, the message is clear: It's a funeral, but at least we'll get some work done. I look down at my own briefcase and wish I'd never picked it up. Then I look over at Pam. She's carrying nothing but a small black purse.

At the front of the line, by the base of the stairs that lead up to the plane, is the Secret Service agent who checks each of our names and credentials. Next to the agent is Simon. Dressed in a black suit and a the-President-wore-one-a-few-weeks-ago silver tie, he greets each of us as we arrive. It's not often the Counsel gets to run such a public show, and from the dumb look on his face, he's basking in the glory. You can see it in the way he puffs out his chest. As the line moves forward, Simon and I finally make eye contact. The moment he sees me, he turns around and walks over to his secretary, who's standing a few feet away, clipboard in hand.

"Asshole," I mutter to Pam.

When I reach the stairs, I give my name to the Secret Service agent. He searches the list he holds in the palm of his hand. "I'm sorry, sir, what was that name again?"

"Michael Garrick," I say, pulling my ID from behind my tie.

He checks again. "I'm sorry, Mr. Garrick, I don't have you here."

"That's impossi—" I cut myself short. Over the agent's shoulder, I notice Simon looking our way. He's wearing that same grin he was wearing the day he sent me home. That motherf—

"Call it in to Personnel," Pam says to the agent. "You'll see he's on staff."

"I don't care if he's on staff," the agent explains. "If he's not on this list, he's not getting on this plane."

"Actually, can I interrupt a moment?" Simon asks. Pulling a sheet of paper from his inside breast pocket, he steps back to the front of the line and passes it to the agent. "In our rush to get this together, I think I inadvertently left out a few people. Here's an updated clearance sheet. I should've given this to you earlier, it's just . . . with this terrible loss . . ."

The agent looks down at the list and checks the code on the clearance sheet. "Welcome aboard Air Force One, Mr. Garrick."

I nod to the agent and shoot my coldest stare at Simon. Nothing needs to be said. To get on board, I better be on board. Anything else is going to have its consequences. He steps aside and motions me forward; I steel myself and climb the stairs.

On a normal day, staffers use the rear staircase—today, we get the front.

When I step into the cabin, I look around for a stewardess, but there's no one there. "First time?" a voice asks. To my left is a young guy in an immaculately starched white shirt. The patches on his shoulder tell me he's Air Force.

"Is it open seating or . . ."

"What's your name?"

"Michael Garrick."

"Mr. Garrick, follow me."

He heads straight down the main hallway, which runs along the right side of the plane and is lined with bolted-down plush couches and fake-antique side tables. It's a flying living room.

As we enter the staff area, rather than shoving everyone into one big hundred-person cabin, the seating is broken into smaller ten-person sections. The seats face one another—five on five—with a shared Formica table between you and the person you're facing. Everyone watches everyone else. Around here, it's the easiest way to encourage work.

"Is it possible to get a window seat?" I ask.

"Not this time," he says as he comes to a stop. He points to an aisle seat that faces forward. On the cushion is a folded white card with the presidential seal. Under the seal, it reads, "Welcome Aboard Air Force One." Beneath that, it reads my name: "Mr. Garrick."

My reaction is instantaneous. "Can I keep this?"

"I'm sorry, but for security purposes, we need it back."

"Of course," I say, handing him the card. "I understand."

He does his best impression of a smile. "That's a joke. I'm joking, Mr. Garrick." As soon as I catch on, he adds, "Now would you like a tour of the rest of the plane?"

"Are you kidding? I'd love t—" Over his shoulder, I see Pam heading our way. "Y'know what, I'll pass for now. I've got some work to do."

Checking the card across from me, Pam finds her name and sits down.

I'm about to throw my briefcase on the table between

us, but instead, I put it below my seat. "How're you doing?" I ask.

"Ask me when it's over."

By seven A.M., we're boarded and ready to go, but since it's not a commercial flight, most people aren't in their seats—they're standing together in small groups or wandering around, exploring the plane. Without question, it looks more like a cocktail party than a plane ride.

Looking up from her newspaper, Pam catches me leaning into the aisle and staring up the hallway. "Don't worry, Michael, she'll be here."

She thinks I'm looking for Nora. "Why do you always assume it's about her?"

"Isn't everything about her?"

"That's funny."

"No, *Charlie Brown* is funny . . ." She lifts her newspaper and snaps it into place. "Yeah, that Charlie Brown . . . he sure does love that Little Red-Haired Girl . . ."

Ignoring her, I get up from my seat.

"Where're you going?" she asks, lowering the paper.

"Just to the bathroom. Be back in a second."

At the front of the plane, I find two bathrooms, both of which are occupied. To my left, on a bolted-down end table is a bolted-down candy dish. Inside the dish are books of matches with the Air Force One logo on them. I grab one for Pam and one for my dad. Before I can get one for myself, I hear the pulsing thumps of incoming helicopters. The bathroom door opens, but I head straight for the windows. Peering outside, I see two identical multipassenger helicopters. The one carrying Hartson is Marine One. The other's just a decoy. By switching him between the two aircraft, they hope would-be assassins won't know which one to shoot out of the sky.

The two copters land almost simultaneously, but one's closer to the plane. That's Marine One. When the doors open, the first person out is the Chief of Staff. Behind him comes a top advisor, a few deputies, and finally, Lamb. The man's amazing. Always has the ear. Nora comes next, followed by her younger brother, Christopher, a gawky-looking kid who's still in boarding school. Holding hands, the two siblings pause a moment, waiting for their parents. First, Mrs. Hartson. Then the President. Of course, while everyone's staring at POTUS, I can't take my eyes off his daugh—

A strong hand settles on my shoulder. "Who you looking at?" Simon asks.

I spin around at the sound of his voice. "Just the President," I shoot back.

"Incredible sight, don't you think?"

"I've seen better," I jab.

He shoots me a look that I know'll leave a bruise. "Remember where you are, Michael. It'd be a real shame if you had to go home."

I'm tempted to fight, but I'm not going to win this one. Time to be smart. If Simon wanted me out, I'd be long gone. He just wants silence. That's what's going to keep this out of the papers; that's what's going to keep me at my job; that's what's going to continue to keep Nora safe. And like she said in the bowling alley, that's the only way we're going to get to the bottom of this.

"We understand each other?" Simon asks.

I nod. "You don't have to worry about me."

"Good," he says with a smile. He motions to the back of the plane and sends me on my way.

I return to my seat feeling like I've been kicked in the stomach.

"See your girlfriend?" Pam asks as I'm about to sit

down. Once again hiding behind the newspaper, her voice is quivering.

"What's wrong?"

She doesn't answer.

I reach over and tug on the paper. "Pam, tell me what's . . ." Her eyes are welled up with tears. As the paper hits the table between us, I get my first look at what she's reading. Page B6 of the Metro Section. Obituaries. At the top is a picture of Caroline. The headline reads: "White House Lawyer Caroline G. Penzler Dies."

Before I can react, the plane starts to move. A sudden lurch forward sends Pam's purse to the floor, and just as it hits, her White House pen slides onto the carpet. After a short announcement, we head down the runway, ready for takeoff. Some people return to their seats; others don't care. The cocktail party continues. The whole cabin's trembling from the final thrust of takeoff. Still, no one's wearing a seatbelt. It's a subtle gesture, but it does imply power. And even en route to a funeral, that's what the White House is all about.

The landing at Duluth International Airport is much smoother than the takeoff. As the runway comes into view, the television monitors in the cabin flicker with life. The TVs are built right into the wall—one over the head of the person on my right, another over the head of the person on Pam's left.

On the monitors, I see a mammoth blue and white plane coming in for a landing. The local news is covering our arrival, and since we're within airspace, the TVs pick up the local stations.

Amazing, I say to myself.

Trusting TV over reality, we keep our eyes on the monitors—and in a moment that turns our lives into the world's greatest interactive movie, when the wheels touch down on TV, we feel them touch down below us.

After the bigshots disembark, the rest of us make our way to the door. It's not a long walk, but you can already feel the mood swing. No one's talking. No one's touring. The joyride on the world's best private plane is over.

Eventually, the line starts to move and I offer Pam my hand. "C'mon, time to go."

She reaches out and accepts my invitation, locking each of her fingers between my own. I give her a warm, reassuring grip. The kind of grip you reserve for your best friends.

"How're you feeling?" I ask.

She squeezes even tighter and says one word. "Better."

Slowly making our way to the front of the plane, we eventually see what's causing our delayed departure. The President's standing inside the main doorway, personally offering his sympathies to each of us.

That human connection . . . his need to help . . . it's exactly why I came to work for Hartson in the first place. If he were shaking hands at the bottom of the jetway, it'd be a purely political move—a staged moment for the cameras and for reelection. In here, the press can't see him. It's every staffer's dream: a moment that exists only between you and him.

As we get closer, I see the First Lady standing to the left of her husband. She knew Caroline before any of us— a fact that I can see in the strain of her pursed lips.

It takes me three more steps before I see the familiar silhouette. Over Hartson's shoulder, I catch my favorite member of the First Family standing in the hallway and taking in the events.

When she looks up, our eyes connect. Nora offers a weak grin. She's trying to look her usual unaffected self, but I'm starting to see through it. The way she glances at her dad . . . then her mom . . . they're no longer the President and First Lady . . . they're her parents. This is what she has to lose. To us, it's a perk. For Nora . . . if there's even an inkling of scandal about her and the money—or even worse, the death . . . it's her life.

I let go of Pam's hand and give Nora a slight nod. *You're not alone.*

She can't help but smile back.

Without a word, Pam forcefully regrabs my hand. "Just remember," she whispers, "every beast has its burden."

CHAPTER 12

Scooping up my newspapers early the following morning, I walk them to the kitchen table and hunt for my name on all four front pages. Nothing. Nothing on me, nothing on Caroline. Even the front photos, which I thought were going to be Hartson at the funeral, are dedicated to yesterday's Orioles no-hitter. With the funeral finished, it's no longer news. Just a heart attack.

Casually flipping through the *New York Times*, I wait for the phone to ring. Thirty seconds later, it does. "You got the fix?" I ask as soon as I pick up.

"Did you see it?" Trey asks.

"See what?"

He pauses. "A14 of the *Post*."

I know that tone. I brush the *Times* from the table and nervously lunge for the *Post*. My hands can barely flip pages. Twelve, thirteen . . . there. "White House Lawyer Depressed, Treated." Skimming through the short article, I read about Caroline's bout with depression, and how she was successfully overcoming it.

As the story goes on, it never once mentions me, but

any political junkie knows the rest. It may be creeping along on the middle pages, but Caroline's story is still alive.

"If it makes you feel any better, you're not the only one getting bad press," Trey says, clearly trying to change the subject. "Have you seen the Nora story in the *Herald*?" Before I can answer, he explains, "According to their gossip columnist, one of Bartlett's top aides called her—get this—'*the First Freeloader*' because she hasn't made her mind up about grad school. Blood-guzzling, reputation-raping muckrakers."

I flip to the *Herald* and pinpoint the story. "Not a smart move," I say as I read it for myself. "People don't like it when you attack the First Daughter."

"I don't know," Trey says. "Bartlett's boys've been polling this one for a while. If they're sending it out, I'm betting people are warm to it."

"If they were, Bartlett would've done it himself."

"Give it a few days—this is just a trial balloon. I can already hear the speechwriters scribbling: *If Hartson can't take care of his own family, how's he going to take care of the country?*"

"That's a big risk, Dukakis. The backlash alone . . ."

"Have you seen the numbers? There's not a backlash in sight. We thought we were going to get a bump from the funeral—Hartson's lead is down to ten. I'm thinking IPO moms love the fighting-for-families idea."

"I don't care. They're gonna draw the line here. It'll never come out of Bartlett's lips."

"Wager time?" Trey asks.

"You really feel that strongly about it?"

"Even stronger than I felt about Hartson's sunglasses-and-baseball-cap-on-the-aircraft-carrier look. Even if it was a little *Top Gun*, I told you we'd use it for the ad."

"Uh-oh, big talk." I look down at the article, thinking

it through one more time. There's no way they'll have Bartlett say it. "Nickel bet?"

"Nickel bet."

For the better part of two years, it's been the best game in town. Around here, everyone loves to win. Including me.

"And nothing sketchy," I add. "No holding back on blasting Bartlett for going after their virgin, innocent daughter."

"Oh, we're going after him," Trey promises. "I'll have Mrs. Hartson's statement ready to go by nine." He pauses. "Not that it's going to help."

"We'll see."

"We'll certainly see," he shoots back. "Now you ready to read?"

I close up the *Herald*, since we always do the *Post* first. But when I look down at the paper, the story about Caroline is still staring me in the face. I can cover it up all I want—it's not going away. "Can I ask you a question?"

"What's wrong? You wanna take back your bet?"

"No, it's just . . . about this Caroline story . . ."

"Aw, c'mon, Michael, I thought you weren't gonna—"

"Tell me the truth, Trey—you think it's got legs?"

He doesn't answer.

I sink down in my seat. For whatever reason, the *Post* is still interested. And from what I can tell, they're just starting to tighten the microscope.

"I'm looking for an Officer Rayford," I say, reading the name from the confirmation of receipt early the following morning.

"This is Rayford," he answers, annoyed. "Who's this?"

As he says the words, I move the phone to my other ear and picture his crooked nose and hairless forearms. "Hi,

Officer, this is Michael Garrick—you stopped me last week for speeding . . ."

"And maybe dealing drugs," he adds. "I know who you are."

I close my eyes and pretend to be unintimidated. "Actually, that's what I wanted to talk to you about. I'm wondering if you've had a chance to check the money, so we could put this all behind—"

"Do you know how much money they photocopied before the drug sweep? Almost a hundred grand. Even at four bills per page, it's going to take me days to make sure the serial numbers on your bills don't match the serial numbers on ours."

"I didn't mean to bother you, I just—"

"Listen, when we're done, we'll give you a call. Until then, leave it alone. In the meantime, say hi to the President for me."

How does he know where I work?

There's a click on the other line and he's gone.

"And that's all he said?" Pam asks, sitting in front of my computer.

I look down at my desk, where I'm fidgeting with the swinging handle of the middle desk drawer. I flip it up, but it keeps falling down.

"Maybe you should tell the FBI about the money," she adds, reading my reaction. "Just to be safe."

"I can't," I insist.

"Of course you can."

"Pam, think about it for a second—it's not just telling the FBI—if it was just them, that's one thing. But you know how they feel about Hartson. From Hoover to Freeh, it's pure hate with every Chief Exec—always a power struggle. And with Nora involved . . . they'll feed it to the press in the bat of an eye. It's the same thing they did with the President's medical records."

"But at least you'd be—"

"I'd be dead is what I'd be. If I start gabbing with the FBI, Simon'll point everyone my way. In a game of he said/he said, I lose. And when they look at the evidence, all they're going to see are those consecutively marked bills. The first thirty grand in Caroline's safe; the last ten grand in my possession. Even *I'm* starting to believe the money's mine."

"So you're just going to sit around being Simon's quiet boy?"

Grabbing a sheet of paper from my out-box, I wave it in front of her face. "Do you know what this is?"

"A tree victimized by the ravenous, death-dealing, cannibal machine we call modern society?"

"Actually, Thoreau, it's a formal request to the Office of Government Ethics. I asked them for copies of Simon's financial disclosure forms, which are filed every year."

"Okay, so you've mastered public records. All that gives you is a list of his stock holdings and a few bank accounts."

"Sure, but when I get his records, we'll have a whole new place to search. You don't just get forty thousand dollars from nowhere. He either liquidated some major investments, or has a debit in one of his accounts. I find that debit and I've got the easiest way to prove the money's his."

"Let me give you an even easier way: Have Nora verify that he was—"

"I told you, I'm not doing that. We already went through this: The moment she's involved, we're all on page one. Career over; election finished."

"That's not—"

"You want to be Linda Tripp?" I challenge.

She doesn't answer.

"That's what I thought. Besides, what Nora saw only takes care of the first night. When it comes to Caroline's death—even if it was a heart attack—I'm still on my own."

Pam shakes her head and my phone starts ringing.

Refusing to get into it, I go for the phone. "This is Michael."

"Hey, Michael, it's Ellen Sherman calling. Am I catching you at a bad time? You talking to the President or anything?"

"No, Mrs. Sherman, I'm not talking to the President." Mrs. Sherman is the sixth-grade social studies teacher from my hometown in Arcana, Michigan. She's also in charge of the annual school trip to Washington, and when she found out about my job, a new stop was added to the itinerary: a private tour of the West Wing.

"I'm sure you know why I'm calling," she says with high-pitched elementary school zeal. "I just wanted to make sure you didn't forget about us."

"I'd never forget about you, Mrs. Sherman."

"So we're all checked in for the end of the month? You put all the names through security?"

"Did it yesterday," I lie, searching my desk for the list of names.

"Howzabout Janie Lewis? Is she okay? Her family's Mormon, y'know. From Utah."

"The White House is open to all religions, Mrs. Sherman. Including Utah's. Now is there anything else, because I really should run."

"As long as you put the names throu—"

"I cleared everyone in," I say, watching Pam continue to smolder. "Now you have a good day, Mrs. Sherman. I'll see you on the—"

"Don't try and chase me off the phone, young man. You may be big and famous, but you're still Mikey G. to me."

"Yes, ma'am. Sorry about that." The Midwest dies hard.

"And how's your father doing? Any word from him?"

I stare at the request for Simon's financial disclosure forms. "Just the usual. Not much to report."

"Well, please send him my best when you see him," she says. "Oh, and Michael, one last thing . . ."

"Yeah?"

"We really are proud of you here."

It's easy, but the compliment still makes me smile. "Thank you, Mrs. Sherman." Hanging up the phone, I turn to my computer screen.

"Who was that?" Pam asks.

"My past," I explain as I find Mrs. Sherman's list. Her school trip was the first time I ever left Michigan. The plane ride alone made the world a bigger place.

"Can't you do that la—"

"No," I insist. "I'm doing it now." Double-clicking on the WAVES folder, I open up a blank request form for the Worker and Visitor Entrance System. Before visitors are allowed in either the OEOB or the White House, they first have to be cleared through WAVES. One by one, I type in the names, birthdates, and Social Security numbers of Mrs. Sherman and her sixth-grade class. When I'm finished, I add the date, time, and place of our meeting, and then hit the Send button. On my screen, a rectangular box appears: "Your WAVES Visitor Request has been sent to the US Secret Service for processing."

"You finally ready to rejoin the discussion?" Pam asks.

I look at my watch and realize I'm late. Hopping out of my seat, I reply, "When I get back."

"Where're you going?"

"Adenauer wants to see me."

"The guy from the FBI? What's he want?"

"I don't know," I say as I head for the door. "But if the FBI finds out what's going on and this thing goes public, Edgar Simon's going to be the least of my worries."

I walk into the West Wing with my mind focused on Mrs. Sherman's school trip. It's a cerebral dodge that I hope'll keep me from panicking about Adenauer and whether or not it's a heart attack. The problem is, the more I think about sixth-graders, the more I worry I won't be here to give the tour.

Approaching the guard's desk at the first security checkpoint, I'm dying for a friendly face. "Hey, Phil."

He looks up and nods. Nothing else to say.

I watch him as I pass, but he still doesn't give me a syllable. It's like the guard outside the parking lot. The more the FBI gets involved, the more strange looks I get. Trying not to think about it, I pass Phil, make a sharp right, and head down a short flight of stairs. After another quick right, I find myself standing outside the Sit Room.

The regular haunt of National Security Council bigwigs, the Situation Room is the most secure location in the White House complex. One rumor holds that as you pass through the door, you're bathed in a thin band of invisible laser light that scans your body for chemical weaponry. Stepping inside, I don't believe a word of it. We're good, but we're not that good.

"I'm looking for Randall Adenauer," I explain to the first receptionist I see.

"And your name?" she asks, checking her scheduling book.

"Michael Garrick."

She looks up, startled. "Oh . . . Mr. Garrick . . . right this way."

My stomach drops out from under me. I lock my jaw to slow my breathing and follow the receptionist to what I assume will be one of the small peripheral offices. Instead, we stop at the closed door of the main conference room. Another bad sign. Rather than bringing me to the FBI's fifth-floor office in the OEOB, he's got me in the most secure room in the complex. It's where Kennedy's staff weighed in on the Cuban Missile Crisis, and where Reagan's staff fought viciously over who should be running the country when the President was shot. Set up in here, Adenauer has something serious to hide.

The click of a magnetic lock grants me access to the room. I open the door and step inside. Visually, it's an ordinary conference room: long mahogany table, leather chairs, a few pitchers of water. Technologically speaking, it's much more. The lining of the room is rumored to keep out everything from infrared spy satellites to electromagnetic surveillance systems that measure telephone, serial, network, or power cable emanations. Whatever's about to happen, there aren't going to be any witnesses.

When the door closes behind me, I notice the soft humming that pervades the room. Sounds like sitting next to a copier, but it's actually a white noise generator. If I'm wearing a wiretap or I'm bugged, the noise drowns it out. He's not taking any chances.

"Thanks for coming down," Adenauer says. He looks different than the last time I saw him. His sandy hair, his slightly off-center jaw—without Caroline's body in the background, both somehow seem softer. Like before, the top button of his shirt is opened. His tie's slightly loose. Nothing intimidating. He's got a red file folder in front of him, but as he sits across the table, his right hand is palm-up and wide open. An outstretched offer to help.

"Is something bothering you, Michael?"

"I'm just wondering why you're doing this here. You could've had me come up to your office."

"Someone's already using it, and if I had you come down to the main office, you would've been seen by every reporter who stakes out our building. At least here, I can keep you safe."

It's a good point.

"I'm not here to accuse you, Michael. I don't believe in scapegoats," he promises in his soft Virginia accent. Unlike last time, he doesn't try to reach out and touch my shoulder, which is one of the real reasons I think he's serious. As he speaks, he's got a fussy professionalism to his voice. It matches his tweed suit—and reminds me of an old high school English teacher. No, not just a teacher. A friend.

"Why don't you take a seat?" Adenauer asks. He points to the chair at the corner of the conference table and I follow his lead. "Don't worry," he says. "I'll make it quick."

He's certainly taking it easy. When I'm seated, he opens the red file folder. Down to business. "So, Michael, do you still maintain that all you did was find the body?"

My head jerks up before he even finishes the question. "What're you—"

"It's just a formality," he promises. "No need to get upset."

I force a smile and take his word for it. But in his eyes . . . the way they narrow . . . he's looking a little too amused.

"All I did was find her," I insist.

"Terrific," he replies, his expression unchanged. All around me, the humming white noise is getting irritating. "Now tell me what you know about Patrick Vaughn," he says, once again relying on old interrogation tricks. Rather than asking *if* I know Vaughn, he bluffs it into the question. But my guard's up. P. Vaughn. First name Patrick. The guy who slipped the note under my door. Hoping for more, I tell Adenauer the truth.

"Don't know the guy."

"Patrick Vaughn," he repeats.

"I heard you the first time. I have no idea who he is."

"C'mon, Michael, don't do it like this. You're smarter than that."

I don't like the sound of that one—it's not a trick—there's real concern in his voice. Which means he has a good reason to believe that I should know this guy Vaughn. Time to fish. "I swear, I'm trying my best. Help me out a little. What's he look like?"

Adenauer reaches into the folder and pulls out a black-and-white mug shot. Vaughn's a short guy with a thin, gang-TV-movie mustache, and slicked-back greasy hair. The identification card he's holding in front of his chest lists a police arrest number and his date of birth. The last line of the card reads "Wayne County," which tells me he's spent some time in Detroit.

"Ringing any bells?" Adenauer asks.

I think back to my neighbor's description of the guy with the gold chains.

"I asked you a question, Michael."

My brain's still stuck on the note under my door. If the guy with the chains . . . if he was Vaughn, why's he asking my neighbor questions? Is he trying to help? Or is he trying to set me up? Until I know the answer, I'm not taking the risk. "I'm telling you, I have no idea who this guy is. Never seen him in my life." It's a lawyer's answer, but it's still the truth. I stare at the mug shot and cast another line. "What was he arrested for?"

Adenauer doesn't move a muscle. "Don't piss on my shoes, boy."

"I'm not . . . I don't know what you want me to say. What'd he do?"

The leather crackles as he leans forward in his seat. He's moving in for the kill. "Take a wild guess . . . I mean, you were first on the scene."

Oh, God. "He's a murderer? This is the guy you think killed Caroline?"

He snatches the photo from my hands. "I gave you your chance, Michael."

"What? You think I know him?"

"I'm not answering that question."

Now I'm starting to sweat. There's something he's not saying. Is this the guy Simon hired? Maybe Simon's using him to point a finger at me. The white noise is making it harder to think. "Did someone tell you something?"

"Forget it, Michael. Let's move on."

"I don't want to move on. Tell me what's making you think that? My father? Is it something with him? Is it because this guy's from Detroit? That we're both from Michi—?"

"What if I told you he's been bagged twice in D.C. for selling drugs?" Adenauer interrupts. "That ring any bells?"

I already don't like where this one's going. "Should it?"

"You tell me—two drug arrests here, and a murder trial two years ago in Michigan. That sound like anyone you know?"

Focused on the drugs, I try not to think about the answer.

"By the way," Adenauer says with a grin. "Did you see that article about Nora in the *Herald* this morning? What'd you think about them calling her the 'First Freeloader'?"

I try to keep it calm. "Excuse me?"

"Y'know, I just figured with you guys dating and all—

is it hard having to always share her with the world like that?"

I'm tempted to say something, but decide to wait it out.

"I mean, going out with the First Daughter—you must have some interesting stories to tell." Crossing his arms, he waits for me to react. I give him a roomful of dead air. The dating's one thing, but I'm not going to let him toss me around about Vaughn and rumors of Nora's drugs. For all I know, it's a bluff based on the *Rolling Stone* story. Or just their old vendetta against Hartson.

"So how long you two been together?" he finally adds.

"We're not together," I growl. "We're just friends."

"Oh. My mistake."

"And what does that have to do with anything anyway?"

"Nothing—nothing at all," Adenauer says. "I'm just talking some current events with a White House employee. This isn't even in my log as an interrogation." Watching me carefully, he puts the picture of Vaughn away and shuts the folder. "Now let's get back to your story. You were fighting with Caroline before you found the body?"

"Yeah, she was—" I cut myself short. Son of a bitch. I never told Adenauer that Caroline and I were fighting. He's walking all over me.

A true Virginian, though, he doesn't gloat about it. "I meant what I said—I'm not here to accuse you," he explains. "Someone in the hallway heard you yelling. I just want to know what it was about." Before I can answer, he adds, "The truth this time, Michael."

There's no way around it. My eyes are locked on Adenauer's red folder. Like before, he doesn't take notes, he just reads my word balloons. Hoping to drown out the white noise with a deep breath, I tell him about my father, his criminal record, and the conflict with his benefits.

Adenauer listens without interrupting.

"I didn't think I did anything illegal, but Caroline thought I should've recused myself. She saw it as a conflict of interest."

He studies me, looking for a hole in the story. "And that's all that happened? When she wouldn't listen, you walked out and went back to your office?"

"That's it. When I came back, she was dead."

"How long were you gone?"

"Ten minutes—fifteen, max."

"Any stops in between?"

I shake my head.

"Are you sure?" he asks suspiciously. Again, I get the feeling he knows something.

"That's all that happened," I insist.

He shoots me a long look, giving me every opportunity to change my story. When I don't, he picks up his file and stands from his seat.

"I swear, I'm not lying—that's the tru—"

"Michael, were you being blackmailed by Caroline?"

"What?" I ask, forcing a laugh. "Is that what you think?"

"You don't want to know what I think," he says. "Now help me out with this one. This wasn't the first time she pulled your file, was it?"

My body's frozen. "I don't know what you're talking about."

"It's right here!" he shouts, pointing to the file. He flips it open and shows me the Request Log stapled to the inside cover. From the two signatures in the Out column, I can see Caroline's pulled mine twice: Last week. And six months after I started work. "Care to tell what the first one's about?"

"I have no idea."

"The more you lie, the more it's going to hurt."

"I'm telling you, I have no idea."

"Do you really expect me to believe that?"

"Believe what you want—I'm giving you the truth. I mean, if I killed her, why didn't I remove my own file? Or at least take the money?"

"Listen, son, I once had a suspect shove a kitchen knife through his own lung—twice—just to take the suspicion off himself. There're no boundaries when it comes to covering up."

"I'm not covering anything up!" I shout. "She had a heart attack! Why can't you just accept that?"

"Because she died with thirty thousand dollars in her safe. And more important, because it wasn't a heart attack."

"Excuse me?"

"I saw the autopsy myself. She had a stroke."

I tighten my jaw and put on my bravest face. "That doesn't mean she was murdered."

"But it does mean it wasn't a heart attack," Adenauer points out, studying my reaction. "Don't worry, Michael—when the tox reports come back, we'll know what caused it. Now it's just a matter of time."

That's what Adenauer was hiding; waiting to see what I'd give up. He's not sure it's a murder, but he's not sure it's not. "What about the press?" I ask.

"That depends on you. Of course, I'm not letting them trample this investigation—especially considering how close we are." He throws me another of his concerned glances. "Wouldn't you and your girlfriend agree?"

I look at him, but I'm lost in the white noise. My head's throbbing. If the reports come back with bad news, and this gets out . . . All this time, I was worried they were going to try and nail me for murder . . . but the way he was teasing me about Nora . . . and linking her to Vaughn . . . I can't help but think he's got his sights on something bigger.

Doing my best not to panic, I go with my best alternative—the one thing I know can't be traced back to me. "Have you checked Simon's bank accounts?"

"Why would we want to do that?"

"Just check 'em," I say, hoping it'll buy some time.

"Anything else you want to tell me?" Adenauer asks.

"No, that's it." I have to get out of here. Leaving Adenauer where he is, I climb to my feet and stagger toward the door.

"I'll call you when we get the tox reports," he says, finally starting to gloat. He brought me here to test my reaction. And now that he's got it, he wants to see what I'll do. "It shouldn't be too long," he adds.

I don't even pause to turn around. The less I see of him, the better. The only thing I want to do now is find out if there's a connection between Nora and Patrick Vaughn.

CHAPTER 13

"So how do you think the FBI found out?" Trey asks from the chair opposite my desk.

"About me and Nora? I have no idea. I'm guessing through the Service. To be honest, though, I'm more concerned with what he implied about her and Vaughn."

"I don't blame you—if they've got something tying him to Nora, the two of them could potentially be—"

"Don't even say it."

"Why?" Trey asks. "You've thought it yourself—she's never spent all her time on the side of the angels."

"That doesn't mean she's out to get me."

"You sure about that?"

"Yes. I am." Shaking my head, I add, "And even if I weren't, what am I supposed to do—assume she's the enemy just because the FBI mentions her in the same sentence as some killer named Vaughn?"

"But the drugs . . ."

"Trey, I'm not doing anything until we get some more facts. Besides, you should've heard Adenauer. The way he was talking, it's like he's got something tying *me* to this guy."

"You think that's why Vaughn's contacting you?"

"I'm not sure what to think. For all we know, Simon left the note, signed it from Vaughn, and is trying to link me up with a killer."

"Sounds a little much," Trey says. Leaning back in his chair, he stretches his arms in the air and lets out an enormous yawn. As his jaw juts side to side, he drops his chair back to the upright position. "Now what about Vaughn's murder trial?" he asks. "Any idea what happened?"

"Not yet. Pam should—"

"I'll have it by tomorrow morning," Pam says, walking into my office.

"Have what?" Trey asks.

"Vaughn's FBI file."

"I don't understand. Since when do you—"

"Until Simon hires a replacement, Pam's taken over Caroline's responsibilities," I explain. "Which means she's the new mistress of the files."

"And guess who I saw on my way to the FBI's office?"

"Simon?" I ask nervously.

"Think deranged girlfriend . . ."

"You saw Nora?"

"She was headed to some function in the Indian Treaty Room—I stepped in the elevator and she was there."

"Did she recognize you?"

"I assume so—she asked me if we were going to the same place. I couldn't help but tell her the FBI wasn't exactly a meet-and-greet. And then—I couldn't believe it—she looks straight at me, and in the softest, sweetest voice says, 'Thanks for helping him.' I swear, I almost hit the Emergency Stop right there."

It's not hard to read the surprise in Pam's voice. "You actually liked her, didn't you?" I ask.

"No, no—now you're just fantasizing. Deep down, I still

think she needs a swift kick in her privileged little ass—
but face-to-face . . . I certainly didn't like her . . . it's just
. . . she's not what I thought either."

"You felt bad for her, huh?"

"I don't pity her, if that's what you're asking . . . but
she's not as simple as she looks."

"Of course she's not simple—she's a lunatic," Trey
shoots back. "What the hell is wrong with you two? You'd
think she's the friggin' Pied Piper. Big deal—she's complex. Welcome to reality. Thomas Jefferson cried freedom,
then had an affair with one of his slaves."

"So? People still separate the two."

"Well they shouldn't!"

"Well I hate to break it to you, but I got a nation of
270 million patriots who disagree."

Shaking his head, Trey knows he's not winning this one.
"Y'know what—why don't we just get back to Vaughn."

Turning to Pam, I ask, "Is there any way to get his file
earlier?"

"I'm trying my best," she says, already downplaying.
"They said it'll take till tomorrow."

"Screw tomorrow," Trey says. "I got Vaughn's number
from information—we can call him right now." He picks
up the phone and starts dialing.

"Don't!" I shout.

Trey stops cold.

"If this is the guy who killed Caroline, the last thing I
need is a call to him originating from my phon—"

Before I can finish, the ringing of my phone cuts through
the room. Pam and I look at Trey, who's still closest to the
receiver.

"What's it say?" I ask as Trey checks the caller ID screen
on the phone.

He shakes his head. "Outside Call," which means that

the person is either calling from an untraceable pay phone, an untraceable cell phone, or the person is one of the few White House bigshots who has a screened identity. I rush to my desk as the advice comes simultaneously.

"Pick it up." "Don't pick it up."

"Let it go," Pam adds. "He'll leave a message."

"If he leaves a message, you're stuck where you are now," Trey says. "Afraid to call him back."

Unsure, I go with instinct. Trey over Pam. "This is Michael," I say as I bring it to my ear.

"Michael, get over here," Nora says on the other end of the line.

"Over where? Where are you?"

"Uncle Larry's office. He just got the dirt on your new friend, Vaughn."

"How'd you find out abou—?"

"C'mon, you don't think the FBI sends him updates?"

I stay silent. Eventually, I ask, "Is it bad?"

"I think you should come up here. Quickly. *Please.*"

Like the day in the bowling alley, there's something completely unnerving about hearing fear in Nora's voice. She's trying hard, but she's not good at hiding it. I hang up the phone and race for the door.

"Where're you going?" Pam asks.

"You don't want to know."

Lawrence Lamb doesn't even look up. Sitting with near-military poise, he's inspecting a red file folder that's spread out on his huge leather-topped desk. I whisper a deferential "Good afternoon," but he's not interested. Nora, staring out the window, whirls around as I walk in.

"What's going on?" I ask her as soon as the door to Lamb's West Wing office slams shut.

"You might want to take a seat," Nora suggests.

"Don't tell me what to—"

"Michael, sit down," Lamb insists in his always-calm voice. With more speed than I'd give him credit for, he whips off his reading glasses and finally looks up. His sharp blue eyes say the rest: I'm in his office now.

Sitting next to Nora in one of the two chairs opposite Lamb's desk, I rephrase the question. "Nora told me you found out more about Vaughn."

"And she told me you're a trustworthy friend. Which means I'm only going to ask this once: Have you ever had any personal dealings with Patrick Vaughn?"

I look over at Nora, who reads my mind. With a subtle nod, she answers my question about Lamb: I can trust him. "I swear to you, I've never seen him, spoken to him, dealt with him . . . nothing. The only reason I know his name is because the investigator at the FBI—"

"I'm well aware of Agent Adenauer," Lamb interrupts. "And I'm also aware of what you did for us that night with the authorities." He shoots me a subtle nod to make sure I understand. In the back-scratch world of politics, this is his way of returning the favor. Lamb slides on his reading glasses and looks back at the file folder. Wearing his suit jacket despite the fact he's in his own office, Lamb has a formal, almost dignified air about him. Like his subdued Brooks Brothers ties, he doesn't need to try. After years of managing a successful health care company, he's made his money—which is why he's just about the only person on staff who doesn't have chewed-apart fingernails.

Letting the red file folder rest in his manicured hand, he begins, "Patrick Taylor Vaughn was born in Boston, Massachusetts, and started out as your basic punk drug dealer. Pot, hash, nothing special. The interesting part, however, is that he's smart. Rather than nickel-and-diming his way through the old neighborhood, he starts servicing the young elites at Boston's many fine universities. It's safer, and they pay their bills. Now he moves up to designer drugs: LSD, Ecstasy, lots of Special K."

My eyes quickly dart at Nora. She's staring at the floor.

"After a few turf battles, Vaughn gets sick of the competition and heads for *your* home state of Michigan."

I give him a sharp look.

"You wanted the story," Lamb says. "In Michigan, he has a few run-ins with the law. Then, two years ago, the police find the body of Jamal Khafra, one of Vaughn's major competitors. Someone stood on the back of Jamal's neck and used piano wire to slice his throat. Vaughn gets fingered for the murder, but swears he didn't do it. Even passes a lie detector. After some prosecutorial blunders, the jury comes back with an acquittal. Feeling lucky, Vaughn hightails it out of Michigan and starts over right here in D.C. He lives in Northeast, off 1st Street. The problem is, when the FBI went to question him about Caroline, they first spoke to one of his neighbors, who apparently tipped him off. Right around then, Vaughn disappeared. He's been missing for almost a week."

"I don't understand. Why's he even a suspect?"

"Because when they examined the WAVES records on the day of Caroline's death, the FBI found that Patrick Vaughn was in the building."

"In the OEOB? You've got to be kidding."

"I wish I were."

"So what does that have to do with me?"

"That's what we have to talk about, Michael. According to the computer records, you're the one who cleared him in."

CHAPTER 14

"*Are you nuts?*" I shout, grasping the armrests of my chair. "I have no idea who he is!"

"It's okay," Nora says as she rubs my back.

"How could I . . . I never heard of the guy!"

"I knew it wasn't you," she says.

Lamb looks less convinced. He's barely moved since he broke the news. Leaning up against his desk, he's studying the scene—watching the two of us react. It's what he does best: surveying first, deciding later.

Making the plea personal, I turn his way. "*I swear to you, I never let him in.*"

"Who else had access to your office?" he asks.

"Excuse me?"

"To have your name on it, the WAVES request had to've been sent from your computer," he explains. "Now after the staff meeting, who else was near your office?"

"Just . . . just Pam," I reply. "And Julian. Julian was there when I got back."

"So either of them could've used your computer."

"It's certainly possible." Yet as I say the words, I don't really believe them. Why would either of them invite a

drug dealer into the— Son of a bitch. My eyes focus on
Nora. I can still picture her little brown vial. That night in
the bar, she said it was headache medicine. I've done my
best to avoid it—but she has to get it from somewhere.

"Is there anyone else who had access to your computer?"
Lamb asks.

I think back to that first night with Nora. She told me
she took the money as evidence. To protect her dad. But
now . . . all that money . . . the cost of drugs . . . if she's
looking for a scapegoat . . .

"I asked you a question, Michael," Lamb reiterates. "Did
Pam or Julian have access to your computer?"

I keep my stare on Nora. "It could've been done without the computer," I explain. "There're other ways to clear
someone into the building. You can call the request in by
an internal phone, or even do it by fax."

"So you're saying it could've been anyone?"

"I guess," I say. Nora finally looks up at me. "But it's
got to be Simon."

"Even if it is, how'd he get this Vaughn guy in?" Nora
interrupts. "I thought the Service does security checks on
all visitors."

"They only stop foreign nationals and people convicted
of felonies. Both of Vaughn's drug hits were reduced to
misdemeanors, and he was acquitted of the murder. Whoever cleared him in, they knew the system."

"Do you know when the request was sent?" I ask.

"Right after our staff meeting. And according to Adenauer's timeline, it could've easily been you."

"It wasn't," Nora jumps in.

"Just relax," Lamb says.

"I'm telling you, it wasn't," she insists.

"I heard you!" he says, his voice booming. Catching
himself, Lamb falls awkwardly silent. It's getting too per-

sonal. "I don't know what you want from me," he says to Nora.

"You told me you'd help him."

"I said I'd *talk* to him." Weighing the facts, Lamb throws me one last look. Like the best of the bigshots, he doesn't give a hint of what he's thinking. He just sits there, his steel features unmoving. Eventually, he says, "Nora, do you mind excusing us for a second?"

"No way," she shoots back. "I'm the one who brought him h—"

"Nora . . ."

"There's no way I'm leaving without a—"

"Nora!"

Like a scolded dog, she shrinks down in her seat. I've never heard Lamb raise his voice. And I've never seen Nora so shaken. That's why he looked after her all those summers—Lamb's one of the few people who can tell her no. Understanding the stakes, Nora rises and heads for the door. As it's about to close behind her, she calls out, "He's going to tell me everything anyway." The door slams shut.

Alone in the office, there's an awkward pause hanging in the air. My eyes jump over Lamb's shoulder as I try to lose myself in office decor. Studying the colonial landscape oil painting behind him, I realize for the first time that he doesn't have an ego wall. He doesn't need one. He's just there to protect his friend.

"Do you care about her?" he asks.

"What?"

"Nora. Do you care about her?"

"Of course I care about her. I've always cared about her."

Rapping his knuckle lightly against his desk, Lamb looks off in the distance, gathering his thoughts. "Do you even know her?" he eventually asks.

"Excuse me?"

"It's not a trick question—do you know her? Do you really know who she is?"

"I-I think so," I stammer. "I'm trying to."

He nods, as if that's an answer. Eventually, his strong voice creaks forward. "When she was younger—seventh, eighth grade—she started playing field hockey. Fast. Heavy contact. They signed her up so she would have some real girlfriends, and she used to play for hours—on the carpets, outside our farm—anywhere she could lug her stick. She used to make Chris play against her. But for Nora, the best part wasn't just the physical side; she loved being on the team. Leaning on each other, having someone to celebrate with—that's what made it worth it. But when her father finally got elected Governor . . . well, security concerns meant that team sports were out. Instead, she got an image consultant who did her clothes shopping for her and her mom. It seems silly now, but that's how they saw it."

"I'm not sure I understand."

"If you care about her, you should know that."

"If I didn't care about her, I wouldn't have lied about the money."

The way his shoulders slack, I can tell that's what he needed to hear. In some ways, I'm not surprised. Now that the FBI knows we're dating, we're all stuck at the epicenter. Nora, Simon, myself . . . one wrong move and we all go down. To be honest, I don't think Lamb would care if I was the one who was sucked in. But from the steely look on his face, and the coldly pragmatic way he asked if I cared about her, he's not letting me take his goddaughter—or the President—along for the ride.

He picks up the FBI folder on his desk and hands it to me. "I assume she told you about the other files in Caroline's office. There were fifteen altogether—some on her desk; others in her drawers. The FBI's treating them as a preliminary suspect list."

"One of the files was mine."

He nods to himself, almost as if it were a test. "In the back of Vaughn's FBI file is the list of everyone they've cleared so far." I flip to the list and see three more judicial nominees. The other two are the names Nora showed me. Five down, ten to go. The suspect list is shrinking. And they still haven't gotten to me.

"I don't have to tell you, Michael—if Nora's linked to a drug dealer . . . much less a murderer . . ."

He doesn't have to finish the sentence. We all know what's at stake here. "Does this mean you're going to help?" I ask.

His voice is slow and methodical. "I'm not going to interfere with this investigation . . ."

"Of course."

". . . but I'll do what I can."

I sit up in my chair. "I appreciate you believing me."

"It's not you," he says matter-of-factly. "I believe *her*." Watching my reaction, he adds, "They're my family, Michael. I held Nora in my arms eight hours after she was born. When she calls me seven times in two hours, demanding that I start taking some action to protect you, I tend to take notice."

"She called you seven times?"

"That's just today," he says. "She's a complicated girl, Michael. She did almost everything you asked. And if she's worried about you . . . that's enough for me."

I look nervously at Lamb. "Does that mean she told the President?"

"Son, if you're asking me about their private conversations, there's nothing for me to say. But if I were you . . ." He pauses, making sure I get the point. "I'd pray that he never finds out. Forget about the fact that with a quiet directive, he can wipe out a small city halfway around the world, or that he's always followed around by a military aide carrying the nuclear codes in a leather satchel. Because when it all comes down, none of that compares to being a father with a hurt daughter."

"What'd he say?" Nora asks as soon as she sees me.

"Nothing." With my chin, I motion at Lamb's assistant, who can hear every word.

Nora turns to her and says, "Do you think you can—"

"Actually, I was about to get myself some coffee," the woman volunteers with that now familiar look in her eyes. You don't say no to the First Daughter. Within thirty seconds, Lamb's assistant is gone.

"So what'd he say?" Nora demands as she wipes her nose. "Is he going to help?"

"He's your godfather isn't he?" I snap.

"What's wrong with you?"

This is no time to hold back. "Did you let Vaughn into the building?"

"What? Are you out of your fucking head? What'd Larry tell you?"

"He didn't tell me anything—I saw it for myself. That brown vial in the bar . . . the rumors of Ecstasy . . . and Special K. Vaughn's dealing both, for chrissakes."

"And that makes me a customer?" she explodes under her breath. "Is that what you think? That I'm a junkie?"

"No, I—"

"I'm not garbage, Michael! Do you hear me? I'm not!"

I stepped over a line with this one. "Nora—calm down."

"Don't tell me to calm down! I take this shit every day from the gossipmongers—I don't need to take it from you! I mean, if I wanted to buy, do you really think I'd bring a drug-dealing murderer *in here?* Do I look that stupid to you? They're after my ass too—not just yours! And even if they weren't, I don't need your name. When I bring someone inside, they don't ID my guests!"

I go to grab her hand, but she slaps me away. Her face is a rage of red. Unable to contain herself, she snaps, "Were you the one who told the FBI we were dating?"

My mouth practically falls open. "You really think I'd—"

"Answer the question!" she demands.

"How can you even think that?"

"Everyone wants something, Michael. Even a little scandal makes you famous."

"Nora . . ." Once again, I reach out for her hand, but when she tries to slap me away, I grab her by the wrist, refusing to let go.

"Get the hell off me!" she growls as she fights against me.

Holding tight, I quickly slide her hand into my own. All of her fingers are taut. Not just now . . . that's how she always is. In her world, with the stakes this high, all she can do is brace for the crash. That's all she knows. "Please, Nora—listen to me."

"I don't want t—"

"Just listen!" Stepping forward, I put my other hand on her shoulder. "I don't want to be famous."

I expect her to come back with a biting remark, but instead, she freezes. That's Nora—on and off with a flick. Before I can react, her arms wrap around me and she collapses against my chest. The embrace surprises me, but it also feels perfectly right. "I didn't do it," she whispers. "I didn't let him in."

"I never said you did. Not once."

"But you believed it, Michael. You believed them over me."

"That's not true," I insist. Grabbing her shoulders, I nudge her back and hold her at arm's length. "All I did was ask you a question—and after everything we've been through, you know I at least deserve an answer."

"So you still don't trust me?"

"If you want to prove it to me, Nora, then prove it. If not, let me know, and I'll move on with the rest of my life."

She cocks her head at the challenge. Her shoulders perk up. For once, it's not handed to her. "You're right," she says, her voice still shaky. "I'll prove it to you." She steps in close and once again takes me around. "I'm not gonna let you down."

Wrapping my arms around her, I think back to the seven calls she made to Lamb. For me. She did it for me. "That's all I ask."

"And you believe that load of horse crap?" Trey asks.

"Trust me, she was really upset."

As we leave the confines of the OEOB, Trey throws me the rub. Not a slow one—just fast enough to tell me I should be careful.

"Now you don't trust Lamb?" I ask as we cross 17th Street.

"Lamb I love—Nora's the one I'm worried about."

"You really think she knows Vaughn?"

"Actually, no, but I think she's lying about the drugs. I've heard too many rumblings to believe she's clean."

"Forget about the drugs. The more important question is: How does Simon know Vaughn?"

"So now you're convinced Simon's the one who let him in?"

"Look at the facts, Trey. Caroline died during the exact same time period that an accused murderer was walking the halls. You think it's all still coincidence? Simon sensed the opportunity the moment he saw me following him. Instead of continuing to pay Caroline, he decides to kill her. He knows I have the money; he knows I won't use my alibi; he knows he can blame it on me. It's the best way to shut me up—invite Vaughn in under my name, then stand back and watch the fireworks."

"And how'd he know you had the money?"

"He could've double-backed and seen us—or maybe Caroline called him when she realized the payment was short."

"I don't know. It's a lot to plan in one night."

"Not when you consider what's at risk," I shoot back. Trey steps out across Pennsylvania Avenue, leaving me two steps behind. I race to catch up as quick as I can.

Reaching the pay phone across the street from the OEOB, Trey pulls out Vaughn's phone number and a handful of change.

"Are you sure this is a smart idea?" I ask as he picks up the receiver.

"Someone's gotta save your ass. If I'm the one talking, they can't trace it to you"—he punches in the first three digits—"and this way, it's not coming from your line."

"Screw the trace—I'm talking about the call in general. If Vaughn's the killer, why's he contacting me?"

"Maybe he has a guilty conscience. Maybe he wants to make a deal. Either way, at least we're doing something."

"But to call him at home . . ."

"No offense, Michael, but you asked for my help and I'm not gonna let you sit on your hands—even if Lamb can delay everything until after the election, you still have the same problems as right now. At least with Vaughn, there's a chance of finding an answer."

"But what if it's just a sucker bet? Maybe that's the trap: They link us together, Vaughn turns state's evidence, and bam, they send me away."

Trey stops dialing. Paranoia cuts both ways.

"You know it's possible," I say.

We both look down at Vaughn's number. Sure, it's creepy for Vaughn to reach out to me. And yeah, it's got me thinking that there's something else at play. But that doesn't mean we can just solve it with a phone call.

"Maybe you should talk to Nora," Trey finally suggests. "Ask her again if she knows him."

"I already did."

"But you can still ask her—"

"I told you, I already did!"

"Stop shouting at me!"

"Then stop treating me like a moron! I know what I'm dealing with."

"See, that's where you're wrong. You don't know her, Michael. You don't know anything about her—all you've seen are the highlight reels."

"That's not true. I know lots abou—"

"I'm not talking flirty political chitchat. I'm talking the real stuff: What's her favorite movie? Or favorite food? How about her favorite author?"

"Graham Greene, burritos, and *Annie Hall*," I rattle back.

"You're trusting the old article from *People* magazine? *I* wrote those answers! Not her! They wanted funky and downtown, so I gave it to them!"

Seeing the rising anger in each other's eyes, we both take a moment and look over our respective shoulders. Eventually, Trey breaks the silence. "What's this really about, Michael? Saving yourself, or saving Nora?"

The question's so dumb, it doesn't deserve an answer.

"It's okay to want to be a hero," he says. "And I'm sure she appreciates the loyalty . . ."

"It's not just loyalty, Trey—if she takes a hit, I go down with her."

"Unless she cuts you loose and you go down alone. So here's the news flash, my friend: I don't care if Pam had a nice encounter in the elevator, I'm not gonna watch you get clobbered as the most likely suspect."

Stepping around Trey, I head back to the OEOB. "I appreciate the concern, but I know what I'm doing. I didn't work this hard and get this far to just give up and lose it. Especially when it's in my control."

"You think you're in control?" He jumps in front of me and blocks my way. "I hate to break it to you, loverboy, but you can't save everyone. Now, I'm not saying you should turn her in—I just think you have to pay a bit more attention to the facts."

"There are no facts! Whoever did this, it's like they've created a whole new reality."

"See, there's the mistake. However you want to delude yourself, there're still a few eternal truths left in the universe: New shoes hurt. Khakis are evil. Bad things happen at air shows. And most important, if you're not careful, protecting Nora is going to blow up in your f—"

"You two doing okay?" a male voice interrupts behind us.

We both spin around.

"I didn't mean to interrupt," Simon adds. "Just wanted to say hello."

"Hi," I blurt.

"Hey," Trey says.

Wondering how long he's been there, both of us start

the dissection. If he knows what we're up to, we'll see it
in his body language.

"So who were you calling?" he asks as he slides a hand
in his left pants pocket.

"Just paging Pam," I reply. "She was supposed to meet
us for lunch."

Simon glances at Trey, then back at me. "And how'd
your meeting go with Adenauer?"

How'd he know about—

"If you want, we can talk about it later," he adds with
just enough force to remind me of our deal. Simon still
wants to keep this quiet—even if he has to make me look
like a killer to do it. Stepping off the sidewalk, he toasts
us with a cup of recently bought coffee. "Just let me know
if there's anything I can do."

CHAPTER 15

I wake up Friday morning feeling like I've been smacked in the back of the head with a skillet. Seven days after Caroline's death, my anxieties are raging and my eyes feel swollen shut. The week of restless sleep is finally taking its toll. Frankenstein-shuffling to the front door, I open my eyes just long enough to pick up my newspapers. It's a couple minutes past six and I still haven't called Trey. It's not going to be long now.

I take two steps toward the kitchen table and the phone rings. Never fails. I pick up without saying hello.

"Who's your momma?" he croons.

I answer with an impossibly long yawn.

"You haven't even showered, have you?" he asks.

"I haven't even scratched myself yet."

Trey pauses. "I don't need to hear that. Understand what I'm saying?"

"Yeah, yeah, just tell me the news." I pull the *Post* from the top of the pile and lay it flat on the table. My eyes go straight to the small headline at the bottom right of the page: "Sperm May Be Real, but Government Says Benefits Aren't."

"What's with the sperm, Trey?"

Again, there's a pause. "You better hope no one's taping these calls."

"Just tell me the story. Is this that lady who was artificially inseminated by her dead husband's frozen sperm?"

"The one and only. She keeps it on ice, has herself a kid after the husband dies, and then applies for the dead husband's Social Security benefits. Yesterday, HHS denied the request since the baby was conceived after the parent's death."

"So let me guess: Now they want the White House to reevaluate the agency's decision?"

"Give the dog a bone," he sings. "And believe me, this one's a dog if ever there was one. Now it's just a question of who's going to get stuck with it."

"Ten bucks says we will." Flipping through the rest of the paper, I add, "Anything else interesting?"

"Depends on whether you think losing a bet is interesting."

"What?"

"Jack Tandy's media column in the *Times*. In an interview with *Vanity Fair* that hits the stands next week, Bartlett says—and I quote—'If you can't take care of the First Family, how can you possibly put family first?'"

I wince at the verbal stab. "Think it's going to stick?"

"Are you kidding? A quote like that—I hate to say it, Michael, but that's a winner talking. I mean, you can feel the shift. Unless the country throws a hissy fit, it'll be in the stump speech by the next news cycle. Voters don't like bad parents. And thanks to your girlfriend, Bartlett just got a brand-new applause line."

Instinctively, I reach for the *Times*. But when I unfold it on the table, the first thing I notice is the front photo: a nice shot of Hartson and the First Lady talking to a group of religious leaders in the Rose Garden. But in the back right corner of the picture, lurking in the last row of the crowd, is the one person without a smile: Agent Adenauer.

I break out in an instant sweat. What the hell is he doing there?

"Michael, you with me?" Trey yells.

"Yeah," I say, turning back to the receiver. "I . . . yeah."

"What's wrong? You sound like death."

"Nothing," I reply. "I'll talk to you later."

Within forty-five minutes, I'm showered, shaved, and two newspapers into the day. But as I leave my apartment, I still can't stop thinking about the photo of Adenauer. There's not a single good reason for an FBI investigator to be that close to Hartson, and the stressing alone has made me a solid fifteen minutes late to work. I don't have time for this, I decide. No more distractions. Heading toward the Metro, I see a homeless man carrying a squeegee. The moment we make eye contact, I realize I'm about to take another kick in the wish list.

"Morning, morning, morning," he says as he holds up his squeegee. He's sporting army green camo pants and the rattiest black beard I've ever seen. Hanging from his pocket is an old Windex spray bottle filled with milky gray water. As he gets closer, I see he's also wearing a worn-out Harvard Law School sweatshirt. Only in D.C. "Where's your Porsche? Where's your Porsche? Where's your Porsche?" he sings, falling in step next to me.

I've seen this guy before. I think it was in Dupont Circle. "Sorry, but I'm not driving," I tell him. "Just me and the Metro."

"No, no, no. Not you, not you. Fancy shoes always take the car."

"Not today. I'm really . . ."

"Where's your Porsche? Wh . . ."

"I told you . . ."

". . . ere's your Porsche? Where's your Porsche?"

Obviously, he's not listening. For more than a block and a half, he's at my side, running his squeegee back and forth along my imaginary windshield. To get him off my back, I reach into my pocket and pull out a dollar bill.

"Ahhh, there he is," Squeegee Man says. "Mr. Porsche."

I hand him the dollar and he finally lowers his squeegee.

"Your change, sir," he says pulling something from his pocket. "Vaughn says you have to talk," he whispers. "Let's try the Holocaust Museum. One o'clock on Monday. And don't bring the black guy from the pay phone."

"Excuse me?"

He smiles and stuffs something in my hand. A folded-up sheet of paper.

"What's this?"

I'm not getting an answer. He's already moved on. Behind me, I see him approach a balding man in a pin-striped suit. "Where's your Porsche?" he asks him, raising the squeegee.

I turn back to the paper and open it up. It's blank. Just a moment's distraction.

Over my shoulder, I look for the Squeegee Man. It's too late. He's gone.

Throwing my briefcase on my desk, I check the digital screen on my office phone. Four new messages waiting. I hit the Call Log button to see who they're from, but every one of them is an outside call. Whoever it is, they're desperate to get in touch. My phone rings, and I jump back, startled. Caller ID reads *Outside Call*.

I lunge for the receiver as quick as I can. "Hello?"

"Michael?" a soft female voice whispers.

"Nora? Is that—"

"Did you see Bartlett's quote?" she interrupts.

I don't answer.

"You saw it, didn't you?" she repeats. Her voice is shaky, and I know that tone. I heard it that day in the bowling alley. She's worried about her dad. "What'd Trey say about it?" she asks.

"Trey? Who cares what Trey said. How're *you?*"

She pauses, sounding confused. "I don't understand."

"How're you doing? Are you okay? I mean, no offense to your dad, but you're the one they're slapping around."

There's another pause. This one a little longer. "I'm fine ... I'm good." There's a change in her voice. "How're you?" she asks, sounding almost happy.

"Don't worry about me. Now what were you saying about Bartlett's quote?"

"Nothing ... nothing ... just par for the course."

"I thought you wanted to talk abou—"

"No. Not anymore," she says with a laugh. "Listen, I really should run."

"So I'll talk to you later?"

"Yeah," she coos. "Definitely."

By the time I get off the phone with Nora, I'm already late for Simon's weekly meeting. Dashing out of my office, I head straight for the West Wing. "Hey, Phil," I say as I blow by the desk of my favorite Secret Service officer.

He shoots out of his seat and grabs me by the arm.

"What're you—"

"I need to see your ID," he says in a cold voice.

"Are you kidding me? You know I'm—"

"Now, Michael."

Pulling away, I remain calm. Reaching for the ID around

my neck, I realize I've tucked it into the front pocket of my dress shirt. It shouldn't matter. He's never stopped me before.

He gives it a quick look and lets me pass. "Thanks," he says.

"No sweat." He's just being careful, I tell myself. Approaching the elevator, I assume he's going to make amends by opening the elevator door for me. I look over at him, but he doesn't care. Pretending not to notice, I hit the elevator call button myself. Word's starting to get out. It's going to be a crappy day.

Slinking to the back of Simon's crowded office, I see that everyone's in their usual places: Simon's at the head of the table, Lamb's in his favorite wingback, Julian's as close to the front as possible, and Pam's . . . hold it right there. Pam's got a seat on the couch. When we make eye contact, I expect her to shrug or wink—some way to acknowledge the ridiculousness of the power shift. She doesn't. She just sits back. At least someone's moving up in the world.

From the sound of things, we're still going around the room. Julian's up.

". . . and they still won't budge on punitive damages. You know how stubborn Terrill's people are—neck-high in their own bullshit and still refusing to smell it. I say we throw it to the press and leak the contents of the deal. Good or bad, it'll at least force a decision."

"I have a conference call with Terrill this afternoon. Let's see where we get then," Simon suggests. "Now tell me what Justice said about the roving wiretaps."

"They're still standing strong on it—they want to be the heroes in Hartson's crime platform." As he continues to explain, Julian glances my way with the most subtle of smirks. That cocky bastard. That's my issue.

"You assigned that project to me," I tell Simon after the meeting. "I've been working on it for weeks and you—"

"I understand you're upset," Simon interrupts.

"Of course I'm upset—you ripped it away and fed it right to the head vampire. You know Julian's going to kill it."

Simon reaches over and puts a soft hand on my shoulder. It's his passive-aggressive way of calming me down. All it does is make me want to put a brick through his teeth.

"Is it because of the investigation?" I finally ask.

He feigns concern at that one, but he's made his point: Keep screwing with me and I'll take your whole life away. Piece by miserable piece. The sad part is, he can do it. "Michael, you're under a lot of pressure right now, and the roving wiretap issues are only going to add to that. Believe me, I really am worried about you. Until this blows over, I think it's best for you to take it easy."

"I can handle it."

"I'm sure you can," he says, taking obvious joy in watching me squirm. "And actually, there's this one that just came in. It concerns a woman who was artificially inseminated by—"

"I saw it. The sperm case."

"That's it," he says with a coal-black grin. "You can get the paperwork from Judy—it shouldn't take you that long. And with Bartlett's new focus on family, maybe this'll turn into something big."

Now he's playing with me. I can see the gleam in his eyes—he's loving every minute of it.

"I'll get right on it," I say, simulating enthusiasm. I'm not giving him this one.

"You sure you're okay?" he asks, once again touching my shoulder.

I look him straight in the eye and smile. "Never been better." Heading for the door, I concentrate on my Monday meeting with Vaughn and wonder if this isn't about more than just a bigshot in a gay bar. Whatever he's hiding, Simon's slowly upping the ante. And from here on in, he'll do anything to stop the bleeding.

Back in my office, I can still see that haunting grin on Simon's face. If there was a point where I saw him as a victim, it's long gone. In fact, that's what scares me most—even if Simon was being blackmailed, he's taking way too much pleasure in what he's done. Which makes me think there's more to come.

I have to admit, though, he's right about one thing: Ever since the onset of this crisis, my work has taken a back seat. My call log is filled with unreturned phone calls, my e-mail hasn't been read in a week, and my desk, with its mountains of paper, has officially become my in-box.

In no mood to clean and even less mood to talk, I head straight for the e-mail. Scanning through the unending list of messages, I see one from my dad. I almost forgot they gave him limited access to a terminal. Opening the message, I read his quick note: "When you coming to visit?" He's got a point with that one—it's been over a month. Every time I go there, I leave feeling guilty and depressed. But he's still my father. I write back my own quick response: "I'll try this weekend."

After deleting over thirty different versions of the President's weekly, monthly, and hourly schedules, I notice a two-day-old message from someone with a *Washington Post* return address. I assume it has to do with the census or one of my other issues. But when I open it up, it says: "Mr. Garrick—If you have some time, I'd be interested in talking with you about Caroline Penzler. Naturally, we can keep it confidential. If you can be of assistance, please let me know." It's signed "Inez Cotigliano, Washington Post Staff Writer."

My eyes go wide and I have a hard time catching my breath. With Caroline's ties to our office and everyone in it, it's no shock that someone was going to start looking my way. But this isn't some conspiracy-cashew-nut Web site. This is the *Washington Post*.

Trying to stop my hands from shaking, I head for calmer ground. Pam's the expert on all-things-Caroline. I dart for the door and pull it open. In the anteroom, however, I'm surprised to find Pam sitting at the usually unoccupied desk right outside my door. The makeshift home of our coffee machine and piles of discarded magazines, the desk has been tenant-less for as long as I can remember.

"What're you—"

"Don't ask," she says, slamming down the receiver. "I'm in the middle of a call with the Vice President's Office, and suddenly my phone goes dead. No explanation, no reason. Now they're telling me there's a backlog for repairs, so I'm stuck out here until tomorrow. On top of that, I don't even understand half of this new stuff—they should've picked someone else—there's no way I'm gonna be able to pull it off." In front of her, the small desk is covered with red files and legal pads. Pam won't turn around, but I don't need to see the deep bags under her eyes to tell she's tired and overwhelmed. Even her blond hair, which is usually exceptionally neat, is breaking loose and looking frizzy. Caroline left tough shoes to fill. And like Trey said, new shoes hurt.

"You know what the worst part is?" she asks without waiting for an answer. "Every single one of these nominees is the same. I don't care if you want to be an ambassador, an undersecretary, or a member of the damn Cabinet—nine out of ten people are cheating on their spouses or floundering in therapy. And let me tell you something else: No one—I repeat—*no one* in this entire government is paying their taxes. *'Oops, I forgot about the housekeeper. I swear, I didn't know.'* You're going to be heading the IRS for chrissakes!"

Raging, Pam spins around to finally face me. "Now what do you want?" she asks.

"Well, I—"

"Actually, now that I think about it, can it wait till later? I just want to finish this stuff."

"Sure," I say, looking down at her makeshift desk. Next to her stack of red file folders, I notice a manila one marked "FOIA—Caroline Penzler." Recognizing the acronym for the Freedom of Information Act, I ask, "Who's the FOIA request from?"

"That *Post* reporter—Inez whatever-her-name-is."

"Cotigliano."

"That's the one," Pam says.

The color fades from my face. I grab the file and rip out the multipage memo. "When did you get this?"

"I-I think it was yester—"

"Why didn't you tell me?" I shout. Before she can answer, I see the heading on the internal memo:

TO: All Counsel Staff
FROM: Edgar V. Simon, Counsel to the President

With the press taking such a quick interest, I bet he's doing this one personally. Flipping past Simon's memo, I notice he's even included Inez's actual request for documents. She's trying to get her hands on personnel files, judicial files, internal memos, ethics memos—every public document that's somehow related to Caroline. Luckily, Counsel's Office communications are generally protected from FOIA disclosure. Then I notice the last item on Inez's list. My heart stops. There it is in black and white—the easiest thing to give to the press—WAVES records. From September 4th. The day I found Caroline dead.

"Michael, before you . . ."

It's too late. By requesting these records, Inez has already lit the fuse. We can stall as long as we want, but it's just a matter of time until the entire world sees that I invited an accused murderer into the building. Which means it's no longer a question of *if* the records are going to get out; it's just a question of *when*.

Unable to speak, I slide my hand into my empty mailbox, wondering where my copy of the memo went. Then I look at Pam.

"I'm sorry," Pam says. "I thought you knew."

"Obviously, I didn't." I toss the memo on her desk and head for the door.

"Where're you going?"

"Out," I reply as I leave the office. "I just remembered something I have to do."

"Cut her some slack," Nora says on the other line. "She sounds avalanched with work."

"I'm sure she is, but she should also know how important it is to me."

"So now's she's supposed to read you all her mail? C'mon, Michael, when she got the memo, I'm sure she assumed you did too."

It's the exact same reaction Trey just gave me, but to be

honest, I was hoping for a different opinion. "You don't understand," I add. "It's not just that she didn't tell me. It's just . . . ever since she started glomming up the ladder, it's like she's a different person."

"Smells like you've got a slight case of jealousy coming on."

"I'm not jealous." Standing at the pay phone across the street from the OEOB, I find myself scanning the crowds of pedestrians, trying to remember that photo I saw of Vaughn.

"Listen, sweet pea, you're starting to sound pathetic. I mean, even if you *are* paranoid, calling me from a pay phone? C'mon. Take a breath, buy a lollipop—do something. It's the same thing with the *Post* reporter. Mountains and molehills, baby."

I'm not sure what's more unnerving—the incident with Pam or the fact that Nora's suddenly acting like there's nothing to worry about. "You think?"

"Of course. Haven't you ever heard how Bob Woodward researched *The Brethren*? He was writing this book about the Supreme Court, but he couldn't get any of the clerks to talk to him. So he writes this six-hundred-page manuscript based on hearsay and rumors. Then he takes the manuscript, makes a few copies, and circulates it around the Court. Within a week, every egomaniac in the building is calling him to point out the inaccuracies. Pow—instant book."

"That's not true. Who told you that?"

"Bob Woodward."

I act cool. "So it's true?"

"It's true that I spoke to Woodward."

"What about the other part? The part with the clerks?"

"He said it's bullshit—one of Washington's great myths. He had no problem getting sources. He's Bob Woodward," she says with a laugh. "This other reporter—the one who e-mailed you—she's just fishing. The whole FOIA thing is just one big expedition. Oop, hold on a second—cleaning lady . . ." She covers the phone and her voice gets muffled—but I can still make it out. "Estoy charlando con un amigo. Puedes esperar un segundito?"

"Disculpe, señora. Solo venía para recojer la ropa sucia."

"No te preocupes. No es gran cosa. Gracias, Lola!" Turning her attention back to me, she asks, "I'm sorry, where were we?"

"You know Spanish?"

"I'm from Miami, Paco. You think I'm gonna take French?" Before I can answer, she adds, "Now let's talk about something else. What're you doing this weekend? Maybe we can get together."

"I can't. I promised my dad I'd visit."

"That's nice of you. Where's he live? Michigan?"

"Not exactly," I whisper.

She recognizes the change in my tone. "What's wrong?"

"No, nothing."

"Then why're you shutting down like that? C'mon, now—you tell me. What's really going on?"

"Nothing," I insist, moving for a change of subject. After her call this morning, I'm tempted to, but . . . no . . . not yet. "I'm just worried about Simon."

"What'd he do?"

I explain how he pulled me off the roving wiretap case. As always, Nora's reaction is instantaneous.

"That dickhead—he can't do that to you!"

"He already did."

"Then make him change it. Get on the horn. Tell Uncle Larry."

"Nora, I'm not going to—"

"Stop letting people push you around. Simon, the FBI,

Vaughn—whatever they say, you accept it. When the food's cold, send it back."

"If you send it back, the cook spits in it."

"That's not true."

"I bused tables at Sizzler for three years in high school. Believe me, I'd rather have the cold food."

"Well, I wouldn't. So if you're not going to call Larry, then I will. In fact, you feast on your cold dinner—I'm going to call him right now."

"Nora, don't . . ."

It's too late. She's gone.

I hang up the phone and notice a quiet clicking. It's coming from behind me. Turning around, I notice a rumpled pudge of a man, with a thin beard that's clearly trying to compensate for a receding hairline. Click, click, click. With a beat-up green camera bag dangling from his shoulder, he's taking pictures of the OEOB. For a split second, though . . . right when I turned around . . . I could swear his camera was pointed at me.

Anxious to leave, I turn my back to him and step off the curb. But I can still hear that clicking. One right after the other. Taking one last look at the stranger, I focus on his equipment. Telephoto lens. Motor drive. Not your average D.C. tourist.

Stepping back to the curb, I slowly move toward him. "Do I know you?" I ask.

He lowers his camera and looks me straight in the eye. "Mind your own business."

"What?"

He doesn't answer. Instead, he spins around and takes off. As he runs, I notice that on the back of his camera bag there're words written in black Magic Marker: "If found call 202-334-6000." Memorizing the number, I stop running and dart back to the pay phone. Shoving change down the throat of the machine, I dial the number and wait for someone to pick up. "C'mon . . ." As it rings, I watch the stranger disappear up the block. This is never going to . . .

"*Washington Post*," a female voice answers. "How may I direct your call?"

"I can't believe this. Why the hell was he—?"

"Michael, calm down," Trey says on the other line. "For all you know—"

"He was taking my picture, Trey! I saw him!"

"Are you sure it was just of you?"

"When I asked him about it, he ran away. They know it, Trey. Somehow, they know to focus on me, which means they're not going to stop digging through my life until they hit either a casket or a . . . Oh, God."

"What?" Trey asks. "What's wrong?"

"When they find out what I did—they're going to rip him apart."

"Rip who apart?"

"I gotta go. I'll speak to you later."

"But what abou—"

I slam down the phone and dial a new number.

Ten digits later, I'm on the phone with Marlon Porigow, a deep-voiced man who's in charge of my father's visitation rights. "Tomorrow should be fine," he tells me in a great Cajun bellow. "I'll make sure he's up and ready."

"Any problems lately? He doing okay?" I ask.

"No one likes being a prisoner—but he manages. We all manage."

"I guess," I say, my left hand clamped ruthlessly to the armrest of my chair. "I'll see you tomorrow."

"Tomorrow it is."

As he's about to hang up, I add, "And Marlon, can you do me a favor?"

"Name it."

"I'm working on some . . . some pretty important stuff over here—some of it a little personal. And since I'm already nervous that the press is sniffing too closely, if you could . . ."

"You want me to keep an extra eye on him?"

"Yeah." I can still see that photographer scurrying up the block. "Just try to make sure no one gets in to see him. Some of these guys can be ruthless."

"You really think someone's gonna—"

"Yes," I interrupt. "I wouldn't ask if I didn't."

Marlon's heard that tone before. "You're up to your knees, now, ain't ya?"

I don't answer.

"Well, don't worry 'bout a thing," he continues. "Meals, showers, lights out—I'll make sure no one gets near him."

Returning the phone to its cradle, I'm alone in the room. I feel the ego walls closing in around me. Between Inez and the photographer, the press is zeroing in a bit too quickly. And they're not alone. Simon, Vaughn, the FBI—they're all starting to look closely. At me.

CHAPTER 16

The Saturday morning traffic out to Virginia isn't nearly as bad as I thought it'd be. I assumed I'd be bumper-to-bumper in I-95's asphalt embrace, but the bad weather leaves me breezing toward Richmond with nothing but dark gray skies and clouds in my eyes. It's the kind of color-less, grim day that feels like it's always about to rain. No, not rain. Pour. The kind of day that scares people away.

Married to the far left lane of the highway, I keep a cautious eye on the rearview mirror until I'm well out of Washington. It's been more than a month since the last time I drove out to see him, and I don't plan on bringing unwanted guests. For almost a half hour, I try to lose my-self in the repetitive views of the tree-lined landscape. But every stray thought leads back to Caroline. And Simon. And Nora. And the money.

"Dammit!" I shout, banging the steering wheel. There's never an escape. I flick on the radio, find some good noisy music with a beat, then crank the volume way up. Ig-noring the still overcast skies, I slide open the sunroof. The wind feels good on my face. For the next few hours,

I'm going to do everything in my power to forget about life. Today's about family.

I spend the last half hour on the highway in a four-car caravan. I'm in second place, with a navy Toyota in front of me and a forest green Ford and a tan Suburban behind me. It's one of the true joys of traveling—linking up with strangers who match your speed. A united defense against the technology of a cop's speed gun.

Two exits away from my destination in Ashland, Virginia, I break from the procession and make my way over to the right-hand lane. Out of the corner of my eye, I notice that the tan Suburban follows. Just a coincidence, I decide. Up ahead, I see the sign for Kings Dominion. It always made me laugh that this place was so close to my dad's. An amusement park—so close; so far. I take a full whiff of the irony and a quick glance in the rearview. The Suburban's still behind me.

He's probably going to get off at the amusement park—there's not much else to see out here. But as we approach the exit, he doesn't have his blinker on. He's not even slowing down. He's just moving in closer.

I look over my shoulder to get a better view of the driver . . . and then my throat goes dry. What the hell is *he* doing here? And why's he alone? Yanking my wheel to the right, I pull onto the shoulder of the road, kicking a cloudful of gravel dust in his face. We're just a few yards shy of the Ashland exit, but with a punch of my leg, I slam the brakes as hard as I can. Behind me, the Suburban is blind from the dust and closer than ever. He comes to a jerking stop, but his front bumper lays a quick bite into mine.

Jumping out of my car, I race to the driver's side of the Suburban. "What do you want!?" I shout, banging the base of my fist against his window.

Turning away, Harry isn't concerned with my question. He's focused on something in the backseat. No, not something. Someone.

She sits up and her laugh rips through me. "And you think *I'm* a psycho driver?" Nora asks as she readjusts her baseball cap. "Honey, you take the cake, the presents, and the whole damn birthday party."

"What do you think you're doing?"

"Don't be mad," Nora says, getting out of the Suburban. "I just wanted to—"

"Just wanted to what? Follow me around? Run me off the road?"

"I . . . I just wanted to see where you were going," she whispers, staring at her feet.

"What?"

"You told me you were going to visit your dad . . . but something about the way you said it . . . I just wanted to be sure you were okay . . ."

I look over at Harry, then back to Nora. Her head's down and she's kicking at a few pebbles in the dirt. She's still hesitating. Afraid to open herself up. Every other time, that's when she's been burned. And with everything going on . . . the way we're tied together . . . she's risking it all just by being here. But she still came.

Even as I move toward her, I know Trey would tell me to walk away. He's wrong. There're some things you have to fight for—even if it means losing it all. No matter what anyone says, there's no easy anything.

Slowly, I lift her chin. "I'm glad you're here."

She can't help but smile. "So you're really going to see your dad?"

I nod.

"Can I meet him?"

"I-I'm not sure that's such a good idea."

She pauses at my reaction. "Why not?"

"Because . . . Why would you want to meet him any-way?"

"He's your dad, isn't he?"

She says it so quick, like there's no other answer. But that doesn't mean she's getting in.

"If you don't want me to, I'd understand."

I'm sure she would—she wrote the book, the prequel, and the sequel on this stuff. And maybe that's part of the problem. Once again, we're back to fear. And loyalty. I can't ask for it if I don't give it. "So you don't care that he's—"

"He's your father," she says. "You don't have to hide him."

"I'm not hiding him."

"I want to meet him, Michael."

It's a hard one to refuse. "Okay, but only if you—"

"Harry, I'm riding with Michael," she calls out. Before I can say a word, she dashes for my car and hops inside.

"Sorry about your bumper," Harry says to me as he heads back to his Suburban. "I have a budget to pay for that if you want."

I'm talking to Harry, but still staring at Nora. "I guess . . . whatever . . . yeah."

As he opens his door, I ask, "You don't still have to watch her, do you?"

"I won't come in, Michael, but I do have to follow."

"That's fine as long as you know one thing. When it comes to my dad, you should steer a little clear. He doesn't like cops."

Pulling off at the Ashland exit, it doesn't take long for us to hit horse country. One minute we're tracing the double-yellow lines of Route One; a left turn later we're riding up and down the peaks and valleys of Virginia's most picturesque rolling roads. Traffic lights become green trees and yellow stalks. Parking lots become lush open fields. The sky's still cloudy, but the sweet smell of the outdoors ... it's suddenly the sunniest of days.

"Not to be an ingrate, but where the hell is this place?" Nora asks.

I don't answer. I want her to see for herself.

Up ahead, the grounds of the facility are located next to a family-owned farm. It wasn't the farmer's first choice for neighbors, but the possibilities for cheap labor quickly changed his mind. When we pass the farm and its cornstalk-covered fields, I make a sharp left through the gate in an unmarked log fence. The car bounces along a dirt road that weaves its way to the front entrance.

As we pull to a stop, I half expect Nora to race out of the car. Instead, she stays where she is. "You ready?" I ask.

She nods.

Somewhat satisfied, I get out of the car and slam the door. For perhaps the first time in her life, Nora follows.

The facility is a one-story 1950s ranch house with a propped-open screen door. So much for security. Inside, it's a normal house, except for the walls, where fire escape routes and state licenses are posted right as you walk in. In the kitchen, a heavy, nappy-haired man is leaning forward on the counter, newspaper stretched out in front of him. "Michael, Michael, Michael," he sings in his deep Cajun accent.

"The world-famous Marlon."

"Momma only made but one." He takes a quick look at Nora, then does an immediate double-take. He's too smart for the baseball cap. Here we go.

"Mmmm-mmm—lookit dat. What you doing this far south?"

"Same thing that Creole accent's doing this far north," she shoots back with a grin.

Marlon lets out a thundering laugh. "Good for you, sister. 'Bout time someone didn't say it was Cajun."

I clear my throat, begging for attention. "Um . . . about my father . . ."

"Been asking about you all morning," Marlon says. "And just so you know, I been lookin' out since you called, but there's nothing to worry about. Whole place hasn't had a visitor since Thursday."

"Who came on Thur—"

"Let it go," Nora says, leaning in over my shoulder. "Just for a few hours."

She's right. Today's supposed to be for family.

"He's waiting for you," Marlon adds. "In his room."

Nora takes the first step. "All set?" she asks.

My fists are clenched and I'm frozen. I shouldn't have let her come.

"It's okay," she says. Prying my fingers open, she takes me by the hand.

"You don't know him. He isn't . . ."

"Stop worrying about it," she adds as she lifts my chin. "I'm going to love him. Really."

Warmed by the confidence in her voice, I hesitantly head for the door.

CHAPTER 17

"Knock, knock," I announce as I enter the small room. There's a bed on my left and a single dresser on my right. My dad's sitting at a desk along the far wall. "Anyone here?"

"Mikey!" my dad shouts with a smile that's all teeth. Jumping out of his seat, he knocks a can of Magic Markers from his desk. It doesn't even register. All he sees is me.

He grabs me in a tight bear hug and tries to lift me off the ground.

"Careful, Dad. I'm heavier now."

"Never too heavy for . . . this!" He picks me up and spins around, planting me in the center of the room. "You are heavy," he says with a slight nasal slur. "Tired-looking too."

With his back to the door, he doesn't see Nora standing on the threshold. I bend over and start picking up the markers from the floor. Noticing the newspaper on his desk, I ask, "What're you working on?"

"Crossword puzzle."

"Really? Let me see." He picks up the paper and hands

it to me. My dad's version of a finished crossword puzzle—he's colored every blank square a different color.

"What d'you think?"

"Great," I tell him, trying to sound enthusiastic. "Your best one yet."

"For real?" he asks, unleashing his smile. It's a bright white grin that lights up the room. With all five fingers extended, he hooks the space between his thumb and pointer finger behind his ear, then folds the top of his ear down and lets it flap up again. When I was little, it reminded me of a cat giving itself a bath. I loved it.

"Will you put in letters?" he asks.

"Not now, Dad," I interrupt. Patting him on the back, I tuck in the tag of his shirt. Over his shoulder, I read the look on Nora's face. She's finally starting to get the picture. Now she knows where my childhood ends. "Dad, there's someone I want you to meet." Pointing to the door, I add, "This is my friend Nora."

He turns around and they check each other out. At fifty-seven years old, he's got the permanent smile of a ten-year-old, but he's still extremely handsome, with a messy swath of gray hair barely receding at the temples. He's wearing his favorite T-shirt—the one with the Heinz ketchup logo on it—and his always present khaki shorts, which are pulled too high around his stomach. Down low, he's got white sneakers and black socks. Watching Nora, he starts rocking on the balls of his feet. Back and forth, back and forth, back and forth.

I can see the surprise on her face. "Nice to meet you, Mr. Garrick," she says, removing her baseball cap. It's the first time she's done that in public. No more hiding.

"Do you know who she is?" I ask, suddenly enjoying myself.

"He's my baby boy," he tells Nora, proudly putting his

arm around me. As he says the words, he looks away from both of us. His always wide eyes go straight to the corner of the room and his shoulders slump awkwardly forward.

"Dad, I asked you a question. Do you know who she is?"

His mouth hangs open as he turns to her with a long sideways glance. Confused, he says, "Pretty girl with small breasts?"

"Dad!"

"She's not?" he asks sheepishly, his eyes darting away.

"Actually, that's just a nickname," she says, extending a hand. "I'm Nora."

"Frank," he blurts with a grin. "Frank Garrick." He wipes his hand against his stomach and offers it to Nora.

I know what she's thinking. The way his mouth gapes open; the way he's always staring in the distance—it's not what she expected. His teeth buck slightly forward, his neck cranes upward. He's an adult, but he looks more like an oversized kid—who happens to have really poor fashion sense.

"Dad, why're you still wearing those black socks? I told you they look terrible with sneakers."

"They stay up better," he says, pulling up each sock to its height limit. "Nothing wrong with that."

"There sure isn't," Nora says. "I think you look handsome."

"She says I look handsome," he repeats, rocking back and forth. As I watch the two of them, he stands right next to her—completely invading her personal space—but Nora never steps back.

I grin at Nora, but she turns away to check out the room. Above my dad's bed is a framed picture from Michigan's Special Olympics. It's an aerial shot of a young man competing in the long jump. On the opposite wall is the framed collage I made for him when he moved into the group home. Built with pictures from the last thirty years, it lets him know I'm always there.

"Is this you?" Nora asks, examining the collage.

"Which one?" I ask.

"Bowl haircut and the pink oxford shirt. The little prepster."

"That's Mikey in his big-boy shirt," my dad says proudly. "Off to school, off to school."

In the corner, she glances at the rows of empty Heinz ketchup bottles that line the bookshelves, and the windowsills, and the side table next to the bed, and every other free space in the room. Following her glance, my dad beams. I shoot him a look. He can show her the ketchup bottles later. Not now.

Next to the bookcase, his bed is made, but his desk's a mess. On top of the clutter is a framed wedding photo. Nora goes right to it.

Right away, my dad starts flicking his middle finger against his thumb. Flick, flick, flick, flick. "She's my wife. Philly. Phyllis. Phyllis," he repeats as Nora picks up the frame. Decked out in their respective tux and wedding dress, my dad looks young and slender; my mom shy and overweight.

"She's very pretty," Nora says.

"She's beautiful. I'm handsome," he says. Flick, flick, flick. "Here's Michael with the President. The real one." Reaching over, he hands Nora a photograph of me and her dad.

"Wow," she says. "And Michael gave this to you?"

"I told you—he's my boy."

After a quick game of Connect Four, we head to the backyard for lunch. Polishing off the remains of our turkey and ketchup sandwiches, the three of us are sitting at an old wooden picnic table. "Want a surprise for dessert?" my dad asks as soon as he's done eating.

"I do," Nora says immediately.

"Michael, what about . . ."

"Sure," I add.

"You got it! Wait right here." He shoots up out of his seat, almost knocking over his plate.

"Where're you going?" I ask as he heads away from the house.

"Next door," he explains without turning around.

My eyes are locked on him as he waddles toward the log fence that separates the two properties. "Be careful," I shout.

He waves back at me, his arm flailing through the air.

"You really get crazy about him, don't you?" Nora asks.

I rip a piece of crust from my bread and crumble it in my hand. "I can't help it. Ever since that photographer took my picture . . . If they're that interested, you know they're going to come out here eventually."

"And what's so terrible about that?"

She thinks I'm embarrassed of him. Even if I am, I wish it were that simple. "Don't tell me there's no reason to worry."

"Maybe it's just a mind game. Maybe it's Simon's way of telling you to keep quiet."

"And what if it's not? What if the press already knows about this guy Vaughn—?"

"I told you before, don't play what-if. You're meeting with Vaughn on Monday—you'll find out soon enough. Until then, we'll talk to Marlon and tell him to keep a close watch."

"But what if . . ." I catch myself. "Maybe I should bring him back to the city. He can stay with me."

"That's a crap idea and you know it."

"You have anything better?"

"I'm going to ask the Service to keep tabs on him out here."

"They'd do that?"

"They're the Secret Service. They'd suck bullets from a tommy gun if they thought it'd keep us safe."

"You mean, if it'd keep *you* safe."

"The benefit cup runneth over," she says, raising an eyebrow. "If something suspicious happens to my friends, I'm supposed to report it. They'll open a file and look into it. That should be more than enough to keep him safe."

I push the crumbs on my plate into a small, neat pile. Time for some order. "Thank you, Nora. That'd be great." Looking up, I notice that she still hasn't put on her baseball cap. "That'd really mean a lot to us."

All she does is nod. Standing from her seat, she picks up her empty plate and starts to clean up.

"Leave it," I tell her. "Marlon likes my dad to do it himself. The group home's goal is self-sufficiency."

"But doesn't he—" Nora cuts herself off.

"What?"

"No, nothing. I just—" Once again, she interrupts herself. She's lived her whole life on the receiving end of this one. Fascination with dad. It's killing her to pry.

"He's mentally retarded," I offer. "And don't worry, I don't mind you asking."

She looks away, but her face is flushed red. She's blushing. So that's what it takes to rattle her. "How long has he suffered with it?" she asks.

"He doesn't 'suffer,' " I explain. "He was just born with a slower ability to learn—which means he takes a little longer with logic and other complex reasoning. The upside, though, is that he'll never lie about his emotions. It's the charm of openness. He means what he says."

"Does that mean I have small breasts?"

I laugh. "Sorry about that one. It sometimes takes its toll on some of his social skills."

"So is your mom . . . ?"

There it is—the first question everyone asks. "No, my mom was normal. At least, by my standards."

"I don't understand."

"Take another look at the wedding photo. She was a full-figured nurse with inch-thick glasses—the kind of sad, heavyset woman you never see out, because she never goes out. She just sat home and read books. Tons of books. All of them fantasies. When my dad went to the hospital with a bladder infection, she took care of him. Penis jokes aside, he adored her—couldn't get enough—kept hitting the call button on his bed so she'd come and visit. His 'butterfly' he called her. That was all she needed. For the first time, someone said she was beautiful and meant it."

"Some people would call that true love."

"No, I agree. My mom loved him for everything he was, and he loved her right back. It was never one way—slow learner doesn't mean brain dead. He's a loving, caring person and she was the one he picked. At the same time, she saw him unobscured by his disability. And the fact that she could take care of him—it's the same thing he did for her— after all those years alone . . . well, everyone wants to be wanted."

"So I guess she's the one who raised you."

Nora's careful the way she says that. What she really wants to know is: How'd I turn out so normal? "However she felt about herself, my mom always found her outlet in me. When I started reading early and asked her if we could subscribe to a newspaper, she did everything in her power to keep me going. She just couldn't believe she and my dad produced . . ." I pause. "She was so shy, she was afraid to talk to the cashier at a Kmart, but she couldn't have possibly loved—or supported me—more."

"And she did it all by herself?"

"I know you're thinking it's impossible, but it happens all the time. Didn't you see the *New York Times Magazine* a few weeks back? They did a whole piece on kids with mentally retarded parents. When I was younger, we had a support group of six people we met with twice a week—now they have comprehensive therapeutic programs. Other than that, we got some help from my mom's aunts and uncles, who were some Ohio wealthy-types. Too bad for us, every one of them was a jerk-off—including the ones who live around here. They tried to get her to divorce my dad, but she told them to go scratch themselves. Hearing that, they told her the same. It's one of the biggest things I respect her for. Born with everything, she went for nothing."

"And what's your twist? Born with nothing, you now want everything?"

"It's better than nothing."

She takes a long look at me, studying my features. Her short fingernails are picking at the edge of her paper plate. I have no idea what she's thinking, but I refuse to say anything. I've always believed people connect in silence. Mental digestion, someone once called it. What happens between words.

Eventually, Nora stops picking at the plate. Something clicked.

"You alright?" I ask.

She shoots me a look I've never seen before. "Do you ever mind taking care of your dad? I mean, do you ever feel like it's a burden . . . or that's it's . . . I don't know, more than you can handle?"

It's the first time I've ever heard her say something's difficult. Even as a thought, it doesn't come easy. "My mom used to tell me that there was always someone who had it much worse."

"I guess," she says. "It's just that sometimes . . . I mean, even coming out here. This place must cost you half your salary."

"Actually, it's barely over a quarter—Medicaid picks up the rest. And even if they didn't, it's not about the money. Didn't you see the way he was walking when he gave us the tour of the kitchen? Chest straight out, ear-to-ear smile. He's proud of himself here."

"And that's enough for you?"

I turn toward the swaying corn stalks in the field next door. "Nora, that's why Caroline pulled my file in the first place." Now it's out there. No regrets. Just relief.

"What're you talking about?"

"My file. We've been waiting for the FBI to clear it, but there's a reason Caroline had it."

"I thought it was the Medicaid thing—since they pay for your dad to stay here, it was a conflict of interest to let you work on the legislative overhaul."

"There's more to it than that," I say.

She doesn't flinch. It's hard to surprise someone who's seen it all. "Out with it," she says.

I lean forward and pull my sleeves up to my elbows. "It was right after I first started in the office. I had just relocated to Washington, and I still hadn't found a place for my dad. You have to understand, I didn't want to put him just anywhere—in Michigan, he had one of the best places in the state. Like this, he was out on a farm, and they made sure he was safe, and stimulated, and had a job—"

"I get the picture."

"I don't think you do. It's not like finding daycare."

"What did you do?"

"If I didn't get him in here, they would've sent him to a training center—an institution, Nora. Forget about a normal life—he'd have languished there and died."

"Tell me what you did, Michael."

I wedge my fingernails into the grooves of the wooden table. "When I first started in the Counsel's Office, I used White House stationery to contact the head of Virginia's residential services program. Three phone calls later, I made it clear that if he accepted my dad into a private group home, he—and the entire mental retardation community—'would have a friend in the White House.' "

There's a long pause after I finish. All I can do is focus on the corn stalks.

"That's it?" she asks with a laugh.

"Nora, it's a complete abuse of power. I used my position here to—"

"Yeah, you're a real monster—you cut the cafeteria line to help your mentally retarded father. Big whoop. Find me one person in America who wouldn't do the same."

"Caroline," I say flatly.

"She found out about it?"

"Of course she found out about it. She saw the letter sitting on my desk!"

"Calm down," Nora says. "She didn't report you, did she?"

I nervously shake my head. "She called me into her office, asked me a few questions about it, then sent me on my way. Told me to keep it to myself. That's why she had my file. I swear, that's the only reason."

"Michael, it's okay. You don't have to worry about—"

"If the press picks up on it—"

"They're not—"

"All Simon has to do is give Inez my file . . . that's all

it takes. You know what they'll do, Nora—he can't survive in an institu—"

"Michael . . ."

"You don't understand . . ."

"Actually, I do." She leans forward on both elbows and looks me straight in the eye. "If I were in your position, I would've done the exact same thing. I don't care what strings I had to pull, you better bet your ass I'd help my father."

"But if . . ."

"No one'll ever find out. I keep my secrets—and yours."

She reaches across the table and motions for my hand. Finger by finger, she pries open my closed fist. It's the second time today she's done that. As her nails skate tiny circles inside my palm, the calm settles on my shoulders.

"How's that?" she asks.

Questions don't come any easier. Behind her, the sun lights the edges of her hair. People wait their whole lives and never get a moment this good. Refusing to let it pass me by, I lean forward and close my eyes.

"Mickey-Mikey-Moo!" my dad shouts at the top of his lungs.

Startled, I pull away. Calmly and with far more poise, Nora does the same. Leaning back, she slowly looks over my shoulder. The moment's lost, and here comes Daddy.

"Got a surprise!" he yells from behind me.

"Where'd you get that?" Nora blurts as a smile lifts her cheeks. In seconds, she's out of her seat.

On the opposite side of the log fence, my dad's holding on to a leather strap, which is attached to a gorgeous chocolate brown horse.

"She's beautiful," Nora says, squeezing between the horizontal logs of the fence. "What's her name?"

"You were gonna kiss him, weren't you?" my dad asks, his eyes even wider than usual.

"Kiss who?" Nora asks as she points at me. "Him?" My dad nods vigorously. "Not a chance," she says.

"I think you're boyfriend and girlfriend," he says, giggling.

"You're very smart."

"You maybe gonna get married?"

"I don't know about that, but I wouldn't rule anythin—"

"Nora," I interrupt. "He doesn't—"

"He's doing just fine." Turning back to my dad, she adds, "You raised a good son, Mr. Garrick. He's the first real friend I've had in . . . in a while."

Hanging on her every word, he's mesmerized. Suddenly, his lips start to quiver. He tucks his thumbs into his fists. I knew this was going to happen. Before it even registers with Nora, his eyes well up with tears and his forehead furrows with anger. "What's wrong?" she asks, confused.

His voice is the enraged cry of a little boy. "You're not gonna have me at the wedding, are you?" he shouts. "You weren't even gonna tell me!"

Nora steps back at the outburst, but within seconds, she extends her hand to reach out. "Of course we'd—"

"Don't lie!" he yells, slapping her hand away with the edge of the leather strap. His face is bright red. "I hate lies! I *hate* lies!"

Nora takes another step toward him. "You don't have to—"

"I do what I want! I can do what I want!" he screams, tears streaming down his cheeks. Like a lion-tamer, he swings at her again with the leather strap.

"Dad, don't hit her!" I shout, racing for the fence. Nora can't handle this one. She backs away just as he swings again. From the look on her face, I can tell she's taken aback, but she's still determined to break through. Counting to herself, she times it just right. He takes another full swing with the strap, and before he can wind up again, she rushes forward. Just as I hop over the fence, she opens her arms and takes him in. He fights to pull away, but she holds tight.

"Shhhhhh," she whispers, lightly rubbing his back.

Slowly, he stops struggling, even as his body continues shaking. "How come you . . ."

"It's okay, it's all okay," she continues, still holding him. "Of course you're invited."

"F-For sure?" he sobs.

She lifts his chin and wipes away the tears. "You're his father, aren't you? You're the one who made him."

"I did," he says proudly as he tries to catch his breath. "He came from me." With all five fingers erect, he picks at the edge of his nose with his middle one. Growing more confident, he once again wraps his arms around her. He's still sobbing, but the gleam in his eyes tells the story. They're tears of joy. He just wanted to be part of it. Not left out.

In a moment, the whole thing's over. Still in Nora's arms, he's pressing his head against her shoulder, rocking back and forth. Back and forth, back and forth, back and forth. She's got it all taken care of, and for the first time, I realize that's her gift. Identifying with what's missing. That's what she knows. A life that's half-complete.

"Is this your horse?" Nora finally asks, noticing my dad hasn't let go of the leather strap of the chocolate horse.

"T-This's Comet," he whispers. "She belongs next door—to Mrs. Holt. Laura Holt. She's nice too."

"She lets you take care of Comet?"

"Clean her, groom her, feed her," my dad says, his voice rising with excitement. "First the curry comb, then the dandy brush, then the hoof pick. That's my job. I have a job."

"Wow—a job *and* a son. What else do you need?"

He shrugs and looks away. "Nothing, right?"

"That's it," she says. "Nothing at all."

As my car leaves the parking lot and bounces along the path of the dirt road, Nora and I each have a hand out the window. We're throwing parade-float waves at my father, who's frantically waving back after us. "Goodbye, Dad!" he shouts at the top of his lungs.

"Goodbye, son!" I reply. He saw the name reversal in an old movie and immediately fell in love with it. Since then, it's become our customary way to say goodbye.

Pulling back onto the rolling roads of Virginia, I check the rearview mirror. Harry and the tan Suburban are right there.

"Wanna try to lose him again?" Nora asks, following my gaze.

"Funny," I say as I turn onto Route 54. Over my shoulder, the sun is finally starting to settle into the sky. Nothing left to do but ask. "So what'd you think?"

"What's to think? He's wonderful, Michael. And so's his son."

She's not one for compliments, so I take her at her word. "So you're okay with all of it?"

"Don't worry—you have nothing to be ashamed about."

"I'm not ashamed. I just . . ."

"You just what?"

"I'm not ashamed," I repeat.

"Who else have you told about him? Trey? Pam? Anyone?"

"Trey knows—and I told him he could tell Pam, but she and I never had the conversation ourselves."

"Ooooooh, she must've been plenty mad when she found out."

"What makes you say that?"

"Are you kidding? The love of her life holding back on her? It must've broken her little heart."

"The love of her life?"

"C'mon, handsome, you don't need X-ray specs to see this one. I saw how she was holding your hand at the funeral. She's dying to put the smoochie on you."

"You don't even know her."

"Let me tell you something—I've met her type a hundred times before. Small town predictable. When you walk into her bedroom, she's already got her clothes picked out for the next day."

"First of all, that's completely wrong. Second, it doesn't even matter. We're just friends. And good friends at that, so don't pick on her."

"If you're such good friends, why weren't you the one to tell her about your dad?"

"It's just the way I deal with it. Whenever I bring it up, people get self-conscious and they suddenly have to prove they're sensitive." Keeping my gaze locked on the power lines along the road, I add, "It's hard to explain, but there're times you just want to let it go. Or maybe grab them by the face and shout, 'Back off, Barnum, it's not a sideshow.' I mean, yes, it's my life, but that doesn't mean it's out there for public consumption. I don't know if that makes any sense, but . . ."

Out of the corner of my eye, I get a quick look at Nora. Sometimes I can be such a dumb bastard. I actually forgot who I was talking to. She's Nora Hartson. Just reading *USA Today*, you'd know who she was named after, her college major, and the fact that she spent her last birthday climbing Mount Rainier with the Secret Service. Turning my way, she raises a single, trust-me-on-this-one eyebrow. To Nora, it makes perfect sense.

"Hiya, Vance," Nora says to the guard at the Southeast Gate of the White House.

"Good evening, Ms. Hartson."

"Nora," she demands. "Nora, Nora, Nora."

With a loud click, the black metal gate swings open. He doesn't need to see my blue pass or my parking permit. He just needs to see Nora. "Thanks, Vance," she calls out, her voice sounding lighter, more open than I've ever heard her.

Pulling up to the South Portico at the base of the mansion, I'm having a hard time containing myself. It's so different than last time. No panic, no hiding, no posturing. No fear. For a few hours, Simon, Caroline, the money—the whole nightmare lowered its voice from a scream to a momentary whisper. All that's left is us.

When we reach the awning that covers the South Portico, I hit the brakes.

"What're you doing?" she asks.

"Aren't I dropping you off?"

"I guess," she says, suddenly losing the confidence in her voice. She's about to get out of the car, but pauses. "Or, if you want, you can come upstairs."

I look up at the shining white facade of the world's most famous mansion. "Are you serious?"

"I'm always serious," she says as the confidence floods back. "You up for it?"

I was wrong before. Questions don't come any easier than *this*. "Where do I park?"

She motions to the expansive South Lawn of the White House. "Anywhere you want."

CHAPTER 18

You ever been in this way?" Nora asks, heading for the south entrance under the awning. We follow the red carpet into the oval-shaped Diplomatic Reception Room, where FDR used to hold his fireside chats.

"I'm not sure—I keep confusing it with my apartment and the red carpet that leads to my futon."

"That's cute. Never heard that one before."

"*Before?* How many guys've you taken on this tour?"

"What tour're you talking about?"

"Y'know, *this* tour. The inside-my-Beltway tour."

She laughs. "Oh, is that what you think you're on?"

"You telling me I'm mistaken?"

"No, I'm telling you you're in full delusion. I'm giving you a cup of coffee and kicking you out on your bee-hind."

"You do what you want, but idle threats aren't the way to get lovin' outta me."

"We'll see."

"Oh, we'll definitely see." I do everything in my power to make sure I get the last word. It's the only time she's excited—when the outcome's out of her control.

Passing through the Dip Room, I'm swinging my shoulders with a strut that tells her she doesn't have a chance. It's such a bad lie, it's pathetic. As we leave the room, we make a sharp left into the Ground Floor Corridor. Across the pale red carpet, there's a guard on the left side of the hallway. I freeze. Nora smiles.

"And you were doing so well there, weren't you?" she teases. "You had the strut going and everything."

"It's not funny," I whisper. "Last time I was here, these guys . . ."

"Forget about last time," she whispers in my ear. "As long as you're with me, you're a guest." Up close, she blows me a taunting kiss.

It's amazing how she can pick the worst moments to turn me on.

As we pass the guard, he barely looks up. He simply whispers three words into his walkie-talkie: "Shadow plus one."

Once we're through the doorway, we can get upstairs by taking either the elevator or the stairs. Knowing that there're guards waiting at the next landing, I head for the elevator. Nora darts for the stairs. She's gone in an instant. I'm left alone with no choice. Shaking my head, I take off after her.

As we reach the next landing, two uniformed officers are waiting. Last time, they stopped me. This time, as I turn the corner of the stairway, they step back to give me more room.

Taking two stairs at a time, I close in on Nora. She leaves the stairs at the next landing and, following her lead, I head into the Residence's main corridor. Like the Ground Floor Corridor, it's a wide, spacious hallway with doors running along every wall. The difference is all in the decor. Painted a warm, pale yellow, and lined with built-in book-cases, half a dozen oil paintings, and plenty of eighteenth-

and nineteenth-century antiques, this isn't a tourist trap. This is a home.

Wandering down the hallway, I scan the paintings. The first one I see is a still-life of apples and pears. "Cézanne rip-off," I almost blurt. Then I notice the signature at the bottom. Cézanne.

"Got it at a flea market," Nora says.

I nod. Across from the Cézanne, I notice an abstract de Kooning. Time to slow down. Taking a deep breath, I get back in my zone.

"You want a quick tour?" she asks.

I pause, pretending to think about it. "If you want," I say with a shrug.

She knows I'm bluffing, but her smile tells me she appreciates the effort. Midway down the hallway, we stop in front of a bright yellow, oval-shaped room.

"Yellow Oval Room," I blurt.

"How'd you guess?"

"Years of Crayola." Pointing inside, I ask, "Now what do you do in a room like this? Is it just for show, or what?"

"This whole floor's mostly for entertaining—after a state dinner, cocktail parties, sucking up to senators, nonsense like that. People always wind up in here because they love the Truman Balcony—makes them feel important when they stand outside and touch the pillars."

"Can we go out there?"

"If you want to be a tourist."

She lets the challenge hang in the air. Man, she knows my buttons. Still, I refuse to give her the satisfaction.

"That's Chelsea's old bedroom," she says, pointing to the door opposite the Yellow Oval. "We turned it into a gym."

"So where's your room?"

"Why? Feeling frisky?"

Again, I'm not giving it to her. I point to the door at the end of the hallway. "What's behind there?"

"My parents' bedroom."

"Really?"

"Yeah," she says, studying my reaction. "Really."

Damn. She's counting that one against me. I should've known better. Her parents are always off limits.

Down the hall, she turns a corner and stops at the wall on her immediate left. Passing her, I'm standing across the hall from the Lincoln Bedroom. "So when're we going to get this coffee?" I ask.

"Right now." She's fidgeting with something on the wall, but I can't tell what it is. "The kitchenette's upstairs."

I assume we'll head back to the staircase, but we don't.

Stepping closer, I see that she's wedging her fingers into a thin crack in the wall. With a sharp pull, the wall swings toward us, revealing an otherwise hidden staircase. Nora looks up and smiles. "We can take the stairs on this side of the house."

"Pay attention," Nora says, "because this's the best part." She heads up a steep carpeted ramp and leads us toward the room directly above the Yellow Oval. "Voilà," she says with a bow. "The Solarium."

Resembling a small greenhouse on top of the mansion, the Solarium's outside walls are made entirely of green-tinted glass. Inside, wicker furniture and a glass-top card table give it the feel of a Palm Beach den. On the left is a kitchenette, on the right, an overstuffed white sofa and large-screen TV. Scattered around the room are dozens of family photos.

On my far right is a short bookcase filled with what looks like homemade arts-and-crafts projects. There's a purple and blue birdhouse that looks like it was made by a seventh-grader—on the side of it are the initials "N.H." in peeling orange paint. There's also a papier-mâché duck or swan—it's too warped to tell which—a ceramic ashtray or cupholder, and a flat piece of brown-painted wood with fifty or so protruding nails that're set up to spell the initials "N.H." To make sure the letters stand out, all the nail-heads are painted yellow. On the bottom of the shelf, I even spot a few trophies—one for soccer, one for field hockey. In all, you can trace the quality of the projects from first grade all the way up to about seventh or eighth. After that, there's nothing new.

Nora Hartson was twelve years old when her father first announced he was running for Governor. Sixth grade. If I had to date it, I'd say that's the same year she made the swan-duck. After that, I'd bet the birdhouse came next. And that's where her childhood ends.

"C'mon, you're missing the good stuff," she says, motioning for me to join her by the enormous window.

Crossing the room, I notice the VCR on top of the TV. "Can I ask you a question?" I begin as I move next to her.

"If it's about the history of the house, I don't really know my—"

"What's your favorite movie?" I blurt.

"Huh?"

"Your favorite movie—simple question."

Without pause, she says, "*Annie Hall*."

"Really?"

She lets out the sweetest of smiles. "No," she laughs. After today, it's not as easy to lie.

"So what is it?"

She stares out the window as if it's a big deal. "*Moonstruck*," she finally offers.

"The old Cher film?" I ask, confused. "Isn't that a love story?"

Shaking her head, she shoots me a look. "What you don't know about women . . . is a lot."

"But I—"

"Just enjoy the view," she says, pointing me back toward the window. When I oblige, she adds, "So whattya think?"

"Sure beats the Truman Balcony," I say, pressing my forehead against the glass. From here, I have a full view of the South Lawn and the Washington Monument.

"Wait until you see it face-to-face." She opens a door in the right corner and steps outside.

The balcony up here is a small one, and although it curves like a giant letter C around the length of the Solarium, there's just a white concrete guardrail to protect you. By the time I get outside, Nora's leaning over the edge. "Time for some fun—let loose and fly!" With her stomach pressed against the railing, she extends her arms and leans forward until her legs are lifted in the air.

"Nora . . . !" I shout, grabbing her by the ankles.

Lowering herself back to earth, she grins. "You're afraid of heights?"

Before I can say another word, she takes off, darting farther around the long, curved balcony. I try to grab her, but she slips through my hands, turns the corner, and disappears. Trying to catch up and trying even harder not to look over the edge, I dash along the far end of the balcony. But as I make my way around the corner, Nora's nowhere in sight. Undeterred, I plow forward, assuming she slipped through another door and went back into the Solarium. There's only one problem. On this side of the balcony, no other door exists. Reaching the corner, I hit a dead end. Nora's gone.

"Nora?" I call out. There aren't many places to hide.

From where I'm standing, the balcony runs flush against the mansion.

I press my hands against the wall, using my nails to search for cracks. Maybe there's another secret door. Within thirty seconds, it's obvious there's nothing there. Nervously, I glance toward the edge. She wouldn't dare . . . Rushing forward, I lock my hands tight around the railing. "Nora?" I call out as my eyes scan the ground. "Where are—"

"Shhhhhhh—lower your voice."

Spinning around, I follow the sound.

"A little higher, Sherlock."

I look up and finally find her. Sitting on the roof of the mansion, she's dangling her feet over the edge. She's low enough that I can touch her swinging legs, but everything else is out of reach.

"How'd you get up there?"

"Does that mean you want to join me?"

"Just tell me how you got there."

She points with her foot. "See where the railing runs into the wall? Stand on that and boost yourself up."

I take a quick look at the concrete railing, then look up at Nora. "Are you out of your mind? That's lunacy."

"To some it's lunacy. To others it's fun."

"C'mon down here—I promise, it'll be more fun."

"No, no, no," she says, wagging a finger. "You want it, you got to come get it."

I take another look at the railing. It's not even that high—it's just my fear I can't conquer.

"You're inches away from climbing the mountain," Nora sings. "Think of the rewards."

That's it. Fear conquered. Straddling the concrete railing, I hold on to the wall for balance. Don't look down, don't look down, don't look down, I tell myself. Slowly, cautiously, I attempt to climb to my feet. First one knee, then the other. As dizziness sets in, my cheek's pressed against the wall and my fingers scurry up the marble like startled spiders. What a stupid way to die.

"Just stand up—you're almost there," Nora says.

Only a few more inches. Balancing on the railing and leaning into the wall, I let my hands scramble for the roof. Within seconds, I lock on to the marble molding and grab that sucker with everything in me. Then, anchored in place, I slowly stand up. Nora's no longer out of my reach. A hop and quick boost finish the job.

As I prop myself up on the ledge, I hear Nora's hushed clapping. Her feet are still dangling over the edge, and she's hiding behind a tall marble structure that looks like an exhaust duct.

"What're you—"

"Shhhhhh," she whispers, motioning across the roof. As she waves me next to her, I realize who she's trying to avoid. On the other side of the roof is a man wearing a dark baseball cap and dark blue fatigues. In the moonlight, I see the outline of the long-distance rifle that's hanging from his shoulder. A countersniper—the executive branch version of Rambo.

"Are you sure this is safe?"

"Don't worry," Nora says. "They're harmless."

"Harmless? That guy can kill me with a roll of Scotch tape and a highlighter. I mean, what if he thinks we're spies?"

"Then he'll stick us down and color us bright yellow."

"Nora . . ."

"Relax . . ." she moans, mimicking my whine. "He knows who we are. As soon as I got up here, he took off to the other corner. As long as we keep it quiet, they won't even report it."

Struggling to act relieved, I scooch next to her and lean against the marble air vent.

"Still worried?" she asks as her shoulder rubs against mine.

"No," I say, enjoying her touch. "But I'm warning you— if I get shot, you better avenge me."

"I think you should be okay. All the times I've been up here, no one's ever shot at me."

"Of course not—you're the crown jewel. I'm the one who's target practice."

"That's not true. They won't shoot at you without a good reason."

"And what kind of reason is that?"

"You know," she says, turning my way. "Assaulting the complex, threatening my parents, attacking one of the First Kids . . ."

"Wait, wait, wait—define *attack*."

"Oh, that's a hard one," she says as her hand flits across my chest. "I think it's one of those know-it-when-you-see-it things."

"Like pornography."

"Actually, that's not such a bad analogy," she tells me.

I reach over and put my hand on her hip. "Does this qualify?"

"As what? Pornography or an attack?"

I take an immensely long look into her eyes. "Either."

She seems to like that one.

"So does it qualify?" I repeat.

She doesn't glance down. "Hard to say."

I slide my hand a little higher, slowly making my way to her untucked shirt. As I sneak beneath it, my fingers dip inside the waistband of her jeans and brush against the edge of her underwear. Her skin is so tight it makes me miss college. As smoothly as possible, I make my way up her stomach.

"Not there," she says, grabbing my hand.

"I'm sorry. I didn't mean to . . ."

"No worries," she says as she offers me a smile. Pointing to her lips, she adds, "Just start a little higher."

I'm about to lean in when I see her pull something from her mouth.

"Everything okay?" I ask.

"Just getting rid of my gum." She reaches into her pocket and pulls out a tiny sheet of paper. As she turns her back to me, she wraps her gum in it and throws in a new piece.

"Want to take out your retainer as well?" I mutter.

Facing me, Nora's sucking on her pointer finger. Pulling it from her mouth, she lets outs a sharp kissing sound. "Come again?"

I don't have a single response that'll do her justice. Instead, I just sit there for a second, enjoying.

For Nora, it's a second too long. In one quick movement, she rolls over, straddles my legs, and, with a slight tug, pulls me toward her and glides her tongue between my lips. Right there, it all comes rushing back. Over the past two weeks, I've had dreams about her smell. Its bittersweetness—almost narcotic. As soon as we kiss, she slides her gum into my mouth. My girlfriend in fifth grade used to do that. I go to chew it, but it feels like it's still wrapped in paper. Caught off guard, I pull away in mid-cough. It's too solid. Unable to pry the gum loose with my tongue, I shove two fingers to the back of my throat, but before I can pull it out, it's gone, accidentally swallowed.

"You okay?" she asks.

"I think so—it's just . . . I wasn't ready for it."

"Don't worry," she says with a sweet laugh. "I don't mind starting over." Once again, she leans forward and slips me her tongue. My fingers run through her hair; her kisses grow more forceful. Eventually, we find each other's flow. From there, it takes me a few minutes of kissing to nerve myself back into exploratory mode, but I eventually smooth my hands along the back of her shirt and feel around for her bra. She's not wearing one. Lost in her kiss, I feel time disappear. It could be fifteen minutes or fifty—but we're starting to burn.

Still on top of me, she pushes me back and slides her hands under my shirt. Unlike her, I don't fight it—I just lie back on my elbows and close my eyes. Her close-cropped nails bite their way up the sides of my chest and behind my shoulders. Where she straddles my legs, I feel her heat up against me. It's a slow rhythm at first, a nearly invisible grind. Slowly, she picks up the pace. In an instant, however, it's all torn away.

Feeling light-headed, I'm hit with a sudden onset of nausea. I try to stop myself from coughing and dry heaving, but the whole world is suddenly blinking on and off. As I look up, everything starts sliding to the right. Across the yellow sky, I see one plane become four. The Washington Monument becomes the neck of a swan. "What's happening?" I ask, though I hear no sound. It's all static.

Struggling to stay conscious, I stand up and stagger to the edge of the roof. It's not that high anymore. Just a small step down. I go to take it, but something pulls me back. Back against the chimney. It hurts, but it doesn't. Sinking down in my seat, I'm having a hard time keeping my head up. My neck keeps sagging, like it's stuffed with grape jelly. In the back of my throat, I still feel the tickle of the swallowed gum. How long ago was that? Twenty minutes? Thirty? The static's getting louder. Unable to hold my head up, I let it crash back against the chimney. I look over at Nora, but all she's doing is laughing. Her mouth's

wide open and she's laughing. Laughing. A mouthful of
teeth. And fangs.

"Son of a bitch," I mumble as the world goes black.
She drugged me.

CHAPTER 19

Michael, are you okay?" Nora asks as I pry open my eyes. "Can you hear me?" When I don't answer, she repeats the original question. "You okay? You feeling okay?" Each time she says it, it sounds less like a question and more like an order.

Blinking my way back to consciousness, I'm trying to figure out how I got tucked into this bed. I pull the cold washcloth from my forehead and take a quick look around. The antique armoire and the built-in bookshelves tell me I'm not in a hospital. The Princeton diploma on the far wall tells me the rest. Nora's room.

"How're you doing?" she asks, her voice racing with concern.

"Shitty," I reply as I sit up in bed. "What the hell happened?" Before she can answer, a wave of vertigo sweeps up from the base of my skull. Reeling from the sudden onslaught, I close my eyes and grit my teeth. My vision goes gray, then comes back again.

"Michael, are you—"

"I'm fine," I insist as I feel it pass. Slowly, my fists tighten. "What the hell did you put in my mouth?"

"I'm so sorry . . ."

"Just tell me, Nora."

"I shouldn't have done that to you—"

"Stop fuckin' apologizing. I felt the paper in the gum!"

Surprised by the outburst, she slinks backwards, moving farther toward the foot of the bed. "I swear, it wasn't supposed to make you pass out," she says, her voice barely above a whisper. "I never meant for that to happen."

"Just tell me what it was."

Staring down at the stark white blanket, she doesn't answer. She can barely face me.

"Dammit, Nora, tell me what it—"

"Acid," she finally whispers. "Just a single tab of acid."

"*Just* a . . . Are you completely out of your head? Do you even realize what you just did?"

"Please don't be mad, Michael—I didn't mean to—"

"You put it in my mouth, Nora! It didn't just get there by itself!"

"I know—and I'm so sorry I did that to you. I shouldn't have violated our trust like that . . . especially after today . . . I just thought . . ." Her voice trails off.

"You just thought *what?* I want to hear the twisted logic behind this one."

"I don't know . . . I figured . . . y'know, outside—while we fooled around—I thought it'd be fun."

"Fun? That's your idea of fun? Drugging me against my will?"

"Believe me, Michael, if you hadn't gotten sick, you would've thanked me for it. It's not like normal sex—it's a life-changing event."

"Damn right it's life-changing—I step off the roof, I die! I could've been killed!"

"But you weren't. When you got near the edge, I pulled

you back. And when you got sick, I had Countersniper bring you down here. All I wanted was to keep you safe."

"Safe!? Nora, what happens if I get called for a drug test? Did you even spend a second thinking about that!? They still randomly test the staff! What do I do then?"

Her eyes narrow. "Is that what it's always about? How it's gonna affect your job?"

Throwing the covers aside, I shut my eyes tight at the head rush, hobble out of bed, and grab my pants from the back of the antique chair.

"Where're you going?" she asks as I pull them on.

Wobbling to pick up my shoes, I refuse to answer. She jumps in front of me, assuming I'll stop. She's wrong. Lowering my shoulder, I'm about to plow into her. She stands her ground. I tell myself that I should knock her over. That I should teach her a lesson. That I shouldn't care. But I do. Just short of impact, I stop myself. "Get out of the way," I growl.

"C'mon, Michael, what else do you want me to say? I'm sorry. I'm so sorry it happened. To work that fast, you must've got a bad one or something."

"Obviously I got a bad one! That's not the damn point!"

"I'm trying to apologize—why're you getting so upset?"

"You want to know why?" I shout. "Because you still don't get it. This isn't about the acid—this isn't even about our trust—it's about the fact that you're a *grade-A quality psycho!* Rationalize all you want, this puts you in a whole new league!"

"Don't you dare judge me!"

"Why not? You drug me; I judge you. The least I can do is return the favor."

She's starting to boil. "You don't know what it's like, asshole—compared to me, you've had it easy."

"Oh, so now you're an expert on my entire childhood?"

"I met your dad. I get the picture," she tells me. "He's retarded. It's frustrating. The end."

Right now I'd love to smack her across the face. "You really think it's that simple, don't you?"

"I didn't mean—"

"No, no, no, don't back down," I interrupt. "You saw *Rain Man*—sure, that was autism, but you know how it works. I just wish you could've had more than a few hours with dear old Dad. Then you would've got the real highlights—like when his medication's messed up and you have to keep him from swallowing his tongue. Or that time in fourth grade when he ran away because he realized I was smarter than he was. Or when he shit his pants for a full month because he was worried about being abandoned if I went off to college. Or how 'bout when an evil little scumbag named Charlie Stupak convinced him that it's okay to take other people's cars as long as you promised to bring them back? Armed with a clueless public defender, Dad can show you just how well the legal system works. Oh, yeah, you saw everything today."

"Listen, I'm sorry your dad's retarded. And I'm sorry your mom ran away . . ."

"She didn't run away—she was gone for treatments. And when those didn't work, she died. Three months after she entered the clinic. She was trying to spare us the pain of watching her deteriorate—she was scared it would slow me down. Now try explaining that to a man with a sixty-six IQ. Or better yet, try protecting him from everything else that's ready to rip him apart in this world."

"Michael, I know it was hard . . ."

"No. You don't. You have no idea what it's like. Your parents are both alive. Everyone's healthy. Besides reelection, you've got nothing to worry about."

"That's not true."

"Oh, that's right, I forgot about your secret horrors: the state dinners, meeting all the bigshots, attending the college of your choice . . ."

"Stop it, Michael."

". . . and let's not forget all the ass-kissing: staffers, reporters, even Johnny Public and Suzy Creamcheese—everyone's got to love the First Daughter . . ."

"I said stop it!"

"Uh-oh, she's getting mad. Alert the Service. Send a memo to her dad. If she throws a fit in public, there'll be some bad press . . ."

"Listen, dickhead . . ."

"We have cursing! The story goes national! That's really as bad as it gets, isn't it, Nora? Bad press that goes national?"

"You don't fucking know me!"

"Do you even remember what a bad day's like anymore? I'm not talking bad press—I'm talking bad day. There really is a difference." She looks like she's about to snap, so I push a little harder. "You don't even have them anymore, do you? Oh, my, to be the First Daughter. Tell me, what's it like when everything's done for you? Can you cook? Can you clean? Do you do your own laundry?"

Her eyes are welling up with tears. I don't care. She asked for this one.

"C'mon, Nora, don't be shy. Put it out there. Do you sign your own checks? Or pay your own bills? Or make your own b—"

"You want a bad day?" she finally explodes. *"Here's your fuckin' bad day!"* Lifting her shirt, she shows me a six-inch scar, running down toward her navel, still red where the stitches used to be.

Dumbfounded, I can't muster a syllable. So that's why she wouldn't let me touch her stomach.

Lowering her shirt, she finally falls apart. Her face contorts in a silent sob and the tears flood forward. It's the first time I've ever seen Nora cry.

"Y-You d-don't know . . ." she sobs as she staggers toward me. I cross my arms and put on my best heartless scowl.

"Michael . . ."

She wants me to open up . . . to pull her close. Just like she did with my dad. I close my eyes and that's all I see. Without another thought, I reach out and take her in. "Don't cry," I whisper. "You don't have to cry."

"I-I swear, I never wanted to hurt you," she says, still sobbing uncontrollably.

"Shhhhhh, I know." As she collapses against me, I feel the little girl return. "It's okay," I tell her. "It's okay."

A full minute goes by before we say another word. As she catches her breath, I feel her pull away. She's wiping her eyes as quickly as possible.

"Want to tell me about it?" I ask.

She pauses. That's her instinct. "New Year's Eve, this past year," she finally says as she sits on her bed. "I'd read that stabbing yourself in the stomach was a great way to kill yourself, so I decided to test the theory for myself. Needless to say, it's no jugular."

Frozen, I'm not sure how to respond. "I don't understand," I eventually stutter. "Didn't they take you to a hospital?"

"Remember where we are, Michael. And know your perks. My dad's doctors are here around the clock—and they all make house calls." Sending the point home, she taps her hand against her mattress. "Didn't even have to leave my room."

"But to make sure no one found out . . ."

"Oh, please. They hid my dad's cancer for ten months—

you think they can't hide his junkie daughter's suicide attempt?"

I don't like the way she says that. "You're not a junkie, Nora."

"Says the guy I just tried to drug."

"You know what I mean."

"I appreciate the thought, but you're working with only half the information." Picking at the lace on her pillowcase, she asks, "Do you have any idea why I'm home?"

"Excuse me?"

"It's not a trick question. I graduated college in June. It's now September. What am I still doing here?"

"I thought you were waiting to hear from grad schools."

Without a word, she heads to her desk and pulls a stack of papers from the top drawer. Returning to the bed, she throws them on the mattress. I take a seat next to her and flip through the pile. Penn. Wash U. Columbia. Michigan. Fourteen letters in all. Every one of them an acceptance. "I don't get it," I finally say.

"Well, it depends who you want to believe. Either I'm still holding out for that final grad school, or my parents are worried I'm going to take another crack at myself. Which do you think is more likely?"

Listening to her explain it, it's not hard to figure out. The only question is: What do I do now? Hunched over on the edge of her bed, Nora's waiting for my reaction. She's trying not to look at me, but she can't help herself. She's worried I'm going to leave. And the way she's rubbing the side of her bare foot over and over against the carpet, it wouldn't be the first time someone's walked out on her.

I pick up the letters and toss them to the floor. "Tell me the truth, Nora—where're your other drugs?"

"I don't—"

"Last chance," I bark.

Without a word, she looks down at the letters, then over to the slightly opened door of her closet. Her voice is soft, beaten. "On the floor is a can of tennis balls. They're inside the middle ball."

I walk to the closet and quickly find the can. Emptying it in my hand, I let the other two balls fall to the floor, then take the middle ball and give it a tight squeeze. Sure enough, like a fish opening its mouth, it spreads wide where the seam is sliced open. Inside is a brown medication vial—there're a few pills at the bottom and, on top, what looks like a roll of seven or eight stamps, but with yellow smiley-faces on them. That's the acid. "What're the pills?" I ask.

"Just some Ecstasy—they're old, though. I haven't taken them in months."

"Months or weeks?"

"Months . . . at least three . . . not since graduation. I swear, Michael."

I stare down at the vial, which is still inside the ball, and let the seam close. Gripping it in a tight fist, I hold it out to Nora. "This is it," I tell her. "No more games. From now on, it's all in your control. If you want to be a headcase, do it on your own. But if you want to be a friend"— I stop and stuff the ball in my pocket—"I'm here to help you, Nora. You don't have to be alone, but if you want to earn my trust, you do have to get it together."

She looks absolutely stunned. "So you're not going to leave?"

I once again picture her cradling my dad in her arms. Identifying with what's missing. "Not yet—not now." As my words sink in, I expect to see her smile. Instead, her brow furrows in distress. "What's wrong?" I ask.

She looks at me, her chin down, her eyes completely lost. "I don't understand. Why're you acting so nice?"

From the foot of the bed, I move in toward her. "Don't you get it yet, Nora? I'm not acting."

Lifting her head, she can't hold back. Her eyes well up and out comes the smile. The real smile.

I lean in and give her a light kiss on the forehead. "I'm just telling you one thing—if you ever do anything like this again . . ."

"I won't. I promise."

"I'm serious, Nora. I see any more drugs, I'll personally put it in a press release."

She looks me straight in the eye. "I swear on my life—you have my word."

CHAPTER 20

Sometimes in my dreams, I'm real small. Six inches small. Simon reaches down and I step into the palm of his hand. He raises me to his cracked lips and whispers in my Barbie Doll–size ears, "It'll all be okay, Michael—I promise it'll be okay." Slowly, his deep voice gets louder, like a churning siren. "Don't cry, Michael—only babies cry!" Then suddenly, he's screaming, his voice thundering as his hot breath blows me back: *"Dammit, Michael, why didn't you listen! All you had to do was listen!"*

I shoot up in bed, startled by the silence. My body's covered in a film of cold sweat—so cold, I'm shivering. The alarm clock says it's only four-thirty in the morning, so I lie back and try to lose myself in Nora. Not the drugs or the scar. The real her. The one underneath; or at least the one I think is underneath. Last night . . . and the day— my God—the roof alone'll keep me going for the rest of my life. NASCAR drivers, paratroopers, even . . . even *pirates* don't have that much excitement. Or that much fear.

Noticing that I'm gripping my sheets, I go for my best fall-back-asleep trick: I put things in perspective. Whatever else is going on, I still have my health, and my dad's, and

Trey's, and Nora . . . and Simon, and Adenauer, and Vaughn, who I still can't figure out. Part of me's worried he's trying to set me up, but if he was in this with Simon . . . and he's now running from the FBI . . . enemy of my enemy and all that. If Simon deserted him, maybe he's got something to offer me. Regardless, I'll have the answer in a few hours. Today's the day we're supposed to meet. Somewhere in the Holocaust Museum.

After twenty minutes of staring at my stucco ceiling, it's obvious I'm not falling back asleep. I kick off the covers and head straight for the coffeemaker. As the smell of caffeine invades my small kitchenette, I pull a map of the museum from my briefcase. Five floors of exhibit space, a research library, two theaters, a learning center . . . How am I ever going to find this guy?

Behind me, there's a noise at the door. It's small—easy to miss—like a tap. Or a thud. "Hello?" I call out. The noise stops. Outside, I hear the pounding of muffled footsteps moving up the hallway. Chucking the map, I fly at the door, flip open the locks, and rip it open. There's another thud. And another. I leap into the hall, anxious to face my attacker. All I find is a teenage delivery boy dropping the first of the day's newspapers. He leaps back from the shock, almost dropping his handful of papers.

"Coño!" he curses in Spanish.

"Sorry," I whisper. "My bad." Picking up my own paper, I slink back into my apartment and shut the door.

Unnerved, I peel off the top section of the paper, hoping to lose myself in current events. But just as I fold back the front page, a small white envelope falls to the floor. Inside is a handwritten note: "Registry of Survivors. Second Floor." I speed back to the museum map, which is still on my linoleum floor. Finally, an exact location.

He's not stupid, I decide. It's a small room tucked away

in a corner of the museum. He'll see everyone coming and going. The meeting's not until one o'clock, but I still look at my watch. Seven more hours.

Bolting out the door of my office, I rush over to the West Wing. I used to pride myself on being early for Simon's staff meetings, but lately, I can't seem to get there on time. And while it's easy to blame it all on forgetfulness, I have to tip my hat to subconscious avoidance.

Inside the West Wing, Phil's at his usual security desk, clearing people in. As soon as I see him, I turn my ID forward and lower my head. It's not that I even care about him calling the elevator—I just hate when he pretends not to know me.

"Hey, Michael," he says as I walk by.

"H-Hey," I reply. "Hi."

"Staff meeting today?"

Before I can even answer, he reaches below his desk and returns my most favorite of privileges. On my left, the elevator door slides open and I step inside. I'm not sure what caused the turnaround, but as the door slides shut, I'm happy to take the favor.

As I step into Simon's office, I expect to find the meeting already in progress. Instead, I see most of the staff swapping stories and sharing gossip. The empty chair at the head of the table tells me why.

I take a quick look around and notice Pam in her now regular spot on the couch. Ever since she's moved up, she's practically disappeared. "You're a real honcho now, aren't you?"

"What do you mean?" she asks, feigning innocence. It's a classic White House power-move: Never acknowledge advantages.

THE FIRST COUNSEL 255

Shaking my head, I make my way to an open seat in the back. "I see right through you, woman—you're not fooling anyone."

"I'm fooling you," she calls out. Her downplaying days are over.

I'm about to shout something back when the door to the room opens. The whole place goes silent, then picks up again. It's not Simon—just another associate—a WASPy, expensive-shoes, Yale-tie-clip-guy who just came over after clerking at the Supreme Court. I hate him. Pam said he's been nice.

As he steps inside, the office is packed. The only open seat is the one next to mine. He takes a quick recon, looking right at me. I move my chair over to make sure he has room. But as he heads toward the back, he passes right by me, continues toward the corner, and leans up against one of the bookcases. He'd rather stand. I glance over at Pam, but she's caught up with her new pals on the couch. No one likes a sinking ship.

With no one to talk to, I sit and wait until the door once again swings open. Simon enters the room and everyone's quiet. As soon as we make eye contact, I look away. He doesn't. Instead, he heads straight toward me and smacks a thick file folder against my chest. "Welcome back," he growls.

I look down at the folder, then back at everyone else in the room. Something's wrong. He's too smart to lose his temper in front of a crowd.

"You whined for it; you got it," he adds.

"I don't even know who—"

He turns and walks away. "They're voting on it Wednesday. Enjoy."

Confused, I read the tab on the folder: "Roving Wiretaps." Inside, I see all my old research. I don't believe it—I'm back on the case.

Looking up, I search for a friendly face to share the news with, but there's only one person looking my way. The person who walked in right behind Simon. Lawrence Lamb. He offers a warm smile and soft nod. That's all he needs to say. Chalk one up for Nora.

"Are you sure Simon's okay with this?"

"He shouldn't have taken you off the case in the first place," Lamb says matter-of-factly as we walk back to his office. Moving with the forcefulness of a man who's always in demand, Lamb somehow still manages to never look rushed. Like the double–Windsor knot in his tie and his cufflinked shirt, he's permanently set on high-sheen polish; the type of man who, when he's in the airport, still looks put together even after a four-hour flight.

Trailing behind him, I'm a complete mess. "But what if Simon—"

"Stop worrying about it, Michael. It's yours. Celebrate."

Passing his secretary's desk, I realize he's right. The thing is, old habits die hard. As we step into his office, I take a seat in front of his desk.

"I don't know what you did, but whatever it is, Nora's happy," he explains. "That alone grants you three wishes."

"Is this my first?"

"If it is, here're the other two." He opens a file folder on his desk and hands me two documents. The first is a single-page memo from the FBI. "They finished investigating two people on Friday, and three more over the weekend," he explains. "All of them appointees—all of them apparently innocent—which brings the total to ten. Only five more suspects to go."

"So they still haven't gotten to mine?"

"Best for last," he says as he cleans his reading glasses with a monogrammed hankie. "It shouldn't be long now."

"What about getting an advance look at the last five names? Is there any way to do that?"

"Why would you . . . ? Oh, I see," he interrupts himself. "Whoever is still on the list—that'll tell us who else was potentially involved."

"If Caroline had their files, she had their secrets."

"Not a bad thought," Lamb agrees. "Let me make a few calls. I'll see what I can do." As he makes a note to himself, the phone rings and he quickly picks it up. "This is Larry," he announces. "Yes, he's right here. I got it . . . I heard you the first fifteen times." There's a short pause. "Don't yell at me! Did you hear me? Stop already!" After a quick goodbye, he hangs up and turns my way. "Nora says hello."

Unreal—Nora puts the word out, and suddenly, I'm at the top of Lamb's dance card. It's amazing what a dozen summers splashing around together can do.

Flipping through the second document, I see that it's a fifty-page computer printout. "Is this wish number three?"

"That depends how you define 'wish.' What you hold in your hands is the official WAVES record on the day Caroline was killed. According to the record, Patrick Vaughn was cleared in at exactly 9:02 A.M."

"By me."

"By you. And he left at 10:05. You know how it works, Michael—once he had that Appointment ID around his neck, he could've wandered through the OEOB for a full hour. And according to the Secret Service, the request to let him in was placed from an internal phone right after you arrived at 8:04 that morning."

"But I never—"

"I'm not saying you made the request—I'm just telling you what the records show."

Shifting uncomfortably in my seat, I replay the facts in my head. "So as soon as I walked in that morning, Simon placed the call."

"They probably watched you walk in the front door. Do you remember anyone in the hallway?"

I pause to think about it. "The only one I saw was Pam, who told me about the early meeting."

"Pam, eh? Well, I guess it is a lot for Simon to pull off by himself."

"Wait a minute—Pam would never—"

"I'm not saying she's involved—I'm just saying be careful. You're dancing on dangerous ground."

"What's that supposed to mean?"

He pauses a moment. There's something he's not saying.

"Is everything okay?" I ask.

"You tell me—ever heard of a *Post* reporter named Inez Cotigliano?"

"The one who did the FOIA request."

Lamb shoots me a look. "How'd you know that?"

"Pam had a copy."

Sitting up in his seat, he makes a quick note to himself.

"Is something wrong with that?"

He ignores the question.

"Was she not supposed to have one?"

"Michael, it took us four days to examine those WAVES records and realize you let Vaughn in the building. According to the Secret Service, Inez has been asking about those same records since the day after Caroline died. One day. It's like she knew—or someone told her."

"So you think Pam—"

"All I'm saying is pay attention. If Inez's even half as

ambitious as she seems to be, it's not going to take her long to find Vaughn. Or you."

My stomach drops. I'm running out of time. "How long do I have?"

"See, there's the problem," Lamb says, his calm voice for the first time sounding uneasy. "You keep forgetting that this isn't just about you." Pausing, he gives me that same anxious look from before.

"Did something happen?" I ask.

He runs his hand against the grain of his still-recent shave. "They called me, Michael. They called me twice."

"Who did? The reporter?"

"The FBI," he says coldly.

I don't say a word.

"Your friend Adenauer wanted to know if she's doing drugs."

"How'd they—?"

"C'mon, son, they see you let Vaughn in the building; and then you're dating Nora . . . All they want now is the last piece of the triangle."

"But she doesn't know Vaughn."

"That's not the question!" he says, raising his voice. Just as quickly, he clears his throat and calms himself down. Family always makes it emotional. "Tell me the truth, Michael. Is Nora doing drugs?"

I stop.

He stays perfectly still. I've seen him use this same tactic before—an old lawyer trick—let the silence drag it out of you.

I sit back in my chair, trying to look unfazed. Is she doing drugs? "Not anymore," I say without flinching.

Across the desk, he nods to himself. It's not the kind of answer you can argue with, and to be honest, I don't think he wants anything more than that. There's a reason no one takes notes in the White House. When it comes to subpoenas and FBI questions, the less you know, the better.

"So what're you going to tell the FBI?" I eventually ask.

"Same thing I told them last time: That even though I know they're hungry to catch the biggest fish in the pond, they damn well better be careful before they start making accusations at the principals."

The principals. The only ones around here worth saving. "I guess that takes care of her part of the problem."

"Her part of the . . . ? Michael, have you been paying attention? We've got an incumbent President who's only nine points ahead in a reelection race where, as pathetic as it sounds, the most resounding issues are the escapades and adventures of *his* daughter—*your* girlfriend. On top of that, we've got the FBI closing in and dying to make the big kill. So if you get sucked down by this investigation, and you give even the slightest impression that Nora's involved—let me put it this way—you don't want to hand Bartlett that ammunition."

"I'd never say a thing."

"I'm not saying you would. I'm just making sure you understand the consequences." He leans forward on his desk, staring straight at me. Then he looks away, unable to hold the pose. It's not just unease in his voice. After two calls from the FBI, it's fear.

Feeling the two-ton weight he just dropped on my shoulders, I rephrase the original question. "So how long do you think we have?"

"That depends on how persistent this reporter Inez is. If she's got a source, I'd say you've got until the end of the week. If she doesn't . . . well, we're doing our best to stall."

End of the week? Oh, God.

"You okay?" he asks.

I nod and climb to my feet.

"Are you sure?" The tone in his voice catches me off guard. He's actually worried about me.

"I'll be fine," I tell him.

He doesn't believe it, but there's nothing left to say. Of course, that doesn't stop him from trying. "If it's any consolation, Michael, she does care about you. If she didn't, you wouldn't be presenting the decision memo."

"What're you talking about?"

"For the roving wiretaps. Didn't you see the list?"

I open the file folder and check for myself. Sure enough, it's in there—next to the word "Participants" are my initials: M.D.G. The wide grin that flushes my cheeks reminds me how long it's been between smiles. I'm not just writing this memo. For the first time in my life, I'm briefing the President.

By the time I get back to my office, I'm in a full-fledged sweat. If Lamb's right, it's only a matter of days. The race is on. If I don't beat Inez to Vaughn and the money . . . Instinctively, I look at the clock on my wall. Not much longer. Luckily, I've got something to pass the time.

My ego keeps telling me it's the single greatest thing that's ever happened to me, but deep down, my brain knows I'm completely unprepared. Two days from now, I'm going to sit across the desk from the President. And the only thing I can think to say is, "Nice office."

I flip on my computer and grab the wiretap folder, but before I can even open it up, I'm interrupted by the ringing of my phone.

"This is Michael," I say.

"Hey, Mr. Hot Shot. Just returning your call."

I immediately recognize the condescending tone. Officer Rayford from the D.C. police. "How's everything going?" I ask, struggling to sound upbeat.

"Don't yank my chain, boy. I'm not in the mood. If you want your money, I've got a new phone number for you."

On the corner of the folder, I write down the number. "Is that Property Division?"

"In your wet dreams. I transferred it over to Financial Investigations. Now you're the pimple on *their* ass."

"I don't understand."

"As long as it's suspicious, we've got a right to hold it—and last I checked, driving late at night with ten grand in cash is still suspicious."

"So what do I have to do now?"

"Just prove it's yours. Bank account, cashed check, insurance policy—show 'em where it came from."

"But what if—"

"I don't want to hear it. As far as I'm concerned, it's someone else's problem." With that, he hangs up.

Lowering the receiver, I'm once again back to Inez. If Simon wants to, he can point her to the money. That's his trump card. Mine, God willing, is a drug dealer named Patrick Vaughn. Looking at my watch, I see it's almost time.

Pulling my jacket from the coat-rack, I head for the door. As I step into the anteroom, though, I'm surprised to see Pam still at the small desk outside my office. "Phone go out again?"

"Don't ask," she says as I pass behind her. "Where you headed?"

"Just over to Trey's."

"Everything alright?"

"Yeah, yeah. Just going to grab some coffee—maybe steal some Ho-Hos from the vending machines."

"Have fun," she says as the door shuts behind me.

*   *   *

"Can I talk to you for a second?" I ask as I poke my head in Trey's office.

"Good timing," he says as he hangs up his phone. "C'mon in."

I stay by the door and motion in the direction of his other two officemates. He knows the rest. "Want to take a lap?" he asks.

"That'd be best."

Without a moment's hesitation, Trey follows me out the door. We take the stairs to the second floor. It goes without saying—no one takes a lap on his home court.

Heading up the hallway, I keep my eyes on the checkered black-and-white marble floor. In the OEOB, life is always a chess match.

"What's going on?" we both ask simultaneously.

"You first," he says.

Trying to look unconcerned, I check over my shoulder. "I just wanted to make sure we were set with Vaughn."

"Don't worry, I got everything we need: tube socks, Band-Aids, Ovaltine . . ."

He's trying to cheer me up, but it's not working.

"It's okay to be nervous," he adds as he puts an arm on my shoulder.

"Nervous I can deal with—I'm just starting to wonder if it's even a good idea to go through with this."

"So now you don't want to meet him?"

"It's not that . . . it's just . . . after Adenauer's picture in the paper and the way they're putting the pressure on Lamb . . . I think the FBI is getting ready to pounce."

"Even if they are, I don't see much of a choice," he points out. "You're taking every precaution we can think of—as long as you're careful, you should be okay."

"But don't you see, it's not that simple. Right now, when

the FBI asks me about Vaughn, I can look them in the eye and say we don't know each other. Hell, I can pass a lie detector if I need to. But once we get together . . . Trey, if the FBI is watching as close as I think—and they see me and Vaughn talking—every defense I ever had goes right down the toilet."

Reaching the end of the hallway, we both fall silent. During laps, you don't talk until you see who's around the corner. As we make the turn, there're only a few people at the far end. Nobody close. "Obviously, it's not the best situation," Trey replies. "But let's be honest, Michael, how else do you plan on getting answers? Right now, you've got about one third of the story. If you get two thirds, you can probably figure out what's going on, but who you gonna get it from? Simon? All that leaves you is Vaughn."

"What if he's setting me up?"

"If all Vaughn wanted was to screw you over, he would've already gone to the police. I'm telling you, if he wants to meet, he's got something to offer."

"Yeah, like copping a plea and serving me up to the FBI."

"I don't think so, Michael—it doesn't make sense. If Simon and Vaughn *were* working together, and they used your name to sneak Vaughn in, why—when he came in the building—would Vaughn link his own name to the one person he knows is about to look like a murderer?"

Trey looks at me and lets the question sink in. "You think Vaughn got screwed over too?" I ask.

"He may not be a saint, but there's obviously something we're missing."

As we walk, I run my fingertips against the hallway wall. "So the only way to save myself . . ."

". . . is to jump in with the lions," Trey says with a nod. "Everything has a price."

"That's what I'm worried about."

"Me too," Trey says. "Me too—but as long as you've kept your mouth shut, you should be fine."

Slowly, we turn another corner of the hallway.

"Please tell me you've kept your mouth shut," he adds.

"I have," I insist.

"So you didn't tell Pam?"

"Correct."

"And you didn't tell Lamb?"

"Correct."

"And you didn't tell Nora?"

I wait a millisecond too long.

"I can't believe you told Nora!" he says, giving me the rub. "Damn, boy, what're you thinking?"

"Don't worry—she's not going to say anything. It only makes things worse for her. Besides, she's good at this stuff. She's full of secrets."

"No crap, she's full of secrets. That's the whole point. Silence—good. Full of secrets—bad."

"Why're you being so paranoid about her?"

"Because while you're up in the Residence drooling all over the First Nipples, I'm the only one who's still planted in reality. And the more I dig, the less I like what I see."

"What do you mean, 'dig'?"

"Do you know who I was on the phone with when you walked in? Benny Steiger."

"Who's he?"

"He's the guy who shines the mirror under your car when you come in the Southwest Gate. I snuck his sister onto the South Lawn for Fourth of July last year, and since he owes me a solid, I decided to call it in. Anyway, remember that first night when you and Nora were trailing Simon? I had Benny do a little check on the guardhouse records for us. According to him, Nora came home alone that night. On foot."

"I dropped her off. Big deal."

"Damn right it's a big deal. Once you lost the Secret Service in your little car chase, you also lost your alibi."

"What're you talking about?"

"I'm talking about the single easiest way for Nora to cover her ass. If she wanted to, there's absolutely nothing preventing her from saying that after you lost the Service, she got out of your car and you went your separate ways."

"Why would she do that?"

"Think about it, Michael. If it comes down to your word against Simon's, who's gonna back up your story? Nora, right? Only problem is, that's bad news for Daddy. This close to re-election—with our lead barely an eyelash above the margin of error—she's not going to put him through that. But if she wasn't there when Simon made the drop—no more problems. You and Simon can scratch each other's eyes out. Of course, in a catfight, he'll eat you like tuna."

"What about the cop who pulled us over? He saw us."

"C'mon, man, you said it yourself: He pretended not to know her. He's the last person I'd count on."

"But for Nora to do all that on purpose . . ."

"Riddle me this, Batman: When you got back to the Southeast Gate, why didn't you drive her through?"

"She figured the Service would be mad, so she said I should—"

"Ding, ding, ding! I believe we have a winner! Nora's suggestion. Nora's plan. The moment you got busted with the money, her brain was churning its way out of it." As we turn another corner of the hallway, he lets the argument sink in. "I'm not saying she's out to get you; I'm just saying she's got her eye on number one. No offense to your love life, but maybe you should too."

"So even though they haven't classified it as a murder, I should screw her over and turn myself in?"

"It's not such a terrible idea. When it comes to a crisis, it's always better to get in front of it."

I stop where I am and think about what he's saying. All I have to do is give up. On myself. On Nora. On everything. My mother taught me better than that. And so did my dad. "I can't. It's not right. She wouldn't do that to me—I can't do that to her."

"Can't do that to . . . Aw, jeez, Michael, don't tell me you're in l—"

"I'm not in love with her," I insist. "It's just not the right time. Like you said, the meeting's this afternoon. I'm too close."

"Too close to what?" Trey calls out as I head back to the stairs. "Vaughn or Nora?"

I let the question hang in the air. It's not something I want to answer.

As I walk from the White House to the Holocaust Museum, the sun is shining, the humidity's gone, and the sky is the brightest of blues. I hate the calm before the storm. Still, it's the perfect day for a long lunch, which is exactly the message I worked into my conversation with Simon's secretary.

According to Judy, Simon's got a luncheon up on the Hill in Senator McNider's office. To be safe, I called and confirmed it myself. Then I did the same with Adenauer. When his secretary wouldn't tell me where he was, I told her that I had some important information and that I'd call back at one-thirty. A half hour from now. I don't know if it'll work, but all it needs to do is slow him down. Keep him by the phone. And away from me.

Yet despite all my planning, as I let the loose change

in my pocket roll through my fingers, I can't stop my hand from shaking. Every lingering glance is a reporter; every person I pass is the FBI. The ten-minute trip is a complete nightmare. Then I reach the Holocaust Museum.

"I have a reservation," I tell the woman at the ticket desk inside the entrance. She has tiny brown eyes and giant brown glasses, enhancing all the worst of her physical features.

"Your name?" she asks.

"Tony Manero."

"Here you go," she says, handing me a ticket. Entrance time: one o'clock. Two minutes from now.

I turn around and scan the lobby. The only people who don't look suspicious are the two mothers yelling at their kids. As I walk toward the elevators, I steal Nora's best trick and pull my baseball cap down over my eyes.

Outside the elevators, a small group of tourists hovers in front of the doors, anxious to get started. I stay toward the back, watching the crowd. As we wait for the elevators to arrive, more people fill in behind me. I stand on my tiptoes, trying to get a better view. This shouldn't be taking so long. Something's wrong.

Around me, the crowd's getting restless. No one's shoving, but elbow room is dwindling. A heavyset man in a blue windbreaker brushes against me, and I jerk my arm out of the way, accidentally elbowing the teenage girl behind me. "Sorry," I tell her.

"No worries," she says in a hushed tone. Her dad nods awkwardly. So does the woman next to her. There're too many people to keep track of. Space is getting tight.

The worst part is, they're still letting people into the museum. We're all pushed forward in a human tide. Frantically, I search the crowd, scrutinizing every face. It's too much. I feel myself burning up. It's getting harder to breathe. The raw-brick walls are closing in. I'm trying to focus on the elevator's dark steel doors and their exposed gray bolts, as if that'll provide any relief.

Finally, a bell rings as the elevator arrives. It's as heavy-handed as they come, but the elevator operator says it best: "Welcome to the Holocaust Museum."

CHAPTER 21

Can you tell me how to get to the Registry of Survivors?"

"Just around the corner," a man with a name tag says. "It's the first door on your right."

As I head toward the room, I take a quick scan for Vaughn. The mug shot I saw was a few years old, but I know who I'm looking for. Thin little mustache. Slicked-back hair. I don't know why he picked this museum. If he's really worried about the FBI, it's not an easy place for us to hide—which is exactly what I'm afraid of.

Convinced that he's not standing outside the room, I pull open the glass door and enter the Registry of Survivors. First I check the ceiling. No security camera in sight. Good. Next I check the walls. There it is, in the back right-hand corner. The reason he picked this room: an emergency exit fire door. If it all goes to hell, he has a way out—which means either he's just as worried about me, or that's part of his deal with the authorities.

The room itself is modest in size and sectioned off by dividers. It houses eight state-of-the-art computers, which have access to the museum's list of over seventy thousand Holocaust survivors. At almost every terminal, two to three people are crowded around the monitor, searching for their loved ones. Not a single one of them looks up as I head to the back. Checking the rest of the room, I reassure myself that leaving Trey back at the office was a good idea. We could've put him in a disguise, but after having him spotted at the pay phone, it wasn't worth the risk. I need my two thirds.

I sit down at an empty computer terminal and wait. For twenty minutes, I keep my eyes on the door. Whoever comes in; whoever goes out—I crane my head above the divider, analyzing everyone. Maybe he doesn't want me to be so obvious, I finally decide. Changing my tactics, I stare at the computer monitor and listen to the voices of all the other people around me.

"I told you she lived in Poland."

"With a *K*, not a *CH!*"

"That's your great-grandmother."

In a museum that's dedicated to remembering six million people who died, this little room focuses on the lucky few who lived. Not a bad place to be.

"I hate this place," I mutter fifteen minutes later. Cowardly son of a bitch is never going to show. Fighting frustration, I stand up and take another quick reconnaissance of the room. By now, we're on our fifth round of tourist turnover. There's only one original member of the band, and I'm it.

Circling the main group of tables, I stare up at the wall clock. Vaughn's over a half hour late. I've been stood up. Still, if I plan on waiting it out, it's best to stay in character and act like all the other strangers in the room. Glancing around, I realize I'm the only one on my feet. Everyone else looks exactly the same—pen in hand, eyes focused on their computers—all they do is type in names . . .

Oh, man.

I race back to the terminal and slide into my seat. Punching at the keyboard, I type thirteen letters into the Registry of Survivors. V-A-U-G-H-N, P-A-T-R-I-C-K.

On-screen, the computer tells me it's "Searching for Matches."

This is it. That's the real reason he picked this room.

"Sorry, no matches found."

What? It's not possible. V-A-U-G-H-N, P.

"Sorry, no matches found."

V-A-U-G-H-N.

Once again, the computer whirs into search mode. And once again, I get the same result. "Sorry, no matches found."

It can't be. Convinced I'm on the right track, I throw it every name I can think of.

G-A-R-R-I-C-K, M-I-C-H-A-E-L.

H-A-R-T-S-O-N, N-O-R-A.

S-I-M-O-N, E-D-G-A-R.

By the time I'm done, I've got tons of matches. Vienna, Austria. Kaunas, Lithuania. Gyongyos, Hungary. Even Highland Park, Illinois. But none of them brings me any closer to Vaughn. Annoyed, I push the keyboard aside and slump back in my chair. I'm about to call it a day when I feel a hand on my shoulder.

I spin around so fast I almost fall out of my seat. Behind me is an olive-skinned woman with kinky black hair. A black T-shirt with the word "Perv" in white letters hugs just tight enough to get a double take, while her faded jeans hang loosely from her hips.

"Let's get out of here, Michael," she says, her voice shaky.

"How do you—?"

"Don't ask the obvious—it's not going to help." As I get out of my seat, she's glancing around the room, her hands fidgeting as she nervously clicks the long nails on her middle fingers against her thumbs. She rubs her nose twice, unable to stand still.

"When is he—?"

"Not today," she blurts. She pushes me from behind, straight toward the door. "Now let's get you out of here in one piece."

I rush forward without another word. She yanks on the back of my shirt to slow me down.

"Only morons run," she whispers.

Pushing open the glass door, I wait until we're back among the crowds. With a sharp left, we're heading down the wide staircase that leads to the main concourse. "So he's not coming?" I ask.

At hyperspeed, she arches her neck in every direction. Over her shoulder, over mine, over the railing of the stairs . . . she can't help herself. "They had his ex-girlfriend's staked out since Tuesday," she explains. "And Vaughn don't even like her."

"I don't understand."

"It's no good," she stutters. "Not here."

"So when do we—"

She lays a sweaty hand on my shoulder and pulls me close. "National Zoo. Wednesday at one o'clock." Letting go, she speeds down the rest of the stairs.

"Is it really that bad?" I ask.

She stops where she is and turns around. "Are you kidding?" she asks, wiping a stray black curl from her face. "You know what it takes to make *him* scared?"

I hold on to the railing to keep myself up. I don't think I want to know the answer.

"So you just let her go?" Nora asks, her eyes wide with disbelief.

"What'd you want me to do? Tackle her and demand an even trade?"

"I'm not sure about tackling, but you gotta start taking some action."

Standing from my seat, I cross Nora's bedroom and lean back on the front edge of her antique desk. On my left, I spot a handwritten note signed by Carol Lorenson, the administrator of the blind trust that holds all of the Hartsons' money. "Weekly allowance—second week September." Next to the note is a small stack with a few twenty dollar bills.

"You don't understand," I say.

"What's to understand? You had her—you let her go."

"She's not the bad guy," I shoot back. "She was even more terrified than I was, and the way she sounded, it was like she was about to have a heart attack."

"Oh, c'mon, Michael. This woman knows the guy you're looking for—the one guy no one can find! No offense, but you should've taken Trey with you—at least that way he could've followed her."

"Don't you get it, Nora? The FBI's got a mad-on to get you on this one—she was already being followed. Besides, I'm not letting anyone else get hurt over this."

"*Anyone?* Who's anyone?"

I don't answer.

"Okay, here we go," she says as her face lights up. "What're you not saying?"

"I don't want to talk about it anymore."

"So this has to do with why you didn't take backup? Is that what's got you all sweaty?"

Again, I don't answer.

"That's it, isn't it? You didn't take Trey because you don't trust him—you think he's working with—"

"Trey's not working with anyone," I insist. "But if I brought him along, I'd be putting him in danger too."

Nora raises an eyebrow, almost confused by the explanation. "So even though you knew you needed backup, you decided not to bring it?"

I stay silent.

"And you did that just to protect a co-worker?"

"He's not a co-worker. He's a friend."

"I wasn't trying to . . . I just meant . . ." She stops, catching herself. "But what if Trey . . ." Once again, she stops. She's trying not to judge. She looks away, then back at me. Eventually, she asks, "You'd really give up meeting Vaughn for a friend?"

It's a silly question. "You think there's a choice?"

As the words leave me, Nora doesn't reply. She just sits there—her mouth barely open, a crinkle on her forehead. Slowly, though, her lips start curling. A grin. A smile. Wide.

"What?" I ask.

She leaps to her feet and moves toward the door.

"Where're you going?"

Putting up her pointer finger, she gives me the *C'mere* motion. Within seconds, she's in the hall. I'm right behind her. A quick left sends her toward a closed door on the far end of the third-floor hallway.

As we step inside, one thought enters my brain: *This little room is ugly.* With its black Formica cabinet emblazoned with the presidential seal, and its too-unaware-to-be-kitschy drapes covered with musical instruments, the place can only be described as a Dollywood-Graceland car crash.

There're some autographed pictures on the wall from famous musicians, as well as a glass case with one of Clinton's saxophones. For some reason, there's also a carpeted three-foot-wide platform that runs along the interior of the room and is set off with a railing. I guess it's supposed to be a tiny stage. The Music Room—where Clinton used to practice.

I'm about to ask Nora what's going on when I see her open the black cabinet with the seal on it. Inside is a pristine, highly polished violin and a bow. Using the stage as a seat, she hops up so her legs are dangling over the edge and rests the violin on her shoulder. Placing the bow on the A string, she spends a moment tuning, then looks up at me.

Since when does she . . .

With an elegant slide of her arm, the bow glides across the strings and a perfect note engulfs the room. Holding the instrument in place with the bottom of her chin, Nora closes her eyes, arches her back, and starts playing. It's a slow song—I remember hearing it once at a wedding.

"When did you learn to play the violin?" I ask.

As before, her answer comes with the song. Her eyes are shut tight; her chin's clenched against the instrument. She just wants me to watch, but despite the calm that the music brings, I can't shake the feeling I'm missing something. When Hartson first got elected, I—like the rest of the country—was force-fed every detail about the First Family's life. Nora's life. Why she went to Princeton, her love for peanut-butter cups, the name of her cat, even the bands she listened to. Yet no one ever mentioned the violin. It's like a giant secret that nobody—

Her chin stays down, but for the first time, Nora looks my way and grins. I freeze. Of everything she does, everywhere she goes, it's the only thing she's still in control of. Her one real secret. With a subtle nod, she tells me the rest. She's not just playing. She's playing for me.

Suddenly light-headed, I take a seat in a nearby chair. "When did you start?" I anxiously ask as she continues to play.

"Whole life," she answers, not missing a beat. "When my dad first became Governor, I was embarrassed about it, so he promised to keep it quiet. As I got older . . . well . . ." She pauses, thinking it over. "You have to keep something."

Up close like this, the vibrations bounce against my chest, almost pushing me back. I lean in closer. "Why the violin?"

"You're telling me *you* didn't think about it when you heard 'Devil Went Down to Georgia'?"

I laugh out loud. As the song peaks, her fingers dance against the strings, pulling the music from its resting place. Slowly, it grows louder, but it never loses its light touch.

With one final, gentle tug, Nora pulls the bow back across the A string. The moment she's done, she looks to me, searching for a reaction. Her eyes are wide with nervousness. Even at this, it's not easy for her. But as soon as she sees the grin on my face, she can't help herself. Lifting herself up on her toes, she bounces up and down on the balls on her feet. And even though she covers her smile with her fingers, her bright eyes blaze through the room, making even the Graceland curtains look like Renaissance art. Those beautiful, beaming eyes—so clear, I can practically see myself. I was wrong all those other times—this is the first time I've seen her truly happy.

I jump to my feet, clapping as loud as I can. Her cheeks flush red and she takes a mock bow. Then the applause gets louder. "Bravo!" someone shouts from behind me— outside, in the hallway.

I spin around, following the sound. Nora looks up, over my shoulder. Just as I spot them, the applause quadruples. Five men—all of them in bureaucratic blue suits and unbearably sensible ties. Leading them is Friedsam, one of the President's top aides. The other four work under him. They must've been up here briefing Hartson, who loves to do after-lunch meetings in the Solarium. From the satisfied looks on their faces, they see their eavesdropping as another perk of the job.

"That was terrific," Friedsam says to Nora. "I didn't know you played."

I turn back to see her reaction. It's already too late. She forces a smile, but it doesn't fool anyone. Her jaw's locked tight. Her eyes glisten with tears. Clutching the violin by its neck, she blows past me toward the door. Friedsam and the white boys part around her like the Red Sea. Racing after her, I make sure to get close to Friedsam. "You leak it and I'll make sure Hartson knows it's you," I hiss as I pass.

Chasing Nora up the hallway, I retrace my original steps back to her bedroom. There're no guards up in the Residence, which means I can run. As I pass the Solarium, I tell myself not to look. But like a modern-day Orpheus, I can't help myself. I glance to my left and spot the President sitting by the wide windows, flipping through paperwork. His back's to me and ... Dammit, what the hell is wrong with me?

Before he turns to face me, I open the door to Nora's room and step inside. She's sitting at her desk, staring at the wall. With the constancy of a human metronome, she's mindlessly bouncing her bow against the front edge of the desk.

"How you doing?"

"How do you think?" she shoots back, refusing to look up.

"If it makes you feel any better, I really loved the song."

"Don't rationalize with me. Even an animal knows it's in a zoo when the visitors show up to gawk."

"So now you're in a zoo?"

"That music was for *you*, Michael. Not them. When they

walk in and see it, it's like they're . . ." She pauses, clenching her teeth. *"Damn!"* she shouts as she pounds the bow against the desk. As it hits, the bow snaps in two, and even though it's still attached by the strands of horse hair, the top half flips forward, knocks over a silver pencil cup, and sends its contents spilling in every direction.

There's a long silence before either of us says anything.

"Now what're you gonna do for an encore?" I finally ask.

Nora can't help but laugh. "You think you're a real Mr. Funnyman, don't you?"

"When you're born with a gift . . ."

"Don't talk to me about gifts."

Stepping toward her, I toss aside the broken bow and take her hands in mine. But as I lean down to kiss her forehead, I realize I had it wrong. It's not that she identifies with what's missing. Nora Hartson identifies with what's destroyed. That's why she can walk into a crowded room and find the one person who's all alone. That's why she found me. She recognized the hurt; she recognized herself.

"Please, Nora, don't let them do this to you. I already told Friedsam that if it leaks, I'll nail him through the toes."

She looks up. "You did?"

"Nora, two weeks ago, I got pulled over with ten thousand dollars in my glove compartment. The next day, a woman who I had just been arguing with was found dead in her office. Three days after that, I learn that I let a known killer into the building on the day she died. This morning, I spend two hours trying to meet with this supposed killer, and I'm eventually stood up. Then, this afternoon, for the first time since this whole damn shitstorm started, you played me that song, and for three whole minutes . . . I know it's cliché, but . . . it didn't exist, Nora. None of it."

Watching me carefully, she doesn't know what to say. She wipes the side of her neck, like she's sweating. Then, finally, she points to the broken bow that's sprawled across her desk. "If you want, I've got another one in the cabinet. I can, uh . . . I know a lot of songs."

I sleep so lightly the following morning, I hear all four newspaper deliveries. Between each one, my mind churns back to Vaughn. When the fourth one hits, I toss aside the covers, head straight for the front door, and gather the morning's reading. Section by section, I open and shake each newspaper, wondering if something will fall out. Nineteen sections later, all I've got are fingers black with newsprint. I guess it's still tomorrow at the zoo.

Waiting for Trey to call, I look over and notice the front photo of the *Herald*. A shot of Hartson from behind the podium as he gives a labor speech in Detroit. Nothing to really e-mail home about—except for the fact that, over his shoulder, there're only five or six people in the audience. The rest of the seats are empty. "Trying to Connect" the caption blares. Someone's going to lose his job for this.

A minute later, I pick up Trey's call on the first ring. "Anything?" he asks, wondering if I've heard from Vaughn.

"Nothing," I say. "What's going on there?"

"Oh, just the usual. I assume you've seen our front-page hari-kiri?"

I look down at the photo of Hartson and the empty crowd. "How did that even—"

"The whole thing is bullshit—there were three hundred people on the left and right of the photo, and the empty seats were for the marching band that was getting into place—the *Herald* just cropped it for effect. We're demanding a retraction for tomorrow—because, you know, a four-line apology buried on A2 is far more effective than an ass-sized full-color on page one!"

"I take it the numbers aren't looking good?"

"Seven points, Michael. That's it. That's our lead. Take away two more—which, once the wires pick up the photo, is exactly where we're gonna be—and we're officially in the margin of error. Welcome to mediocrity. Enjoy your stay."

"What about the *Vanity Fair* story? Any response on that?"

"Oh, you didn't hear? Yesterday in California—California of all places!—Bartlett apparently used his *First Family/family first* quote on a religious radio station. The callers ate it up."

"I didn't know they still had religion in California."

There's a long silence on the other line. He must be getting reamed for this one.

"I assume you're planning something drastic?" I add.

"You should hear it around here. Last night, it got so bad, someone actually suggested putting the whole First Family on TV for a live prime-time all-of-them-at-once interview."

"And what'd they decide on?"

"Live prime-time all-of-them-at-once interview. If America's really concerned that Nora's out of control or that the Hartsons are bad parents, the only way to tackle it is to prove it wrong. Show 'em the entire family unit, throw in a couple *Aw, Dad*s, and pray that all's well once again."

"It's that easy, huh?" I ask with a laugh. "So I assume you'll have nothing to do with this transparent attempt at public pandering?"

"Are you kidding? I'm in the center ring—my boss and I are in charge of it."

"What?"

"I don't know what you're finding so funny, Michael. There's nothing to laugh at. We're bottoming out in every key battleground state. California, Texas, Illinois . . . If we don't start converting some undecideds, we're going to be out of our jobs."

I freeze as he says the words. "You really think—"

"Michael, no sitting President's ever done a First Family interview. Why do you think we are? It's the same reason Lamb asked you to keep quiet. This is it—if the numbers don't turn, Nora and company are heading back to sunny Flori—"

"Just tell me who you're going with—*20/20* or—"

"*Dateline,*" he blurts. "I suggested *60 Minutes,* but everyone thought it was too Clinton. Besides, the First Lady likes Samantha Stulberg—she did a nice piece on her after the Inauguration."

"And when is this all going to take place?"

"Eight P.M. this Thursday, which also, lucky for us, happens to be the First Lady's fiftieth birthday."

"You're not wasting any time."

"We can't afford to. And no offense, boyo, but the way we're headed, neither can you."

It's barely seven A.M. as I open the door to Room 170, and the darkness in the anteroom tells me I'm the first one in. With a cup of coffee in one hand and my briefcase in the other, I elbow on the light switch and start another fluorescent day. I count all three flickers before the light actually comes on—which is exactly how long it takes me to shut the alarm, pull the mail from my mailbox, and reach the door to my office.

Heading toward my desk, I peer out the window and take in the view. Hugged by the sun, the White House shines in the morning. It's right out of the press kit. Green trees. Red geraniums. Glowing marble. For one glorious moment, everything's right in the world. Then it's interrupted by the quiet knock on my door.

"Come in," I shout, assuming it's Pam.

"Mind if I take a seat?" a man's voice asks.

I spin around. Agent Adenauer.

He closes the door and extends an open handshake. "Don't worry," he says with a warm smile. "It's only me."

CHAPTER 22

W hat are you doing here?"

"Just got back from fishing," Adenauer says, in his easy-going Southern drawl. "Three-day trip to the Chesapeake. Man, did it just take my breath—you got to get over there sometime." With his cheap suit and his playful Keith Haring tie, he really does seem genuinely friendly. Like he wants to help.

"Take a seat," I offer.

He tosses me a nod of appreciation. "I promise, I'll make this one quick." Sliding into the chair, he explains, "As I'm kicking through the grease, there's just one thing I can't get my head for." He pauses a moment. "What's going on with you and Simon?"

I've heard that tone before—it's not an accusation; he's worried for me. Still, I play dumb. "I'm not sure I understand the question."

"Last time we spoke, you suggested that we check Simon's bank accounts. When we went to see Simon, he said we should take a look at yours."

I feel it all the way down to my groin. The rules are starting to change. All along, I thought Simon would keep it quiet. But now, détente's beginning to crumble. And the more I fight against it, the more Simon's going to point the finger at me. Forget about my job. He's going to take my life.

"Don't try to do it by yourself, Michael—we can help you with this one."

"What'd you find in his bank accounts?"

"Not much. He sold some stock recently, but he said it was to remodel his kitchen."

"Maybe he's lying."

"Maybe he's not." Even if I'm not showing it, Adenauer knows I'm squirming. Hoping to help me along, he adds, "I'll tell you one thing, though—if you want to see an interesting account, you should see Caroline's. For a woman on the moderate side of the pay scale, she was flush full of cash. More than five hundred thousand to be exact—fifty of it hidden in a box of tampons in her apartment."

Now we're getting somewhere. "So Caroline's the blackmailer?"

"You tell me," he says.

"What's that supposed to mean?"

"We checked your account as well, Michael. Pardon my saying so, but things are looking a little thin."

"That's because a quarter of every check goes direct deposit to my dad. Check it out—you'll see."

He rubs his hand along the length of his tie, looking almost hurt. He doesn't enjoy pushing buttons. "Please, Michael, I'm just trying to help. What about your mom's family? Don't they have some money? What are they up to now—forty stores nationwide?"

"I don't talk to my mom's family. Ever."

Leaning forward in his seat, he sharpens a dark smile. "Even if it's an emergency?"

The lawyer in me snaps to attention. "What kind of an emergency?"

"I don't know—what if your dad were in trouble? What if Caroline were about to open her mouth and send him to one of those white-coat institutions? If she asked for forty grand to stay quiet, would you call them then?"

"No." My stomach shifts as I realize where he's going. Forget Simon—*I'm* the suspect. Trying to cover my ass, I add, "Besides, where're you getting forty grand from? I thought you only found thirty?"

His hand continues to stroke his tie. "I guess it could be either," he replies.

I hate that tone in his voice. He's got something. "What's your point?" I ask.

"No point—just a hypothesis. See, when we checked out the thirty thousand in Caroline's safe, we realized it was consecutively numbered. Only problem is, about halfway through, there's a skip in the digits. Based on the sequencing, we figure there might be another ten grand that's still unaccounted for. Now you wouldn't happen to know anything about that, would you?"

Behind my desk, my foot's tapping nervously against the carpet. "Maybe the original bank teller grabbed the piles of money out of order."

"Or maybe the extra ten grand was used to pay Vaughn. It's an easy transaction—take the money from the victim. Only problem is, one of you grabbed the wrong pile."

"*One* of us?"

He runs his tongue against the inside of his bottom lip. Now he's having fun. "So how's everything going between you and Nora? Still getting along?"

"Better than ever," I shoot back.

"That's good—because dating a woman in her position— it puts a lot of unnecessary strain on a relationship. And when problems come up? You can't turn to anyone on the outside; it's almost like you have to deal with them yourself. I mean, that's the only way to keep her happy, right?"

Is that his theory? That I had Caroline killed for Nora?

"I'm not here to make accusations, Michael. But if Caroline found out one of the principals was doing drugs ... and that principal had access to a person like Vaughn ... it's not much to ask you to bring him inside, now is it?"

"If you're going to keep harassing me—"

"Actually, I'm trying to protect you. And if you'd help us out, you might actually be able to see that."

Lamb was right about one thing: As much as they're after me, I'm just bait for the big fish.

"She doesn't care about you," he continues. "To people like her, all we are are dictionaries—useful when you need them, but any one'll do."

He's using "we" to make me feel comfortable. I don't buy it for a second. "You obviously know nothing about her."

"You sure about that?"

I look up. He doesn't blink.

"For all you know, we've already spoken twice. Once on the telephone; once in the Residence. In fact, she might've already pushed me in your direction."

I know it's a lie. "She'd never do that."

"She wouldn't save herself? Everyone's human, Michael. And when you think of the circumstances ... if she goes down, you both go down. That's part of cleaning house. But if *you* go down—if *you're* the one to blame—she's not going anywhere." He pauses, letting it grind into my brain. "I know you don't want to hurt her, but there's only one way to help yourself ... and if you can get us Vaughn—"

"How many times do you need to hear it? I didn't do anything and I don't know Vaughn!"

Adenauer flicks a tiny piece of lint from the knee of his slacks. The easygoing English teacher is long gone. "So you've never been in contact with each other?"

"That's correct."

"You're not lying to me, are you?"

I can either tell him about tomorrow's meeting, or I can call his bluff. I'm not ready to give it up just yet. "I've never seen or spoken to the guy in my life."

He shakes his head at the news. "Michael, let me give you a piece of advice," he says, once again sounding concerned. "I've got Vaughn's profile down to a gnat's ass. Whatever he's got with Nora—they'll both sell you out in a second."

I stop my leg from shaking and take a mental deep breath. Don't let him get to you. "I know what it says in the WAVES report, but I swear to you, I didn't let him in." Hoping to grab the reins, I dart for my own change of subject. "Now what about the death itself? Have you got Caroline's results yet?"

"I thought you said it was a heart attack."

The man never lets up. "You know what I mean—is the tox report back from the lab yet?"

He tilts his head just enough for me to see the arch in his eyebrow. "I don't know. I haven't checked in a while."

It's a blatant lie and he wants me to know it. He's not giving me that one. Not unless I cooperate. And especially not when he's this close.

"You sure you don't want to tell me what really happened?" he asks, once again playing the teacher.

I refuse to answer.

"Please, Michael. Whatever it is, we're willing to work with you."

It's a tempting offer—but it's not a guarantee. Besides, if Vaughn comes through . . . it's not only the fastest way to prove it's Simon, it's also the best way to protect Nora. And myself. Still silent, I turn away from Adenauer.

"Your choice," he says. "I'll see you on Friday."

I pause. "What's Friday?"

"C'mon, boy, you think we're going to just sit around, waiting on you? If I don't hear from you in the next three days, I'm taking you and Vaughn public. That'll be more than enough to flush Nora out. Friday, Michael. That's when America meets you."

"Was he serious?" Trey asks through the phone.

Staring at the blank TV in my office, I don't answer. On-screen, all I see is my reflection.

"Michael, I asked you a question: Was Adenauer serious?"

"Huh?"

"Was he—"

"I-I think so," I finally say. "I mean, since when does the FBI make empty threats?"

Trey takes a second to answer. He knows what I'm going through, but that doesn't mean he's going to hold back. "This isn't just a bad hair day," he warns. "If even a hint of what happened gets out . . ."

"I know, Trey. Believe me, I know—you read me the polls every morning—but what am I supposed to do? Yesterday you're telling me to turn myself in so Nora doesn't bury me; today, you're crying that if anything gets out, I single-handedly wreck the presidency. The only thing that's consistent is that either way I'm screwed."

"I didn't mean to—"

"All I can do is go for the truth—find Vaughn and figure out if he's got some insight into what really happened. If that doesn't work . . ." I stop, unable to finish the sentence.

He gives me a few seconds to calm down. "What about Simon's financial disclosure forms?" he eventually asks, still determined to help. "I thought we were going to look through those to see where he got the money."

"According to Adenauer, there's nothing in his bank accounts."

"And you're going to take his word for it?"

"What else you want me to do? I put the request in over a week ago—it should be here any day."

"Well, I hate to break it to you, but *any day*'s not gonna cut it. You've only got three days left. If I were you, I'd put on my nice-guy voice and have a long overdue talk with Nora."

Silently, I once again stare at the TV, rolling the option around my brain. He has a point. Still, if Vaughn comes through . . . if he's also been screwed by Simon . . . That's the door to a brand-new reality. Maybe Vaughn was the one Simon met in the bar. Simon could've been borrowing the cash. Maybe that's why there was nothing in his bank accounts.

"So whattya say?" Trey asks.

I shake my head even though he can't see it. "Tomorrow's my meeting with Vaughn," I say hesitantly. "After that, I can always talk to Nora."

By the long pause, I can tell Trey disagrees.

"What?" I ask. "I thought you wanted me to meet with Vaughn?"

"I do."

"So what's the problem?"

Again, there's a pause. "I know it's hard for you to accept this, Michael, but just remember that, sometimes, you should be looking out for yourself."

*   *   *

It takes me a good half hour to turn my attention back to the briefing, but once there, I'm consumed. The wiretap file is spread out in front of me, and my desk is buried in a pile of law review articles, op-ed pieces, scientific studies, and current opinion polls. I've spent the last two months learning everything I could about this issue. Now I have to figure out how to teach it. No, not just teach it—teach it to the leader of the free world.

Two hours later, I'm still working on my introduction. This isn't high school debate with Mr. Ulery. It's the Oval Office with Ted Hartson. President Hartson. With a dictionary at my side, I rewrite my opening sentence for the seventeenth time. Each word has to be just right. It's still not there.

Opening sentence. Take eighteen.

Working straight through lunch, I hit the heart of the argument. Sure, we're trained to present an unbiased view, but let's be honest. This is the White House. Everyone's got an opinion.

As a result, it doesn't take me long to make a list of reasons for the President to come out against roving wiretaps. That's the easy part. The hard part is convincing the President I'm right. Especially in an election year.

At five o'clock, I take my only break: a ten-minute round-trip dash to the West Wing for the first batch of fries that comes out of the Mess. Over the next four hours, I skim through hundreds of criminal cases, looking for the best ones to make my point. It's going to be a late night, but as long as things stay quiet, I should be able to get through it.

"Candy bars! Who wants candy bars?" Trey announces, striding through the door. "Guess what just got added to

292   Brad Meltzer

the vending machines?" Before I can answer, he adds, "Two words, Lucy: Hostess. Cupcakes. I saw 'em downstairs— our childhood trapped behind glass. For seventy-five cents, we get it back."

"Now's really a bad time . . ."

"I understand—you're knee-deep. Then let me at least tell you about—"

"I can't . . ."

"No such thing as *can't*. Besides, this is impor—"

"Dammit, Trey, can't you ever take a hint?"

He's not happy with that one. Without a word, he turns his back and heads for the exit.

"Trey . . ."

He opens the door.

"C'mon, Trey . . ."

At the last second, he stops. "Listen, hotshot, I don't need the apology—the only reason I came by was because your favorite *Post* reporter just called us about the WAVES records. Adenauer may be waiting until Friday, but Inez's cashing in every press favor she has. So no matter how badly you're trying to smudge elbows with the President, you should know the clock's ticking—and it may explode sooner than you think." He wheels around and slams the door shut.

I know he's right. By Adenauer's count, I'm almost down to two days. But with everything else going on, it's going to have to wait until tomorrow. After the President, and after Vaughn.

By eight o'clock, the howling in my stomach tells me I'm hungry, the searing pain in my lower back tells me I've been sitting too long, and the vibration of my pager tells me someone's calling.

I whip it out of the clip on my belt and look at the message. *"Emergency. Meet me in the theater. Nora."*

As I read the words, I feel my whole face go white. Whatever it is, it can't be good. I take off without even thinking.

Within three minutes, I'm on a mad dash through the Ground Floor Corridor of the mansion. At the far end of the hallway, I push through a final set of doors, cut through the small area where they sell books on the White House public tour, and see the oversized bust of Abraham Lincoln. During the day, the hallway is usually filled with tour groups checking out the architectural diagrams and famous White House photos that line the left-hand wall. For the most part, visitors and guests think that's pretty interesting. I wonder how they'd react if they knew that on the other side of that wall is the President's private movie theater.

I run my open palm against my forehead, hoping to hide the sweat. As I approach the guard who's stationed nearby, I motion to my destination. "I'm supposed to meet—"

"She's inside," he says.

I rip open the door, smell the slight remnants of popcorn, and dart into the theater.

Nora's sitting in the front row of the empty fifty-one-seat theater. She has her feet hiked up on the armrest of her chair, and a big bag of popcorn on her lap.

"Ready for a surprise?" she asks, turning my way.

I'm not sure whether I'm angry or relieved.

"For once, stop looking so depressed. Just sit," she says, patting the seat next to her.

Dumbfounded, I head over to the front row. There're nine rows of traditional movie theater seats, but the front row consists of four leather La-Z-Boy recliners. Best seats in the house. I take the one to Nora's left.

"Why'd you send that messa—?"

"Hit it, Frankie!" she shouts the moment I sit.

Slowly, the lights go down and the flickering stutter of the projector fills the air. The walls of the theater are draped with *Soul Train*-era burnt-orange-colored curtains with beige bird designs. Like the Music Room, Elvis would've loved it.

As the opening credits roll, I realize we're watching the new Terrance Landaw movie. It's not going to be out in theaters for another month, but the Motion Picture Association makes sure that the White House gets on the hottest new releases delivered every Tuesday. Subliminal lobbying.

"Is there a reason we're—"

"Shhhhh!" she hisses with a playful smirk.

For the rest of the opening credits, I stay silent, trying to figure it out. Nora shovels popcorn into her mouth. Then, when the opening shot hits, she reaches over and tickles the hair on my forearm.

I look over at her and she's gazing at the screen, a mesmerized movie zombie.

"Nora, do you have any idea what I'm working on right now?"

"Shhhh . . ."

"Don't shush me—you said it was an emergency."

"Of course I did," she says, again tickling my arm. "Would you've come down if I didn't?"

I shake my head and start to get up. Before I get anywhere, she wraps both arms around my biceps, holding on like a little girl. "C'mon, Michael, just the first half hour. A quick mental break. I'll pause it and we can finish tomorrow."

I'm tempted to tell her that you can't pause a movie theater, then I remember who I'm talking to.

"It'll be fun," she promises. "Ten more minutes."

It's hard to argue with ten minutes—and the way it's been going, it'd be good to recharge. "Ten," I threaten.

"Fifteen, max. Now shut up—I hate missing the beginning."

I gaze up at the screen, still thinking about the decision memo. For two years, I've been doing legal analysis on the President's hottest policies and most cutting-edge proposals—but not a single one of them thrills me as much as ten minutes in the dark with Nora Hartson. Sitting back in my seat, I lock my fingers between hers. With everything going on, this is exactly what we need. A nice, quiet moment alone where we can finally take a breath and rela—

"Nora . . . ?" someone whispers. Behind us, a blade of white light slices through the dark.

We both turn around, surprised to see Wesley Dodds, the President's Chief of Staff. With his pencil neck already leaning into the room, he lets the rest of his body follow.

"Get out!" Nora barks.

Like most bigshots, Wesley doesn't listen. He heads straight down to the front row. "I apologize for doing this, but I've got the head of IBM and a dozen CEOs standing in the lobby, waiting for their screening."

Nora doesn't even look at him. "Sorry."

He raises an eyebrow.

"*Sorry,*" she repeats. "As in, *Sorry you're gonna be disappointed.* Or even better: *I'm sorry, but you're interrupting me.*"

He's too hypersmart to pick a fight with the boss's daughter, so he just pulls rank. "Frankie, turn the lights on!"

The projector warps to a halt and the lights come on. Shading our eyes, Nora and I squint our way to adjustment. She's the first out of her seat, sending the bag of popcorn flying.

"What the hell're you doing?" she shouts.

"I already told you, we have a CEO event waiting outside. You know what time of year it is."

"Take 'em to the Lincoln Bedr—"

"I already did," he shoots back. "And if it makes you feel better, we reserved the room a month ago." Catching himself, he realizes it's getting too hot. "I'm not asking you to leave, Nora—in fact, if you stay, it'll actually be better. Then they can say they watched a movie with the First Dau—"

"Get out of here. It's my house."

"I'm sure it is—but if you want to live in it for another four years, you better move over and make some room. Understand what I'm saying?"

For the first time, Nora doesn't answer.

"Forget about it," I say, putting a hand on her shoulder. "It's not that big a—"

"Shut up," she barks, pulling away.

"Rewind it, Frankie!" Wesley calls out.

"Don't you—"

"It's over," he warns. "Don't make me call your dad."

Oh, shit.

Her eyes narrow. Wesley doesn't move. She reaches back, and I swear to God, I think she's about to clock him. Then, out of nowhere, a devilish grin takes her face. She lets out a whispered throaty cackle. We're definitely in trouble. Before I can even ask, she picks up her purse and races for the door.

In the hallway outside, a dozen fifty- to sixty-year-old men are milling around, staring at the black-and-white photographs along the hallway. She flies past them before they can even react. But they all know who they've seen. Even as they try to play cool, their eyes are wide with excitement as they elbow and wink the message through the small crowd. *Didja see? That was you-know-who.*

It's amazing. Even the most powerful . . . in here, they're just kids in a schoolyard. And from what I can tell, the first rule of the schoolyard still holds true: There's always someone bigger.

Weaving my way back to the Ground Floor Corridor, I'm only a few feet behind her. "Nora . . ." I call out. She doesn't answer. It's just like that first night with the Service. She's not stopping for anybody.

With her arms swinging forcefully at her side, she plows forward up the red-carpeted hallway. I assume she's heading up to the Residence, but she doesn't turn at the entrance to the stairs. She just keeps going—straight up the hall, through the Palm Room, and outside, up the West Colonnade. Just before she reaches the door that leads into the West Wing, she takes a sharp left and sidesteps a dark-suited agent. "Oh, no," I mutter, watching her plow along the concrete terrace outside the West Wing. There's only one place she's going. The back entrance of the Oval. Straight to the top.

Knowing that no one goes in that way, I slam on the brakes. In case there's any doubt, the agent shoots me a look of confirmation—Nora's the only exception. Leaning against one of the enormous white columns that leads up to the West Wing, I watch the rest from here.

Fifty feet away, without looking back, Nora stops at two tall French doors and, pressing her nose against the glass paneling, peers inside the Oval. If she were anyone else, she'd be shot by now.

The lights from inside the room illuminate her like a raging firefly. She raps loudly on the paneling to get some attention, then reaches for the doorknob. But as soon as she opens the door, her entire demeanor changes. It's like she flipped off a switch. Her shoulders lose their pitch and her fists open. Then, instead of stepping inside, she motions for him to come out. The President's got someone in there.

Still, when his daughter calls . . .

The President steps out on the terrace and shuts the door behind him. He's a solid foot taller than Nora, which allows him to lean forward over her with full parental intimidation. The way he crosses his arms, he doesn't like being interrupted.

Realizing this, Nora quickly makes her case, her arms gracefully gesturing to drive home her point. She's not frenzied—not even angry—her movements are subdued. It's like I'm watching another woman. She barely even looks up as she talks to him. Everything's restrained.

As he listens, he puts a hand on his chin, resting his elbow against the arm that's wrapped around his waist. With the Rose Garden in the foreground, and the two of them in the back, I can't help but think of all those black-and-white photos of John and Bobby Kennedy, who had their famous discussions standing in the exact same spot.

Next thing I know, Hartson shakes his head and puts a tender hand on Nora's shoulder. As long as I live, I'll never forget it. The way they connect—the way he reassures her by rubbing her back. An arm over her shoulder. In silhouette, the power's gone—just a father and his daughter. *"I'm sorry,"* his body language says as he continues to rub her back. *"That's the way it's going to have to be on this one."*

Before Nora can argue, the President reopens the door to his office and waves someone else out. I can't see who it is, but quick introductions are made. *"This's my daughter, Nora."* She snaps to attention, trained her whole life in campaign-trail etiquette. The President knows what he's doing. Now that a guest's around, there's nothing Nora can say.

As she turns to leave, the President looks my way. I

spin around and step behind a white column. I don't need to make my entrance until tomorrow.

"Fuck him!" Nora shouts as we race back along the empty Ground Floor Corridor out of earshot.

"Just forget about it," I tell her again, this time keeping pace with her. "Let 'em have their schmoozefest."

"You don't get it, do you?" she asks as we cross back through booksellers and approach the oversized bust of Lincoln outside the theater. "I was actually having fun! For once, it was fun!"

"And we'll make up for it tomorrow. We were only going to be there another ten minutes anyway."

"That's not the point! It was *our* ten minutes! Not theirs! I picked out the movie, and made them pop popcorn, and sent you the message—and then . . ." Her voice starts to crack. She rubs her nose vigorously, but her hands are shaking. "It's supposed to be a house, Michael. A real fuckin' house—but it's always like the Music Room"—she wipes her eyes—"always a show." Biting her lip, she's trying to fight back tears. The redness of her eyes tells me it's not going to work. "It's not supposed to be like this. When we first got here, everyone talked about the perks. *Oh, you'll get perks. Wait'll you see the perks.* Well, I'm still waiting! Where are they, Michael? Where?" She looks over each of her shoulders as if she's physically looking for them. The only thing she sees is a uniformed guard, sitting at his checkpoint outside the theater and staring straight at us.

"What?" she screams at him. "Now I can't cry in my own house?" Her voice cracks even louder with that one. It doesn't take a shrink to spot the breakdown coming.

I motion to the guard with a can-we-have-a-second-here? look. Deciding it's time for a break, he gets up and disappears around the corner. At least someone in this place has some sense.

Waiting for him to leave, Nora's about to crumble. I haven't seen her like this since the night she showed me the scar. Her chest is heaving, her chin's quivering. She's dying to finally let it out—to tell me what it's really like. Not about *her;* about *here.* Still, she inhales as deep as she can and sniffles it all back in. Some things are too ingrained.

Wiping her nose with her hand, she slumps back against the wall and rests her shoulder against a white metal utility box that looks like it houses one of the Service's emergency telephones.

"You want to talk about it?" I ask.

She shakes her head, refusing to look at me. Over and over, she continues the motion. No, no, no, no, no. Her breathing's wet—saliva through gritted teeth—and with each movement of her head the motion gets faster, more adamant. Within seconds, it's too much. Still leaning against the wall, she lifts her left hand and pounds her fist back against the plaster. *"Damn!"* she shouts. The single word echoes through the hall, and like a bookend to her original reaction, anger that became despair once again turns to anger.

"Nora . . ."

It's too late. With a quick shove of her hips, she pushes herself off the wall and away from the telephone. There's a slight ripping noise and she stops. Her shirt's caught on a sharp edge of the metal utility box. "Motherf—" She jerks her shoulder, enraged at the delay, and there's another loud rip. We both follow the noise. From the top of her shoulder, down to her armpit, her black lace bra strap emerges through the hole in her shirt.

"Nora, take it eas—"

"Son of a bitch!" Spinning around, she swings her arm into the side of the metal box. Again. And again. I race in and grab her in a bear hug from behind.

"Please, Nora . . . the guard'll be back in a—"

Struggling against me, she swings her left elbow around and clips me in the jaw. I let go and she wriggles free. In a rabid rage, she raises both fists in the air and delivers a death blow to the box. Pile-driving down, she connects with a hollow, metal bang that sends the door on the small box flapping open. Inside, there's no phone. Just a gun, shiny and black.

Nora and I freeze, equally surprised.

"What the . . . ?"

"Storage in case of emergency," she hypothesizes.

I take a few steps back and look up the hallway that runs around the corner. The guard's nowhere in sight.

Nora couldn't care less. Without even looking, she reaches forward, her eyes completely lit up.

"Nora, don't . . ."

She grabs the pistol and yanks it out of its hiding spot.

CHAPTER 23

What the hell're you doing?"

"I just want to see it," she says, admiring the gun in her hand.

Up the hallway, around the corner from us, I hear a door slam. The guard's shoes click against the marble floor.

"Put it back, Nora. *Now!*"

She motions to the theater and flashes me one of her darkest grins. "If you hold them down, I'll pull the trigger. We can kill 'em all, y'know."

"That's not funny. Put it back."

"C'mon—Bonnie and Clyde—me and you. Whattya say?"

She's enjoying this way too much. "Nora—"

Before I can finish, she reaches back and tosses the gun through the air. At me. By the time I realize what's happening, my arms feel like weights at my side. Fighting to lift them, I catch the gun in my fingertips, like a kid playing hot potato. I barely have it three seconds. Oh, shit. My fingerprints. Hearing the guard get closer, I toss it as quickly as I can back to Nora . . .

No! What if she doesn't . . .

She catches it with a laugh. I can barely breathe. I turn the corner and see the guard coming down the hallway. He's less than thirty feet away.

"Nora, no more psycho games!" I hiss, struggling to keep it at a whisper. "I'm giving you three seconds to put it back!"

"What'd you say?"

I ignore the question. "One . . ."

Her hands go to her hips. "Are you threatening me?"

The guard's got to be less than ten feet away. "No . . . I'd never threaten . . . C'mon, Nora . . . not now. Please put it back!"

I spin around just as the guard turns the corner. Behind me, I hear Nora cough loud enough to cover the sound of the metal box slamming shut.

"Everything okay?" the guard asks me.

Turning around, I look at Nora. She's standing right in front of the box, blocking it with her body. The guard's too busy staring at her bra, which is still peeking through the rip in her shirt.

"Sorry," she laughs, pulling her sleeve up to cover her shoulder. She steps forward and coyly slides her arm around my waist. "That's what happens when they kick you out of the face-sucking section of the theater." Before I can object, she adds, "We'll take it upstairs."

"Good idea," the guard says dryly. Without a second glance, he returns to his post behind the desk.

Walking back toward the Ground Floor Corridor, with her arm still around my waist, Nora slides her thumb through the hook on my belt. "So what's more exciting—that or working on a decision memo?"

Convinced we're well out of earshot, I quickly pull away. "Why'd you have to do that?"

"Do what?" she taunts.

"Y'know, the . . ." No, don't get into it with her. I take a deep breath. "Just tell me you put it back."

She looks up and laughs. Instinctively, I step back. After four years of eating with kings and royalty, the only thing that thrills her anymore is risk—take what you love and risk losing it. Light and dark in the same breath. But now . . . the mood swings are starting to flip too fast.

"C'mon, Michael," she teases. "Why would you think I—"

"Nora, playtime's over. Answer the question. Tell me you put it back."

We reach the entrance that'll take her back up to the Residence, and she flicks me back with her wrist. "Why don't you go do some work. You're obviously stressed out."

"Nora . . ."

"Relax," she sings. She turns into the entryway and heads for the stairs. "What'm I gonna do? Hide it in my pants?"

"You tell me," I call out.

She stops where she is and glances over her shoulder. The laugh, the smile—they're gone. "I thought we were already past that one, Michael." Our eyes connect and she drives it home. "I'd never hide anything from you."

I nod, knowing that she's finally back in control. "Thank you—that's all I wanted to hear."

When I eventually finish at quarter to four in the morning, I'm a bleary-eyed mess. Except for a twenty-minute break for dinner and a ten-minute begging session to get an extension from the Staff Secretary, I've been sitting in my chair for almost eight hours straight. A new personal record. Yet as the laser printer hums with the fruits of my labor, I find that I'm oddly wide awake. Not sure of what to do, and in no mood to go home, I casually flip through my still unopened mail. Most of it's standard: press clips, meeting announcements, going-away party invitations. But at the bottom of the pile is an interoffice envelope with a familiar handwriting in the address box. I'd recognize that bubble cursive anywhere.

Opening the envelope, I find a handwritten note with a single key Scotch-taped to it: "For when you're done— Room 11. Congrats!" At the bottom is a heart and the letter N. As I pull off the key, I can't help but laugh. Room 11. It's even better than parking inside the gate.

The sign on the door of Room 11 reads "Athletic Unit," but everyone knows it's far more than that. Built by Bob Haldeman during the Nixon administration and limited to only the biggest of the bigshots, the Senior Staff Exercise Room is easily the most exclusive private gym in the country. Indeed, fewer than fifty people have keys. On an average day, I'd be slaughtered if I set foot in here. But at four in the morning, in desperate need of a shower and on the eve of my most important professional moment, I'll take my chances.

With one last look around the deserted hallway, I slide the key in the door. It opens without a hitch. "Cleaning crew!" I shout, just to be safe. "Anyone here?" No one answers. Inside, it doesn't take long to tour around. There's a beat-up StairMaster, an outdated stationary bicycle, a broken treadmill, and an odd pile of rusty weights. The place is a shithole. I'd kill for a regular pass.

After a quick workout on the bike and a fifteen-minute stop in the sauna, I'm standing in the shower, letting the hot water run over me. Every time I get accustomed to the temperature, I turn it up a little more. With my eyes closed and my palms pressed firmly against the tile, I'm lost in the steam and completely relaxed. Every day should start this way.

Back in my office, I lie on the couch, but there's no way I'm falling asleep. I've got less than four hours to go, and the testosterone alone is like a twin-pack of Vivarin. All I can think about are my opening words.

Mr. President, how are you?

Sir, how are you?

President Hartson, how are you?

Dad! How 'bout a loan?

At six-thirty, as the orange sun begins to slice through the morning sky, the newest version of the President's schedule arrives via e-mail. I skim through it until I see what I'm looking for. There it is on the second page.

10:30 to 10:45—Briefing—Oval Office. Staff Contact: Michael Garrick. My fifteen minutes of fame.

Outside, groundskeepers are prepping the lawn and the morning-show reporters are arriving in the press room. On the other side of the iron gates, a family of four early-risers poses for an Instamatic moment. The flash of their camera catches my eye like a bolt of lightning. It's going to be a big day.

CHAPTER 24

"Nervous?" Lamb asks, watching me sit completely still across from his desk, my palms resting on my knees.

"No, not at all," I reply.

He smirks at the lie, but he doesn't call me on it.

"I appreciate you seeing me like this," I add as quickly as I can. It's the understatement of the year. In the halls of the OEOB, there're staffers who'd kill for private lessons with the White House's best-dressed old pro.

"The first one's always the hardest. After that, it'll come naturally."

I know I'm supposed to be listening, but my brain keeps practicing my opening line—*Good morning, Mr. President. Good morning, Mr. President. Good morn—*

"Just remember one thing," Lamb continues. "When you get in there, don't say hello to the President. You walk in; he looks up; you start. Anything else is a waste of time, which we all know he doesn't have."

I nod as if I knew it all along.

"Also, don't get thrown by his reactions. The first answer he gives is always going to be provocative—he'll yell, he'll shout, he'll scream, 'Why are we doing it this way?' "

"I don't understand . . ."

"It's how he vents," Lamb explains. "He knows it's always going to be a compromise, but he needs to show everyone—including himself—that he's still got his hand on the moral compass."

"Anything else?"

He nods his standard nod. "Just don't forget what you're there for."

Once again, I'm lost.

"Michael, when it comes to advice, there're three types: legal advice, moral advice, and political advice. What you can do, what you want to do, and what you should do. You may be trained in the first, but he's going to want all three. In other words, you can't just go in there and say, 'Kill the wiretaps—it's the right thing to do.'"

I'm still anxiously palming my knees. "But what if it *is* the right thing to do?"

"All I'm saying is, don't get married to a victory—my gut tells me this thing's a vote-getter."

I don't like the sound of that. If Lamb says it, it's truth. "Is there any chance I'm going to convince him otherwise?"

"Time'll tell," Lamb says. "But I wouldn't bet on it."

With nothing left to say, I get up to leave the office.

"By the way," he adds, "I've been trading calls with Agent Adenauer's second in command. I have a meeting with him later today, so I'm hoping to have the final list of suspects by this afternoon—tomorrow morning at the latest."

"That's great," I say, trying to stay focused. I'm about to switch back to the Oval, but I realize there's something else I should tell him. "I had another meeting with the FBI."

"I know," he says wearily. He rests both elbows on his desk. "Thanks for keeping me up-to-date."

It's moments like this, with the even-more-pronounced-than-usual bags under his eyes, that Lawrence Lamb really starts to show his age.

"It's not good, is it?" I ask.

"They're starting to develop theories—I can tell by the way they've been asking their questions."

"They gave me a deadline of Friday."

Lamb looks up. That part he didn't know. "I'll make sure we have the list by tomorrow." Before I can even say thank you, he adds, "Michael, are you sure she doesn't know Vaughn?"

"I think so—"

"Don't give me guesses!" he shouts, raising his voice. "You think so, or you know?"

"I-I think so," I repeat, well aware that I'll have the real answer in a few hours. It's a panicked question from a man who never panics. But even Lawrence Lamb can't predict Nora.

I cross over to the West Wing with fifteen minutes to spare, and while I know it's considered bad form to show up early, I really don't care.

Clutching an inch-thick file folder in my sweaty hand, I enter the small waiting room that connects to the Oval. "I'm Michael Garrick," I say proudly as I approach Barbara Sandberg's desk. "I'm here to see the President."

She rolls her eyes at the enthusiasm. As Hartson's personal secretary, she hears it every day. "First time?" she asks.

It's a cheap shot, but it lets me know who's boss. A short, no-nonsense New Yorker who enjoys chewing the stem of her reading glasses, Barbara's been with the President since his Senate days in Florida. "Yeah," I reply with a forced grin. "Is he running on time?"

"Don't sweat it," she says, warming up. "You'll survive. Take a seat; Ethan will call you when he's ready. If you want, have some fudge. It'll calm you down."

I'm not hungry, but I still take a toothpick and spear a small square of fudge from the glass bowl on Barbara's desk. I've spent two years hearing about this stuff. *Oh, you have to taste the fudge. You won't believe Barbara's fudge.* For the bigshots, it's braggart's shorthand for a visit with the President. For those of us on the outside, it brings brownnosing jokes to a rude, crude low. As I take a seat in one of the wingback chairs, though, I finally have my answer. The fudge . . . is awesome.

Five minutes later, I'm fighting massive fudge dry mouth and doing everything in my power not to look at my watch. The only thing keeping me calm is the enlarged photo over Barbara's desk—a spectacular shot of the President the night he won the election. On a stage in Coconut Grove, Florida, he's got the First Lady on his right and his son and Nora on his left. As the seconds tick down, that's who I focus on. Nora. She's frozen mid-scream with a wild smile on her face, one arm pumped in the air, and the other one wrapped around her brother's neck. It's a victory cheer—no pain, no sadness—just true, wide-eyed euphoria. She had no idea what she was in for. Neither do I.

"Want some more fudge?" Barbara asks. With nothing else to do, I get up and head for her desk. Before I get there, though, she looks over my shoulder and smiles. Someone just walked in.

I turn around just in time to see him step in front of me. He's facing the other way, but I know that posture anywhere. Simon.

"Hey, sweetie," he says as he swipes a piece of fudge. "We running on time?"

"Actually, pretty close," Barbara replies. "Shouldn't be long now."

"Morning, Michael," he says, taking my seat in the wingback chair.

I feel like someone just punched me in the chest. An octopus of rage is already crawling its way across the back of my shoulders.

"Oh, c'mon," he responds to the look on my face. "You didn't really think you were going alone, did you?"

Before I can answer, he throws a manila file folder into my chest. Inside is what already went to the President: a copy of my decision memo, with the Staff Secretary's summary attached to the top. Below my memo, I notice something else. The original letter I wrote to the Office of Government Ethics about Simon. I don't believe it—that's why I never got any of Simon's financial disclosure forms. The letter never even made it out of the building.

"There's a typo in the second paragraph," Simon points out, eyeing me carefully. "I thought you might want it back."

How the hell did he—?

Behind me, I hear the door to the Oval open. "He's ready for you," Barbara announces. "Go on in."

Shoving his way past me, Simon heads straight for the door. Feeling as if I'm about to vomit, I follow.

"How'd it go?" Pam asks as I stand in front of her desk.

"I don't know, it was kinda like—"

The ringing of her phone interrupts my thought. "Hold on a second," she says, picking it up. "This is Pam. Yeah. No, I know. You'll have it by next week. Great. Thanks."

She hangs up and looks back up at me. "I'm sorry—you were saying . . ."

"It's hard to describe. When Simon got there, I thou—"

Once again, her phone interrupts.

"Don't worry—let it ring," she tells me.

I'm about to continue when I see her glance at the caller ID. I know that panicked look on her face. This is an important call.

"It's okay," I say. "Pick it up."

"It'll just take a minute," she promises as she lifts the receiver. "This is Pam. Yeah, I . . . What? No—he won't. I promise he won't." There's a long pause as she listens. This is going to be longer than a minute.

"Why don't I come back later," I whisper.

"I'm really sorry," she mouths, covering the receiver.

"Don't worry. It's not a big deal." Leaving Pam's office, I try to tell myself that's the truth.

Crossing through the anteroom, I decide to call Trey, who's probably still mad at me. As I head to my office, I see a pair of men's white Fruit-of-the-Loom underwear hanging from the doorknob. Above it is a laser-printed sign:

Welcome Home Brief(ing)Master!
                    Butterfly kisses,
                    All of Your Adoring Fan

I pull off the underwear and open the door. Inside, it only gets worse. On my chair, covering my couch, hanging from my lamps and every picture frame—there's men's underwear everywhere. Boxers, briefs, even a little silk fruit-smuggler. To top it off, a dozen tighty-whities spell out the word "Mike" across my desk.

"All hail Briefmaster!" Trey shouts from his hiding spot

behind the door. He drops to his knees and bows at my feet. "What say you, Master of the Brief . . . ing?"

"Unbelievable," I tell him as I admire the effort.

"I even stuffed them in your drawers," he says proudly. "Get it? Drawers?"

"I got it," I say, picking three more pair off my chair. "Where'd you get all these anyway?"

"They're mine."

"Skanky!" I say, tossing them across the room.

"What, you think I'm going to buy all new underwear for a one-time joke? Humor has a price, boy." He sniffs the air twice. "And now you're paying it."

I have to admit, it's just what I needed. "Thanks, Trey."

"Yeah, yeah, yeah, now tell me how it went. Were you in good positioning for the photo?"

"What photo?"

"Oh, please, Michael—it's me. You know they take your picture on your virgin visit. I don't care how scared you are, everyone here's always got one eye on the camera. Always."

I let out the smallest of grins.

"I knew it!" Trey laughs. "You're more predictable than a bank calendar! What'd you do? Stiff jaw? Squinty eyes?"

"Are you kidding? I pulled out the big guns—stiff jaw, pursed lips, *and* I pointed at the memo, just to solidify the student-teacher dynamic."

"Nice touch," Trey nods. "Did that convince him about the wiretaps?"

"Let me put it this way: Y'know that feeling right before you get a haircut? When you wake up one morning and suddenly you've got a bathroom mat for hair? And every day, it gets that much worse? But then, on the actual day you're supposed to get the haircut, you wake up and magically, spontaneously, your hair looks great?

Y'know what I'm talking about? It's like all your fears were for nothing?" Trey nods as I pause for effect. *"Well, not today!"* I shout at the top of my lungs. "My hair looked crappy all day long!"

"It couldn't have been that bad," Trey says, laughing.

"No, it was worse than bad. It was awful. Tragic. So tragic it approached poetic."

"Poetic's good. Everyone loves a good rhyming couplet."

"You weren't there, Trey. I was nervous enough by myself—I didn't need Simon showing up. And when he took my information request and crammed it down my throat—son of a bitch saved it up just to rattle me. That's why we haven't gotten his records; somehow, he knew what was going on. After that, I lost my center. Every time the President asked me a question I felt like all I could do was blink back at him."

"Trust me, that's how everyone feels with the President."

"That's not—"

"It *is* true—the moment he enters the room—Bam!—instant bedwetter."

I'm still not convinced, but I have to smile. "If you say so."

"You know it's the truth. There's nothing small around the President—and when he asks you a question, you want to have the answer. Now tell me what else happened. Did you get to filch anything cool? Pencils? Pens? I've-got-presidential-power-coursing-through-my-veins T-shirts?"

"Not really," I say, sitting down. "Just these . . ." I reach into my pocket and pull out a pair of presidential seal cufflinks.

"Don't tell me he—"

"Took them right off his shirt—I think it was his way of calming me down."

"Calming you down? You dope, you just got Grand Poobah cufflinks! He must've liked what you said!"

"We'll see when he makes his decision. They should be voting on it as we sp—"

The ringing of my phone cuts me off. Caller ID reads Outside Call. This could be it.

"Aren't you going to pick it up?" Trey asks.

"This is Michael," I answer.

"So, did he ask you about us?" Nora says with a laugh.

"What do you mean?"

"My dad—did he ask you if you groped my goodies?"

"He decided to leave that one out," I say, still wondering how Simon found out about my request. "He probably already had enough reasons to hate me."

"I'm sure you did fine. He gave you the cufflinks, didn't he?"

"How'd you—"

"Unless you're a jerk-off, he gives them to everyone on their first briefing. He has dozens of them in his desk. Nixon used to do the same thing. Story for your kids."

I grab the cufflinks and slide them back in my pocket. Unsure of what else to say, I'm relieved to see the little red indicator light that signals call waiting. "Hold on a second," I tell Nora. I switch to the other line without even checking caller ID. My mistake. "This is Michael."

"Nice job today," a smug voice says. It's Simon.

"T-Thanks."

"I mean it, Michael. You stumbled in the beginning, but now I think you learned your lesson. Am I right?"

He's asking me if I'm going to keep it quiet. After hearing that he sicced Adenauer on me, it's obvious what the alternative is. Still, there's something he's missing. If he knew I was meeting with Vaughn, he would've said something. Which means one of two things: Vaughn's truly got something to offer—or he's setting a hell of a trap. "Yeah," I stutter. "I learned my lesson."

"Good. Then let's talk about the wiretaps."

"Hold on a second." The touch of a button clicks me back to Nora. "Listen, I gotta run—that's Simon."

"What's he—"

Too late. I'm gone. "You were saying about the wiretaps . . . ?" I ask as I click back.

"It was certainly interesting," he replies. "When you left, I went over to the Roosevelt Room for the preliminary vote. Problem was, FBI, Justice, even the policy boys . . . they were all against us."

I hate the way he says *us*. "So what happened?"

"Just what I said." Referring to the Chief of Staff, he explains, "When Wesley was done counting the votes, he looks at me and says, 'Seven to two. You lose.' Proud of himself, he goes back to tell Hartson. Ten minutes later, Wesley returns. Looking my way, he says, 'I just spoke to the President. The vote's now seven to *three*. You win.'"

It takes a minute before it registers. Then, suddenly, it hits me. "I won?"

"*We* won," Simon replies. "Hartson said it wasn't the right thing to do. Consider it a gift." The next thing I hear is a click. He's gone.

"You won?" Trey asks.

I'm still speechless.

"C'mon, Michael, I'm giving you thirty seconds to—"

Damn—the time. I check my watch and race for the door, shouting to Trey over my shoulder. "We won! Hartson pushed it through!"

"So where're you going now? Victory party?"

"I'm late for Vaughn."

Getting up from his seat, Trey starts to follow. "Are you sure you don't want me to—"

"No. Not with the FBI watching."

Trey's eyes narrow.

"What?" I ask. "Now you don't think I should go?"

"No, but after what happened at the museum, I just think you should have some backup."

"I appreciate you offering, but . . . no . . . no way." I'm not putting him at risk. As I say the words, he's got an annoyed, almost hurt look on his face. I've known him long enough to know what he's thinking. "You think I'm out of my league, don't you?"

"You want to know what I think?" He slaps his palm flat against my desk. Then he flips his hand, so his knuckles hit the desk. Then back to his palm. Then back to his knuckles. Palm, knuckles, palm, knuckles, palm, knuckles. "Fish out of water."

"Thanks for the wonderful mime imitation, but I'll be fine."

"What if it's an ambush? You're out there all by yourself."

"It's not an ambush," I insist as I pull open the door. "I have a good feeling about this one."

Rushing down the steps of the OEOB, I'm swimming against the steady stream of co-workers returning from lunch. Outside the gate, I bob and weave through the crowd, making my way to 17th Street. There's no time to wait for the Metro. "Taxi!" I shout as I throw an arm in the air. The first two cabs pass me by. I jump into the street waving. *"Taxi!"*

An emerald green cab honks his horn and stops dead in front of me. Just as I'm about to get in, I hear someone call my name.

"Michael?"

Looking up, I see a woman with stark black hair making her way toward me. I look at the ID around her neck. It's everyone's first instinct—scan the badge. I don't like what I see. Her ID's got a tan background. Press.

"You're Michael Garrick, aren't you?" she asks.

"And you are . . . ?"

"Inez Cotigliano," she says, extending a hand. "I contacted you by—"

"I got your message. And your e-mail."

"But you still haven't replied," she teases. "You're going to hurt my feelings."

"Don't take it personally. I've been busy."

"So I hear. Schedule said you had the briefing today. How'd it go?"

Typical reporter—nothing but questions. I decide to give her typical White House—nothing but nothing. "I don't mean to be rude, but you know the drill—call the Press Office."

I shut the door to the cab, and Inez leans in the window. Pressed against her chest is a clipboard and a file folder. The tab on the folder says "WAVES." She looks down to see what I'm staring at. Then she grins. "I meant what I said, Michael. We're still interested. And this way, you get to put out *your* side of the story."

I'm not that stupid. "If you want someone who gives good quote, you're betting on the wrong horse."

"Would it make it easier if there were some financial incentives involved?"

"Since when does the *Post* pay for stories?"

"They don't," she shoots back. "This is just between us—consider it my way of saying thank you."

"You don't get it, do you?" I ask, shaking my head. "Some things aren't for sale."

Laughing to herself, she throws me a wry smile. "Whatever you say," she replies as the cab begins to pull away from her. "Though I wouldn't be so sure of that."

Ten minutes later, I'm surrounded by children. Fat ones, quiet ones, crying ones, even one in a forest green sweatsuit who's picking at his crotch something fierce. Located straight up Connecticut Avenue and final home of Hsing-Hsing, Nixon's most-famous panda, the National Zoo is easily one of the best family attractions in the city. And one of the worst places to hold an inconspicuous meeting. Pacing across the bench-lined concrete promenade that serves as the public entrance to the zoo, I'm a dark pin-striped suit amid a rainbow sea of pigtails and camcorders. If I were on fire, I couldn't stick out more. Maybe that was Vaughn's hope—if the FBI is here, they'll find it just as hard to hide. Riding that theory, I try to spot people without kids. By the ice-cream cart are two young adults. And there's a single woman getting out of a cab.

"Popcoooorn," someone wails behind me. Startled, I spin around. In front of me is an eighteen-year-old kid with two red-and-white-striped boxes of popcorn in each hand. "Popcoooorn!" he announces, whining the last syllable.

"No, thanks," I say.

Undeterred, he's on to the next tourist. "Popcoooorn . . . !"

Hoping to drown out the sales pitch while also getting a better view of the area, I eventually head over to one of the nearby wooden benches. I'm about to sit down when I notice a small red-and-white sign: THIS AREA MONITORED BY SURVEILLANCE CAMERAS. Instinctively, I look up at the trees, trying to spot the cameras. I don't see them anywhere. It doesn't matter; they're out there. Watching me. Watching us. Vaughn, wherever you are, I pray you know what you're doing.

*   *   *

A half hour later, I'm sitting on the same wooden bench, studying the crowd. It doesn't take long to spot the pattern. Family in, family out. Family in, family out. Still, throughout the constant flux of people, one thing remains: "Popcoooorn . . . Popcooorn!" Over and over, the refrain is grating. "Popcoooorn . . . Popcoooo—"

"I'll take one," a deep voice says. I look up, but he's facing the other direction—a tall man in dark jeans and a bright red polo shirt. Handing the kid a dollar, he grabs a box of popcorn. Without another word, he readjusts his sunglasses and heads to a bench on the opposite side of the promenade. I'm not sure what it is—maybe it's the fact he's alone; maybe it's my own paranoia—but something tells me to watch him. Yet, just as I'm about to get my first good look at him, someone steps in front of me, blocking my view.

"Popcoooorn!" the kid announces, holding his red-and-white box in front of my face.

"Out of the way!" I shout.

He couldn't care less. "Popcoooorn!" he continues. "Peeeee Vaaaaughn!"

I do a quick double take. "What'd you just say?"

"Popcoooorn . . . !"

As he steps aside, I look across the promenade. The man in the red shirt is gone. Turning back to the kid, I ask, "Was that—?"

He holds out his last red-and-white-striped box. "Popcoooorn . . . Pop—"

"I'll take it." One dollar later, the kid's moved on, and I'm alone on the bench. I'm tempted to check over my shoulder, but it's more important to appear calm. As casually as possible, I open the box. Inside, there's barely any popcorn—just a handwritten note taped inside. I have to angle the box just right to read it. *"Four P's Pub. Three blocks north. Next to the Uptown."*

Closing the box, I can't fight my instinct. I check to see who's watching. As far as I can tell, no one's there. A quick survey of the promenade shows everything's normal. Family in, family out. Family in, family out. As the parade of smiles marches on, I walk back toward Connecticut and pass the popcorn cart. "Popcoooorn . . . !" Fully restocked, the kid doesn't give me a second look. Instead, he heads back into the crowd. And I head three blocks up the street.

Sticking to the shady side of Connecticut Avenue, I try to keep my pace as quick as possible. At this speed, if someone's behind me, they should be easy to spot. Still, my eyes dart from every parked car, to every tree, to every storefront. It all looks suspicious. Coming toward me, I see a woman jogging with her black Labrador. As she's about to pass, I step into the street and look away. I'm not taking any chances—as long as I keep my head down, she can't make an ID. When she's gone, I get back on track.

In the distance, I can already see the red neon sign of the Uptown, the city's greatest old-fashioned movie house and the neighborhood's most popular monument. To its left, half a dozen restaurants and shops fight for attention. Dwarfed by the Uptown, they rarely get a second glance. Today, however, one jumps out: Ireland's Four Provinces Restaurant and Pub.

Under the run-down green and red sign, I take a quick look up the block. Everything checks out—no khakis or polos in sight; none of the nearby cars have government plates. I even brush my eyes past the roof of the Uptown. Far as I can tell, no one's taking photos. Heading for the entrance, I know this is it. Time to meet Vaughn.

As I pull open the door, I'm slapped in the face with

bar whiff. It immediately reminds me of my first night with Nora. Inside, it's set up like a real Irish pub. Sixteen to twenty tables, some framed stained glass Irish crests, and an old oak bar along the back wall. To my surprise, the place is packed. One guy's wearing a mailman uniform. Another's dressed by FedEx. I like this place. No tourists. Local crowd.

"Take a seat at the bar," a waitress says as she blows by me. "I'll have a table in a second."

Following her instructions, I pull up a stool and scan the lunchtime group. Nothing too suspicious.

"How you doing?" the bartender asks as he pours a couple of sodas.

"Okay," I say. "And you?"

Before he can answer, I hear a door on my far right creak open. Following the sound, I see a muscular guy wearing a ratty black T-shirt step out of the men's room. He's got a great Neanderthal brow that puts Darwinism to the test. Focused on the box scores of his folded-up newspaper, the man seems startled when he looks up and notices me.

"Wat you looking at, putzhead?" he asks in a heavy Brooklyn accent.

"No, nothing," I reply. "Nothing."

Shrugging me off, he moves back to his table in the corner. "Where the hell's my san'wich?" he asks his waitress.

"Don't bitch at me," she warns. "They're backed up in there."

Convinced the waitress is going to spit in his food, I'm content to let him study his box scores. But just as I'm about to look away, I see him lay his folded-up newspaper back on the table. It hits with an unusual thud. That's when I see it. There's something hidden inside the paper.

The tip of it peeks out toward the top. Like a thick black Magic Marker. Or the top of a walkie-talkie antenn— A cold chill runs down my back. Son of a bitch. That guy's FBI.

I look away as fast as I can, pretending I haven't seen anything. Just then, the front door swings open, shooting a flash of sunlight into the dark bar. When it closes, one person's standing there. The guy with the red shirt who bought the popcorn. The sunglasses give him away. More FBI. Any minute now, Vaughn's going to walk in that front door. And the moment he does, every agent in this room is going to be all over us.

My mind's racing. The guy in the red shirt is heading toward me. Like it or not, I've got to abort this meeting. As quick as I can, I hop off the stool and head for the door. The agent with the walkie-talkie stands up at the same time, his chair screeching against the beer-stained floor. One in front of me; one on my right. They're both moving, just in case I run. No matter how fast I am, I'm not going to lose them without a distraction. I point at the agent with the walkie-talkie. "FBI! He's FBI!" I shout at the top of my lungs, assuming Vaughn's listening.

Instinctively, the agent does exactly what I was hoping he'd do. He pulls his gun. That's all it takes. Instant chaos. Everyone's screaming. Both agents are mobbed by the crowd's mad rush for the door. I'm about to join in when I feel someone grab me by the back collar of my shirt. Before I realize what's happening, he throws me through the swinging doors of the kitchen. I crash to the ground in front of the industrial refrigerator. Stumbling to my feet, I get a quick look at my attacker. It's the bartender.

"What're you—"

He grabs me by the knot of my tie and drags me to the back of the kitchen. I'm trying to fight, but I can't get my balance. My flailing arms are pulling pots and pans from every counter. "Sorry, kid," he says. In one quick movement, he kicks open the back exit and shoves me out into the alley behind the restaurant.

Across the alley, the door to the building next door opens. "In here!" someone shouts in a Boston accent. I limp in, still struggling to catch my breath. Once inside I see that I'm in a dingy gray hallway that has all the charm of an unfinished basement. A single fluorescent light twitches from above. In the background, I hear the hum of two people talking. Like a movie. At the other end of the hallway is a metal door. Judging by the location, I'm in the emergency exitway for the Uptown.

Leaning back against the wall, I slowly sink to the floor.

"Having fun?" my host asks.

As soon as I look up, I recognize him from his mug shot. Finally. Vaughn.

He whips out a gun and presses the barrel against the center of my forehead. "You have exactly three seconds to tell me why you killed Caroline Penzler."

CHAPTER 25

What the hell's going on?" I ask.

"*One . . . !*"

"Are you nuts!?"

"*Two . . . !*"

"I didn't kill her!" I cry as he pulls back the hammer on the gun. "I swear, I didn't kill her! Why would you—"

"*Three!*" he shouts. "Sorry about this, Michael."

His finger tightens and I clench my eyes shut.

"*Itwasn'tme! Itwasn'tme! Iswearitwasn'tme!*" I shout.

He pulls the trigger, but there's no shot. Just a hollow click. I open my eyes. The gun's empty.

Vaughn stands over me, studying my reaction.

"Are you insane?" I shout. My chest's heaving and the sweat's pouring down my face.

"Had to see for myself," he says, stuffing his gun in the back of his pants.

"See *what* for yourself?"

He doesn't answer, but whatever the test was, I passed. I think.

Unlike his mug shot, Vaughn no longer has the tiny mustache and the slicked-back hair. Today, he's all style.

Sharp haircut, Gucci loafers, and a slightly creased but otherwise beautiful silk shirt. His pants also look expensive but way too wrinkled. Like they've been worn too long. Or slept in.

"Sorry 'bout the mess," he says like nothing happened. He points to his clothes and flashes a toothy grin. "Things're a little tense since I'm . . . on the go."

"Don't you mean, on the run?" I ask.

"You got that right," he agrees. "Now what kept you so late?"

"Talk to your popcorn clients—those kids had me waiting for a half hour."

"No, no, no," he says in full Boston accent. "I don't sell to kids. Ever."

"Oh, so you're one of those dealers who cares?"

"Listen, shortie, if some rich little college girl wants to shove daddy's money up her nose, I don't sweat it for a second. After all their years of shoving the peace pipe into my neighborhood, I figure that makes us even."

"You're a real humanitarian."

"Shit, man, you work in the White House. Who you think's putting more poison out there, me or you?"

I refuse to answer.

"No fun bein' judged, now, is it?" Vaughn asks. "'Sides, if you're countin' brownie points, you're the one should be thankin' me."

"Thank you?" I ask. "Why should I thank you? For setting me up? For sneaking in under my name? For killing Caroline Penzler and acting like I'm the one who—"

"Stop where you are, pretty boy. Don't blame that shit on me."

"You telling me you weren't in the building?"

"No, I was there. I was walkin' halls for an hour. But I never put a finger near that woman."

"What're you talking about?"

"Now you deaf? Listen up, here: I don't know dick about that lady. Never met her in my life."

"What about Simon? You ever met him?"

"Simon who?"

"C'mon, Vaughn, you know who he is."

"You callin' me a liar?"

I pause a moment. "All I'm saying—"

"All you're sayin' is I'm bullshitting; I can hear it in the back of your throat. You better readjust your glasses, though, boy—I'm just tryin' to give you some conversation."

"Oh, so first you point a gun at my head, and now you're gonna sweep me up and play Oprah?"

"I don't like that tone."

"I don't have a tone. All I know is you've been running me around for the past two weeks. Holocaust Museum, paperboys, squeegee men—I'm sick of the Spy vs. Spy mind games. So drop the tough guy act and tell me what the hell is going on wi—"

He grabs me by the front of my shirt and slams me against the concrete wall. "What'd I tell you 'bout raising your voice? Huh, boy? What'd I tell you!?"

"You said you don't like it."

"Damn right I don't like it!" he screams in my face. "You think this is only 'bout you!? Shit, kid, at least you're still sleeping in your own apartment—I'm on the D.C. shelter tour."

"You make your bed; you lie in it."

"I didn't make the damn bed! They threw me in it!" He lets go of my shirt and takes a step back. "Just like they threw you."

I study his eyes, looking for a lie. He knows I don't see it. "You're serious about this, aren't you?"

"Would I be sneaking 'round if I weren't? Son of a bitch FBI trashed my life, ruined my business . . . I never met this guy Simon in my life."

Unsure of how to respond, I look away.

"What?" he asks. "You think I'm bluffing 'bout that too?"

I can't help but hesitate. "To be honest, I don't know what to think."

"Well, Wonder Bread, that makes two of us."

I take another look at his creased shirt and wrinkled pants. There're some things you can't hide. "So you weren't trying to frame me?"

He shakes his head and puts his hands on his hips. "I look like Jack Ruby to you? The only reason I came to that building was because my man Morty was busy. He had something cookin' in Southeast, so he asked me to do him a favor."

"And Morty works for you?"

"Nah, he's a—how can I say it?—a fellow independent contractor."

"He's a drug dealer."

"He's into pharmaceuticals. Anyway, he asked me to make a drop for him—I had nothing doing—so I told him I'm in. 'Course, when I found out where it was, I almost had myself an infarction, know what I'm saying? I mean, that's just plain stupid—next door to the White House?"

"But you still did it?"

"Morty put up three Bennys in cash. For that kind of money, I'll kick Hartson in his big white ass. Besides, Morty said you were one of his cash cows."

"I never met the guy in my—"

"I'm just telling you what he said. He told me you were some presidential whiz kid with a taste for the white stuff—and that you went DEFCON One if you didn't get your weekly visit. According to Morty, all I had to do was go to the front desk and give 'em your name. When you cleared me in, I was supposed to head up to the second floor and walk the halls till you found me—he said your schedule was so busy, you couldn't do exact times—presidential crap and all that. Soon as I heard it, I shoulda known that shit was trouble."

"What about the person who cleared you in? Who was that?"

"I thought it was you."

"It wasn't me!" I insist. "They just used my name on the ph—"

"Relax, little man—I'm just relaying how it happened. I told the guard we had a meeting; the guest pass was waitin' for me. Looking back, it obviously wasn't my finest hour."

I nod and suddenly think of my dad. "So all you did was spend an hour taking laps around the hallway?"

"That's what I got paid to do. When you didn't show, I left. Next thing I know, that woman Caroline's dead and the FBI's sniffing 'round my place and hasslin' my neighbors. My cousin across the hall says they mentioned two names to her—the woman who just died and some fool named Michael Garrick. Soon as I heard that, I was gone—smelled that setup a mile away."

Shading my eyes with my hand, I rub my temples and let it all sink in. If it wasn't Vaughn I saw in the bar with Simon, it must've been this guy Morty. That's who Simon was working with.

"You really thought I killed her, didn't ya?" Vaughn asks.

I keep quiet.

"It's okay," he says. "I don't take offense. I thought the same 'bout you."

"What?"

"You heard me. I figured you and Morty set it up. I walk in; you kill Caroline; I eat the blame."

I almost want to laugh. "I already told you, I didn't kill anyone. You've got it all mixed up."

"Then why don't you alphabetize it for me?"

I think about it for a sec, but decide not to answer.

"Oh, you best not be yankin' my rope," Vaughn says. "Is that how you play it? You can hear my side, but I can't hear yours?"

Again, I stay silent.

"Listen, Garrick, my boys took major risk to get to you— the least you can do is tell me how ya got sucked in."

"Why, so you can use it against me? No offense, but I've had enough stupidity for one week."

"You still caught up on that one? 'Cause if that's the case, your stupidity's just gettin' started."

"What's that supposed to mean?"

"You got the big brain—use it. If I were the rough-and-tough bad guy, why would I spend all this time tryin' to track you down?"

"Are you kidding? To set me up."

He looks around at the empty passageway we're standing in. "You see anyone settin' you up?"

"That doesn't prove anything."

"Okay, so you want proof? How 'bout this one—if I came in that building to kill someone, you really think I'm dumb enough to use my real name?"

"You used it for a drug deal, didn't you?"

He rolls his eyes. "That's different and you know it."

"Not to me it—"

"Don't give me the legal bullshit!" he shouts, annoyed by my challenge. "If I want to kill someone, I kill 'em!

That goes with the job. But I'm tellin' ya right now, I didn't do this one!"

"And that's supposed to convince me?"

"What the hell else you want me to—" He cuts himself off and clenches his jaw. For at least a full minute, he stands there, stewing. Searching for a convincing explanation. Eventually, he looks up. "Answer me this, shortie. If I killed her and I'm tryin' ta blame it on you, why'd I attach my own name to the one guy I know is about to look like suspect number one?"

There's the question. The one that brought me right here.

"I'm waitin'—oh, yeah—just sitting here and waitin'."

The problem is, even with all this new information, I can't come up with a single good answer.

"You know I'm on target. You know it."

Again, I give him nothing but silence.

"Tell me what happened—I'll figure what's up," he offers, suddenly sweet. "Did it have somethin' to do with that Simon guy? 'Cause whoever it was, they knew their shit and they knew how to pin the blame. On both of us."

I take another look at Vaughn. The man's smart—and though I don't want to admit it—he may be right. "If I tell you this . . ."

"Who'm I gonna tell? The police? Don't flake—your secret's safe."

"Yeah . . . maybe." With everything to lose, I take the next ten minutes to explain what happened—from spotting Simon in the bar, to finding the money, to Adenauer's Friday deadline. I leave out the parts about Nora. When I'm done, Vaughn lets out a deep, thundering laugh.

"Damn, boy," he says, covering his bright white teeth. "And I thought I was screwed."

"It's not funny—this's my ass on the line."

"Mine too," he says. "Mine too."

He hits it on the head with that one. For the past week, I'd assumed that Vaughn was going to be the missing piece. That when we finally got together, it'd all make sense. But listening to his story . . . I can't help but feel like I'm back where I started.

"So whatta we do now?" he asks.

Realizing that I've got less than forty-eight hours until it goes public, I lean back against the wall and once again feel myself slipping to the floor. "I have no idea."

"Nuh-uh, no way," he says, reading my expression. "This ain't the time to crumble."

He's right. Get it together. Pushing away from the wall, I feel around for a toehold. It's got to be there somewhere. "What about your buddy Morty? He's the one who set us up."

"Morty hasn't been in much of a talkin' mood lately."

"What do you mean?"

"His neighbors sniffed the smell late last week. When the super kicked in the door, they found Morty facedown on his white shag carpet. Throat sliced with piano wire."

I look nervously at Vaughn. "You didn't . . ."

"I look like that much of a hump to you?"

"I didn't mean . . ."

"Sure you did—that thought hit your brain lickety-split. *Sure, he's fool enough to use that piano wire trick twice.* Like I'm some dumb-ass piece of street trash beneath your Ivy League loafers."

"I went to a state school."

"I don't care where you went," he shoots back. "Unlike you, it don't matter to me."

"What're you—"

"I looked you up, Michael. Don't forget where you're from."

"I don't know what you're talking about."

"I listened to ya from word one."

"You had a gun to my head!"

"Don't gimme that—I didn't press you 'bout Simon or quiz you 'bout Caroline. I took one look in your scaredy eyes and knew you were telling truth. Now I may not be one of your Brainiac buddies—but if I'm crazy enough to sniff the lines you're sellin' me, I expect you to return the favor and hand me the benefit of the damn doubt."

"I wasn't trying to judge you, Vaughn, it's just the way you . . ." I stop myself. One foot in my mouth is enough. "Why don't we just get back to figuring this out?"

"Yeah . . . right." Looking away, he stuffs his hands in his pockets. And in that moment, I finally realize what he's thinking. It's not in his eyes. It's in the slump of his stance and the clench of his jaw. He'd never say it—he's got a tough-guy act to think about. But lately, I've seen my share of fear. When they catch him, he knows they're going to stomp on him. No fancy lawyer to protect him. No resources but the creased shirt on his back.

"So where does that leave us?" I ask.

"With my sniff-pinkie shoved straight in the eye of whoever did this. Soon as we find that raunchbag, I'm giving 'em—"

"Guaranteed proof that you're the killer they say you are. No offense, but take a breather. We need better evidence than that."

"Howzabout where Simon was when Caroline got inanimate? Any holes there?"

The question catches me off guard. "His alibi? I-I don't know."

"Whatchu mean you don't know?"

"I never bothered to ask. Until now, I thought you were the killer. I figured Simon set it up and let you in to do the dirty work."

"But if it ain't me . . ."

"It's not a bad idea," I say excitedly as my voice picks up speed. "We should find out where he was."

"And who he's with."

"You think he had some help?" I ask.

"Don't know. But how else would Mr. Lawyer-to-the-President know his local dealers?"

There's an easy answer to that one, but I don't want to believe it. Still, I can't just pretend she doesn't exist. In the background, I hear music swelling. If the movie's about to end, I don't have much time. I turn to Vaughn before I can talk myself out of it. "Can I ask you a question about an unrelated subject?"

"Hit me."

"Have you ever sold drugs to anyone in the First Family?"

He raises an eyebrow just enough to make me worry. "Why?"

Already, I know I'm in trouble. "Just answer the question."

"Personally, I never met Nora, but I heard 'em whisper. Supposed to be a crazy little bitch."

Under the metal door, I see the house lights come up.

"That's our cue," Vaughn says. "Out with the crowd." As we head for the door, he adds, "You think she's playin' in all this?"

"No. Not at all."

He nods. For some reason, he's letting me get away with it. As he marches forward, I notice the cocky strut that haunts his walk.

"You really think we have a chance?" I ask.

"Trust me, the big boys don't like playing rock-'em-sock-'em. Too worried 'bout protectin' their face."

"And we're not?"

"Not anymore. They're the ones got something to lose."
Picking up speed, he adds, "Same thing in a turf war—you
wanna win, you gotta bring a little fight to them."

I raise my shoulders and stick my chest out. It's been
too long since I shoved back.

"Ass-kissing bureaucrats think they can get away with
tossin' me in the street," Vaughn adds as we head into the
theater. "It's like my granddad used to say—you gonna take
a shot at the king . . . you better kill 'im."

"What do you mean you want me to prove it?" I ask
late Thursday afternoon.

"Exactly what I said," the detective explains on the other
line. "Show me a receipt, a bank account, a stock certifi-
cate—anything that'll prove the cash is yours."

"I already went through this with the cop who took it.
It's my personal savings—it's not like I have a receipt."

"Well you better find one. Otherwise the whole thing's
going to forfeiture."

From the shortness in his tone, I can tell this is one of
hundreds of cases he'd rather not deal with. Which means
if I can stall him a few days, that's a guarantee of at least
another week to keep this part quiet. It takes a bureaucracy
to know one. "Now that I think about it, there might be
one way for me to prove it."

"Why doesn't that surprise me?"

"I'm just going to have to go through my files," I say
as Trey walks in the room. "I'll call you next week."

"How goes the stonewalling?" Trey asks as I hang up.

"I'm not stonewalling; I'm stalling. There's a difference."

"Tell that to Nixon."

"What do you want me to do, Trey? I've got Inez paying people for stories; the FBI threatening to go public to-

morrow. If I get caught with this money . . . stuck between a drug dealer and Nora . . . they'll bury me with Simon's version of the story."

"And Nora's. Don't forget, you guys split up after you lost the Secret Service. That's why she came home alone that night."

I burn my worst annoyed look into his forehead. I know he's only trying to help, but now's not the time. "Just tell me what Simon's secretary said."

"More bad news. According to her schedule, on the day Caroline died, Simon left the staff meeting and spent the rest of the morning in the Oval." Reading my reaction, he adds, "I know. If you tried, you couldn't come up with a better alibi."

"That's not possible! Is there a way to check it?"

"I'm not sure what you mean."

"Just because Judy says he was in the Oval doesn't mean he was actually there. I mean, when I had my appointment, I stood around for twenty minutes before I finally got called in."

"I can call the President's secretary," Trey suggests. "As the gatekeeper, she records the actual times people go in there."

"When I walked into the Oval, I remember her making a note."

"Then that's our best bet. I'll check it out." Wasting no time, Trey reaches for my phone, but just as he's about to pick it up, it starts to ring.

I check caller ID. Outside Call. I'm betting on Lamb. He said he might have something.

"I should take this," I say.

"Is there another phone I can call Barbara on?"

"In the anteroom," I say as I point to the small desk

that Pam's been using. Answering the phone, I add, "This is Michael."

"Michael, it's Lawrence."

I mouth "Lamb" to Trey. He nods and heads for the phone in the anteroom.

"Find anything out?" I ask Lamb.

"I spoke to the FBI," he begins in his slow, methodical voice. I can practically hear the starch in his French-cuffed shirt. "They still won't release their list of the last five files . . ."

My whole body deflates.

"However," he continues, "I told them we were having some security concerns in assigning new cases, and that we would therefore appreciate—at minimum—a list of all the people in our office whose files Caroline had in her possession. As we discussed, I think that's the best way to figure out who she was blackmailing—and who else would therefore want her dead."

"And were they helpful?"

"They gave me the list."

"That's great," I say, my voice cracking.

"It certainly is," Lamb replies. Even with a breakthrough, he's too careful to be excited. "The first two names were exactly what we expected. She had your file and Simon's."

"I knew it. I told you he—"

"But it was the third name on the list that caught me by surprise."

"Third? Who?"

He's about to answer when I hear the loud touch-tone beeps of someone calling on the line. Looking up, I see Trey punching in a phone number in the anteroom. "Ooops—sorry," he says as his voice comes through the earpiece on my phone. I look up, astounded. The phone in the anteroom is supposed to be on a separate line.

"Michael, is everything okay?" Lamb asks.

"Yeah. I just leaned on the keypad." Trying to stay focused, I can't stop thinking that the phone in the anteroom could've been used to listen in on my conversations.

"Back to Caroline's files," Lamb begins. "The third name on the list . . ."

There's only one person who uses that phone. A sharp pain rips through the back of my neck. My legs are already numb. Please don't let it be her.

Lamb voices my fear as succinctly as possible. "The last file . . . was Pam Cooper's."

CHAPTER 26

Whatd he say?" Trey asks as I hang up the phone.

"I don't believe it," I say, collapsing in my seat.

"What? Tell me."

"You heard him—we were all on the same line."

"I meant after I hung up."

"What else is there to say? Caroline had Pam's file."

"I don't believe that."

"You think he's making it up?"

"Maybe he— Did he say what was in it?"

All I can do is shake my head. "FBI wouldn't give it to him."

"You really think Pam was being blackmailed by Caroline?"

"Can you think of any other reason why Caroline would need her file?"

"What about if Pam had an ethics question? Didn't Caroline do those?"

"It doesn't matter what she did—you saw the phone—Pam's been listening on my line."

"Just because you shared a line doesn't mean—"

"Trey, in all the time we've been in this office, Pam's

never once used the phone in the anteroom. Then, as soon as I start sniffing around for Caroline's killer, she's on it full time."

"But if she were listening in, don't you think you would've heard her by now?"

"Not if she hit the mute button. She could pick up and I wouldn't hear a thing." Jumping out of my seat, I head for the door. "I bet she even turned off the ringer so I couldn't hear when someone—"

"It's off," Trey whispers, turning away.

"What?"

"I checked it when I hung up. The ringer's off."

"This better be good," Nora says, bursting into my office. She blows past the couch, but my eyes are still on the door.

She doesn't even have to ask—she knows who I'm looking for. The Service.

"They're not coming," she says.

"Are you sure?"

"What do *you* think?"

"So they—"

"They only follow if I leave the grounds. Otherwise, in here, they leave me . . ." Her voice trails off. She notices something behind my desk. The ego wall. Damn. Charging toward it, she goes straight to the photo of me and her dad. It's the same one I gave to my dad, but this one's signed.

"What?" I ask.

Studying the photo, she doesn't answer.

"Nora, can't you—"

"He must've been in a good mood . . . the signature's real."

"I'm thrilled—now can you stop for a second?"

Ignoring the request, she's too busy checking out the rest

of my office. The crazy part is, most people get intimidated when they're not on their own turf. Nora thrives. "So this is where it all happens, huh? This is where you bust your ass for a signature on a glossy prin—"

"Nora!"

She looks up and grins, enjoying the outburst. "I'm just joshing with you, Michael."

"Now's not the time."

She knows that tone. "Listen, I'm sorry . . . just tell me what the big deal is. Who's on fire?"

I quickly relay everything that's happened with Pam and the files. As always, Nora's judgment comes quick.

"I told you," she says, taking a seat on the corner of my desk. "I said it from the start. That's how it always is in this place. It's all about competition."

"It has nothing to do with competition."

"Oh, so now you're going to ignore the fact that Caroline's death meant a huge promotion for Pam?"

"That's only for the interim. They'll hire someone new after the election."

"So you think she was being blackmailed? That she killed Caroline to hide whatever's in her file?"

I don't answer.

"And Jill came tumbling after," Nora says. "And let's not forget Vaughn's file. Didn't Pam promise she was going to pull that for you? Last I checked, you still don't have it."

"I don't need it. Lamb gave me most of it; Vaughn told me the rest."

"That still doesn't change the facts. Pam promised it and never delivered."

"Can you please just drop it?"

She crosses her legs and shakes her head. "So when you

accuse her, it's fine; and when I accuse her, it's bad? Is that how it—"

"I don't want to talk about it," I interrupt, raising my voice. For the next few seconds, we sit in awkward silence. I eye the envelope that's resting on her lap. Finally, I say, "Did you get the information?"

"What do you think?" she asks, dangling it from her fingertips.

I snatch it away and rip it open. Inside is a four-page photocopy from the President's Oval Office appointment book. When Trey put in a request for the same information, he got nothing but goose-egg. Undeterred, we pulled out the big gun. Ten minutes later, Barbara was more than happy to fulfill Nora's request.

"What'd you tell her?" I ask, flipping through the pages.

"I told her we thought Simon was a killer, and we wanted to see if he was really in the Oval when Caroline died."

"That's cute."

"I didn't have to say anything—I told her it was personal. Before I could get another verb out of my mouth, she had copies in my hand."

The four pages of photocopies cover the four hours from eight A.M. until noon on the day Caroline died. One page for each hour. Looking at it, it's a true marathon.

8:06—Terrill enters. 8:09—Pratt enters. 8:10—McNider enters. 8:16—Terrill leaves. 8:19—Pratt and McNider leave. 8:20 to 8:28—phone calls. 8:29 —Alan S. enters. 8:41— Alan S. leaves. The meetings run through the entire morning. Hartson doesn't have to go anywhere. They all come to him.

Flipping to the next page, I quickly find what I'm looking for.

9:27—Simon enters.

My finger scrolls through the rest of the list, looking for

its match. My heart drops as soon as I see it. 10:32—Simon leaves. Damn. I didn't find the body until at least 10:30. That means he's got it. The perfect alibi.

There's a sad look on Nora's face. "I'm sorry," she says. When I don't answer, her voice starts to race. "Though it sure puts a hell of a finger on Pam, don't you think?"

"For once in your life, can you just stop?"

She doesn't appreciate that one. "Listen, Archie, just because you got dicked over by Betty doesn't mean you have to be an ass to Veronica." Before I can respond, she's on her way to the door.

"Nora, I'm sorry for snapping like that."

She doesn't care.

"Please, Veronica, don't leave. I can't do it without you."

She stops in her tracks.

"You mean that?" she asks, surprisingly serious.

I nod. "I could really use your help."

Hesitantly, she heads back to my desk. Her fingers stroll along the photocopied pages. Studying them, she eventually says, "Do you have any idea what they were meeting about? An hour's a long time to have in there."

I smile a thank-you. "I checked the old schedule—the first twenty minutes were for a briefing with some National Security folks. The last forty were listed as a leadership ceremony for some bar association hotshots. Probably some kind of schmoozefest for big donors—show them around the Oval, send them an autographed picture; a week later, ask them for a donation."

"Whatever it was, it tied Simon up for an hour."

"I don't know. There're plenty of other doors to the office. Maybe Simon snuck out and Barbara never noticed."

"Or maybe Pam—" She cuts herself off, learning from before. Even so, Nora knows what I'm thinking. "Have you asked her about it yet?"

"Who? Pam?"

"No, Nancy Reagan. Of course, Pam."

"Not yet. I checked her office, but she's not there."

"Then get off your ass and find her. Beep her, send an e-mail. You need to figure out what's going on."

"I tried. She won't answer."

"I bet she's at the party."

"What party?"

"Six o'clock in the Rose Garden. For my mom. Trey put together the event."

I almost forgot. Today's the First Lady's fiftieth birthday—and the live *Dateline* interview. "You really think Pam'll be there?"

"Are you kidding? Every clutch in the building'll be there. Pam'll be right at home." Nora looks down at her watch and adds, "Speaking of which, I should get going."

There's a moment of hesitation in her voice. "Is everything okay?" I ask.

"Yeah. Fine."

I know that tone. "Say what you're thinking, Nora."

She stays quiet.

I reach over and take her hand. As softly as possible, I pry open *her* fist. This can't be about the party—she's a pro at the staged stuff. "You nervous about the interview?"

"No, Michael, I love being judged by the whole damn country. I love when ten thousand letters flood in telling me I don't wear enough makeup and that my lipstick sucks. And the fact it's live? Ain't that the rotten cherry on top— one bad answer away from my very own *Saturday Night Live* sketch. I mean, my parents asked for this crap—I was just born into it."

She stops to catch her breath and I don't say a word.

"You have to understand," she adds. "I mean . . . I can

live with all the other bullshit—I just don't like being the issue."

"Who says you're the—"

"Please, Michael, they send me the poll numbers too. There's a reason they want the whole family there."

"Nora, that doesn't mean you—"

"Whatever you're about to say, Romeo, I got a hundred million voters who disagree with you. And every vote counts."

"It may count, but it doesn't matter. There's a difference."

She looks up and stops. "You really think that, don't you?"

"Of course I do."

"Yeah, well, that's you." With one last glance at her watch, she pushes herself away from my desk and heads for the door. "Torturous or not, I gotta be there. Press Office asked me to wear a dress; they're lucky they're getting underwear."

In a blur, Hurricane Nora blows out of the office and leaves me alone in the wake of silence. Still, I know where I am. I've been here plenty of times before. The roar of absolute quiet. The calm before the storm.

"Anyone here?" I call out as I step into the anteroom. No one answers. I tap a loud knuckle on Julian's door. "Julian, you in there?" Still nothing. At Pam's door, I knock even louder. "Pam, you there?" No response.

Convinced I'm alone, I move toward the main door that leads to the hallway. With a flick of my wrist, I twist the lock above the doorknob. A loud deadbolt thunks into place. All three of us have the key, but it should buy me at least a few seconds of warning time.

As I head toward Pam's office, I tell myself this isn't a

violation of trust; it's just a necessary precaution. It's not a great rationalization, but it's all I've got. "Pam, are you there?" I call out one last time. Again, no one answers. I press my sweaty palm against the cold doorknob and slowly push open her office door. "Pam? Hello?" The door swings into the wall with a dull thud. The scent of her apricot shampoo still lingers in the air.

All I have to do is step in. The thing is . . . I can't. It's not right. Pam deserves better than that. She'd never do anything to hurt me. Of course, if she did . . . if she was being blackmailed and then realized my Nora stuff gave her an alibi and an easy out . . . I'd be in trouble. End-of-my-life kind of trouble. In truth, that's the best reason to get in there. I mean, it's not like I'm going to take anything. I just want to look around. For Caroline to have her file, Pam must've had something big to hide. Leaving hesitation at the door, I step into her office. My eyes go right to the red, white, and blue flag over her desk. Saving my own ass. It's the American way.

Approaching her desk, I take a quick look over my shoulder and recheck the anteroom, just to be safe. I'm still alone.

I turn back to the desk and feel my heart pound against my rib cage. The silence is overwhelming. I hear the ebb and flow of my own labored breathing. It's a steady ocean tide. In . . . and always out. Just like that first night watching Simon. Across the hall, my phone starts ringing. I spin around in a panic, thinking it's someone at the door. It's okay, I tell myself as it continues to ring. Just stay on course.

Trying to be systematic, I ignore the pile of files on her desk. She's too smart to leave anything in the open. Luckily, there're some things you can't hide. Heading straight for her phone, I hit the Call Log button and keep my eyes on the digital screen. In an instant, I have the names and phone numbers of the last twenty-two people who called her.

Scrolling through the list, the first thing that jumps out is how many Outside Calls she has. She's either getting called from a lot of pay phones or a lot of bigshots. Neither one is good. When I'm done with the list, there're at least five people I can't identify. I search around for a pad and pen to jot them down. But before I can even get near her "Ask Me About My Grandchildren" pencil cup, I hear a key in the main door of the anteroom. Someone's there.

I race out of Pam's office as fast as I can, bounding into the anteroom just as the main door swings open.

"What the hell's going on?" Julian asks. "Why'd you lock the door?"

"Nuh . . . Nothing," I say, out of breath. "Just straightening the anteroom."

"I get it," he says with a laugh. "*Straightening* the anteroom."

I refuse to acknowledge what's got to be Julian's oldest joke. Adding an "-ing" to create euphemisms for masturbation. *Straightening* the anteroom. *Faxing* the document. *Filing* my memo. It really does work, but I'll never give him the pleasure of knowing it.

"Have you seen Pam?" I ask, in no mood to play around.

"Yeah, she was headed over to the First Lady's party."

I move toward the door without another word.

"Where you going?" Julian asks.

"To check out the Rose Garden—I have to speak to her."

"I'm sure you do, Garrick," he says with a wink. "You do what you have to."

"Huh?"

"*Checking out* the Rose Garden."

*   *   *

It's a five-minute walk from my office to the Rose Garden. Or a two-minute run. Cutting through the West Wing and looking at my watch, I'm already twenty minutes late. Accounting for the First Family's guaranteed lag time, that should put me there right on time. As I push open the doors to the West Colonnade, I expect to see a crowd. I find a mob.

There must be at least a couple hundred people—all of them angling toward the podium at the far end of the Rose Garden. Instinctively, I start glancing at ID badges. Most people have orange backgrounds—limited to the OEOB. A few have blue. And the ones who're hiding their badges in their shirt pockets—those're the interns. That's why the garden's so full. Everyone's invited. The odd part is, even young staffers don't usually get this excited by an event.

Behind me, I hear a man's voice say, "I been standing in lines like this my entire life."

I stand on my tiptoes and crane my neck to see over the crowd. That's when I realize this isn't your standard event. With the President's lead shrinking, they need the next few hours to be back-to-back grand slams. First the family party; then the live interview. They're putting on the ultimate pretty face for America—and sparing no expense to pull it off.

Next to the podium is the object of everyone's attention: an enormous vanilla-frosted sheet cake with an uncanny likeness of the First Lady drawn in different colored icings. To the right of the cake, behind a long velvet rope, is the *Dateline* team, collecting footage for tonight's intro. In front of them are two men with cameras. White House photographers. Damn, Trey's ruthless. Get a slice of cake; have your picture taken with Mickey and Minnie. In the final months before the election, they want us all to look like family. Family first.

Ignoring the photo-op, I step deeper into the crowd. I

need to find Pam. I elbow my way through the sea of fellow staffers, searching for her blond hair.

Without warning, the mob begins to rumble. The cheers start up front and work their way to the back. In one sudden rush, the whole group presses forward. Clapping. Shouting. Whistling. The First Family's here.

With the President on her right and Nora and Christopher on her left, Susan Hartson greets the crowd as if she's surprised by the two hundred people on her lawn. As always, there's a velvet rope that separates them from the staff, but the President shakes every hand that's extended over it. Wearing a red-striped tie and a light blue shirt under his standard navy suit, he looks more relaxed than I've ever seen him. Behind him, the First Lady is beaming with requisite joy, followed by Christopher, who's wearing the same color shirt as his dad but without the tie. Nice touch. Finally, bringing up the rear, in a tasteful black skirt, is Nora. She's carrying a birthday present with red, white, and blue wrapping paper. As they move toward the podium, three TV crews, including the *Dateline* team, capture the moment. It's a brilliant event. Everyone—the staff, the Hartsons, all of us—we're one big happy family. As long as we stay on our side of the rope.

Truly, the definition of "tone deaf" is a herd of White House staffers singing "Happy Birthday" at the top of their lungs. By the time we're done with the song, I'm about a quarter way through the crowd. Still no Pam.

"Time for presents," the President announces. On cue, Christopher and Nora step up to the podium. For this, I stop.

She stands in front of us with a convincing smile. A month ago, I would've believed it. Today, I'm not even close to fooled. She's miserable up there.

Brushing his dark hair from his eyes and approaching the microphone with adolescent pride, Christopher lowers it to his height. "Mom, if you'd join us . . ." he says. As the First Lady steps forward, Nora leans awkwardly into the mike. "This is a present from me, Chris, and Dad," she begins. "And since we didn't want you to return it, we decided that I'd be the one to pick it out." The crowd fills in the sitcom laugh track. "Anyway, this is from us to you."

Nora picks up the red, white, and blue box that I know she didn't wrap and hands it over. But as the First Lady peels off the wrapping paper, something happens. There's a new expression on Nora's face. Her eyes dance with nervous excitement. This isn't part of the script. It's no longer Nora and the First Lady. It's just a daughter giving her mom a birthday present. The way Nora's bouncing on her heels, she's dying for Mom to like it.

The moment the box is opened, the crowd oooohs and ahhhhs. The TV crews pull in for the close-up. Inside is a handmade gold bracelet studded with tiny sapphires. Taking it out, Mrs. Hartson's first reaction—the first thing she does—is pure instinct. In slow motion, she turns to *Dateline*'s camera with a radiant look and says, "Thank you, Nora and Chris. I love you."

Almost an hour and a half later, I'm back in my office, attempting to sort through the nightly pile of mail. I beeped Pam two more times. She hasn't answered. Trying to squash the migraine that's ricocheting through my skull, I open my top drawer and finger through my collection of medicines: Maalox, Sudafed, cetirizine . . . always prepared. I grab a plastic bottle of Tylenol and fight with the childproof lid. In no mood to get water, I tilt my head back and swallow them on the spot. They don't go down easily.

"C'mon, campers, it's time for a sing-along!" Trey shouts

as he kicks open the door to my office. "Spell it out, Annette! Who's the leader of the club that's made for you and me? T-R-E Y-Y-Y Y-Y-Y-Y-Y!"

"Can't stop with the Disney references, can you?"

"Not when they're this good. And, boy, is this Kingdom Magic! Did you see how well that event went over? Already on CNN. Cued up for the nightlies. Nancie's predicting front page of the Style section. And in less than an hour—live on *Dateline*. Can I get any better? No! No, sir, I cannot!"

"Trey, I'm thrilled that you and your necromancers were able to brainwash half the nation, but please . . ." I stare at my pencil cup and lose my thought. It's all unimportant.

"Don't give me that pouty face," he scolds, taking a seat in front of my desk. "What's wrong?"

"I just . . . I don't know. The whole event left a bad taste in my mouth."

"It's supposed to leave a bad taste—that's how you know it's good! The more syrup, the better. It's what America eats for breakfast."

"It wasn't just the sappy parts. You saw when she got the present. Nora picked out a beautiful gift for her mother. And what does the First Lady do? She thanks the camera instead of her daughter."

"I swear, right there, I cried."

"It's not funny, Trey. It's pathetic."

"Can you please jump off the high horse? We both know the real reason you're cranky."

"Stop telling me how to feel! You're not the master of my thought process!"

Silently sitting back in his seat, he gives me a second to calm down. "Don't take it out on me, Michael. It's not my fault you didn't find Pam."

"Oh, so you're not the one who crowded two hundred wannabes behind the vanilla-frosted Pied Piper?"

"It wasn't frosting; it was icing. There's a difference."

"There's no difference!"

"There could be a difference—we just don't know it."

"Stop fucking around, Trey! You're starting to piss me off!"

Rather than shout back, he gives me the rub. It's a medium one, done more as a way to restrain himself. A lesser friend would head for the door. Trey stays right where he is.

Eventually, I look across the desk. "I didn't mean to . . ."

He lowers his gaze to his lap and pulls something from his belt. His pager's going off.

"Anything important?" I ask.

"One hour till *Dateline*—they want me over there to do the run-through."

I nod, and he heads for the anteroom.

"When I get back, we'll sit down and figure it out," he offers.

"Don't worry," I say. "I'll be okay."

Stopping at the door, Trey turns around. "I never said you wouldn't."

I give Pam another half-hour to answer two more pages. She doesn't. At this point, I should call it a night, but instead, I flip on CNN for one last look at today's news. All day, the lead story's been the *Dateline* interview, but as the picture blooms into focus, I'm staring at a clip from today's Bartlett rally. Wherever it is, the place is going crazy—jumping, shouting, screaming with excitement and home-painted signs. When a graphic comes on that reads MIAMI, FLORIDA, I almost fall over. Hartson's home state. That's a ballsy move by Bartlett, but it looks like it's paying off.

Not only is he getting press for the confrontation, but compared to last week, his music's louder, his crowd's bigger, and, as the anchorwoman says, "When it was all over, he stayed and shook hands for almost a full hour." Now I know we're in trouble. Candidates only stay when the getting's good.

Flicking off the TV, I decide to head over to the Dip Room, where Trey's *Dateline* opus is getting ready to roll. Whatever else Bartlett's up to, tonight's interview is still the biggest game in town. So why watch it on TV when Trey can clear me in to see it in person? Besides, after what Nora said earlier, she can use the support.

From the west end of the Ground Floor Corridor, I see that, as usual, I'm not the only one who had the idea—a small crowd of staffers is already gathering. Going live in the White House is no small task, and the way everyone's running around, it's got its usual circus feel. Peering over the shoulder of the guy in front of me, I get my first look at the set.

With the room's wallpaper—nineteenth-century landscapes of North America—as the warm-fuzzy backdrop, the whole thing's set up around two sofas and an antique chair. But instead of the cold, wood-back sofa that's usually in the Dip Room, they've replaced it with two plush, comfy sofas that, if memory serves, are from the second floor of the Residence. It's gotta look like a real family. No one— not the parents, not the kids—sits alone.

Surrounding the makeshift living room are five separate cameras that're set up in a wide semicircle—the twenty-first-century firing squad. Beyond the cameras, on the other side of the reams of black wiring that zigzag across the floor, the President and Mrs. Hartson are schmoozing with Samantha Stulberg and a stylish, late-thirties woman dressed all in black and wearing a headset. The producer. Hartson lets out a hearty laugh—he's putting in his final bid to keep the interview on soft focus. I look at my watch and realize they have a full ten minutes to go. This is big for him. If it weren't, he'd never be down here this early.

In the background, amid the sound people, cameramen, and makeup artists, I spot Trey talking on the phone. Looking anxious and almost panicked, he walks over to Nora's brother, Christopher, who has taken his seat on the sofa. It's not until Trey starts whispering in his ear that it hits me. The President, Mrs. Hartson, Christopher, their staff, the TV crew, the producer, the interviewer, the satellite experts . . . everyone's here. Everyone but Nora.

Finished with Christopher, Trey gingerly tiptoes behind the First Lady and taps her on the shoulder. As he pulls her aside, I can't hear what he's saying. But the First Lady's face says it all. For one slight, barely noticeable nanosecond, she lapses into a red rage, then—just as quickly—it's back to a smile. She knows those cameras are on her; there's a guy with a handheld taping for a local newscast. She has to keep it cool. Still, I can read the growl on her lips from here.

"Find her."

Holding his head high, Trey walks calmly out of the room, shoving his way past us. No one really pays much attention—they're all watching POTUS—but as soon as Trey sees me, he shoots me that look. That this-is-gonna-cause-me-sexual-dysfunction-I'm-so-scared look. I leave the crowd and fall in right behind him. The farther he gets down the hallway, the faster he goes.

"Please tell me you know where she is," he whispers, still in speed walk.

"When was the last time you—"

"She said she was going to the bathroom. No one's seen her since."

"So she went to the—"

"That was a half hour ago."

I stare silently at Trey. As we blow through the doors to the West Colonnade, he starts to run. "Have you checked her room?" I ask.

"That's who I was on the phone with. The guards by the elevator said she never went upstairs."

"What about the Service? Have you notified them?"

"Michael, I'm trying to convince a fifteen-person *Dateline* crew and one hundred million viewers that Hartson and his family are Ozzie-Harriet clones. If I tell the Service, it'll be a manhunt. Besides, I called my friend at the Southeast Gate—according to him, Nora hasn't left the grounds."

"Which means she's either in the OEOB or on the first two floors of the mansion."

"Do me a favor and check your office," Trey says.

"I was just there. She's not—"

"Just check it!" he hisses, his forehead covered with beads of sweat.

As we enter the West Wing, Trey darts for the Oval. I keep going—taking off for the OEOB and checking my watch. Eight minutes to go. Turning around to run backwards, I ask, "How long is the—"

"There's a one-minute intro, thirty seconds for credits, and two minutes of B-roll footage from the birthday party." His voice is shaking. "Michael, you know the numbers. If this turns into a crisis . . ."

"We'll find her," I say as I start to run. "I promise."

CHAPTER 27

I throw open the door to the anteroom and it slams into the wall. "Nora? Are you here?"

No answer.

I keep going, flinging open the door to my office. "Nora?" Again there's no response. I check for myself. Couch, desk, fireplace, couch. Nowhere in sight. Seven minutes to go.

Spinning around, I race through Julian's and Pam's offices. "Nora?" Julian's is empty. So is Pam's—though her light is on. That's means she's still in the . . . No, not now. If Nora's not here and she's not upstairs, where could she . . . ? Yeah. Maybe.

Tearing back into the hallway, I run full speed to the exit, burst out onto West Exec, and descend the stairs in a few large jumps. But as I squeeze past Simon's car in the parking lot, I don't head for the usual entrance under the awning. Instead, I snake around to the north side of the mansion, along the length of the West Wing, past the kitchen, and into the tradesmen's entrance. My blue pass gets me past the guard, and I take a sharp left, down toward the one place we've never been interrupted.

I reach for the knob of the heavy metal door, knowing it's supposed to be locked. When I turn it, there's a thunk. And it gives. It's open. I pull open the door and leap inside.

My eyes quickly scan the length of the bowling alley. Lane, pins, rack of balls. "Nora, are you—"

My heart stops and I take a step back, bumping into the door just as it slams me from behind. There. On the floor. Hidden behind the scorekeeper's table—her legs dangle out and I see the edge of her skirt. Her body's motionless. Oh, God.

"Nora!"

I race around the table, slide down on my knees, and scoop her into my arms. From her nose, two thin streams of blood run down her face, collecting on her top lip. Her face is white. "Nora!" I lift her head and shake her. She lets out a soft moan. Unsure of my CPR, I slap her on the cheek. Again. And again. "Nora! It's me!" Out of nowhere, she starts to laugh—a dark little giggle that sends a cold chill down my back. She flips her right arm wildly through the air, crashing it down over her head and slamming her wrist into the polished floor. Before I can say another word, her laugh turns into a cough. A wet, hacking wheeze that comes straight from the lungs.

"C'mon, Nora, pull it together." Frantically, I grab the front of her blouse, including her bra straps, and pull her up straight. As she flops forward, a wave of clear vomit shoots out of her mouth, all over my shirt. Startled, I let go, but as her coughing gets louder, she's able to sit up by herself.

I wipe her insides from my tie, and she looks up, her eyes half closed, her neck bobbing and sagging uncontrollably. Her whole body is in slow motion.

She starts talking, but nothing makes sense. Just mum-

bles and slurred words. Slowly, it starts coming back. "Then
... I'm not ... you gotta be ... Special K ... Just some
K ..."

Special K. Ketamine. Congrats to *Rolling Stone*. I remember the article like it was yesterday. Snort it like cocaine and, depending on how much you take, you're gone
from ten to thirty minutes.

"How much did you do, Nora?"

She doesn't answer.

"How much, Nora? Tell me!"

Nothing.

"Nora!"

Right there, she looks at me—and for the first time, I
see recognition in her eyes. Blinking twice, she cocks her
head. "Did we fool 'em?"

"How much did you take!?"

She closes her eyes. "Not enough."

Okay, that's a response—she's coming back. I glance
down at my watch—five minutes to start, plus four minutes of intro. I race to the phone, call the operator, and ask
her to beep Trey with a message. Rushing back to Nora, I
help her to her feet.

"Lemme alone," she says, pulling away.

I grab her by the shoulders. "Don't fight me on this!
Not now!" Seeing that she's about to fall, I shove her onto
the seat at the scorekeeper's table and slap her again on
the cheek—not too hard—I don't want to hurt her. Just
enough to ...

"Please don't hate me for this, Michael. Please."

"I don't want to talk about it," I shoot back.

On the scorekeeper's table, I see her open purse. I dump
out its contents as fast as I can. Keys, tissues, and a small
metal lipstick tube that, thanks to the incline of the table,
is now rolling toward me. I catch it just as it falls. Looks

like lipstick, but ... I pull off the lid and see the white powder. How can she simultaneously be so smart and so stupid? Unable to answer, I reseal the tube and shove it into the small groove that holds pencils. Right now, there are more important things to deal with.

Snatching the tissues, I rip them open, spit into one of them, and like every mother does to every kid, wipe Nora's face. The blood from her nose is fresh. It rubs away easily. With my right hand, I brush the hair from her face, but it falls right back. I brush it again and tuck it behind her ear. Anything to make it stay. Once the hair is out of the way, I hold up her chin and get a better look. The edge of my shirtsleeve takes the last bit of throw-up from the corner of her mouth. The way her lips are sagging, I know she's still not there. But appearance-wise, as I check the rest of her, it's not too bad. She's leaning forward, with her elbows resting on her knees. Crash position. Still, all the vomit's on me. She's clean. And *Dateline*'s waiting.

I run back to the phone and once again call the operator. She tells me my message was sent to Trey. He still hasn't responded. They must be starting. "Nora, get up!" I shout, rushing to her side. I grab her by her wrists and try to pull her to her feet. She won't help; she just sits there. "C'mon!" I yell, pulling harder. "Get up!" She still won't budge.

Circling around to the back of the scorekeeper's seat, I throw my tie over my shoulder, slide my arms under her armpits, and when I have her in full Heimlich, I lift as hard as I can. She's all deadweight. There's a sharp pop in my back, but I ignore it. Sure, I'm tempted to just leave her and let her hang—fourteen strikes and you're out. The thing is, if I don't get her on this show ... Shit. Sometimes I hate myself in this place. It's a damn TV show. All this bullshit for a TV show. *"Nora, for Godsakes, stand up!"*

With one final yank, she's up and out. We can still make it, I tell myself, but the second I get her upright, her legs give out under her. We tumble forward, completely off-balance. With a thud, she's back on the floor—both of us flat on our asses.

As I watch her, we're both breathing heavily. However we got here, our chests rise and fall at the exact same pace. Searching for distinction, I slow my breathing and break away. For the next thirty seconds, I keep her sitting upright, watching the color come back to her face. I don't have a choice—if we want to get out of here, she needs a minute. Slowly, she picks her head up. "I mean it, Michael—I didn't mean to break my promise to you."

"So this just happened by itself?"

"You don't understand."

"*I* don't understand? You're the one who—"

Before I can finish, the door to the bowling alley swings open and Trey steps in carrying a compact and a blush brush. I'm tempted to be relieved—until I see who's following him. Susan Hartson. Despite the atomic hairspray, her light brown hair bobs angrily against her shoulders, and in the fluorescent light of the bowling alley, her facecake of makeup no longer hides her sharp features. Refusing to touch anything, she steps into the room like a mother stepping into a fraternity house.

"Can she make it?" she barks.

"They just hit the intro," Trey tells me, rushing forward. "We've got three minutes."

I pull Nora to her feet, but she's still off-balance. Catching her, I let her take a second. She's propped against my shoulder with her arms hooked around my neck. It takes her a moment, and she's still leaning, but she quickly wins the battle to stand up straight.

At the same time, the First Lady fights her way past

Trey, stepping forward until she's face-to-face with her daughter. And me. Without a word, Mrs. Hartson licks her thumb and angrily spit-shines the last remnants of blood from Nora's nose.

"Sorry, Mom," Nora says. "I didn't mean to—"

"Shut up. Not now."

I feel Nora tense up. Within a breath, she's standing on her own. She lifts her chin and looks her mother in the eye. "Ready to go, Mom."

Following the acidic smell, the First Lady glares down at the vomit on my shirt, then, without moving her head, lifts her steady gaze to look me straight in the eyes. I'm not sure if she's blaming me or just studying my face. Eventually, she blurts, "Think she can do it?"

"She's been doing it for years," I shoot back.

"Mrs. Hartson," Trey jumps in, "we can still—"

"Tell them we're on our way," the First Lady says, her eyes never leaving me.

Trey darts for the exit. Turning back to her daughter, the First Lady grasps Nora's arm and pulls her toward the door. There's no time for goodbyes. Nora leaves first and Mrs. Hartson follows. I just stand there.

When they're gone, I look over my shoulder and see Nora's purse on the scorekeeper's table. So damn stupid. Shoving the keys and tissues back inside, I notice the silver metal tube that looks like lipstick. If I leave it out, someone'll find it. Good—maybe that's the best way to help her. For a full minute, I don't move, my mind playing through the consequences. This isn't a rumor about a backseat in Princeton. This would be drugs *in* the White House. My eyes focus on the shiny metal tube, watching it gleam as the ceiling lights bounce off it. It's so polished, so perfect—in its convex curve, I see a warped version of myself. Me. It's all up to me. All I have to do is hurt her.

Right.

Like a little kid playing jacks, I scoop up Nora's tube, grip it in my fist, and with a short prayer, shove it deep down in my pants pocket, praying this isn't the moment I'll forever look back on with regret.

A quick stop in the men's room sends the rest of Nora's Special K down the sink before I finally head back to my office. For the next hour, my eyes are glued to my small TV. Hartson's schmoozing must've worked—Stulberg's opening ran over by a solid two minutes, giving Nora just enough time to change into a new dress and put some blush on her cheeks.

As expected, most of the questions go to the President, but Stulberg's no dummy. America loves the family—which is why the sixth question goes to Nora. And the seventh. And the tenth. And the eleventh. And the twelfth. With each one, I hold my breath. But whatever she's asked, whether it's about her indecisive post-graduation plans, or what it's like moving back into the White House, Nora takes it in. Sometimes she stutters, sometimes she tucks her hair behind her ear, but for every answer, she's all poise and smiles—never an argument. She even gets in a joke about being called the First Freeloader, a subtle moment of humility that'll have the Sunday talk show pundits gushing over themselves with praise.

At nine o'clock it's over, and I'm honestly amazed. Somehow, as always, Nora pulled it off—which means any minute now, someone's going to . . .

"What kind of medal do I get?" Trey asks as my office door swings open. "Purple Heart? Medal of Honor? Red Badge of Courage?"

"What's the one for when you take it in the gut?"

"Purple Heart's for when you're wounded."

"Then that's the one you get."

"Fine. Thank you. You get one too." Reaching my sofa, Trey collapses in it. We're both deathly silent. Neither of us has to say a word.

Eventually, though, I give in. "Did the First Lady say anything to you?"

Trey shakes his head. "Like it never happened."

"What about Nora?"

"She mouthed a *thank you* on the way out." Sitting up straight, he adds, "Let me tell you something, my friend— that girl is Queen of the Psychos, know what I'm saying?"

"I don't want to get into it."

"Why? You're suddenly so busy?"

There's a loud knock on my door.

I glance over at Trey. "Who is it?" I call out.

The door opens and a familiar figure steps inside. My mouth goes dry.

Reading my expression, Trey looks over his shoulder. "Hey, Pam," he says nonchalantly.

"Nice job on the interview," she replies. "They're still celebrating in the Dip Room. Even Hartson looked relaxed."

Trey can't help but beam. My eyes stay locked on Pam. I can read it in her smile. She has no idea what we've seen. Or what we know.

"What's going on?" I ask.

"Nothing," she replies. "Meanwhile, did you see the on-line poll NBC did with the *Herald*? After the interview, they asked one hundred fifth-graders if they wanted to be Nora Hartson. Nineteen said yes because they could get away with whatever they wanted. Eighty-one said no because it wasn't worth the headache. And they say our education policy is having no effect? Please—eighty-one of them are Einsteins."

Avoiding a response, I keep it calm. "Trey, don't you have to get Mrs. Hartson off to that fund-raiser?"

"No." He's hoping to stay and watch the show.

I give him a look. "Don't you have a hobby or something you're supposed to be working on?"

"Hobby?" he asks with a laugh. "I work *here*."

I tighten the look.

"Fine, fine, I'm out of your way." Heading to the door, he adds, "Nice seeing you, Pam."

Cat's out of the bag. She knows something's up. "What was that about?" she asks.

I wait for Trey to shut the door. With a slam, he's gone. Here we go.

CHAPTER 28

W hat's going on?" Pam asks, standing in front of my desk.

I'm not sure where to begin. "Are you . . . Have you ever . . ."

"Spit it out, Michael."

"Have you been listening in on my phone line?"

She drops her briefcase, letting it sag to the floor. "Excuse me?"

"Tell me the truth, Pam—have you been listening in?"

Unlike Nora, Pam doesn't detonate. Instead, she's confused. "How could I possibly listen in?"

"I heard your phone—I saw how it works."

"What're you . . . What phone?"

"The phone in the anteroom!"

"What are you talking about?"

I push myself away from my desk and storm through the anteroom, into Pam's office. Picking up the phone, I dial my extension. Two phones ring simultaneously. The one in my office and the one on the anteroom's small desk. "They're the same lines!" I shout. "Did you really think I wouldn't notice you had the ringer turned off?"

"Michael, I swear on my life, if those lines are the same, I never knew it. You've seen me when I sit out there—it's just to use the phone."

"That's my point."

"Wait a minute," she says, finally getting annoyed. "You think I was *faking* those conversations? That that was some secret ploy to fool you?"

"You tell me. You're the one who was on the line."

"On the . . . ? I can't believe you, Michael. After all we've . . . Who fed you this one? Was it Nora?"

"Don't bring her into this."

"Don't tell me what to do. Regardless of what you saw with Simon, the world's not out to get you. You know how our system runs here—it's still the federal government. Maybe the lines got crossed when they did the repair."

"And maybe it's been like that all along."

"Stop saying that!"

"Then tell me the truth."

"I already have, dammit!"

"So that's it? The lines were separate, and when they made the last repair, they crossed yours into mine?"

"I don't know what else you want me to say! I didn't know!"

"And you never listened in?"

"Never! Not once!"

Watching her get riled doesn't make it any easier. "Then I can take you at your word?"

She takes a few steps toward me. "Michael, this is me."

"Answer the question."

She still can't believe it. "I wouldn't lie to you," she insists. "Ever."

"Are you sure?"

"I swear."

She asked for this one. I look her straight in the eye

and smack her with it. "Then why didn't you tell me Caroline had your file?"

Pam stops dead in her tracks. She's too smart to come any closer.

"C'mon, Pam, you're a bigshot now—where's your bigshot answer?"

Refusing to reply, she clenches her jaw in silence.

"I asked you a question."

Still nothing.

"Did you hear what I said, Pam? I asked y—"

"How'd you find out she had it?" Her voice is barely above a whisper. "Tell me who told you."

"It doesn't matter who told me, I—"

"I want to know!" she demands. "It was Nora, wasn't it? She's always butting—"

"Nora had nothing to do with it. And even if she did, it doesn't change the facts. Now why did Caroline have your file?"

She walks across the anteroom and rests against the small table that houses the fax machine. Leaning forward, she holds her side like she has a stomachache. It's a vertical fetal position.

"I knew it was her," she says. "I knew it."

"Knew it was who?"

"Caroline. She was the one with the access. I just didn't want to believe it."

"I don't understand. What's in the file?"

"Nothing's in the file. That's not how she worked."

"Pam, stop being cryptic and tell me what the hell she did."

"I'm assuming she picked apart the fine print. That's what she was good at. I mean, it's not like your file says 'Son pulled strings for retarded father.' She probably just noticed that all your dad's residences were group homes. A little legwork later, she had everything she needed."

"So what was in your fine print?"

"You have to understand, it was right when I first started. I was still . . ."

"Tell me what you did," I insist.

Pausing, she takes her knuckle and lightly knocks it a few times against her cheek. Penance. "Do you promise you won't tell anyone?"

"Pam . . ."

She knows me better than that. Eventually, she asks, "Do you remember what Caroline was working on when I got here?"

I think about it for a second and shake my head.

"Here's a hint—when Blake announced his resignation . . ."

". . . Kuttler was nominated. She was filling Blake's seat on the Supreme Court."

"That's the one," Pam says. "And you know how it is when a Justice gives up his seat. Every lawyer worth his pinstripes starts thinking he's pretty. So when Senior Staff started working on the list of nominees, it fell to us to check them out. Around the same time, I got smacked with my first law school loan bill. With ninety-thousand dollars in loans, that's over a thousand dollars every month. Add that to the first and last months' rent on the apartment I had just moved into, plus security deposit, plus car payments, plus insurance, plus credit card debt, plus the fact that it takes a month before you get your first paycheck—I was here a total of nine days and I was already sinking hard. Suddenly, I'm contacted by a *Washington Post* reporter named Inez Cotigliano."

"That's the woman who—"

"I know who she is, Michael. She was my next-door neighbor during my senior year of college."

"So you're the one who—"

"I never told her about you. I swear on my mother's life. We had one dance and that was it. Believe me, that was more than enough."

I cross my arms. "I'm listening."

"Anyway, as I was vetting all the potential Court nominees, Inez, like every hungry reporter in the city, was trying to find out who was on the short list."

"Pam, don't tell me you—"

"She offered me five thousand dollars for confirmation that Kuttler was the front-runner. I didn't know what else to do. I'd be fine once the paychecks started flowing, but that was three weeks away." As she tells the story, she refuses to face me.

"So the *Post* fronted the cash?"

"The *Post*? They'd never let that happen. It was all out of Inez's own pocket—she was dying to make it big. Her dad's some Connecticut trust-fund guy. Family has the patent on aspirin or something ridiculous like that."

"That was confidential information."

"Michael, she showed up on the worst day of my life. And if it makes you feel any better, I was so wracked with guilt, I eventually paid her back the money. Took me almost a year to do it."

"She still had the infor—" I cut myself short. It's so easy to judge; just grab the gavel. The only catch is, I know what it's like to get my fingers pounded. "Must've been a big day for Inez."

"Her first front-page story—below the fold, but on A1— 'Hartson Down to Three; Kuttler Leading Pack.' It didn't matter, though. The *Herald* beat her to the punch. They ran a similar story the same day, which I guess means I wasn't the only one leaking."

"That's pure rationalization and you know it."

"I never gave her anything concrete; I just told her the front-runner."

"So what happened? Caroline found out?"

"Took her less than a week," Pam says. "Flipping through my file, Caroline probably spotted the connection. Inez Cotigliano. College neighbor. New reporter. As soon as she found it, she could've fired me, but that's her MO—keep the people with the problems around and cash in on their secrets. Next thing I know, I'm stuck in the web."

"What'd she do?"

For the first time since we started talking, Pam looks up at me. Her eyes are wide with the fear of judgment.

"What'd she do?" I repeat.

"Four days after the story ran, I got an anonymous note asking me to pay ten thousand dollars. Two payments. Six months apart." Looking wobbly, she takes a seat. "I didn't sleep for days. Every time I closed my eyes, I'm telling you, I can still see it: Everything I worked for—dangling right there in front of me. It got so bad, I started coughing up blood. But in the end . . . there was no way around it . . . I couldn't afford to start from scratch." Shading her eyes with her hands, she rubs the top of her forehead in slow, tense circles. "I left the money in an Amtrak locker in Union Station."

"I thought you didn't have any—"

"Sold my car, went delinquent on my loans, and maxed out the cash advances on every credit card I could find. Better to have bad credit than no career."

She says something else, but I'm not listening. A swell of rage crashes against the base of my skull. Even my toes clench for this one.

"What?" she asks, reading the anger on my face.

"You knew," I growl. "You knew the whole time she was the blackmailer!"

"That's not—"

"You sent me right to her! When I came in that first day, I asked you if Caroline could be trusted. You said yes! What the hell were you thinking?"

"Michael, calm down."

"Why? So you can talk through your teeth some more? Or serve me back up to Inez? You lied to me, Pam! You lied about the phone, you lied about the file, and you lied about Caroline! Think about it for once—if I hadn't gone to see her that day, none of this—" Once again, I cut myself off and take a careful look at Pam. Cocking my head, I watch the prism shift. She knows what's running through my brain.

"Hold on a second," she interrupts. "You don't think I . . . ?"

"You telling me I'm wrong?"

"Michael, are you nuts? I didn't kill her!"

"You said it, not me."

"I'd never hurt her! Never!" she insists. "I swear—I thought she was my friend!"

"Really? So do all your friends blackmail you for large sums of cash? Because if that's the case, I could use a few extra grand. Small bills, of course."

"You're an asshole."

"Call me whatever you want—at least I'm not squeezing you for hush money. I mean, if that's a friend, I'd hate to see your enemies."

"I didn't have any enemies. Not until now."

"What about—"

"Don't you get it, Michael? Have you even been listening? All I got was a note and a location. I never knew who it was."

"But you knew Caroline had access to the files."

"That didn't matter—she's my—" She stops. "She was like family."

It takes me a second to process the information. "So you never suspected her?"

"I suspected you before I suspected her."

I'm not sure how to deal with that one.

"Besides," Pam continues, "you don't need FBI files to find out Inez and I went to school together. I figured someone else put two and two together, then did the research on their own."

"Well, didn't you think it was odd when Caroline showed up dead with thirty grand in her safe and all our files on her desk? I mean, if you're looking for a blackmailer . . ."

"I swear to you, that's the first I ever thought of it. It wasn't until that moment that I even raised an eyebrow."

"Raised an eyebrow? It's a damn DNA print—all she's missing is blood on her fingertips and a forehead tattoo that says 'Will Victimize for Cash'!"

"Don't make a joke of this!"

"Then stop acting stupid! Once Caroline was killed, you knew she was the blackmailer. I've been chasing my tail all this time, and you never gave me a clue! Not once!"

"You already knew, Michael."

"I didn't—"

"You did!" she shouts with newfound rage. "You said it that night we had Thai food. You wondered whether Simon was being blackmailed."

"And you could've told me the answer. *Yes! He probably was! Just like me!* Instead, you left me to rot!"

"How dare you say that? I've been by your side since the moment this thing started!"

"Then why didn't you tell me about what happened with Inez?"

"Because I didn't want you to know!" she yells, her voice booming through the office. "There! Is that what you want? I was mortified when it happened—sick to my stomach. Then, as if the act alone weren't bad enough, Caroline took my worst moment and humiliated me with it. You of all people should understand—dirty laundry's better kept in the closet."

"It still doesn't—"

"That's the only thing I hid from you, Michael. My own personal black eye. Everything else, I told the truth. And if you didn't guess blackmail on your own, I would've pushed you there myself."

"You still sicced Inez on me."

"You don't believe that for a second."

She's right. I was bluffing to see her reaction. Near as I can tell, she passes. "So you've never spoken to Inez about this?"

"She called me the day after it happened. I told her even less than I told the FBI. Trust me, if I wanted to screw you over, I would've done the easiest thing of all."

"And what's that?"

She looks me dead in the eye. "I would've told them about you. And the money. And Nora. I could've made at least twenty grand on that one." There it is. Guerrilla honesty. If it weren't so disconcerting, I'd probably laugh.

"So you *never* knew it was Caroline demanding the money?" I ask again.

"I don't think anyone did. Walk through it—why else would Simon drop that money in the woods? If he knew it was Caroline, he could've paid her face-to-face."

It's not a bad theory. "Maybe that's why he killed her. When he went to tell her his bullshit side of the story, she made some snide comment and he realized she was Miss Moneypenny."

"But to kill her for that? No offense, but, so what? She knows he's gay. Who cares?"

"Certainly not Simon. If he did, he never would've shown up undisguised at a gay bar. Which is why I think it's more than just the gay part—don't forget, Simon's got a wife and three kids. Whatever you think, that's still a life-wrecker."

We both sit in silence, nodding in agreement. Eventually, Pam says, "I still think Caroline knew something about Nora."

"I don't want to talk about it."

She pauses a second. "And if she weren't dead, I bet she would've blackmailed you. That's why she had your file."

"We'll never know," I say, glad to change the subject. "That's her secret."

"Speaking of secrets, what about mine?" Pam asks, leaping at her own segue. "You plan on turning me in?"

"You're the new Queen of Ethics. You plan on ratting out my dad?"

We look at each other for a long moment and then dip our heads in an awkwardly relieved bow.

"Can I ask you one last question," I add as she turns to leave. "What ever happened with Vaughn's FBI file? You said you were going to get it for us."

"I thought you got it from Lamb."

"I did. I just want to know why I didn't get it from you."

Just like that, her smile's gone. Her eyebrows tighten and her mouth sags open in pain. No, not pain. Sadness.

Disappointment. "You still think I . . . After all we just . . ." Her voice once again trails off.

"What? What'd I say?"

She's done giving me answers. Rushing toward the main door of the office, she covers her mouth with her hand and fights back tears. "I tried my best, Michael."

I'm about to follow when I'm interrupted by the ringing of my phone. The ring echoes simultaneously from my office and out here in the anteroom. I check out the caller ID. Outside Call. A few feet away, Pam grabs the door and pulls it open. In a second, she'll be gone. It's a hard one, but I make my choice.

"This is Michael," I say as I pick up the phone.

As Pam leaves, the door slams with a thunderclap. I shut my eyes tight to avoid the noise.

"Ready to put on the fear face?" an excited voice asks on the other line.

I recognize it instantly. Vaughn. "Are you crazy?" I shout. "They could be—"

"Takes 'em eighty seconds ta trace a phone call. They're not gonna find nothin'."

"This better be good."

"Would I be botherin' you if it weren't?"

I ignore the question. "Twenty seconds."

He gets right into it. "So I started askin' my boys 'bout your li'l lady friend—y'know, with the powerful daddy?"

"I got it," I snap.

"Found a couple people who know her. Seems that she's still got a little bit of an ear, nose, and throat problem—emphasis on the nose. And when it comes to Special K? She's buyin' like it's double coupon days—buddy of my buddy Pryce says that's their favorite."

"*Their? Who's *they?*"

"See, that's where the shoe pinches," he says as his

voice gets serious. "She's too smart to buy her candy herself, so she sends her boyfriend out for it."

"Her boyfriend?"

"That's why I wanted to call. I'm thinkin' you got a little suckered that night in the bar. Accordin' to my best source out here—and he swears on his cousin's life it's the truth . . ."

"Tell me who it is," I demand.

He throws it right at my gut. "No easy way to say it, Michael. She's sleeping with the old man. Your favorite boss."

Simon. I don't . . . He can't . . . The wind's knocked out of me so fast, I almost drop the phone. My arm goes numb and slides down the side of my chest. It can't be.

"I know," Vaughn says. "Makes you want to reach for the Charmin, don't it?" Before I can answer, he adds, "My boy said when they first met him, he thought he was all sly—like we don't watch CNN or nothin'. Anyway, they staked him out—worried he was bein' followed. When the deal's done, he goes back to his car—and one of my boys who's lurkin'—he swears he sees Nora hidin' in the front seat. Big kiss on the lips when Sugar Daddy comes home—she was all over him. And when they climb in the back—Action Jackson, baby. He does her right there—up against the side window. My boy says she's wild too. Likes to take it in the—"

"I don't want to hear it."

"I'm sure you don't, but if she's tuggin' your ya-ya, you gotta know where she's goin' with it. Which means we better make some time to get together."

"What about Si—"

"Ten seconds," he interrupts. "Write this down. A week from Friday. Seven at night. Woodley Park Marriott—Warren Room. Ya got it?"

"Yeah, I—"

"Five seconds. Plenty to spare."

"But we—"

"See you next Friday, Mikey. It'll be worth it." With a click, he's gone.

Alone in the anteroom, I'm pounded by silence. It doesn't make any sense. If she ... she can't. There's no way. With a tight fist, I tap my knuckles against the desk. It can't be. I hit a little harder. And harder. And harder. I hammer the desk until my knuckles are raw. The middle one's starting to bleed. Just like Nora's nose.

Searching for answers, I reread the note I jotted for myself. A week from Friday. Seven P.M. Woodley Park Marriott. Warren Room. I still can't shake the nausea that's choking me, but I remember what he told me right before we split up in the movie theater. Always subtract seven. Seven days, seven hours. In the blink of an eye, seven P.M. becomes twelve noon. A week from Friday becomes this Friday. Tomorrow. Noon tomorrow at the Woodley Park Marriott.

The code was all Vaughn's idea. If the FBI was able to get that close to our meeting at the zoo, it was going to take more than another popcorn kid to buy us some privacy. I take the extra few seconds and scribble in the revised time. Stuffing the handwritten note in my pocket, I dash back to my office—and back to the one person who can answer my questions.

According to the toaster, Nora's in the Residence, but a quick phone call to her room suggests otherwise. I flip through my copy of the President's schedule and see why. In fifteen minutes, the First Family is taking off so they can spend all of tomorrow morning at breakfast fundraisers. New York and New Jersey. Five stops in all, including the overnight. I glance at my watch, then back at

the schedule. If I run, I can still catch her. I tear out of
my office. I have to know. As I pull the main door open,
however, I see someone standing between me and the
hallway.

"How're you doing?" Agent Adenauer asks. "Mind if I
come in?"

CHAPTER 29

"Why so out of breath?" Adenauer asks as he backs me into the anteroom. "Worried about something?"

"Not at all," I say with my bravest face.

"What're you doing here so late?"

"I was going to ask the same thing of you."

He keeps moving forward, pushing toward my office. I stand my ground in the anteroom.

"So where're you running to?" he asks.

"Just going to watch the departure. Takeoff's in ten minutes."

He studies my answer, annoyed that it came so quick. "Michael, can we sit down for a second?"

"I would, but I'm about to—"

"I'd like to talk about tomorrow."

He doesn't blink. "Let's go," I say, turning toward my office. I head for my desk; he heads for the couch. I already don't like it. He's too comfortable. "So what's going on with you?" I ask, trying to move us along.

"Nothing," he says coldly. "I've been looking at those files."

"Find anything interesting?"

"I didn't realize you were originally pre-med," he says. "You're a man of many parts."

I'm ready to mouth off, but it's not going to get me anywhere. If I plan to talk him out of going public tomorrow, he'll need some honesty. "It's the dream of every kid with sick parents," I tell him. "Become a doctor; save their lives. Only problem was, I hated every minute of it. I don't like tests with right answers. Give me an essay any day."

"Still, you stayed with it until sophomore year—even made it through physiology."

"What's your point?"

"No point at all. Just wondering if they ever taught you anything about monoamine oxidase inhibitors."

"What're you talking abou—"

"It's amazing, really," he interrupts. "You have two medications that separately are harmless. But if you mix them together—well, let's just say it's not a good thing." He's watching me way too carefully. Here it comes. "Let me give you an example," he continues. "Let's pretend you're a candidate for the antidepressant Quarnil. You tell your psychiatrist you're feeling bad; he prescribes some, and suddenly you're feeling better. Problem solved. Of course, as with any drug, you have to read the warning label. And if you read the one on Quarnil, you'll see that, while you're taking it, you're supposed to stay away from all sorts of things: yogurt, beer and wine, pickled herring . . . and something called pseudoephedrine."

"Pseudo-what?"

"Funny, that's what I thought you'd say." Losing his smile, he adds, "Sudafed, Michael. One of the world's best-selling decongestants. Mix that with Quarnil and it'll shut you down faster than an emergency brake on a bullet train.

Instant stroke. The strange part is, on the surface it'll look like a simple heart attack."

"You're saying that's how Caroline died? A mixture of Quarnil and Sudafed?"

"It's just a theory," he says unconvincingly.

I give him a look.

"The Sudafed was dissolved in her coffeepot," Adenauer explains. "A dozen tablets, judging by the strength of the sample we scooped up. She never saw it coming."

"What about the Quarnil?"

"She's been taking it for years. Ever since she started working here." He pauses. "Michael, whoever did this did their homework. They knew she was already on Quarnil. And they had to have more than a basic understanding of physiology."

"So that's your grand theory? You think they taught me this at Michigan? Poison 101: How to Kill Your Friends with Household Products?"

"You said it, not me."

We both know it's a stretch, but if he's been through my college transcript, it means they're tearing my life apart. Hard. "You're on the wrong track," I tell him. "I don't play around with drugs. Never have; never will."

"Then what were you doing yesterday at the zoo?" That's what he was waiting for. I walked right into it.

"Watching the monkeys," I say. "It's amazing now—they all have walkie-talkies."

He shakes his head with parental disapproval. "You have no idea who you're dealing with, do you? Vaughn's not just the local bully. He's a killer."

"I know what I'm doing."

"I'm not sure you do. He'll slice you open for fun. You heard what he did to his buddy Morty—piano wire through his—"

"I don't think he did it."

"Is that what Vaughn told you?"

"Just a theory," I say.

He stands up from the sofa and walks toward my desk. "Michael, let me paint a little picture for you. You and Vaughn are standing on the edge of a cliff. And the only way to safety is a rickety bamboo bridge that leads to the other side. Problem is, this bridge is only strong enough to hold one more person. After that, it's going to crumble into the canyon. You know what happens next?"

"Let me guess—Vaughn runs across."

"No. He stabs you in the back, then he takes your canteen, then he swipes your wallet, *then* he runs across. Laughing all the way."

"That's a pretty complex analogy."

"I'm only trying to help you, Garrick. I really am. According to eyewitnesses, you were the last one who saw her. According to the tox reports, she was killed by someone who knows their drugs. According to WAVES records, you let Vaughn in. Now I don't care what your little arrangement was with Nora—either way, I've got him linked to you. You're standing on the edge of a cliff. What do you want to do?"

I don't give him an answer.

"Whatever they're telling you is cow-pie. They don't care about you, Michael."

"And you do?"

"Despite what you think, I don't want to see you throw your life away on this—I respect how you got here. Make it easy on us and I promise you, I'll make it easy on you."

"What do you mean 'make it easy'?"

"You know what we're after. Tie Nora to Vaughn—drug user to drug dealer to drug-related death. Give us that and we're done."

"But they don't—"

"Don't tell me they don't know each other—I'm sick of the bullshit. If you don't give us Nora's link to Vaughn, we'll just use Vaughn's link to you."

"Even if you know it's not true?"

"Not true? Garrick, the only reason I'm holding out this long is because she's the President's daughter—the proof has to be airtight. If I can't get it on her, though, like I said, I'm just as happy to start with you. Y'see, once I put you out there—once the press realizes you're dating—it doesn't take a genius to fill in the rest. It may take an extra step, but Nora's not going anywhere." Pressing the tips of his fingers tightly against my desk, he leans in close. "And unless you give us the link, neither are you."

As he pulls away, I'm speechless.

"I can still help you, Michael. You have my word."

"But if I—"

"Why don't you think about it overnight?" he suggests. He's not changing his deadline, but I still need to stall—until after my noon meeting with Vaughn.

"Can I at least have until the end of the day tomorrow? There's one last thing I want to ask Nora about. If I'm right, you'll understand. If I'm wrong and it doesn't come through—you can slap a big red ribbon on me and I'll personally hand myself to the press."

He takes a moment to think about it. A promise with actual results. "Five o'clock tomorrow," he finally says. "But remember what I told you—Vaughn's just looking for another sucker. As soon as you're in harm's way, he's going to duck out."

I nod as he heads for the door. "I'll see you at five o'clock."

"Five o'clock it is." He's about to leave when he turns

around, his hand still on the doorknob. "By the way," he says. "What'd you think of Nora on *Dateline*?"

My stomach sinks as he pulls tight on the noose. "Why do you ask?"

"No reason. She was pretty good, huh? You'd never know they were in the margin of error—it was like she was holding the whole family together."

I study his eyes, trying to read between the lines. There's no reason for him to bring up poll numbers. "She's strong when she needs to be," I say.

"So I guess that means she doesn't need much protection." Before I can respond, he adds, "Of course, maybe I have it backwards. These media things always make it look like more than it is, don't you think?" With a knowing nod, he turns back to the anteroom, flips off the light switch, and leaves the room. The door slams behind him.

Alone in the dark, I replay Adenauer's last words. Even if we're both still missing a few pieces, he's got enough to make a picture. That's why he's made his decision: No matter what I do, for me, it's over. The only question now is who I'm going to drag down with me.

I wait a full minute after he leaves before I go for the door myself. Regardless of what the schedule says, when it comes to trips, almost nothing moves on time. If they're running late, I can still catch her. Following my usual path, I tear toward the West Wing. But as soon as I hit the night air, I know I'm cutting it close. There's no Marine guard standing under the light outside the West Lobby. The President's not in the Oval. Rushing full speed through the West Colonnade, I fly into the Ground Floor Corridor. As I run, I hear clapping and cheering echoing through the hallway. In the distance, there's the chug of a steam train. First slow, then fast. Faster. As it picks up speed, it's pulsing. Whirring. Humming. The helicopter.

Halfway down the hallway, I make a sharp right into the Dip Room and crash head-on with the last person I expect to see at a departure.

"Where're you heading?" Simon asks, sounding unsurprised.

My jaw tightens. I can't help but picture him and Nora in the backseat. Still, I fight it down. "To watch the departure."

"Since when are you such a tourist?"

I don't answer. I need to hear it from her. Turning away, I step around him.

He seizes me by the arm. It's a tight grip. "You're too late, Michael. You can't stop it."

I pull away. "We'll see."

Before he can respond, I push forward, shoving open the doors of the South Portico. On the driveway, a small crowd of twenty-five is still cheering. Remnants of the post-*Dateline* celebration. On the South Lawn, Marine One is about to take off. I have to squint against the swirling winds, but I still see the fat army-green copter lift off the ground. As my tie and ID are whipped over my shoulder, the force of the wind from the spinning blades crashes against my chest like a wave. Behind bulletproof glass, and in his armor-lined seat, the leader of the free world waves goodbye to us. Two seats back, Nora's caught up in a conversation with her brother. I lift my chin and watch their ascent. Simon's right. There's no way to stop it. It's out of my control. In a heartbeat, the helicopter's lights go off, and the First Family disappears in the black sky. With nothing left to cheer for, the crowd starts to disperse. And I'm left standing there. Alone. Back to a world of one.

*   *   *

"This is stupid," I say as the waitress delivers a pitcher of beer to our table.

"Don't talk to me about stupid," Trey says, pouring himself a glass. "I was there today—I saw it myself. The best thing now is to plan your way out."

As he says the words, my eyes are locked on the waitress who's clearing the table next to us. Like the crane in the old carnival game, she lowers her arm and lifts all the important stuff: glassware, menus, a dish of peanuts. Everything else is trash. With a sweep of her arm, empty bottles and used napkins are brushed into the busboy's plastic bin. With one quick move, it's gone. That's what *she* did—after the fun, jettisoned the trash. Still, I refuse to believe it. "Maybe Vaughn had it wrong. Maybe when Nora gets back—"

"Wait a minute, you're gonna give her a chance to explain? After what she did tonight . . . Are you out of your head?"

"It's not like I have a choice."

"There're plenty of choices. Whole shopping-carts-ful of them: Hate her, despise her, curse her, scorn her, pretend you're nature and abhor her like a vacuum—"

"Enough!" I interrupt, my eyes still locked on the waitress. "I know what it looks like . . . I just . . . We don't have all the facts."

"What else do you need, Michael? She's sleeping with Simon!"

My chest constricts. Just the thought of it . . .

"I'm serious," he whispers, looking suspiciously at the tables around us. "That's why Caroline got killed. She found out the two of them were doing the horizontal Electric Slide, and when she started blackmailing them, they decided to push back. The only problem was, they needed someone to blame."

"Me," I mutter. It certainly makes sense.

"Think about the way it played out. It wasn't just a co-incidence that you wound up in the bar that night; it was a setup. She took you there on purpose. The whole thing—losing the Service, pretending to be lost, even taking the money—that was all part of their plan."

"No," I whisper, pushing myself away from the table. "Not like that."

"What're you—"

"C'mon, Trey, there's no way they knew the D.C. police were going to pull us over for speeding."

"No, you're right—that was pure chance. But if you didn't get pulled over, she would've planted it in your car. Think about it. They set Vaughn up and make it look like you let him in the building. Then when Caroline shows up dead the next morning, between Vaughn and the money, you've got the smoking gun."

"I don't know. I mean, if that's the case, then why haven't they turned me in? I've still got the 'gun.' It's just in po-lice custody."

"I'm not sure. Maybe they're worried the cop'll iden-tify Nora. Maybe they're waiting until after the election. Or maybe they're waiting for the FBI to do it on their own. Five o'clock tomorrow."

We sit in silence and I stare at my beer, studying its ris-ing bubbles. Eventually, I look up at Trey. "I still have to speak to her." Before he can react, I add, "Don't ask me why, Trey—it's just . . . I know you think she's a whack-job—believe me, I *know* she's a whack-job—but under-neath . . . you've never seen it, Trey. All you see is someone you work for—but behind all the tough-stuff posturing and all the public-face nonsense, in a different set of circum-stances, she can just as easily be you or me."

"Really? So when was the last time we did Special K in the bowling alley?"

"I said *underneath*. There's still a girl underneath."

"See, now you're sounding like Mithridates."

"Who?"

"The guy who survived an assassination attempt by eating a little bit of poison every day. When they finally put it in his wine, his body was immune to it."

"And what's so bad about that?"

"Pay attention to the details, Michael. Even though he survived, he still spent every day eating poison."

I can't help but shake my head. "I just want to hear what she says. Your theory's one possibility; there're plenty of others. For all we know, Pam's the one who—"

"What the hell is wrong with you? It's like you're on permanent autopilot!"

"You don't understand . . ."

"I *do* understand. And I know how you feel about her. Hell, even forgetting Nora, I still have my own questions about Pam—but take a step back and put on your rational pants. You're trusting Nora and Vaughn—two complete strangers you've known less than a month—and questioning Pam, a good friend who's been by your side for two years. Please, Michael, look at the facts! Does that make any sense to you? I mean, today alone . . . what're you thinking?"

My eyes drop back to my beer. I don't have an answer.

Early Friday morning, I tear through all four newspapers, checking to see if Adenauer kept his word. The *Herald* has a short piece on some of the conspiracy theories that're starting to develop around Caroline's death, but that's to be expected. More important, Hartson bounced up six points in the polls, a giant leap that takes him out of the margin of error. It's not hard to see why. The front photo in the *Post* is a shot of the whole family on *Dateline*. On the far right, Nora's laughing at her mother's joke. Just another day in the life.

Beyond that, as far as I can tell, it's all okay. Nothing by Inez. Nothing by anyone. Now all I have to do is the hard part. According to the schedule, they should be landing any minute. I tighten my tie and pull it extra tight. Time to see Nora.

Once the Secret Service waves me in, I head straight to her bedroom on the third floor. I stop at her door, my hand poised to knock. Inside, I hear her talking to someone, so I lean in close. But just as I do, the door flies open and there's Nora, radiant in a tight black T-shirt and jeans, cradling a cell phone to her ear, and grinning at me for all of a split second.

"I don't care if he raises *two* million," she shouts into the phone. "I'm not going to dinner with his son!" As I step in, she puts up her pointer finger and gives me the "one more minute" sign.

Based on the schedule, this must be about yesterday's donor receptions. When we first met, she told me it's always like this after the fund-raisers. Every letch with a checkbook starts calling in favors. For the President, they're usually business requests. For Nora, they're personal.

"What the hell is wrong with these people?" she says into the phone, continuing to pace. She gestures me to the daybed, to sit down. "Why can't they buy a Humvee and some Ralph Lauren furniture like everyone else?" With a swing of her arm, she adds, "Tell them the truth. Tell them I think Daddy's little stock baron is a roach and that . . ." She pauses, listening to the person on the other line. "I don't care if he went to Harvard—what the hell does that—" She cuts herself off. "Y'know what? That actually does matter. It matters a lot. Do you have a pencil, because I just figured out what you should say. Are you writing this down? When you get his parents back on the line, tell them that while I am keenly excited by the prospect of having their son cop a feel while sticking his tongue in my ear, I regret that I will not be able to make it. Indeed, while a student at Princeton, I took a vaginal oath that forbids me to date two types of people: First, men from Harvard. And second"—here she starts shouting—"sons of self-important, pretentious, trumpeteering parents who think that just because they know how to get preview-night seats at the trendiest restaurant-of-the-moment, the entire free world must have a price tag on it! Sadly, their darling Jake qualifies for both! Sincerely yours, Nora. P.S.—You're not hot shit, the Hamptons are overrated, and no matter what the maître d' says, he hates you too!" Glaring furiously at the receiver, she shuts off the phone.

"Sorry about that," she says to me, still breathing heavily.

I'm breathing heavily myself and can hardly hear over the thump of my own heartbeat. "Nora, I have something impor—"

Once again, the phone rings.

"Damn!" she shouts, grabbing it. "Yes . . . ?"

As Nora grudgingly agrees to another round of fund-raiser appearances, my eyes roll over to the two framed letters on her nightstand. The first one's in bright red crayon and reads, "Dear Nora: You're hot. Love, Matt, age 8." The other reads, "Dear Nora: Fuck 'em all. Your friends, Joel & Chris." Both are dated during the first months of her father's administration. When everything was fun.

"You've got to be kidding," she says into the phone. "When? Yesterday?"

Listening, she walks across the room toward an antique desk and rifles through a pile of newspapers on top. As she pulls out one of them, I see that it's the *Herald*. "What page?" she asks. "No, I got it right here. Thanks—I'll call you later."

Putting down the phone, she thumbs through the paper and finds what she's looking for. A wide smile breaks over her face. "Have you seen this?" she asks, shoving the paper in my face. "They asked a hundred fifth-graders if they wanted to be me. Guess how many said yes?"

I shake my head. "We'll talk about it later."

"Just guess."

"I don't want to guess."

"Why? Afraid to be wrong? Afraid to compete? Afraid to—"

"Nineteen," I blurt. "Nineteen said yes. Eighty-one would rather keep their souls."

She throws the paper aside. "Listen, I'm sorry about yesterday . . ."

"This isn't about yesterday!"

"Then why're you acting like I stole your Big Wheel?"

"Nora, this isn't the time for jokes!" I seize her by the wrist. "Come with—"

Once again, the phone rings. She freezes. I refuse to let go. We look at each other.

"Are you sleeping with Edgar Simon?" I blurt.

"What?" Behind her, the phone continues to ring.

"I'm serious, Nora. Say it to my face."

Nora crosses her arms and stares blankly at me. The phone finally quits. Then, out of nowhere, Nora laughs. She laughs her heartfelt, deep, little-girl laugh—as honest and free as they come.

"I'm not playing around, Nora."

She's still laughing, panting, slowing down. Now she looks into my eyes. "C'mon, Michael, you can't be—"

"I want an answer. Are you sleeping with Simon?"

Her mouth clamps shut. "You're serious, aren't you?"

"What's your answer?"

"Michael, I swear to you, I'd never . . . I'd *never* do that to you. I'd rather die than be with someone like that."

"So that means no?"

"Of course it means no. Why would I—" She cuts herself off. "You think I'm working against you? You really think I'd do that?"

I don't bother to reply.

"I'd never hurt you, Michael. Not after all this."

"What about *before* all this?"

"What're you saying? That I had my own reason to kill Caroline? That I set this whole thing up?"

"You said it, not me."

"Michael!" She grabs me by both hands. "How could you think that . . . I'd never . . . !" This time, she's the one who won't let go. "I swear to you, I've never touched him—I'd never want to touch him"—her voice cracks—"in my life." She drops my hands and turns away.

"God," she says. "How'd you even get that in your head?"

"It just seemed to make sense," I say.

She stops where she is. Her whole body locks up. Facing just her back, I can tell that one hurt. I didn't mean to—

"Is that what you think of me?" she whispers.

"Nora—"

"Is that what you think?" she repeats, her voice quivering. Before I can answer, she turns back to me, searching for the answer. Her eyes are all red. Her shoulders sag. I know that stance—it's the same one my mom had when she left. The posture of defeat. When I don't answer, the tears trickle down her cheeks. "You really think I'm that much of a whore?"

I shake my head and go to reach out. When I'd thought about how she'd react, I always assumed it'd be raging anger. I never expected a breakdown. "Nora, you have to understand . . ."

She's not even listening.

Stepping into my arms, she curls into a ball and presses her face against my chest. Her body's shaking. Unlike with Pam, I can't argue. Nora's different.

"I'm sorry," she sobs, her voice once again cracking. "I'm sorry you even had to think it."

As her fingers brush against the back of my neck, I hear the hurt in her voice and see the loneliness in her eyes. But as she nuzzles in close, for once, I hold back. Unlike before, I'm not as easily convinced. Not yet. Not until I talk to Vaughn.

Although my destination is the Woodley Park Metro stop, I hop off the train at Dupont Circle. Throughout the twenty-minute walk between the two, I weave through side-streets, cut across traffic, and race against the grain of every one-way I can find. If they're following me in a car, they're lost. If they're on foot . . . well, at least I have a chance. Anything to avoid a rerun of the zoo.

Walking past the restaurants and cafés of Woodley Park, I finally feel at home. There's Lebanese Taverna, where Trey and I came to celebrate his third promotion. And the sushi place where Pam and I ate when her sister came to town. This is where I live—my turf—which is why I notice the unusually clean garbage truck that's coasting up the block.

As it stops on the corner, I barely give it a second glance.

Sure, the driver and the guy emptying the nearby trash cans
look a little too chiseled, but it's not a weak man's job.
Then I notice the sign on the side of the truck—"G & B
Removal." Below the company's name is its phone number, which starts with a 703 area code. Virginia. What's a
Virginia truck doing this far in D.C.? Maybe the work's
contracted out. Knowing D.C.'s public services, it's certainly possible. But just as I turn away, I hear the broken-
glass-raining-bottle-sliding-garbage sound of the metal-can
being emptied into the back of the truck. Sound of the city.
A sound I hear every night, just as I go to b— My legs
cramp up. At night. That's when I hear it. That's when they
come. Never during the day.

I spin around and look down the block. On the far corner, there's a trash can overflowing with garbage. That's
where the truck was coming from. A full trash can. *Behind*
the truck. Pretending not to notice, I dart into the video
store midway up the block.

"Can I help you?" a girl wearing head-to-toe black asks.

"No." Holding imaginary binoculars in front of my eyes,
I press them against the plate glass window, block out the
glare of the sun, and stare out at the truck. Neither of the
two men has given chase. They're just sitting there. While
the loading guy fidgets with something in the back, the
driver twists open his thermos, as if he's suddenly decided
to take a break.

The video clerk is getting anxious. "Sir, are you sure I
can't—"

Before she can finish, I rush out of the video store and
into the dry cleaners next door. There's no one at the
counter, and I don't ring the bell for service. Instead, I dash
to the window and stare outside. Still haven't moved. This
time, I wait a full minute before I bolt next door to the
coffee bar.

A girl wearing an "Eat the Rich" T-shirt asks, "Can I help you with something?"

"No thanks." Glued to the front window, I give it two minutes and a third "Can-I-help-you?" before I race out the door and into the storefront on my left. I keep it going for two more stores—dart inside, wait, then out and to the left; dart inside, wait, then out and to the left. That's how I make my way up the block. Each one I go into, I wait a little longer. Let them think it's a pattern. One more store to go.

At the end of the block I run for the local drugstore, CVS. The way I figure it, I'm up to about a five-minute wait. But this time, after I push open the doors, I just keep running. Straight up the cosmetics aisle. Shampoos on my left, shaving cream on my right. Pharmacy-whiff floats through the air. Without stopping, I dash to the back of the store, around a bend, and down an undecorated back hall. That's when I spot my destination—it's what only a local would know, and what the guys in the garbage truck would never guess—that this CVS is the only store on the block with two entrances. Smiling to myself, I throw open the back door and blow out of there like a cannonball. I look back only once. No one's in pursuit.

Crossing 24th Street, I'm a rage of adrenaline. My body's flushed with the raw energy of victory. Around the corner is the side entrance of the Woodley Park Marriott. Nothing's going to get in my way.

Inside the lobby, I reach into my pants pocket, looking for the note with the exact location. Not there. I reach into my left pocket. Then inside my jacket. Oh, crap, don't tell me it's . . . Frantically, I pull apart each of my back pockets and pat myself down. It's not in my wallet or my . . . I close my eyes and retrace my steps. I had it this morning; I had it with Nora . . . but when I got up to leave . . . Oh, no. My lungs collapse. If it fell out of my pocket, it could still be sitting on her bed.

Struggling to stay calm, I remember the operator's instructions from when I called this morning. Somewhere on the Ballroom Level. As I approach the Information Desk, I stare suspiciously at the three bellmen in the front corner of the lobby. Dressed in starched black vests, they look right at home, but something seems off. Just as the tallest one turns my way, I notice the closing elevator on my immediate right. A quick burst of speed lets me squeeze through the doors just as they're about to slam shut. Whipping around, the last thing I see is the tall bellman. He's not even watching. I'm still okay.

"You got a favorite floor?" a man with a bolo tie and cowboy hat asks.

"Ballrooms," I say, studying him carefully. He hits the appropriate button. He's already pressed 8 for himself.

"You okay there, son?" he quickly asks.

"Yeah. Just great."

"You sure about that? Looks like you can use a little . . . commune with the spirits . . . if you know what I mean." He throws back an imaginary shot of whiskey.

I nod in agreement. "Just one of those days."

"Loud and clear; loud and clear."

The doors slide open on the ballroom level. "Have a good one now," the man with the cowboy hat says.

"You too," I mutter, stepping out. Behind me, the doors slam shut. Straight ahead, at the end of the long corridor, I cross over into the Center Tower of the hotel, where there's an escalator marked "Up to First Floor Ballrooms." I hop on.

At the top, there must be at least three hundred people, mostly women, milling around the hallway. They all have name tags on their shirts and canvas bags dangling from their arms. Convention-goers. Just in time for lunch.

As fast as I can, I weave my way through the crowd of women smiling, boasting, and waving their arms in excitement. Draped across the wall of the main corridor hangs an enormous banner: "Welcome to the 34th Annual Meeting of the American Federation of Teachers." Underneath the banner, I spot the hotel directory. "Excuse me, I'm sorry, excuse me," I say, trying to get there as quickly as possible. Squinting to read the directory, I find the words "Warren Room" followed by an arrow pointing right.

Warren Room. That's it.

I turn to the right so fast I slam into a woman with a small rhinestone-encrusted chalkboard pinned to her blouse. "Excuse me," I say, racing past her.

Outside the entrance to the room, a crowd of teachers is gathered around an oversized corkboard that's resting on a wooden easel. At least a hundred folded-up sheets of paper are tacked to the board—each of them with a different name written on it. Miriam, Marc, Ali, Scott. As I stand there, a flurry of notes are added and retrieved. Anonymous and untraceable. Message board. Warren Room. No doubt about it; this is the place.

As I fight my way through the crowd and toward the board, I'm blocked by a fake redhead who smells like a hairspray bomb went off. Craning my neck to check out the messages, I try to be as systematic as possible. My eyes skim across the notes, scrutinizing names. There it is: *Michael*. I wedge a fingernail behind the pushpin and pull off the note. Inside, it reads, "Dinner's bad tonight. How about tomorrow at Grossman's?" It's signed Lenore.

Scanning names on the message board, I find it again. *Michael*. I stick the first note back on the corkboard and pull out this one. "Breakfast is great. Eight it is. See you then, Mary Ellen."

Frustrated, I jam the note to the board and continue the search.

I find three more notes addressed to Michaels. The only one that's remotely interesting is one that reads "I shaved for you," from a woman named Carly.

Maybe he put it under another name, I think as I stare at the board. Starting over in the top left-hand corner, I take another pass, this time looking for something familiar: Nora, Vaughn, Pam, Trey—none of them come up. Desperate, I open one that's addressed with nothing more than a smiley face. Inside it reads, "Made you look."

I crumple it in a sweaty fist. Teachers. Biting my bottom lip, I scour the board. All around me, dozens of people are adding and removing notes . . . This is no time to lose it . . . I'm sure he's just being careful . . . which means there's something on here that makes sense—

I don't believe it. There it is, right in the center of the board. The name is written with a pen that looks like it's running out of ink. In thin, capital letters. L.H. Oswald. The ultimate patsy. That's me.

I pull the note off as fast as I can and step away from the lunchtime crowd. Rushing down the hallway, I head straight for the bank of elevators at the end of the hall. As I alternate between jogging and speed-walking, I unfold the Oswald note one crease at a time. At the top of the page it reads, "How long before you picked up this one?" Always the smart-ass. Right below that it reads "1027." Exactly what I expected. A room number. When I subtract seven, it's Room 1020.

Inside the elevator, I go straight for the button marked 10. Over and over, my finger attacks it woodpecker-style. Clamping the elevator's brass rail in tight fists, I can barely contain myself. Nine floors to go. My eyes are glued to the digital display, and the moment I hear the ping of arrival, I push forward. The doors are still sliding open when I squeeze through and step out on the tenth floor. Almost there, almost there. But as I trace the logical ascent of room numbers to 1020, I feel the hallway closing in. It starts with a sharp pain in my shoulders and works its way up the back of my neck. For better or worse, Vaughn's going to tell me the truth about Nora. And I'm finally going to get my answer. Of course, I'm not sure what he has, but he said it was worth it. It better be—because I'm counting on taking it straight to Adenauer. No matter how deep it cuts. My stomach starts making noises that are usually reserved for major illnesses. A cold chill slithers up my rib cage and I curse the hotel's air-conditioning. It's freezing in here.

Finally, I'm standing in front of Room 1020. I grasp the doorknob, but before I can turn it, I stop. For the past two days, my mind's been flooded with dozens of questions I couldn't wait to ask. Now, I don't know if I want the answers. I mean, how can they possibly help? Can I believe him? Maybe it's like Adenauer said. Maybe Vaughn can't be trusted.

I think back to our meeting behind the movie theater. His wrinkled clothes. His tired eyes. And the fear on his face. Over and over, I replay the question: If he was trying to set me up, why would he link his name to *me*— the one person he knew was going to look like the murderer? I still can't answer it. So am I ready to take the next step? As with everything lately, I don't have much choice. I wipe my hand on my pants and knock on the door.

To my surprise, it opens a crack when I hit it. I knock

again, opening it a little more. "Vaughn, you in there?" There're some faint voices, but no one answers.

Down the hallway, I hear the return of the elevator. Someone's coming. This is no time to be shy. I push open the door. Blinding sunlight pours through the windows at the far end of the room. As soon as the door slams shut behind me, I notice the TV blaring. No wonder he didn't hear me.

"Whattya doin'? Watching soaps?" I move forward to step into the room, but my foot catches on something and I lose my balance and lurch forward. Putting my hands out to stop my fall, I hit the carpet with a hard thud. And an unnerving squish. My legs are askew, lying over some obstacle.

"What the . . . ?" The whole carpet's soaked. Sticky. And dark red. My hands are covered in it. I roll back to see what I tripped over. No, not what. Who. Vaughn.

"Oh, God," I whisper. His mouth is slightly open. Red spit-bubbles collect in the gap between his teeth and his lower lip. Move, move, move! I scramble furiously to get up, pushing myself away from his body, but my hands slip, sending me straight back toward the floor. At the last second, I catch myself on my elbow, with my tie pinned underneath. Now it matches my hands. More blood.

Shutting my eyes, I let my legs do the rest. They scramble their way across Vaughn's rigid torso, my right knee rubbing against his rib cage. Staggering to my feet, I spin around and get a better look at him lying lengthwise in the entryway. His left forearm is tight against his chest, but his hand's still reaching upward, frozen in a half-open fist. The bullet hole is in his forehead—off center, above his right eye. It's a tight wound—dark and crusted. Blood mats his thick black hair to the bone gray carpet. On his face, one eye stares straight forward; the other skews cock-eyed to the side. Like Caroline's. Just like Caroline's. And all I can think of is the gun inside that utility box by the movie theater. The gun and that damn note—sitting there on Nora's bed.

CHAPTER 30

Trying not to panic, I dart through the open door of the bathroom and yank a white towel from the wall rack. Anything to get rid of the blood. After two minutes of frantic scrubbing, my hands come as clean as they're going to get. I can turn on the faucet, but . . . no, don't be stupid . . . if even a tiny chip of my skin hits the sink . . . Don't give them anything else to trace you to it. Keeping the towel wrapped around my hand, I race out of the bathroom and step over Vaughn without looking down.

I'm at the door. No fingerprints, no physical evidence. All I have to do is leave. Just turn the knob and . . . No. Not like this.

Fighting every fear that's swirling through my gut, I turn around and take a step toward the body. Whatever he did, Vaughn died for this one. For me. For trying to help me. He deserves better than a knee in the ribs.

I squat down next to him and use my towel-wrapped hand to shut his eyes. Patrick Vaughn. The one person who was supposed to have all the answers. "Sleep well," I whisper. It's not the world's best eulogy, but it's better than nothing.

Through the door, I hear a group of voices up the hallway. Whoever did this knew Vaughn was going to be here. Which means they probably knew I was going to— Oh, crap . . . time to leave. I pull open the door and race outside. Two people are waiting for me. Startled, I jump back.

"Sorry, man," one of them says. "Didn't mean to freak you out."

The woman next to him starts to giggle. She's wearing a baby-doll white T-shirt with a little rainbow across her chest. They're just a young couple.

"I-It's okay," I say, trying to hide the towel that's still around my hand. "My mistake."

Brushing past them, I go straight for the elevators. All four are stuck at the lobby. Thirty seconds later, none has moved. "C'mon!" I shout, as I pound the call button. What the hell is taking so long? Down the hallway, I see the giggling couple coming back my way. That was a quick stop— maybe they just forgot something. Whatever it was, they're no longer laughing. As they get closer, there's a new purposefulness in their walk. I'm not sticking around to see what's causing it.

Scanning the hallway, I spot a red-and-white exit sign above what looks like the door to the stairs. On the door is a yellow sticker with bright red letters: "WARNING: Alarm will sound if fire door is opened."

Damn right it will. I shove the door open and hit the stairway. Two steps in, a shrill scream pierces through the horizontal cavern, echoing off the concrete. Most people aren't in their rooms, but I can already hear the results down the stairway, from the ballroom level. Leaving their convention behind, three hundred teachers flood the fire exit. That's what I was counting on: strength in numbers. Thundering down the circular stairs, the human wave of educators absorbs me as one of their own. There's no panic or screaming—these people wrote the book on fire drills. And by the time we pour into the lobby, I've got all the cover I need. Lost amid the canvas bags and colored name tags, I slide out the front door and, at a brisk walk, keep on going. I can't let anyone see me. The best-case scenario now is that they blame Vaughn's death on me. Worst-case . . . I can still see the dark and crusted hole above Vaughn's right eye.

I don't slow down until I'm at least four blocks away. There's a narrow alley with a phone booth in it. Catching my breath, I pull apart my pockets, searching for loose change. I gotta get some help. Trey, Pam, anyone. But just as I pick up the receiver, I slam it back down. What if someone's listening on the other end? No time to take a chance. Do it face-to-face. Keep going. Run.

I crane my neck out of the alley and check the span of the block. No one's there. Bad sign for a usually busy area. On the street, there's a cab stopped at a red light. I wait until the light's about to turn green, then make a mad dash for it. My dress shoes pound against the pavement, and just as the cab starts to inch forward, I reach out and grab the handle of the rear door. The driver slams on the brakes, and I slam into the door.

"Sorry," he says as I clamber inside. "I didn't see y—"

"The White House. Fast as you can go."

"Stop the car!" I shout a few blocks from my destination.

The car jerks to an immediate halt. "Here?" the driver asks.

"Up a little further," I say, eyeing the McDonald's on 17th Street. "Perfect. Stop."

Noticing the newspaper that someone left in the backseat, I pull off my tie and wrap it around the blood-smeared towel.

When I'm done, I stuff both inside the Metro section of the paper, hop out of the cab, and toss a ten-dollar bill in the driver's window. As the cab pulls away, I take a breath and walk as calmly as I can toward McDonald's. Skirting around the line inside, it doesn't take me long to reach the trash cans. With a quick push, I shove the ball of newspaper into the garbage. In here, every red stain is ketchup.

Three minutes later, I'm climbing the stairs of the OEOB. I've got four hours before Adenauer sends me public, and I'm going to need them. Until I can think of something better, keeping the story quiet is all I've got. And when it comes to keeping stories quiet, Trey's the master. My eyes scan the nearby bushes and scrutinize the surrounding columns. Whoever killed Vaughn, if they're going to blame it on me, they might've already notified the Service. From the outside, however, everything looks okay. As I pull open the heavy glass door, I see a small line waiting to get through security—the after-lunch crowd getting back to work. Last in line, I count and study the four uniformed officers on duty. Do they know? Did word get out? Standing there, it's hard to tell. There're two behind the desk who're caught up in small talk and two more by the X-ray machine.

Slowly, I inch closer to the front of the line. Hoping to avoid their gaze, I bury my head in the remaining sections of the newspaper. Almost there—just keep it quiet.

"Always working, aren't you?" a man's voice asks as I feel a hand on my shoulder.

"What the—" I spin around and grab his wrist.

"Sorry," he laughs. "Didn't mean to scare you." Looking up, I see the blond hair and warm smile of a young lawyer, Howie Robinson. Sweetheart of a guy; works in the VP's office.

"N-No, it's okay." I peek over my shoulder and check

out the guards. All of them are watching us. Too much movement.

"You at the party yesterday?" Howie asks.

"Yeah," I say, taking another glance at the guards. The two at the desk are starting to whisper.

"You shoulda seen it, Garrick," Howie says. "I snuck my sister and nephew in. This kid—let me tell you, he went nuts—I think he's in love with Nora."

"Yeah . . . great," I mutter. The guard at the desk gets up and walks over to the two at the metal detector. Something's wrong.

"You okay?" Howie asks as we inch forward. I'm next in line.

"Sure," I nod. I should get out of here right now. Go home and—

"Next!" the uniformed officer says. All eyes are on me.

Refusing to look up, I pull out my ID, punch in my code, and step through the turnstile. Bolting as fast as I can through the metal detector, I don't even hear the sound of the alarm going off. The uniformed officer grabs me tightly by the arm. "Where you going, hotshot?"

I don't believe it. "You don't understand . . ."

"Empty your pockets. Now."

I catch myself before I say another word. It's not a security alarm; it's just the metal detector. "Sorry," I say, snapped back to reality. "Belt. It's my belt."

A wave of his handheld detector verifies the rest.

"Take it easy, man," Howie says as he pats me on the back. "You gotta get out of here once in a while—join us for basketball or something. It's good for the soul."

"Yeah, I'll do that," I say, forcing a grin.

He heads to the right, while I make my way to the left. Although I'm surrounded by fellow employees, the hallway's never felt more empty. As I'm about to turn the corner, I take one last look at the uniformed officers. The two behind the desk are focused on the line. The one by the X-ray is still watching me. Pretending I don't notice, I hold my breath and make a quick right. The moment I'm out of sight, I take off. Straight for Trey's.

I throw open the door to Trey's office and check his desk. He's nowhere in sight.

"Can I help you?" his officemate Steve asks.

"Have you seen Trey?" I shoot back, struggling to look like I'm not out of breath.

"No, I—"

"I saw him," a third officemate interrupts. "I think ... uh ... I think he had his head stuck up the First Lady's rear end."

"That's right," Steve says, laughing. "Hell of a photo-op. We brought in some kids. Put her in a living room setting. Fluffy throw pillows. Soft focus on the camera. Real deliverable."

Press secretaries. Always comedians.

I grab a Post-it, jot a quick note, and slap it against Trey's computer screen. "Find me. 911!"

"Great code," Steve says. "Way better than Morse."

Storming back to the hallway, I slam the door as I leave. Once again, I'm drowning in silence. I have to talk to someone—even if it's just to figure out the next step. As I nervously check the marble hallway, the first person who comes to mind is Pam. I can go to her and ... What am I thinking? I can't. Not after what happened. Not yet. Besides, with Vaughn dead, this whole thing's about to jackknife. Which means the last place I want to be is behind the wheel of the truck. I don't care if it's an election year— I've been avoiding it since I left the hotel—I need to go upstairs.

*   *   *

Racing across the soft red carpet of the Ground Floor Corridor, I see a phalanx of sightseers in the middle of a VIP White House tour led by one of the Secret Service tour guides. As I blow past them, two people take my picture. They think I'm famous. If things keep going in this direction, they're going to be right.

I don't stop until I reach the uniformed guard who sits outside the movie theater. "Can I ask you a favor?" I beg, my voice racing.

He doesn't answer. He just looks at me, judging.

"I know this is going to sound crazy," I begin, "but I was using the bathroom in the OEOB . . ."

"Which one?"

"On the first floor—the one near Cabinet Affairs. Anyway, I'm in the stall and I hear two interns bragging about the . . . uh"—I motion over my shoulder toward the utility box—"about the gun you keep in there." He sits up straight. "Maybe I heard it wrong—they were whispering the whole time—but it sounded like they either *knew* a gun was there, or that they *had taken* a gun from there. It may just be bragging but . . ."

He leaps from his seat, sending his chair sliding backwards across the marble floor. Warning me to stand back, he pulls a set of keys from his belt and heads for the still semidented utility box. I watch silently as he fights with the lock—it's stuck. My whole body's burning up. It's like someone's pounding on my skull. All I hear is the jingling of keys. He's standing in front of me—I can't see a thing. It looks like he's pulling on the door. Harder. Harder. Then . . . I hear the scratch of rusted metal. The door swings open, and the guard looks back at me. Stepping out of the way, he lets me see it for myself. The gun is sitting right where it's supposed to be.

"Sorry," I say with forced relief. "I must've heard it wrong."

"It appears that way, doesn't it?"

I shrug and turn around, backtracking past the Lincoln statue. The moment I turn the corner, I shoot out of there, running as fast as I can through the Ground Floor Corridor. It's a good sign, but she could've easily put it back.

Three-quarters down the hallway, as I approach the main staircase to the Residence, I finally slow down. As always, my ID and a decisive nod get me past the downstairs guard. "One up," he whispers into his walkie-talkie.

I fly up the stairs two at a time knowing I'm going to be stopped. I could've called her to clear me in, but I didn't want anyone to know I was coming. Surprise is all I have left—and despite the gun, I still want to see her reaction myself. Sure enough, as I reach the State Floor, two Secret Service officers block my way.

"Can I help you?" the one with black hair asks.

"I need to see Nora. It's an emergency."

"And you are . . ."

"Tell her it's Michael—she'll know."

Checking me out, he takes a quick look at my ID. "I'm sorry—she asked not to be disturbed."

I try to keep calm. "Listen, I don't mean to be a pain. Just give her a call. It's important."

"You already got your answer," the second officer adds. "What word didn't you understand?"

"I understood all of them. I'm just trying to save us some headache."

"Listen, sir . . ."

"No, you listen," I push back. "I came here completely civilized—you're the one who picked the fight. Now I've got a real crisis to deal with, so you have one of two choices: You can make a simple phone call and explain that it's an emergency, or you can brush me away and deal with the wrath of Nora yourself when she finds out that you're the one who caused this shithouse of a mess. Personally, I'm partial to the latter—I love bloodsports."

He studies me carefully, moving in close. Eventually, he growls, "Those're my orders . . . sir. She's not to be disturbed."

Refusing to give in, I look up at the small surveillance camera hidden in the air-conditioning vent. Time to go over his head. "Harry, I know you're watching . . ."

"I'm asking you to leave," the officer warns.

"Just call her," I plead toward the ceiling. "All you have to do is—" Before I can finish, three plainclothes officers run up the stairs. Leading the way is Harry.

"We told him she didn't want to be bothered," the officer explains.

"I have to see her, Harry. I—" The officer cuts me off by seizing the back of my neck in a tight grip.

"Loosen up," Harry warns.

"But he—"

"I want to hear what he has to say, Parness." Parness gets the picture. Uniformed officers don't argue with plainclothes.

Following instructions, he relaxes just a bit.

"Now where's the fire?" Harry asks.

"I have to speak to her."

"For personal reasons or official White House business?"

"C'mon, you know what it's about. You were there that night."

He throws me the most subtle of nods.

"It's important, Harry. I wouldn't come like this if it weren't. Please."

The other officers stare him down. They all know Nora's

orders. She didn't want to be bothered. Still, it's all in his court. Finally, he says, "We'll call her."

I smile faintly.

He heads into the nearby Usher's Office and picks up the phone. I can't hear what he's saying, and to make sure we don't read his lips, he turns his back to us.

When he's done, he comes back into the stairwell. He looks at me deadpan. "Today's your lucky day."

I breathe deeply once and run for the stairs. Out of the corner of my eye, I catch sight of the officer with the black hair opening the visitors log to record my name. Shaking his head, Harry stops him. "Not this one," he says.

CHAPTER 31

A<small>S</small> I enter Nora's room, I see her quickly close a desk drawer. Spinning around to face me, she puts on a big smile. It fades almost instantly. "What's wrong?"

"Where've you been for the past two hours?"

"R-Right here," she says. "Signing letters. Now tell me what's—"

"Don't lie to me, Nora."

"I'm not lying! Ask the Service—I haven't left once."

It's a hard one to argue, but there's still . . . "Have you seen a little scrap of paper?" I ask, scouring her bed.

"What're you—"

"A scrap of paper," I repeat, raising my voice and checking the hand-sewn carpet. "I think I dropped it this morning. It had the words 'Woodley Park Marriott' on it."

"Michael, calm down. I don't know what you're talking about."

"I'm not doing this anymore, Nora. That's it. It's over. I'm sorry if it's going to get you in trouble, but you're the only one who can back me up. All you have to say is Simon had the money, and then I can—"

She grabs me by the shoulders and stops me in my place. "What the hell are you talking about?"

"They killed him, Nora. Blew a hole straight through his forehead."

"Who? Whose forehead?"

"Vaughn. They killed Vaughn." As I say the words, a geyser of emotion erupts up my throat. "His eyes . . ." I say. "Why did he . . . He was helping me, Nora. *Me!*"

Her mouth quivers and she steps away from me.

"What're you . . ."

Before I can finish the thought, she backs into the bed and sits down on the mattress. Her hand is cupped over her mouth; her eyes well up with tears. "Oh my God."

"I'm telling you, they're going to come straight at me for this one . . ."

"Okay, hold on a second," she says, her voice shaking. "When did this . . . Oh, God . . . Where did it happen?"

"At the hotel . . . we were supposed to meet at the Marriott. But when I walked in the room—he was just lying there, Nora—no one to blame but me."

"How did he . . ."

"A bullet. Right in his head. He probably opened the door and—one shot. That's all it took. Where he fell . . . everything . . . his brain . . . He was all over the carpet."

"And you . . ."

"I fell over him . . . on him. They'll find my prints everywhere—the doorknob . . . his belt . . . all they need's a hair follicle. He was just lying there. Blood was foaming at his mouth . . . hardened bubbles . . . but he wouldn't move . . . couldn't. It was everywhere, Nora . . . my hands . . . my tie . . . everywhere . . ."

She quickly looks up. "Did anyone see you?"

"I was worried the FBI was there, but I don't think I would've gotten this far if they—"

The sound of her telephone screams through the room. Both of us jump.

"Just let it ring," she tells me.

"But what if it's . . ."

The two of us look at each other. Safe versus sorry. Naturally, she's the first to react. "I should . . ."

". . . pick it up," I agree.

Slowly, Nora heads for her desk. The ringing continues, insistently.

She lifts the receiver. "Hello?" she says, hesitating. In an instant, she looks my way. Not good. "Yeah. Yeah, he is," she adds as she holds out the phone in an outstretched arm. "It's for you."

Anxiously, I take the phone. "This is Michael," I say, fighting vertigo.

"I knew you'd be there. I knew it! What the hell is wrong with you?" someone shouts. The voice is familiar.

"Trey?"

"I thought you were going to stay away from her."

"I-I was . . . I just—"

"It doesn't matter. Get out of there."

"You don't understand."

"Trust me, Michael—you're the one who's missing it. I just got a call from—"

"They put a hole in Vaughn's head," I blurt. "He's dead."

Trey doesn't even pause. After four years riding shotgun to the First Lady, he's used to bad news. "Where did it happen? When?"

"Today. At the hotel. I walked in and found the body. I didn't know what to do, so I ran."

"Well you better keep running. Get out of there, now."

"What're you talking about?"

"I just got a call from a friend at the *Post*. They're

breaking the story on their Web site—Caroline's murder, the tox reports, everything."

"Are they naming a suspect?"

Trey gives me another long pause. "He said you're gonna take a hit. I'm sorry, Michael."

I close my eyes. "Are you sure? Maybe he was fishing for—"

"He asked me how to spell your name."

My legs go numb and I lean back on the desk. That's it. I'm dead.

"Are you okay?" Trey asks.

"What's he saying?" Nora demands.

"Michael, are you there?" Trey's voice squawks from the phone.

"Michael, are you okay?"

The whole world blurs in front of me. It's like that night on the roof—only this time, it's reality. My reality. My life.

"Listen to me," Trey says. "Get out of the Residence— get away from Nora. Come down here and we can—" He falls suddenly silent.

"What?" I ask.

"Oh, no," he moans. "I don't believe this."

"What? Is it about the story?"

"How'd they—"

"Just tell me, Trey! What is it?"

"I'm watching it scroll across the AP screens—it's on the wire service, Michael. They must've picked it up from the *Post*'s site."

Son of a bitch. There's no stopping it now. "I have to get out of here."

"Where're you going?" Nora asks.

"Don't tell her!" Trey shouts. "Just go! Now!"

Panicking, I slam down the phone and run for the door. Nora follows.

"What'd Trey say?" she asks.

"It's out. The story's out. Caroline. Me. Everything. He says it's all over the wires."

"Did they mention me?"

I stare at her. "For God's sake!"

"You know what I mean."

"Actually, Nora, I don't." Turning my back on her, I stride to the main staircase.

"Michael, I'm sorry!" she calls out.

I don't stop.

"Please, Michael!"

I keep going.

I'm about to leave the hallway when she gives it her last shot. "That's not the best way out!"

For that, I stop. "What do you mean?"

"If you take the stairs, you'll run right into the Service."

"You got any better ideas?"

She takes me by the hand, leading me farther up the hallway. I resist just enough to let her know I'm not her puppet.

"Spare me the power-play, Michael. I'm trying to get you out of here."

"You sure about that?"

She doesn't like being accused. "You think I did this?"

I'm not sure what to think and this is no time to get into it. "Just lead the way."

In the far corner of the hallway, she shoves open two swinging doors as we bound into what looks like a small pantry. Mini-refrigerator, bar sink, a few glass cabinets full of cereal and snacks. Just enough to save you from walking down three flights to the kitchen. In the corner of the room, on top of the counter, are two square metal panels with compact-disc-size windows cut into them. Grabbing the handles at the bottom of one of the panels, Nora lifts it open like a stubborn window. Behind the panel is a small crawl space that looks big enough for two people.

"What?" Nora asks. "You've never seen a dumbwaiter before?"

I quickly piece together the floor plan in my head. The President's dining room is right below us, and the kitchen's on the Ground Floor. Seeing that I get it, she adds, "Even Presidents have to eat." She motions her chin toward the tiny elevator.

"Hold on—you don't expect me to . . ."

"You want to get out of here?" she asks.

I nod.

"Then get in."

CHAPTER 32

We ride down to the kitchen in complete darkness and absolute silence. As we arrive on the Ground Floor, the tiny round window is filled with light. Nora peeks out, lifts the door, and looks both ways. "Let's go," she says.

As she fights her way out of the dumbwaiter, her knee digs into my rib cage. All I can think about is Vaughn.

Crawling into the light, I see that we're in the back corner of the kitchen—in a small room by the banks of industrial freezers. Through the doorway, I spot a uniformed guard outside the tradesmen's entrance. Closer to us, a chef and an assistant are prepping dinner on the stainless steel countertops. Caught up in their motions, they don't even notice us.

"This way," Nora says, pulling me by the hand.

She opens the door to our far right and leads us out of the kitchen, back into the Ground Floor Corridor.

"There!" someone shouts from the hallway.

Fifty flashbulbs explode in our eyes. Instinctively, Nora steps in front of me, shielding me from the— Wait . . . it's not the press. Not with Instamatics. It's just another tour group.

"Nora Hartson," the guide announces to what looks like a group of diplomatic VIPs. "Our own First Daughter!"

The crowd breaks into spontaneous applause and the guide unsuccessfully reminds them that they're no photos allowed. "Thank you," Nora says, excusing herself from the still snapping group. She stands in front of me, trying to keep me hidden the entire time. I know what she's thinking: If my photo's going to be in all of tomorrow's papers, the last thing she needs is a group shot. As the tour group moves on to its next destination, Nora seizes my wrist. "Let's go," she whispers, trying hard to stay in front of me. "Hurry."

I duck my head low and follow her lead. We speed-walk up the hallway past my favorite uniformed officer. He doesn't move; he doesn't touch the walkie-talkie. As long as we avoid the stairs to the Residence, he apparently doesn't care. That's why she didn't take us out the back of the kitchen.

Making a sharp left outside the Dip Room, Nora opens a door flanked by bronze busts of Churchill and Eisenhower, which leads into a long hallway with at least forty six-foot-high stacks of chairs. Storage for state dinners. As we make our way down the hall, the floor starts to slant downward. We pass a pyramid of crated produce and then the bowling alley on our left. Nora maintains her swift pace as she takes us deeper down into the labyrinth. I'm starting to feel far from daylight.

"Where are we going?"

"You'll see."

As the hallway levels off, it leads into another perpendicular corridor, but this one is far dingier. Low ceilings. Not as well lit. The walls are dank and smell like old pennies.

It doesn't make any sense. We're in the basement—

Nora's running out of room. And I'm running out of time. Still, she isn't slowing down. She makes a hairpin right and keeps going.

My eye starts twitching. My heart feels like it's going to burst out of my chest. "Stop!" I shout.

For the first time, she stops and listens.

"Tell me where we're going, for God's sake!"

"I told you, you'll see."

I don't like the dark. "I want to know now," I say suspiciously.

Once again, she stops. "Don't worry, Michael," she says in a soft voice. "I'll take care of you."

I haven't heard that tone since the day with my dad. Still, now's not the time. "Nora . . ."

Without a word, she turns away, striding to the far end of the basement hallway. There's a steel door with an electronic lock. If the rumors are right, I'm pretty sure it's a bomb shelter. Nora punches in a PIN code and I hear the thunk of locks tumbling.

With a sharp tug, Nora pulls open the door. Instantly, my eyes go wide. It can't be. But there it is in front of me. The greatest myth in the White House—a secret tunnel.

Nora looks me in the eye. "If it's good enough for Marilyn Monroe, it's good enough for you."

CHAPTER 33

With my mouth hanging down by my ankles, I'm staring into a secret tunnel below the White House. "When did . . . Where . . . ?"

She steps in close and takes me by the hand. "I'm here, Michael. It's me." Reading my bewildered expression, she adds, "They may get it wrong in the movies, but that doesn't mean it's bullshit."

"Still, the—"

"C'mon, let's go." By the time I blink, she's gone. Zero to sixty. Instantly.

The tunnel itself has cement walls and is better lit than I would have expected. It looks like a straight shoot under the East Wing. "Where does it let out?"

She doesn't hear me. Either that or she's not telling.

At the end of the tunnel is another steel door. Frantically, Nora taps in her code. There's a noticeable shake in her hands. We stare at the electronic lock, waiting anxiously for the thunk of access. It doesn't come.

"Try again," I say.

"I'm trying!" Once again, she enters a code. Again, nothing.

"What's the problem?" I ask. I'm clenching my fists so hard, my arms are aching.

"Let us out!" Nora shouts, lifting her head.

"Who—?" I follow her gaze to the corner of the ceiling. There's a small surveillance camera pointed right at us.

"I know you're watching!" she continues. "Let us out!"

"Nora," I say, gripping her arm, "maybe we shouldn't—"

She pushes me away. She's looking at that camera the same way she looked at the Secret Service our first night out.

"I'm not playing around, asshole. He's just my boyfriend. Call Harry—he cleared him in."

Now she's gambling. Harry may've cleared me in, but he certainly doesn't know we're running out.

"Can you believe this?" she says to me, forcing a flighty laugh and flipping her hair back. "I'm *so* embarrassed." I get the idea. But it takes a superhuman effort to relax my hands and slow my breathing.

"No, don't sweat it." I casually rest one arm against the wall. "Same thing happened last time I was in the Gulag."

It's a great moment. It's also fake. That's probably how it's always been.

Nora looks at me with a small, appreciative grin, then glances up at the camera. "So? Did you call him?"

Silence. I'm almost faint with the desire to turn and run. Then, out of nowhere—the pop of a churning lock. Nora pulls open the door and lets me out. The camera can't spot us anymore.

"We're in the basement of the Treasury Building," she whispers.

I nod. Next door to the White House.

"You can walk up the parking ramp to East Exec, or

take the stairs and leave through Treasury. Either one'll lead outside."

I go straight for the stairs. Nora follows. Turning around, I hold my arm up and stop her, keeping her at the threshold of the tunnel.

"What?" she asks.

"Where're you going?"

She looks at me with the same look she gave my dad when he was hysterical. "I meant what I said. I'm not leaving you, Michael. Not after all this."

For the first time since we started running, my eye stops twitching. "Nora, you don't have to—"

"Yes. I do."

I shake my head. "You don't, Nora. And while I appreciate the offer, we both know what'll happen. If you're caught running around with the press's main suspect . . ."

"I don't care," she blurts. "For once, it's worth it."

Stepping in close, I try to force her back toward the door. She doesn't budge. "Please, Nora, it's no time to be stupid."

"So now it's stupid to want to help?"

"No, it's stupid to shoot yourself in both feet. The moment the press puts us together, they're going to leap for your throat. On every page one. Above every fold. 'First Daughter Linked to Murder Suspect.' It'll make your *Rolling Stone* story look like the back page of *People* magazine."

"But—"

"Please—for once—don't argue. Right now, the best thing I can do is lay low. If you're around . . . it'll be impossible, Nora. At least this way, we're both safe."

"You really think you're safe?"

I don't answer.

"Please be careful, Michael."

I smile and head for the stairs. Hearing her like that . . . it's not easy to leave.

"So where're you going?" she calls out.

I freeze. My eyes narrow. And slowly, I turn around. Behind her, the outside of the reinforced steel door is disguised to look like an ordinary exit. The whole thing's an illusion. "I'll tell you when I get there," I reply. With nothing left to say, I turn away and start walking. Then jogging.

"Michael, what about—"

Then running. Keep going. Don't look back. Behind me, I hear her calling my name. I let it roll off.

Bounding upstairs two at a time, I race up the interior stairwell of the Treasury Building. Nora's voice has all but faded away and the only thing I'm focused on is the small black-and-white sign that reads "Exit—Lobby Level." Approaching the door, I want to kick it open and make a mad dash out the front. But, afraid of the attention, I inch it open and peek out—just enough to figure out where the hell I am. Down the hall in front of me is a metal detector and a sign-in desk. Behind the desk, with their backs to me, are a pair of uniformed Secret Service. Damn—how am I going to get through— Wait—I don't have to get through anything. I'm already in. All I have to do is leave.

Stepping out of the stairwell, I lift my shoulders, stuff confidence into my posture, and move firmly toward the turnstile at the exit. As I get closer, the officers are checking IDs and clearing in visitors. Neither of them has noticed me.

I'm less than ten feet from the turnstile. Do I need to swipe my ID to get out? Studying the woman in front of me, I don't think so. I step into the turnstile, but just as the metal bar presses against my waist, the officer closest to me turns my way. I force a smile and give him a two-fingered salute. "Have a good one," I add.

He nods back without a word. But he's still staring. As I pass through the turnstile, I feel his eyes on the back of my head. *Ignore him. Don't panic. Only a few more steps to the glass door that leads outside. Almost there. A little farther.* Across the street, I see the white-and-gold entrance of the Old Ebbitt Grill. This is it. If he's going to stop me, it's going to be in the next five seconds. Four. Three. I lean into the door and push it open. Two. This is his last chance. One. The door swings back behind me, leaving me alone on 15th Street. I'm out.

The first one I spot is right outside the building—heavy build, dark suit, dark sunglasses. There's another midway up the block. And two uniformed officers on the corner. They're all Secret Service. And from what I can tell, they've got the whole block covered.

Panic sends me spiraling as I struggle to stay on my feet. They mobilized so quickly . . . Of course, that's their job. Avoiding the agent in front, I move as fast as I can down the block. *Keep your head low—don't let them get a good look.*

"Stop right there!" the agent shouts.

I pretend I don't hear him and keep going. Fifty feet away, there's another agent waiting. "Sir, I'm asking you to stop moving," he says.

My hands quickly fill with sweat. My breathing's so labored, I feel it reverberate. He whispers something into the collar of his shirt. In the distance, I hear the shrill wail of a police siren. It's coming my way. Closer. I check every direction for a way out. I'm surrounded. Shooting out of the Southeast Gate, two motorcycle cops fly toward me. I freeze as soon as I see them. Instinctively, I raise my hands to surrender.

To my surprise, however, they blow right by me. Followed by a limo, followed by another limo, followed by a Blazer, followed by a dark van, followed by an ambulance, followed by another two motorcycle cops. As they disappear up the street, the agents follow. Within seconds, the clouds clear and a blue calm is returned to the block. Frozen in place, I let out a nervous laugh. It's not a manhunt—it's a motorcade. Just a motorcade.

With no time to wait for the Metro, I hop in a cab and head back to my apartment. The note with Vaughn's meeting place wasn't in Nora's room, which means she either picked it up, or it's still sitting on my bed. It may be risky to go back home, but I need to know which. Before the cabbie drops me off, I ask him to circle the block—just so I can check license plates. No press passes; no federal plates in sight. So far, so good.

"Right here's fine," I tell him as he approaches the service entrance around back. I toss him a ten-dollar bill, slam the door, and bolt up a short flight of stairs. I do my best to look around, but I can't afford to waste time and risk getting caught. With the *Post* reporting that I'm the main suspect, Adenauer won't wait till five o'clock to pick me up. He's going to try and do it now. Of course, the only reason I agreed to go in was because I thought I'd have the info from Vaughn. After what happened, though . . . well . . . not anymore.

Walking cautiously through the back of the lobby, I keep an eye out for anything that's out of the ordinary. Mailbox room, welcome area, front desk—it all looks undisturbed. Sticking my head around the corner, I scan the main entrance of the lobby and look out the front door. This time tomorrow, the press is going to be camped out there—unless I can figure out a rock-solid way to prove it's Simon.

Convinced that I'm alone, I rush past the front desk, toward the elevator. I push the call button, the doors slide open, and I move forward.

"Where you going?" a deep voice asks.

I spin around, crashing into the now-closing elevator doors.

"Sorry, Michael," he laughs. "Didn't mean to startle you."

I take a deep breath. It's just Fidel, the doorman. He's watching TV behind the front desk—and with the sound turned off, he's easy to miss.

"Damn, Fidel, that was a full heart attack!"

He just smiles as wide as he can. "Orioles are beating the Yanks—top of the second."

"Wish them luck for me," I say, turning back to the elevator. I push the call button and once again the doors slide open.

As I step inside, Fidel calls out, "By the way, your brother stopped by."

Just as the elevator's about to slam shut, I shove my arm between the doors. "What brother?" I ask.

Fidel looks alarmed. "W-With the brown hair. He was here ten minutes ago—said he had to grab something from your apartment."

"Did you give him my key?"

"No," Fidel says, stammering. "He said he had it." Picking up the phone, he adds, "Do you want me to call the—"

"No! Don't call anyone. Not yet." I jump back into the elevator and let the doors close. Instead of pressing the button for the seventh floor, I press six. Just to be safe.

When the elevator opens on the sixth floor, I dash directly toward the stairs that are straight across the hall. Quietly, I run up to the seventh. If it's the FBI hoping to catch me by surprise, I shouldn't be here. But if it's Simon—if he killed Vaughn to keep things quiet, he could be planting somethi— I cut myself off. Don't think about it. You'll find out soon enough.

On the landing of the seventh floor, I peer through the small window in the stairwell door. The problem is, my apartment's all the way at the end of the hall, and I can't see there from here. There's no way around it—I have to open it for a look. I put my hand on the doorknob and take a deep breath. It's okay, I tell myself. Just turn it. Nice and easy. Not too fast.

I slowly pull the heavy metal door toward me. Each creak sounds like a tiny scream. Down the hall, I hear voices mumbling. More like arguing. Using my foot as a doorstop, I prop open the door and carefully peer into the hallway. As I ease the door backwards, the hall starts to come into view. The elevator . . . the trash room . . . my neighbor's door . . . my door—and the two men in dark suits fidgeting with my locks. Sons of bitches are breaking in. My upper body is about halfway into the hall when a loud ping announces the arrival of the elevator. The doors slide open, and the two men in dark suits look straight up—at me.

"There he is!" one of them shouts. "FBI! Stay where you are!"

Directly across from me, Fidel steps out of the elevator, oblivious to what's going on. "Michael, I wanted to make sure you—"

"Grab him!" the second agent shouts.

Grab him? Who's he talking t— My head jerks back as I'm plowed into from behind. I feel an arm slide across my throat, and another under my armpit. These guys came prepared.

Panicking, I jab my elbow backwards as hard as I can

and connect squarely with my attacker's gut. He lets out a throaty gasp, and as his grip goes weak, I slip free.

"What the . . . ?" Fidel blurts. Down the hallway, the other two agents are charging toward us.

"Get back in the elevator!" I shout at Fidel. The doors are about to close.

Before anyone can react, I dive forward, tackling Fidel and hurling us both toward the elevator. We squeeze in just as the doors slam shut. Over my shoulder, I swing my arm back and pound the button marked Lobby. As we start moving, I hear the FBI agents pounding on the elevator door. It's too late.

My hands are shaking as I help Fidel up from the floor.

"T-That's the guy who said he was your brother," Fidel says.

Still shaking, I barely hear what he's saying.

"Are they really the FBI?" he asks.

"I think so . . . I'm not sure."

"What did you—"

"I didn't do anything, Fidel. Whoever comes, you tell them that. I'm innocent. I'll prove it." Looking up, I see we're almost at the lobby.

"Then why're they—?"

"They'll be coming down the stairs," I interrupt. "When you see them, tell them I went out the back. Okay? I went out back."

Fidel nods.

The moment the elevator doors open, I dart out toward the front of the lobby. As an escape route, it may be more conspicuous, but Connecticut Avenue is the only place I'm going to catch a cab. Of course, as I bound out of the building, there's not a single one around. Damn. I start running up the block. Anything to get away. If I plan on saving myself, I need to catch my breath and think.

A minute into my mad dash, I turn around just as two of the FBI agents burst out the front door. They didn't believe Fidel—they only sent one out back.

Across the street, there's a cab coming in the opposite direction. *"Taxi!"* I scream.

Finally, something goes my way. He pulls a wide, illegal U-turn and stops right in front of me.

"Where you going?" he asks in a loose Midwestern accent. As he turns around to face me, he's got a thick arm wrapped around the back of the passenger seat.

"Anywhere . . . Straight . . . Just get out of here," I say, kicking myself for coming to find the note. I knew this would happen.

He slams the gas and sends me flying backwards in my seat.

I turn to look back. The agents are shouting something, but I can't hear them. It doesn't matter—they've answered my question. The word's out. And all eyes are on me.

Ten minutes later, we pull into an above-ground parking garage right off Wisconsin Avenue. The cabbie swears it's the closest pay phone that can't be seen from the street. I take his word for it.

"Do you mind waiting?" I ask as I hop out to the phone.

"You pay, I stay—American way."

I pick up the receiver and dial Trey's number. His line rings twice before he picks up.

"This is Trey."

"How we doing?" I ask.

"Mi—" He stops himself. Someone's in the office. "Where the hell are you? Are you okay?" he whispers.

"I'm fine," I say unconvincingly. In the background, I hear the other phones in his office ringing. "What's happening there?"

Another two phones go off. "It's a friggin' zoo—like nothing you've ever seen. Every reporter in the country has called us. Twice."

"How bad am I going to be hit?"

There's a short pause on the other line. "You're Dan Quayle."

"Have they issued—"

"No statements from anyone—Simon, Press Office, not even Hartson. Rumor is they're going live at five-thirty—to make sure they have something for the nightlies. I'm telling you, man, I've never seen anything like it—the place is paralyzed."

"And your friend at the *Post*?"

"All I know is they got a photo of you standing outside the building—probably the one taken by that photographer. Unless they get something better, he says it's running A1 tomorrow."

"Can't he—"

"I'm trying my best," he says. "There's just no way around it. Inez got everything—you leaving Caroline's office, the WAVES records, the tox reports, the money . . ."

"She found the money?"

"My buddy says she knows someone at D.C. police. They typed your name in and it came up under 'Financial Investigations.' Ten thousand big ones seized from Michael Garri . . ." Trey's voice trails off. "What?" he asks, sounding muffled. He's got a hand over the receiver. "Says who?"

"Trey!" I shout. "What's going on?"

I hear people talking, but he doesn't answer.

"Trey!"

Still nothing.

"*Trey!*"

"Are you there?" he finally asks.

I'm so sick, I'm going to vomit. "What the hell's going on?"

"Steve just got back from the Press Office," he says hesitantly.

"Is it bad?"

I can't hear it, but I know I'm getting the rub. It's a record-breaker. "I wouldn't panic until they confirm—"

"Just tell me what it is!"

"He says they found a gun in your car, Michael."

"What?"

"Wrapped in an old map; hidden in your glove compartment."

I feel like I just took a kick in the neck. My body's reeling. I hold on to the phone booth to stand up. "I don't own a . . . How did they . . . Oh, jeez, they're going to find Vaughn . . ."

"It's just a rumor, Michael—for all we know, it's—" Once again, he stops short. So does everyone in the background. The place is silent. All I hear are phones ringing. Someone must've walked in.

"What're they saying?" a female voice demands. I recognize it instantly.

"Here you go, Mrs. Hartson," another voice says.

"I gotta run," Trey whispers into the phone.

"Wait!" I shout. "Not y—" It's too late. He's gone.

Lowering the phone to its cradle, I look over my shoulder for help. The only one there is the cab driver, who's already lost in his newspaper. I hear the taxi coughing and wheezing from years of abuse. The rest of the garage is silent. Silent and abandoned. I put my hand over my stomach and feel the knife twisting in my gut. I have to . . . I have to get help. I pick up the receiver and stuff another set of coins in the pay phone. Without even thinking, I dial her number. It's the first thought that comes to my brain.

Forget what happened—call her. I need the front lines; I need to know what's going on; and more than anything else, I need some honesty. Guerrilla honesty.

"This is Pam," she says as she picks up the phone.

"Hey," I say, trying to sound upbeat. After our last conversation, she's probably ready to rip me apart.

She pauses long enough to let me know she recognizes my voice. I close my eyes and get ready for the tongue-lashing.

"How you doing, Pete?" she asks with a strain in her voice.

Something's wrong. "Should I—"

"No, no," she interrupts. "The FBI never called—they wouldn't trace the phone lines . . ."

That's all I need to hear. I slam the phone back into its cradle. I have to hand it to her—regardless of how pissed she was, she came through. She'll be taking major heat for that one. But if they've already closed in on my closest friends . . . Damn, maybe Trey didn't even know. Maybe they already . . . I back up from the phone and race toward the cab. "Let's get out of here," I shout to the driver.

"Where to?" he asks as the tires screech toward Wisconsin Avenue.

I've only got one other option. "Potomac, Maryland."

CHAPTER 34

"Almost there," the cabbie announces twenty minutes later.

I raise my head just enough to peek out the left window. Flower beds, manicured lawns, plenty of cul-de-sacs. As we drive past the recently built McMansions that dot Potomac's way-too-conscious-to-be-natural landscape, I slouch down in the seat, trying to stay out of view.

"Not a bad neighborhood," the driver says with a whistle. "Check out the lawn frogs on that one."

I don't bother to look. I'm too busy trying to come up with other places to run. It's harder than I would've thought. Thanks to the FBI's original background check, my file is filled with my entire network. Family, friends. That's how they check you out—they take your world. Which means if I'm looking for help, I have to step outside the maze. The thing is, if someone's outside the maze, there's usually a good reason for it.

"There it is," I say, pointing to what I have to admit is a stunning New England–style colonial on the corner of Buckboard Place.

"Turn here?" the cab driver asks.

"No, keep going straight." As we pass the house, I turn

around and watch it through the back window. About two hundred yards away, I point to the empty driveway of a messy little rambler. Unkempt lawn, peeling shutters. Just like our old place. The black eye of the block. "Pull in here," I say, studying the dusty front windows. No one's home. These people work.

Without a word, we roll into the driveway, which runs perpendicular to the street. He pulls the cab in so that everything but the back window and the trunk are hidden by the house next door. It's a great hiding spot—a room with a view.

Diagonally down the block, I keep my eyes on the old colonial. It's got a spacious two-car garage. The driveway's empty.

"So how long until he gets back?" the cabbie asks. "You're running up some serious tab."

"I told you, I'll cover it. Besides," I add, looking down at my watch, "he'll be here soon—he doesn't work full days anymore."

Settling in for the wait, the cab driver reaches for the radio. "How about I turn on the news, so we can—"

"No!" I bark.

He raises an eyebrow. "Whatever you want, man," he says. "Whatever you want."

Within fifteen minutes, Henry Meyerowitz turns onto the block in his own personal midlife crisis—a 1963 jet black Porsche roadster convertible. I shake my head at the SMOKIN personalized plates. I hate my mother's family.

To be fair, though, he's the only one who ever reached out to me. At the funeral, he told me I should give him a call—that he'd love to take me out to a nice dinner. When he heard I got a job at the White House, he reiterated the offer. Hoping for a family connection that might mean something, I took him up on it. I remember trekking out here the week after I started work—even used a AAA map to negotiate the side streets—but it wasn't until I was weaving my way through the actual neighborhood that I realized they didn't invite my dad. Just me. Just the White House.

Too bad for them it's always been a package deal. I don't care if they're the other side of the family—they did the same thing with my mom. If they didn't want my parents, they couldn't have me. After sitting parked around the corner for close to an hour, I drove to a gas station pay phone and told him something had come up. I never contacted him again. Until now.

As Henry makes a left onto Buckboard Place, I reach for the taxi door handle. I'm about to open it when I notice the black sedan that follows him into his driveway. Two men get out of the car. Dark suits. Not as built as the Secret Service. Just like the guys in my building. Approaching my cousin, they open a folder and show him a photograph. I'm pretty far up the block, but I can read the body language from here.

I haven't seen him, my cousin says with a shake of his head.

Do you mind if we come in anyway? the first agent asks, pointing toward the door.

Just in case he shows up, the second agent adds.

Henry Meyerowitz doesn't have much of a choice. He shrugs. And waves them in.

The front door of the New England–style colonial is about to slam in my face.

"Let's get out of here," I tell the driver.

"Huh?"

"Just get out of here. Please."

The FBI agents are following my cousin inside. Instinctively, the cabbie turns the ignition and the engine roars.

"Not yet!" I yell. It's too late. The car coughs to life. The agent closest to the door stops. I don't move. From the doorway, the agent turns around and looks our way. He's squinting hard, but doesn't see a thing. It's okay, I tell myself. From this angle, I think we're—

"There!" he shouts, pointing right at us. "He's up there!"

"FBI!" the first agent yells, pulling out a badge.

"Get out of here!" I shout to the cab driver.

He doesn't move.

"What're you waiting for!?"

The sad look in his eyes says it all. He's not risking his livelihood for a fare. "Sorry, kid."

I look out the back window. Both agents are closing in. The decision's easy. I'm not going to be a prisoner. Out here, I still have a chance. And if I give myself up, I'll never find the truth.

I kick open the door and scramble out. Knowing that there's only a few dollars left in my wallet, I tear off my presidential cufflinks, toss them in the cabbie's window, and take off. Unsure of where to go, I dart farther up the driveway and around the side of the house. Behind me, the cab driver pulls backwards at a 45-degree angle—just enough to block the driveway and get in the agents' way.

"Get this piece of crap out of here!" one of the agents yells as I tear into the backyard. I grab two posts of the wooden fence surrounding the yard and hoist myself over. Landing in the backyard of the abutting house, I hear the FBI climbing over the cab, their shoes thunking against its metal hood.

"He's in the other backyard!" one of the agents shouts.

I dash out toward the front of the house and find myself on a neighboring block. Rushing across the street, I run up a driveway toward the backyard of a third house. In this yard, the fence at the rear of the property is too high to scale, but the ones at the sides are shorter. I go over one into the backyard on the right. From there I hurdle the back fence and exit out onto another new block. From the quick look I got as they ran toward the cab, both agents appeared to be in their early forties. I'm twenty-nine. That should be all it takes.

"Give it up, Garrick!" one of them shouts, only a backyard behind.

That's when I remember I'm a lawyer.

House by house, he's closing in. I feel it at each fence. His voice keeps getting louder. When I started running, he was at least a minute behind. Now it's less than thirty seconds. But as I land in the backyard of a beige Tudor-style home, I look up just in time to see my best way out: an enormous blue-and-white Metro bus blows past the driveway trailing a smokescreen of black exhaust. As it passes, its brakes scream. It's stopping! I sprint down the driveway. Sure enough, as I turn onto the street, it's waiting at the corner.

"Hold it!" I scream at the top of my lungs.

On board, an old woman carrying a mesh bag of groceries is teetering down the stairs.

I'm running full speed; it's almost within reach. She reaches the sidewalk and waves goodbye to the bus driver. My hand brushes against the bus's back right tire as I lunge for the door.

"FBI!" the agent shouts behind me. "Don't let him in!"

I reach out my hand . . . almost there . . . If I make it in, I'm as good as—

The door slams before I get there. That's the end. I missed it . . . I can't believe I missed it. The bus lurches forward, kicking a cloud of black smoke in my face. I turn around and spot the FBI agent less than fifty feet up the block. I'm too out of breath . . . I can't . . . But there's no choice. I dash across the street and up the driveway of the nearest house. Within seconds, I'm in the backyard. Unlike the others, this yard is enclosed by a black wrought iron gate. At six feet, it's too high to climb. I look for another way out. The agent's already in the driveway. Nowhere to go but up.

Grabbing a nearby patio table, I shove it against the back of the fence and hop on top of it. It's just the boost I need. From this height, I wrap my hands around two of the black metal spikes and pull myself up. Behind me, the agent's closing in. As I cautiously maneuver my body over the fleur-de-lis-shaped spikes, I feel them pressing against my thigh. Slowly . . . slowly . . .

"Got you!" the agent shouts. He grabs my ankle as I straddle the tall fence.

I lash out and kick him directly in the face. He reels backwards and lets go just as I clear the fence, but as I hop down to the ground I'm off balance. I land on my ankle and it twists below me. A hot spasm shoots up my left leg. Stumbling to my feet, I ignore the pain and limp forward. On the other side of the fence, the agent's already on the table.

My ankle's throbbing, but I run. Keep running.

He scurries up the fence in a mad dash and throws one leg over. He's wobbling, but all he has to do is—

"*Aaaaah!*" he screams.

I spin around. On top of the fence, he's got a spike straight through his thigh. Blood's slowly running down his leg. I cringe just looking at it.

"Are you okay?" I call out.

He doesn't answer; his face is contorted in pain.

In the distance, I hear the second agent. "Lou, are you there? Lou!?" He'll find his partner soon enough. Time for me to leave.

Throwing all my weight on my good leg, I limp out of

there as fast as I can. Five blocks later, I spot another bus. This time, I make it on board. As the doors slap shut, I hear the howl of a nearby ambulance. That was fast. Standing at the front of the bus, I stare out the windshield and watch the flashing lights head our way.

"You gonna pay the fare, or what?" the bus driver asks, snapping me back to reality.

"Y-Yeah," I say. As the ambulance shoots past us, I reach into my wallet and slide a dollar into the fare machine. On my way to the back of the bus, I feel my pager go off in my pocket. Pulling it out, I recognize the number instantly. It's my own. Whoever it is, they're in my office.

It takes twenty minutes before the bus pulls into the back parking lot of the Bethesda Metro station. From here, I have access to the subway and all its connections—downtown, out of town, and anywhere in between. But first, I have to find a phone.

Ducking inside the Metro building, I avoid the crowd that's headed for the absurdly long escalators, and instead head for the bank of pay phones on my right. There're still a few coins floating around my pocket, but after my conversation with Pam, I'm not taking any chances. Rather than dialing my number directly, I pick up the receiver and call the 800 number that'll connect me with Signal. Once I'm routed through the White House phone system, it'll be that much harder to trace my call.

"You have reached the Signal switchboard," a mechanical female voice says. "For an office extension, press one." I press 0.

"Signal operator 34," someone quickly answers.

"I just got paged by Michael Garrick—can you connect me?"

"What's the last name again?"

She sounds honest about that one. Good—it's not everywhere yet. "Garrick," I say. "In the Counsel's Office."

Within seconds, the phone to my office is ringing. Whoever's in there, they're getting nothing but the word "Signal" on caller ID.

"Pretty smart," Adenauer answers. "Going through Signal like that . . ."

My fist tightens around the receiver. I knew it was going to be him. In fact, I'm surprised it took him this long. "I didn't do it," I insist.

"Why didn't you tell me about the money, Michael?"

"Would you've believed me?"

"Try me. Where'd you get it from?"

I'm sick of him jerking me around. "Not until I get some guarantees."

"Guarantees are easy—but how am I going to know you're telling me the truth?"

"I had a witness. I wasn't alone that night."

There's a short pause on the other line. Remembering Vaughn's advice about tracing calls, I look at the second hand on my watch. Eighty seconds max.

"You're lying to me, Michael!"

"I'm not—"

Adenauer interrupts with what sounds like the buzz of a tape recorder.

"Last night being Thursday the third," a female voice says.

Oh, no, I think to myself. Before she stopped the tape . . .

"I mean, that's correct," my recorded voice says. *"Anyway, I was driving along 16th Street when I saw—"*

"Before we get there, was anyone with you?"

"That's not the important part—"

"Just answer the question," Caroline says.

"No. I was alone."

"Did you forget we had the tape?" Adenauer asks, sounding way too self-satisfied.

The second hand's spinning. Thirty seconds to go. "I-I swear to you . . . that's not the—"

"We found Vaughn," Adenauer says. "And the gun. No more lies, Michael. Did you do it for Nora?"

"I'm telling you—"

"Stop bullshitting me!" Adenauer explodes. "Every time, it's a new damn story!"

Twenty seconds. "It's not a story! It's my life!"

"All you have to do is come in." Worried that I'm going to run, he's trying to make nice. "If you help us—if you give us Nora—I promise you, the whole process'll be a lot easier."

"That's not true."

"It *is* true. Be smart about it, Michael. The longer you're out there, the worse it looks."

Ten seconds. "I have to go," I say, my voice shaking. "I need . . . I need to think."

"Just tell me you're going to come in. You give the word and we're there for you. Now what do you say?"

"I have to go."

He's out of patience and I'm about to hang up. "Let me tell you something, Michael—remember when Vaughn said it took eighty seconds to trace a phone call?"

"How'd you—"

"He was wrong," Adenauer says. "See you soon."

I slam down the phone and slowly turn around. Behind me is a mob of commuters angling for space on the escalators. At least three people are staring directly at me—a woman with Jackie O sunglasses and two men looking up from their newspapers. Before I can react, all three disappear on the escalators. Half the crowd's going down to the subway; the other half's going up to the street exit. I scan the rest of the mob, looking for suspicious glances and forceful strides. This is Washington, D.C., at rush hour. Everyone qualifies.

My body tenses. I'm tempted to run, but I don't. It doesn't make sense. They can't trace a call through Signal. It's impossible—he just wants me to panic; make a mistake. Calling his bluff, I take a hesitant step toward the crowd. I don't care how good they are, nothing's that fast. I keep telling myself that as I slide onto the escalator and get absorbed by the mob.

Clenching my jaw, I try to ignore my ankle. Nothing to make me look out of place. I glance around as we reach the top, but everything's quiet. Cars whiz by; commuters disperse. Following two other passengers to the nearby taxi stand, I wait in line and hail a cab. Just another normal day at work.

"Where to?" the cabbie asks as I slide inside.

Ignoring the question, I look nervously left, then right. Searching for a security blanket, my hand moves instinctively for my tie. As I reach for it, though, I realize it's gone. I almost forgot. It was covered in blood.

"Let's hear it," the cabbie calls out. "I need a destination."

"I don't know," I finally stammer.

He looks at me in the rearview. "You okay back there?"

Once again, I ignore the question. I can't believe Adenauer has the tape—I knew I should've never let Caroline start recording—even with my stopping it early, there's enough on there to . . . I don't even want to consider it. Leaning forward on the stained cloth seats, I cuff my hands around my swollen ankle and feel like I'm about to collapse. I may've made my way out of the suburbs, but I've got to figure something out. I still need somewhere to go. Somewhere to think.

Home's no good. Neither is Trey's apartment. Or Pam's. There're a few friends from college and law school, but if the FBI's sending people out to my cousin, that means they're covering my file—and then some. Besides, I'm not going to put any more friends—or relatives—at risk. Once again, my eye starts twitching. There's no way around it. Everything's on me.

All that leaves is a nearby motel. It's not a bad option, but I have to keep it safe. No credit cards—nothing they can trace me with. I open my wallet and see that I'm flying on fumes; all that's left is twelve dollars in cash, my lucky two-dollar bill, and a Metro farecard. First things first. "How about a cash machine?"

"Now you're talkin'," the cabbie says.

Sliding my card into the ATM, I punch in my four-digit PIN code. Even with the bank's daily limit of six hundred dollars on withdrawals, that should be more than enough to get me through the night. Then I can start working on a solution.

Entering the dollar amount, I wait as the machine whirs through its motions. But instead of hearing the shuffling of bills being distributed, I see a digital message appear on-screen: "Transaction cannot be processed at this time."

Huh? Maybe I tried to take out too much. I hit the Cancel button to start again. This time, a new message appears: "To retrieve your card, please contact your branch manager or your local financial institution."

"What?" I hit Cancel again, but there's no response. The machine resets itself and the words "Please insert card" appear on-screen. I don't understand. How'd they . . . I look straight at the ATM and remember that the FBI's background check includes a disclosure of all current bank accounts. "Damn!" I shout, pounding my fist against unbreakable glass. They took my card. Refusing to give up, I pull out a credit card and shove it into the machine. All I need is a cash advance. Once again, though, the words flash up on-screen: "Transaction cannot be processed at this time."

The sun has barely started to set, so when I turn around, it's still light enough for the cabbie to read the expression on my face. He puts the car in gear. He knows a dead fare when he sees one.

"Wait . . . !" I call out.

The tires screech. He's gone. And I'm out on the street.

The last time this happened, I was seven. On the way home from the local barbershop, Dad decided to take a new shortcut through the repaved schoolyard. Two hours later, he'd forgotten where we lived. He could've picked up a pay phone and called my mom, but that thought never occurred to him.

Of course, back then, it was an adventure. Lost among the labyrinth of apartment buildings, he kept joking that wherever we were, it was going to be his new spot for hide-and-seek. I couldn't stop laughing. That is, until he started to cry. Frustration always did that to him. That high-pitched wail of adult desperation is one of my earliest memories— and one I wish I could forget. Few things slice as deep as a parent's tears.

Still, even as he fell apart, he tried to protect me, shielding me inside the glass walls of a phone booth. "We have to sleep here until Mom finds us," he said as it started to grow dark. I sat down in the booth. He leaned against it outside. At seven years old, I was rightfully scared. But not half as scared as I am now.

CHAPTER 35

By a quarter to six, I'm tucked away in the best Metro-accessible, high-traffic, twenty-four-hour hiding spot I could think of—Reagan National Airport. Before settling on my current location, I made one stop at the luggage store outside Terminal C. For two dollars and seventy-two cents, I cashed in my lucky two-dollar bill and all the change in my pocket for a defective black plastic garment bag that was about to be sent back to the manufacturer. Who cares if the zipper never opens?—it's not like I need it for travel. I just need to look the part. And when I combine it with a canceled ticket I fished out of the garbage, it does the job.

Since then, I've been huddled in the far corner of Legal Seafood—the only restaurant in the airport that airs the local news, and therefore the best place to nurse my last twelve dollars.

"Here's your soda," the waitress says, lowering the glass to my table.

"Thanks," I say, my eyes glued to the TV. To my surprise, the local affiliate has preempted its programming to cover the daily press conference live. It's a power move by the stations—putting pressure on the Press Office to get on with the story. Naturally, the White House pushes back. CNN is one thing, but they can't have the whole nation going live—it sets people into a panic and sends votes to Bartlett. So they do the best thing they can think of—they run the agenda backwards. Start with the small stories; work up to the home run.

As a result, we're watching a wire-rimmed State Department bureaucrat explaining to eighty-five million people the benefits of the Kyoto Accords and how they'll affect our long-term trade positions with Asia. In one massive collective yawn, thirty million people change the channel. For the networks, it's a ratings nightmare. For the Press Office, it's a TKO. The message is sent—don't fuck with the White House.

Convinced that only the diehards are left, Press Secretary Emmy Goldfarb and the President approach the podium. She's there to speak; he's there to let us know it's serious. A candidate who can handle a crisis.

No more wasting time—she gets right into it. Yes, Caroline Penzler's death was not from natural causes. No, the White House never knew. Why, because the toxicology reports were only recently completed. Everything else can't be discussed because they don't want it interfering with the current investigation. Like before, she tries to keep it short and sweet. She doesn't have a chance. Once the smell of blood's in the air, the press licks their chops.

In nanoseconds, the reporters in the room are on their feet and shouting questions.

"When'd the tox reports come back?"

"Is it true the story was leaked to the *Post*?"

"What about Michael Garrick?"

Reaching for my soda, I inadvertently knock it over. As it waterfalls off the table, the waitress runs to my side.

"Sorry about that," I say as she throws down a rag.

"Not a big deal," she replies.

On-screen, the Press Secretary explains that she doesn't want to interfere with the FBI's ongoing investigation, but there's no way the reporters'll let her avoid it that easily. Within seconds, the questions once again fly.

"Have you confirmed murder, or are you still considering suicide?"

"What about the ten thousand dollars?"

"Is it true Garrick's still in the building?"

She's getting hammered up there. Someone's got to save her. Sure enough, the President steps in. To the American people, he looks like a hero. To the press—as soon as they saw him in the room, they knew they were going to get him. The President doesn't just hang out at briefings. Still, it quiets the crowd.

Locking his hands on to the sides of the podium, he picks up where Goldfarb should've never left off. This is an FBI case. Period. *They* investigated; *they* ran the tests; and *they* kept it quiet to prevent exactly what's happening from happening. Within seconds, he's passed the buck. He's so good at this, it's scary.

When he's convinced he's clean, he tackles the questions. No, he can't comment on Vaughn or myself. Yes, that would greatly impede the investigation. And yes, in case the press corps forgot, people are still innocent until proven guilty, thank you very much.

"However," he says as the room falls silent. "I do want to make one thing perfectly clear . . ." He pauses just long enough to get us all salivating. "If this is a murder . . . whatever it takes, we will find the person who killed my friend, Caroline Penzler." He says it just like that. *"My friend,* Caroline Penzler." Right there, it all shifts. From defense to offense in a matter of syllables. I can feel his

poll numbers rocket. Screw Bartlett. There's nothing America loves more than a little personal vengeance. When he's done, he looks straight at the camera for the big closer. "*Whoever* they are, *wherever* they are, these people will pay."

"That's all we have to say," the Press Secretary jumps in. Hartson leaves the room; the press keeps shouting questions. It's too late, though. It's six o'clock. For now, the local news is going to have to pick up the pieces, and all they have is Hartson's positively flawless sound bite. I have to hand it to them. That thing was choreographed better than the First Lady's birthday party. Every moment was brilliant—right down to Goldfarb pretending she was overwhelmed. The President steps in, sounds fair, and saves the day. Play up the dead friend; sprinkle in some retaliation. Tough on crime never had it so good.

Of course, as the smoke clears, all I can focus on is who the press was asking about. Not Simon. And thankfully, not Nora. Just me. Me and Vaughn. Two dead men.

By eight o'clock, to avoid the glut of Friday night little-kid sitcoms, the restaurant switches to CNN—just in time to watch the story run again. When they're finished showing Hartson's sound bite, the anchorwoman says, "Tomorrow's *Washington Post* reports that this man, Michael Garrick, is currently being sought for questioning by authorities." As she says my name, my ID photo flashes on-screen. It happens so fast, I barely react. All I can do is look away. When she's done, I pick my head up and check the bar. Waitress. Bartender. Businessmen expense-accounting their salmon dinners. No one knows but me.

Having overstayed my welcome with the waitress, I eventually move over to the restaurant bar, where the bartender's used to stranded commuters who just want to watch a little TV. "Do you have a lost-and-found?" I ask him. "I think I left some stuff here during my last trip."

He pulls a cardboard Heinz ketchup box from behind the bar and plops it in front of me. Amid the keychains and lost paperbacks, I pick out a pair of sunglasses and a Miami Dolphins baseball cap. My dad would've taken the box.

"All set?" the bartender asks.

"It's a start," I say, plastering the Dolphins on my head.

By nine o'clock, I've seen the story run four times. By ten, it's double that. I'm not sure why I'm still watching it, but I can't help myself. It's like I'm waiting for it to change—for the newscaster to come on and say, "This just in—Nora Hartson admits drug problem; Counsel's Office is completely corrupt; Garrick innocent." So far, it hasn't happened.

When the neon lights of the restaurant blink off, I take the hint and limp out toward the boarding gates. My ankle's better, but it's still stiff. Adjusting my glasses, and with my garment bag trailing behind me, I sink into a corner seat and crane my neck to see the televisions suspended from the ceiling. Three more hours of CNN brings the total up to twenty. Each time, the words are identical. Sure, there're some permutations—the anchorperson changes adjectives and intonations just to keep things lively—". . . *this* man, Michael Garrick . . ." ". . . this *man*, Michael Garrick . . ." ". . . this man, *Michael Garrick . . .*"—but the message is always the same. It's my face up there; my life; and as long as I sit here in my own little pity party, it's only going to get worse.

At two-fifteen in the morning, a delayed flight from Chicago arrives at the US Airways terminal. When the crowd clears off the plane, two security guards approach and tell me that the terminal is now closed.

"I'm sorry, but we're going to have to ask you to leave," the second guard says.

Trying to make sure they don't get a good look at my face, I keep my head down and give them nothing but Dolphins logo. "I thought you were open twenty-f—"

"The gates close for security purposes. The main terminal's open all night. If you want to wait out there, you're welcome to."

Refusing to look up, I take my paper-thin garment bag and leave CNN behind.

By three A.M., I'm spread out on a small bench next to the information booth, with the garment bag draped over my chest. In the past fifteen minutes, the guards have chased away two homeless men. I'm wearing a suit. They leave me alone. It's not the best hiding spot, but it's one of the few that'll let me sleep. Unlike New York, the subway here closes at midnight. Besides, if the authorities *are* searching, they're looking for someone trying to leave. I want to stay.

Over the next fifteen minutes, I'm having a hard time keeping my head up, but I can't calm myself enough to actually welcome sleep. Naturally, I'm wondering about Nora and how she's going to react, but the real truth is, I can't stop thinking about my dad. By now, the press is already bulldozing through the rest of my life. It's not going to take long to find him. I don't care how independent he is, he's not built for something like this. None of us are. Except maybe Nora.

Fading out, my mind trips back to Rock Creek Parkway. Trailing Simon. Getting caught with the money. Saying it was mine. That's where the snowball started. Barely two weeks ago. From there, the images rush forward.

Vaughn dead in the hotel room. Nora on the White House roof. Caroline's eyes, one straight, one cockeyed. The moments blur together, and I mentally sketch how it could've been different. There was always a simple way out, I just . . . I didn't want to take it. It wasn't worth it. Until now.

In Washington . . . No. In life . . . there're two separate worlds. There's the perception of what's important, and then there's what actually is. It's been too long since I realized there's a difference.

As my eyelids sway shut, I pull the garment bag all the way up to my chin. It's going to be a cold night, but at least I've made my decision. I'm sick of being stuck in a phone booth.

CHAPTER 36

Simon wakes up at four-thirty in the morning and hustles through a quick shower and shave. On most days, he sleeps until at least five-thirty, but if he wants to beat the press today, he's going to have to get out early. Naturally, there's no paper on his doorstep yet, but he checks anyway.

Outside, where I'm sitting, it's still completely dark, so as he goes from bedroom to bathroom to kitchen, I follow the trail of lights. As near as I can tell, he's got a tasteful house in a tasteful neighborhood. It's not the best of Virginia's sprawling suburbs, but that's why he chose it. I remember him telling the story during the last staff retreat. The day he and his wife were going to bid on the house, their Realtor called about a brand-new home in a coveted section of McLean. Sure it was more expensive, Simon's wife argued, but they could afford it. Simon wanted nothing to do with it. If he was going to teach his kids proper values, they had to have something to shoot for. There's nothing gained by always being on top.

Looking back, the story's probably bullshit. Up until a few weeks ago, Simon was a man to be taken at his word.

Which, in a strange way, is precisely why I'm now sitting in the passenger seat of his black Volvo.

It's still pitch dark as Simon steps out the back door of his house. I watch him lock up and check the yard. It's still early. No reporters in sight. Moving toward the driveway, he's wearing the strut of a man without a care. More like a careless man to me. He doesn't even see me as he heads to the driver's side of his car. He's too busy thinking he got away with it.

Tossing his briefcase into my lap, he slides into the leather seat like it's just another day.

"Morning, Mr. Worm—I'm the early bird," I announce.

Startled, he clutches his chest and drops his keys. Still, I have to hand it to him. Within seconds, his ironing-board shoulders rise in irritation. As he brushes a hand through his salt-and-pepper hair, his unshakable calm flows back even faster than it left. He turns my way, and the light in the car shines in his face. With an angry tug, he slams the door shut and darkness falls.

"I thought you'd wait until I got to the office," he says in a voice that's pure gravel.

"You think I'm that stupid?" I ask.

"You tell me—who's the one sleeping in my car?"

"I didn't sleep here, I was . . ."

". . . just stalking your boss at five in the morning? C'mon," Simon adds. "You didn't really think you were going to get away with it, did you?"

"Get away with—?"

"It's over, Michael. Better to plead insanity than innocence." Laughing to himself, he adds, "I was right, though, wasn't I? Caroline set it up; you collected the cash?"

"What?"

"I wouldn't have even thought it if I hadn't spotted you

that night. Then when I heard what happened to my payment—when the cops confiscated the ten grand, that's where it all fell apart, isn't it? She thought you were holding out on her. That's why you did it, right? That's why you killed her?"

"*I* killed her?"

"It's a fool's way out, Michael—it was *then* and it is *now*. You'll never pull it off twice."

"*Twice?*" I don't know what he's talking about, but it's clear he's got his own version of reality. Time to call bullshit. "I'm not a moron, Edgar. I saw you at Pendulum that night. I was there."

"There's a good expla—"

"Spin it whichever way you want, you were still paying the blackmail. Forty grand to keep a lock on the closet." He shoots me a look. "Does your wife know? Have you—"

"Are you wearing a wire?" he interrupts. "Is that why you're here?" Before I can react, his arm springs out, slapping an open palm against my chest.

"Get the hell off me!" I shout, pushing him away.

Realizing there's nothing in my shirt, he sits back in his seat.

I shake my head at the man who used to be my boss. "You haven't even told her yet, have you? You're out playing around and she still doesn't know. What about your kids? You lying to them too?" Realizing I have his attention, I motion over my shoulder toward his house. "They're the ones who pay for it, Edgar."

Once again, he runs his hand through his hair. For the first time since I met him, the salt-and-pepper doesn't go back in place. "I have to tell you, I didn't think you had it in you, Michael." The way his voice slowly lingers on each word, I assume he's talking out of shock. Maybe even fear.

But it's not. It's disappointment. "All this time, I always figured Caroline as the ruthless one. Now I know better."

"I didn't—"

"Tell whoever you want," he says, staring straight out the front windshield. "Tell the papers; tell the whole damn world. I'm not embarrassed."

"Then—"

"Why'd I pay the money?" He looks over my shoulder, back at his tasteful house. "How do you think the other sixth-graders are going to react when the newscaster says Katie's daddy likes to sleep with other men? And what about the ninth-grade boys? And the one who's about to hit college? It was never about me, Michael. I know who I am. It's for them."

Listening to his strained words, I notice how tightly he's holding the steering wheel. "So that's why you told Caroline that I was the one who had the money?"

"What are you talking about?"

"The next morning. After the meeting. You told her the forty thousand dollars was mine—that I made the drop."

He lets go of the wheel and looks at me completely confused. "I think you have it backwards. All I told her was that I wanted to see your file. I figured if you were the blackmailer . . ."

"Me?"

"Dammit, Michael, stop lying to my face! You picked up the money—you're a co-conspirator. I know that's why you killed her."

He says something else, but I'm not listening. "You never told her the money was mine?" I ask.

"Why would I do that? If Caroline was in on it—which I always thought she was—and she knew I found out—she'd have gutted me to keep me quiet."

I feel the blood rush from my face. I don't believe it

. . . all this time . . . she made it up to keep me quiet—and to point the finger at Simon. It's perfect when you think about it; she was playing us against each other. Searching for solid ground, I wrap my fist around the door handle. Slowly, painfully, I turn to look at Simon. And for the first time since we followed him out of the bar, I entertain the thought that he might be innocent.

"Are you okay?" he asks, reading my expression.

It doesn't make any sense. "I didn't do it—I never killed anyone. V-Vaughn . . . and Trey . . . even Nora said . . ."

"You told Nora about this?"

Behind us, up the street, a bright light cuts through the darkness. A car just turned onto the block. No, not a car. A van. As it gets closer, I notice the broadcasting antenna attached to its roof. Oh, shit. That's no mom-mobile. That's a news van. Time's up.

I throw open the door, but Simon grabs me by the arm. "Does Nora know? Did she tell Hartson?"

"Let go!"

"Don't do this now, Michael! Please! Not while my kids are in the house!"

"I'm not telling anyone. I just want to get out of here!" Jerking my arm free, I scramble out of the car. The news van is almost in front of the house.

"Ask Adenauer! I didn't do anything wrong!" Simon shouts.

I'm about to take off, but . . . it's hard to describe . . . there's pain in his voice. With seconds to spare, I turn back for one last question. Until now, it's the only one I've been afraid to ask. "Tell me the truth, Edgar. Have you ever slept with Nora?"

"What?"

That's all I need to hear.

The door to the news van slides open and two people

hop out. It's hard not to miss the interior glow of Simon's car. "Up there!" a reporter shouts as the cameraman turns on his light.

"Start the car and get out of here," I tell him. "And tell Adenauer I'm innocent."

"What about—"

I slam the car door and dart for the wooden fence in the backyard. Like a spotlight in a prison break, a blast of artificial light floods through the back window of Simon's car and lights the right side of his face. By the time they pan across the rest of the backyard, I'm gone.

"Operator 27," a male voice says, answering the phone.

"I just got paged," I say to the Signal operator. "Can you please connect me to Room 160½."

"I need a name, sir."

"It's not assigned to anyone. It's an intern room."

He puts me on hold to verify the rest. Typical White House operator. No time for—

"I'm connecting you now," he announces.

As the phone rings, I huddle close to the gas station's pay phone and thank God for 800 numbers. Looking down, I notice that the leather on my shoes is beginning to rip. Too many fences. Story of my life. When the phone rings for the third time, I start getting nervous. They should've picked up by now—unless no one's there. I take a quick glance at my watch. It's past nine o'clock. Someone's got to need copies. It's the—

"White House," a young man's voice answers.

I can hear it in the seriousness of his tone. Intern. Perfect.

"Who am I speaking with?" I bark.

"A-Andrew Schottenstein."

"Listen, Andrew, this is Reggie Dwight from the First Lady's Office. Do you know where Room 144 is?"

"I think—"

"Good. I want you to run down there and ask for Trey Powell. Tell him you need to speak to him and bring him back here to me."

"I don't understand. Why—"

"Listen, man, I've got about three minutes before the First Lady issues her statement on this Garrick fiasco, and Mr. Powell's the only one who has the new draft. So get your butt out of the copy room and get your heinie running down that hallway. Tell him it's Reggie Dwight, and tell him I need to speak to him."

I hear the door slam as Andrew Schotten-something rushes out of his office. As an intern, he's one of the few people who'll actually fall for that one. More important, as chairman of the Elton John Fan Club, Washington Chapter, Trey is one of the few people who will recognize the singer's real name.

I'm counting on both as I scrutinize each car that rolls into the gas station. "C'mon, already," I mutter, grinding my shoe against the concrete. He's taking too long. Something's up. To my right, a dark gray sedan pulls into the station. Maybe the kid got suspicious and called it in. Watching the sedan, I slowly lower the phone back to its cradle. The door opens and a woman gets out. The smile on her face and the snug fit of her sundress tell me she's not FBI. Raising the phone to my ear again, I hear a door slam.

"Hello?" I ask anxiously. "Anyone there?"

"I knew it," Trey answers. "How're you feeling?"

"Where's the intern?" I ask.

"I sent him to Room 152—figured you'd want to talk alone."

I nod at the response. There is no Room 152. He'll be searching for at least half an hour.

"Now you want to tell me how you're doing?" Trey asks. "Where'd you sleep last night? The airport?"

As always, he knows it all. "I probably shouldn't say— in case they ask."

"Just tell me if you're okay."

"I'm fine. How're things there?"

He doesn't answer, which means it's worse than I thought.

"Trey, you can—"

"Did they really shut down your bank accounts? Because I went to the ATM this morning and took out everything I could get. It's not a lot, but I can leave three hundred for you at—"

"I spoke to Simon," I blurt.

"You did? When?"

"Early this morning. Surprised him as he got in his car."

"What'd he say?"

It takes me ten minutes to relay our five-minute conversation.

"Wait a minute," Trey eventually says. "*He* thought *you* were the killer?"

"He had it all worked out in his head—all the way down to the fact that Caroline and I were blackmailing people together."

"So why hasn't he turned you in?"

"Hard to say. My guess is he was afraid of his own sexual activities coming out."

"And you believe him?"

"You have any reason not to?"

"I can think of one. Starts with an N; ends with an A; her daddy's President . . ."

"I got it, Trey."

"You sure about that? If he's sleeping with Nora, he'll say anything to make you—"

"He's not sleeping with her."

"Aw, c'mon, Michael—we're right back where we started."

"Trust me on this one. We're not."

He can hear the change in my voice. There's a short pause on the other end. "You know who did it, don't you?"

"It doesn't mean anything without the proof."

This time, Trey doesn't pause. "Tell me what you need me to do."

"You sure you're up for it?" I ask. "Because it's going to be a bitch and a half to pull off."

CHAPTER 37

Running down my fourth flight of stairs in the concrete stairwell, I'm starting to feel sick. I don't like being this far underground. My head's throbbing; my balance is out of whack. At first, I assumed it was the repetitious pattern of my downward descent. But the closer I get to the final sub-basement, the more I start thinking about what's waiting for me at the bottom. I pass the door marked B-5 wondering if it's going to work. It all depends on her.

The stairwell ends at a metal door with a bright orange B-6 painted on it. I pull it open and step into the lowest level of the underground parking garage. Surrounded by dozens of parked cars, I check to see if she's already here. Judging by the silence, it appears I'm first.

A quick breath fills my lungs with chalky air, but as a meeting place, the garage fits the bill. Close by, yet out of sight.

A shriek of screeching tires slices through the silence. It's coming from a few floors above but echoes all the way down. As the car tears around the ramp's turns, the echo gets louder. Whoever it is, they're coming my way—and driving like a maniac. Running for a hiding spot, I dash back into the stairwell and peer through the window in the door. A forest green Saab leaps toward an open parking spot and jerks to a sudden halt. When the door opens, a parking garage attendant gets out. Finally, I exhale, wiping my face on my jacket sleeve.

The moment he leaves I hear the screeching start again—barreling down from the street level, growing louder as it goes. These guys are psychopaths. But as a black Buick careens off the ramp, it doesn't head for a parking space. Instead, it bucks to a dead stop right in front of the stairwell. As before, the door to the car swings wide open. Ah.

"Heard you want to get into my house," Nora says with a grin.

Already, she's having too much fun. "Where's the Service?"

"Don't worry—we got fifteen minutes till they realize I'm gone."

"Where'd you get the car?"

"Woman who does my mom's hair. Now, you want to continue grilling me, or do you want to be nice?"

"I'm sorry," I offer. "It's just been a hard—"

"You don't have to say it. I'm sorry too. Even if you wanted it, I shouldn't have let you leave like that." Taking a step toward me, she opens her arms.

I put a hand up and push away.

"What're you—"

"Nora, let's just save it for later. Right now, there're more important things to deal with."

"Are you still mad about Simon? I swear we—"

"I know you didn't sleep with him. And I know you'd never hurt me." Looking her straight in the eyes, I add, "I believe you, Nora."

She stares at me, weighing every word. I'm not sure what she's thinking, but she's got to know I'm all out of options. It's either this, or I dance for the police. At least here, she's still in control.

Her eyes narrow and she makes her decision. Naturally, I have no idea what it is. "Get in the car," she finally says.

Without a word, I circle around to the passenger's side and open the door.

"What're you doing?"

"You said to get in."

"No, no, no," she scolds. "Not with your face on every front page." She pushes a button on her keychain and pops the trunk. "This time, you're riding in back."

Curled up in the trunk of the First Beautician's Buick, I'm trying to ignore the damp-carpet smell. Lucky for me, there're plenty of distractions. Besides the jumper cables that I'm nervously squeezing in each hand, there's a full chess set—which I've just realized was never properly closed. As Nora ascends the circular ramp out of the garage, pawns, knights, bishops, and rooks bombard me from every direction. A knight hits me in the eye and bounces into my hand, just as a sharp right turn tells me we're back on 17th Street.

Wrapped in darkness, I try to mentally follow the path of the car, twisting and turning its way toward the Southwest Appointment Gate. There's no question she could be delivering me right to the authorities, but I think the last thing she wants is to be caught with the current "It" boy. At least, that's what I'm counting on.

Including wheelchair entrances, there're eleven different ways to get into the White House and the OEOB. The ones that involve walking require a valid ID and a stroll past at least two uniformed officers. The ones that involve driving require a bigshot and a kick-ass parking permit. I've got Nora. More than enough.

As the sound of traffic disappears behind us, I know we're close. The car slows down as we approach the first checkpoint. I expect them to stop us, but for whatever reason, they don't. Now comes the actual gate. This is the one that counts.

I roll forward as we come to an abrupt halt, grinding a few chess pieces into the carpet. There's an electric hum as Nora's window opens. I strain to hear the muffled voice of the uniformed guard. The night we went up on the roof, they never checked the trunk. Nora got in with nothing more than a wave and a smile. But in the last twenty-four hours, times have changed. I'm barely breathing.

"I'm sorry, Miss Hartson—those're the rules. The FBI asked us to check every car."

"I'm just picking up something from my mom. I'll be in and out in a—"

"Whose car is this anyway?" he asks suspiciously.

"The woman who does my mom's hair—you've seen her—"

"And where're your agents?" he adds as I shut my eyes.

"Down by the checkpoint—even they know it's only gonna take me a second. Now do you want to call them, or do you want to let me in?"

"Again, ma'am, I'm sorry. I can't—"

"They're waiting right down there."

"It doesn't matter—pop your trunk, please."

"C'mon, Stewie, do I look dangerous to you?"

No, don't flirt with him! These guys're too smart to—

There's a loud click and the car rolls forward. Nora—one; guards—nothing. We're in.

As we move up West Exec, I can't tell if there're people running across the narrow street that separates the OEOB and the White House. Even if it's empty, though, someone could easily walk out. Hoping to avoid surprises, and following my earlier instructions, Nora makes a sharp left up the concrete driveway and pulls right under the twenty-foot archway that leads to the ground floor of the OEOB. Out of sight and used mostly as a loading zone, it's more obscure than the wide-open area of the West Exec parking lot. As the car levels off, I know we're there. Nora shuts the engine and slams the door. Now comes the hard part.

She's got to time this one just right. The archway may lead through to a courtyard, but it's still physically part of the OEOB's massive hallway. Which means there're always plenty of people crisscrossing in and out of the automatic doors that're cut into the base of the arch. If I'm going to get out of here without being seen, she's going to have to wait until the hallway is clear.

Inside the trunk, I twist around on my stomach, slowly getting into position. My muscles are tensed. As soon as she opens the trunk, I'm out. I wrestle the jumper cables out of the way and brush chessmen away from my face. Nothing to trip me up. I don't hear anything, but she hasn't come to get me. There must be people nearby. That's the only reason she'd wait. As the seconds turn into a full minute, my fingers pick anxiously at the trunk carpet.

I try to prop myself up on my elbows as a minor revolt, but the space is too small. And dark. It's like a coffin. The walls of the trunk are pressing in. The silence is sickening. I hold my breath and listen closer. The final click of the engine as the car shuts down. Whispered friction as my shoe slides along the trunk's carpet. In the distance, a car door slams. Is Nora even out there? Did she leave? Oh, God, I panic as I lick a tiny pool of sweat from my top lip. She could be anywhere by now. Back in the Residence; pit stop in the Oval. All she needs is a head start to feed me to the wolves. Outside, I hear a group of footsteps approach the car. Just as quickly, they stop. They're waiting. Out there. For me. Son of a bitch.

The trunk pops open and a shot of daylight slaps me in the face. Squinting and using my forearm to block the sun, I look up, expecting to see the FBI. But the only one there is Nora.

"Let's go," she says, waving me out. She grabs my jacket by the shoulder and pulls me along.

My eyes scan the loading zone. No one's around.

"Sorry about the wait," she says. "There were a few stragglers in the hall."

I catch my breath as Nora slams the trunk. Reaching inside her shirt, she pulls a metal chain with a laminated ID badge from around her neck and tosses it to me. A bright red badge with a big white letter *A* on it. *A* for appointment; my very own scarlet letter. I quickly put it on. Now I'm just another White House guest—completely invisible. Wasting no time, I dash for the automatic doors on my right. The moment my body steps past the electronic eye, the doors swing wide. I'm in. So's Nora. Right behind me.

"So you're all set?" she asks as we stop in the hallway.

"I guess," I reply, my eyes glued to the floor.

"You sure you don't need anything else?"

I shake my head. "I think I'll be okay."

"I guess I'll see you at Trey's office," Nora adds.

"What?"

"That's the plan, isn't it? I go back and check in with the Service, then we'll meet up in Trey's office?"

"Yeah. That's the plan," I say, trying to sound upbeat. Turning around, I can't face her anymore. Better to walk away.

"Are you sure you don't want to tell me what you're looking for?" she asks hesitantly.

"I don't know if it's smart to talk about it out here."

"No, you're right." She looks around at the abandoned hallway. "Someone could overhear."

I nod in agreement.

"Good luck," she says, reaching out for my hand.

I reach back and our fingers slide together. Before I can react, she pulls me close and presses her lips against mine. I open my mouth and take one last taste. It's like cinnamon with a shot of brandy. She grabs me by the back of my head as her nails scratch the short hairs on my neck. Her breasts press against my chest; the entire world doesn't exist. And I'm once again reminded why Nora Hartson is completely overwhelming.

When she finally pulls away, she wipes her eyes. Her trembling lips are slightly open and she anxiously tucks a stray section of hair behind her ear. As a soft crinkle spreads across her forehead, the pained look on her face is the same as the night we were pulled over. Her seen-it-all eyes are fighting back tears.

"Are you okay?" I ask.

"Just tell me you trust me."

"Nora, I—"

"Tell me!" she pleads, a tear rolling down her cheek. "Please, Michael. Just say the words."

Once again, I take her by the hand. "I've always trusted you."

She can't help but fight back the smile. "Thank you." Wiping her eyes, she squares her shoulders and puts her mask back in place. "Clock's ticking, handsome. I'll meet you back at Trey's office?"

"That's where I'm headed," I reply, my voice trailing off.

She kisses her fingertips and slaps me on the cheek. "Stop worrying. It'll all work out." Without another word, she gets back in the car and heads down the loading ramp.

I turn away and dash for the stairs. Don't look back—
it's not going to help.

Racing up the stairs, I have a clear path to Trey's office. The moment Nora's gone, though, I spin around and
head downstairs. My stomach stings from lying to her, but
if I'd told her the truth, she'd never have brought me in.

As I rush down to the basement of the building, the
staircase narrows, the ceiling lowers, and I start to sweat.
With no windows, and not a single air-conditioning unit in
sight, the hallways in the basement are at least fifteen degrees hotter than the rest of the OEOB.

Rushing past the rotting concrete in what now feels like
an underground sauna, I take off my jacket and roll up my
sleeves. I have to duck down to avoid knocking my head
against the pipes, wires, and heating ducts that hang down
from the ceiling, but it doesn't slow me down. Not when
I'm this close.

When Caroline died, all of her important files were confiscated by the FBI. Everything else was put here: Room
018—one of the many storage areas used by Records Management. As the bureaucratic pack-rats of the Executive
Branch, they catalogue every document produced by the
administration. By all accounts, it's a suck job.

Turning the doorknob and stepping inside, I see that
they live up to their reputation. Floor to ceiling—stacks of
file boxes.

Weaving my way through the cardboard catacombs, I
move deeper into the room. The boxes just keep on going.
On the side of each one is an employee's name. Anderson,
Arden, Augustino . . . I follow the alphabet around to my
right. It must be somewhere toward the back. Over my
shoulder, I hear the door suddenly slam. The room's fluo-

rescent lights shudder from the impact. I'm not alone anymore.

"Who's there?" a man's voice barks as he approaches through the cardboard alleys.

I squat down, my hands flat against the tile floor.

"Just what the hell do you think you're doing?" he asks as I spin around.

"I . . ." I open my mouth but nothing comes out.

"You have a maximum of three seconds to tell me why I shouldn't pick up the phone and call Security—and don't give me some lame excuse like you were lost or something equally insulting." As soon as I see the handlebar mustache, I recognize Al Rudall. A true Southern gentleman who refuses to deal with low-level associates, Al is well known for his love of women and distaste for lawyers. When subpoenas came in, and we needed to gather old memos, we used to make sure that all our document requests came with a female bigshot signature at the bottom. Considering that we've never met, combined with the Y-chromosome that's floating in my genes, I knew he wasn't going to give me access to the room. Lucky for me, though, I know his kryptonite.

"It's okay," Pam says as she steps out from behind Al. "He's with me."

CHAPTER 38

Within ten minutes, Pam and I are sitting in the back of the room with fourteen boxes of Caroline's files spread out across the floor in front of us. It took a bucketful of assurances to convince Al to let us take a look, but with Pam being the new keeper of the files, there wasn't much room to argue. This is her job.

"Thanks again," I say, looking up from the files.

"Don't worry about it," Pam says coldly, refusing to make eye contact.

She has every right to be mad. She's risking her job to get us through this. "I mean it, Pam. I couldn't—"

"Michael, the only reason I'm doing this is because I think they stabbed you with this one. Anything else is just your imagination."

I turn away and stay quiet.

Flipping through the files, I'm left with the remnants of Caroline's three years of work. In each folder, it's all the same—sheet after sheet of cover-your-ass memos and filed-away announcements. None of them changed the world; just wasted paper. And no matter how fast I leaf through it, it just keeps going. File upon file upon file upon file.

Wiping sweat from my forehead, I shove the carton aside. "This is never going to work," I say nervously.

"What do you mean?"

"It's going to take forever to look at every sheet—and Al's not giving us more than fifteen minutes with this stuff. I don't care what he said, he knows something's up."

"You have any other ideas?"

"Alphabetically," I blurt. "What would she file it under?"

"I keep mine under *E. Ethics*."

I look down at the manila folders in my box. The first is labeled *Administration*. The last is *Briefing Papers*. "I got *A* through *B*," I say.

Seeing that she has *B* through *D*, Pam walks on her knees to the next box and pulls off the cardboard lid. *Drug Testing* to *Federal Register*. "Here!" she calls out as I hop to my feet.

Hunched over Pam's shoulder, I watch as she rifles through the folders. *Employee Assistance Program . . . EEO . . . Federal Programs*. Nothing labeled *Ethics*.

"Maybe the FBI took it," she suggests.

"If they did, we'd know about it. It's got to be here somewhere."

She's tempted to argue, but she knows I'm running out of options.

"What else could it be under?"

"I don't know," Pam says. "*Files . . . Requests . . .* it could be anything."

"You take *F*; I'll take *R*." Working my way down the line, I flip off the cover of each box. *G* through *H . . . I* through *K . . . L* through *Lu*. By the time I reach the second to last box, most of which is allocated to *Personnel*, I know I'm in trouble. There's no way the last quarter of the alphabet is fitting in the final box. Sure enough, I pull off the top and see that I'm right. *Presidential Commis-*

sions . . . Press . . . Publications. That's where it ends. Publication.

"There's nothing under *Files*, " Pam says. "I'm going to start at the—"

"We're missing the end!"

"What?"

"It's not here—these aren't all the boxes!"

"Michael, calm down."

Refusing to listen, I rush to the small area where Caroline's files were originally stacked. My hands are shaking as they skim down the stacks of every surrounding box. Palmer . . . Perez . . . Perlman . . . Poirot. Nothing marked Caroline Penzler. Frantic, I zigzag through the makeshift aisles, looking for anything we may've overlooked.

"Where else could they be?" I ask in a panic.

"I have no idea—there's storage everywhere."

"I need a place, Pam. *Everywhere* is a little vague."

"I don't know. Maybe the attic?"

"What attic?"

"On the fifth floor—next to the Indian Treaty Room. Al once said they used it for overflow." Realizing we're short on manpower, she adds, "Maybe you should call Trey."

"I can't—he's stalling Nora in his office." I look down at the fourteen boxes laid out in front of us. "Can you—"

"I'll go through these," she says, reading my thoughts. "You head upstairs. Page me if you need help."

"Thanks, Pam. You're the best."

"Yeah, yeah," she says. "I love you too."

I stop dead in my tracks and study her barbed blue eyes. She smiles. I don't know what to say.

"You should get out of here," she adds.

I don't move.

"Go on," she says. "Get out of here!"

Running for the door, I look over my shoulder for one

last glimpse of my friend. She's already deep into the next box.

Back in the halls of the basement, I keep my head down as I lope past a group of janitors pushing mop buckets. I'm not taking any chances. The moment I'm spotted, it's over. Following the hallway around another turn, I duck under a vent pipe and ignore two separate sets of stairs. Both are empty, but both also lead to crowded hallways.

A quarter-way down the hall, I slam on the brakes and push the call button for the service elevator. It's the one place I know I won't run into any fellow staffers. No one in the White House thinks of themselves as second-class.

Waiting, I anxiously check up and down this oven of a hallway. It's got to be ninety degrees. The armpits of my shirt are soaked. The worst part is, I'm out in the open. If anyone comes, there's nowhere to hide. Maybe I should duck into a room—at least until the elevator gets here. I look around to see what's— Oh, no. How'd I miss that? It's right across from the elevator, staring me straight in the face—a small black-and-white sign that reads "Room 072—USSS/UD." The United States Secret Service and the Uniformed Division. And here I am, standing right in front of it.

Looking up, I search the ceiling for a camera. Through the wires, behind the pipes. It's the Secret Service—it's got to be here somewhere. Unable to spot it, I turn back to the elevator. Maybe no one's watching. If they haven't come out yet, the odds are good.

I pound my thumb against the call button. The indicator above the door says it's on the first floor. Thirty more seconds—that's all I need. Behind me, I hear the worst kind of creak. I spin around and see the doorknob starting to turn. Someone's coming out. The elevator pings as it finally arrives, but its doors don't open. Over my shoulder, I hear hinges squeak. A quick look shows me the uniformed agent stepping out of the room. He's right behind me as the elevator opens. If he wanted to, he could reach out and grab me. I inch forward and calmly step into the elevator, praying he doesn't follow. Please, please, please, please, please. Even as the doors close, he can stick his hand in at the last second. Keeping my back turned, I squint with apprehension. Finally, I hear the doors close behind me.

Alone in the rusty industrial elevator, I turn, push the button marked 5, and let my head sag back against the beat-up walls. Approaching each floor, I tense up just a bit, but one after another, we pass them without stopping. Straight to the top. Sometimes there're benefits to being second-class.

When the doors open on the highest floor of the OEOB, I stick out my head and survey the hallway. There're a couple young suits at the far end, but otherwise, it's a clear path. Following Pam's instructions, I dart straight for the door to the left of the Indian Treaty Room. Unlike most of the rooms in the building, it's unmarked. And unlocked.

"Anyone here?" I call out as I push open the door. No answer. The room's dark. Stepping inside, I see that it's not even a room. It's just a tiny closet with a metal-grated staircase leading straight up. That must be the attic. I hesitate as I put my foot on the first step. In any building with five hundred rooms, there're always gonna be a few that inherently seem off-limits. This is one of them.

I grab the iron handrail and feel a layer of dust under the palm of my hand. As I climb higher up the stairs, I'm encased in another sauna caused by the lack of air-conditioning. I thought I was sweating before, but up here . . . proof positive that heat rises. Every breath in is like a full gulp of sand.

As I continue up the stairs, I notice two deflated Winnie-the-Pooh mylar balloons attached to the banister. Both of them read "Happy Birthday" on them. Whoever was up here last, it must've been a hell of a private party.

At the top, I turn around and get my first good look at the long, rectangular attic. With high, slanted ceilings and exposed wooden beams, it gets all its light from a few skylights and a set of miniature windows. Otherwise, it's a dim, crowded room filled with leftovers. Discarded desks in one corner, stacked-up chairs in another, and what looks like an empty swimming pool cut into the center of the floor. As I get closer, I realize that the recessed part of the floor is actually the casing for a section of stained glass that's surrounded by a waist-high guardrail.

As soon as my eyes hit it, I know I've seen it before. Then I remember where I am. Directly above the most ornate room in the building—the Indian Treaty Room. Looking down, I can see its outline through the huge sections of stained glass. The marble wall panels. The intricate marquetry floor. I was there for the AmeriCorps reception, when I first met Nora. The attic runs right over it. Their stained glass ceiling; my stained glass floor.

Deeper into the room, I finally find what I'm after. Beyond the guardrail, in the far left corner, are at least fifty file boxes. Right in the front, in a horizontal stack, are the six I'm looking for. The ones marked *Penzler.* My stomach constricts.

I grab the top box from the pile and rip off the cardboard lid. *R* through *Sa.* This is it. I pull out each file as I go. *Racial Discrimination . . . Radio Addresses . . . Reapportionment . . . Request Memos.*

The folder is at least three inches thick, and I tear it out with a sharp yank. Flipping it open, I see the most recent memo on top. It's dated August 28th. A week before Caroline was killed. Addressed to the White House Security Office, the memo states that she "would like to request current FBI files for the following individual(s):" On the next line is a single name, Michael Garrick.

It's not much in the way of news—I've known she requested my file since the day I saw it on her desk. Still, there's something odd about seeing it in print. After everything that's happened—everything I've been through—this is where it started.

No matter how ruthless Caroline was or how many people she blackmailed, even she knew it was impossible to get an FBI file without a request memo. Thinking about it, she probably didn't see it as that big a deal—as Ethics Officer for the White House, she had fifty ways to justify each request. And if anyone tried to use a request against her . . . well, every one of us *was* guilty of something. So who cares about a little paper trail?

Remembering that Caroline had fifteen folders on her desk, I flip to the next memo and take a closer look at the other files she'd requested. Rick Ferguson. Gary Seward. Those are the two nominees Nora told me about in the bowling alley. Including me, that's three. Twelve more to go. The next eight are presidential appointees. That brings it to eleven. Pam's was requested a while back. That's twelve. Thirteen and fourteen are both judicial nominees—people I've never heard of. That leaves only one more name. I turn the page and look down, expecting it to be Simon. Sure enough, he's there. But he's not the only one. There's an extra name on the last sheet.

My eyes go wide. I can't believe it. I sit down on a box, the sheet trembling in my hand. Simon was right about one thing. I had it all backwards. That's why Simon was clueless when I quizzed him about Nora. And why I couldn't rip a hole in his alibi. And why . . . all this time . . . I had the wrong guy. Vaughn hit it right on the money. Nora *was* sleeping with the old man. I just had the wrong old man.

Caroline had requested a sixteenth file—a file that must've been snatched from her desk—snatched by the killer—so it was never seen by the FBI. That's why he was never a suspect. I reread his name half a dozen times. The calmest among us. Lawrence Lamb.

A fit of nausea punches me in the throat and my chest caves in. The folder I'm holding sags to the floor. I don't . . . I don't believe it. It can't be. And yet . . . that's why I— And he—

I shut my eyes and clench my teeth. He knew I'd buy it—all he had to do was open the inner circle and wave a few perks. Fudge outside the Oval. Briefing the President. The chance to be the bigshot. Lamb knew I'd lick up every last drop. Including Nora. That was the cherry on top. And the more I relied on him, the less likely it became that I'd search things out for myself. That's all he needed. That's all I had. Blind faith.

Bent over, I'm still struggling to digest what's running through my head. That's why she brought me to see him. They gave me the list of suspects; I took it as fact. Without Vaughn, I never would've questioned it. There's only one problem with the picture—it's all coming together a bit too easily. From the box being up here, to the file being in its exact place . . . I can't put my finger on it, but it feels a little too force-fed. It's almost as if someone's trying to help me. As if they want to be found out.

"I never meant to hurt you, Michael," a voice whispers behind me.

I spin around, recognizing it immediately. Nora. "Is that the lie of the moment? Some maudlin disclaimer?"

She walks toward me. "I wouldn't lie to you," she says. "Not anymore."

"*Not anymore?* That's supposed to make me feel better? The first fifty things you told me were bullshit, but from here on in, it's all sunshine?"

"It wasn't bullshit."

"It was, Nora! All of it was!"

"That's not—"

"*Stop lying!*"

"Why're you—"

"Why'm I *what?* Shattered? Enraged? Devastated? *Why do you think, Nora!?* That night we outran the Service, you weren't lost! You knew where that bar was, and you knew Simon'd be waiting inside for the drop point!"

"I wasn't—"

"You *knew*, Nora. You *knew*. After that, all you had to do was sit back and watch it play out. I follow; you leave the ten grand in my car; the next day, once Caroline's dead, you've got an instant scapegoat."

"Michael . . ."

"You're not even denying it! Trey was right, wasn't he? That's why you took the money—to plant on me! That's all you had to do!"

For once, she decides not to fight back.

I take a second, catching my breath. "Must've been a real monkey-wrench when we got pulled over by the cops. You may've lost the Service, but now you had a witness."

"It was more than that," she whispers.

"Oh, that's right—when I said the money was mine, it was also the first time anyone was ever nice to you. How'd you put it that night? *People don't do nice things for you?* Well, no offense, Sybil, but I finally understand why."

"You don't mean that," she says, putting a hand on my shoulder.

"Get the hell off me!" I shout, pulling away. "Dammit, Nora, don't you get it? I was on your side! I looked past the drugs; I ignored every rumor. I took you to see my father, for chrissakes! I loved you, Nora! Do you have any idea what that means?" I can't help it—I start choking up.

She looks at me with the saddest eyes I've ever seen. "I love you too."

I shake my head. Too little. Too late. "Are you at least gonna tell me *why?*"

All I get is silence.

"I asked you a question, Nora. Why'd you do it?" My shoulders are shaking. "Tell me! Are you in love with him?"

"No!" Her voice cracks with that one.

"Then why're you sleeping with him?"

"Michael . . ."

"Don't *Michael* me! Just give me an answer!"

"You wouldn't understand."

"It's sex, Nora! There are only so many reasons to do it—you're in love . . ."

"It's more complicated th—"

". . . you're horny . . ."

"This isn't about you."

". . . you're desperate . . ."

"Stop it, Michael."

". . . you're bored . . ."

"I said stop it!"

". . . or it's against your will."

Nora falls dead silent.

Oh, God.

Crossing her arms, she wraps them around her torso and tucks her chin toward her chest.

"Did he . . ."

She raises her eyes just enough for me to see the first tears. They stream down her face and slowly trickle down her thin neck.

"He molested you?"

She turns away.

A sharp fire rips a hole in my stomach. I'm not sure if it's rage or pain. All I know is it hurts. "When did it happen?" I ask.

"You don't underst—"

"Was it more than once?"

"Please, Michael, please don't do this," she begs.

"No," I tell her. "You need this."

"It's not what you think—it's only since—"

"Only!? How long has it been going on?"

Once again, dead silence. A piece of wood creaks in the corner. She keeps her eyes locked on the floor. Her voice is tiny. "Since I was eleven."

"Eleven?" I cry. "Oh, Nora . . ."

"Please—please don't tell anyone!" she begs. "Please, Michael!" Floodgates open. The tears come fast. "I . . . I have to . . . I don't have money!"

"What do you mean you don't have money?"

She's breathing heavily—panting through her sobs. "For the drugs!" she sobs. "It's just the drugs!"

As she says the words, I feel the blood drain from my face. That sick dominating bastard. He keeps her trapped by drugs in exchange for—

"Please, Michael, promise you won't say anything! Please!"

I can't stand hearing her beg. Sobbing uncontrollably, with her arms still wrapped around herself, she just stands there—in her self-made cocoon—afraid to reach out.

Since the day we met, I've seen a side of Nora Hartson that she'd never reveal to the public. As a friend and a liar, a lunatic and a lover. As a bored rich kid, a fear-nothing thrill-seeker, an odds-defying gambler, and even, for the briefest of moments, as a perfect daughter-in-law.

I've seen her everywhere in between. But never as a victim.

I won't let her go through this alone. There's no need for alone. I cover her with my embrace.

"I'm sorry," she cries as she crumbles in my arms. "I'm so sorry."

"It's okay," I tell her, rubbing her back. "It's all going to be okay." But even as I say the words, both of us know it's not. However it started, Lawrence Lamb has ruined her life. When someone steals your childhood, you never get it back.

Rocking back and forth, I use the same technique I use on my dad. She doesn't need words; she just needs soothing.

"Y-You should . . ." Nora begins, her head buried against my shoulder. "You should get out of here."

"Don't worry. No one knows we're—"

"He's coming," she whispers. "I had to tell him. He's on his way."

"Who's on his way?"

There's a steady thunk as he bounds up the stairs. I spin around and the answer comes from the deep, calm voice in the corner of the room. "Get away from her, Michael," Lawrence Lamb says. "I think you've already done enough."

CHAPTER 39

At the sound of his voice, I feel every muscle in Nora's back tense. First, I think it's anger. It's not. It's fear.

Like a child caught stealing from her mother's purse, she pulls away from me and wipes her face. Lightning speed. Like nothing ever happened.

I turn toward Lamb, wondering what she's so afraid of.

"I tried to stop him," Nora blurts, "but he—"

"Shut up," Lamb snaps.

"You don't understand, Uncle Larry, I—"

"You're a liar," he says in a low monotone. Moving toward her, his shoulders are pitched, barely restrained in his flawlessly tailored Zegna suit. He glides like a panther. Slow, calculating, as his ice blue eyes drill into Nora. The closer he gets, the more she shrinks backwards.

"Don't touch her!" I warn.

He doesn't stop. Straight at Nora. That's all he sees.

She races to the files, pointing down at the open box. She's shaking uncontrollably. "S-See . . . here it is—j-j-just like I . . ."

He points at her, extending a single, manicured finger. His voice is a whispered roar. "Nora—"

She shuts up. Dead silent.

Thrusting his hand at her throat, he grabs her by the neck, holds her at arm's length, and scans the pile of files at her feet. Her arms go ragdoll; her legs are quivering. She can barely stand up.

I'm paralyzed just watching it. "Get off her!"

Once again, he doesn't even look my way. All he does is glare at Nora. She tries to squirm free, but he grips her tighter. "What did I tell you about fighting?" She goes back to ragdoll, her head lowered, refusing to face me. Lamb looks to the floor and smiles that thin, haunting grin. I can read it in the smug look on his face. He's seen the files. He knows what I found. Reaching into his pocket, he pulls out a silver Zippo lighter with the presidential seal on it. "Take this," he says to Nora. She stands frozen. *"Take it!"* he shouts, forcing it into her hands. "Listen to me when I talk to you! Do you want to be unhappy? Is that what you want?"

That's it. Enough melodrama. I race toward them at full speed. "I said, get the hell off h—"

He spins around and pulls out a gun. A small pistol. Pointed right at me. "What'd you say?" he asks.

I stop in my tracks and raise my hands.

"Exactly," Lamb growls.

Next to him, Nora's trembling. But for the first since Lamb arrived, she's looking at me.

Lamb yanks her chin, jerking her head back toward him. "Who's talking to you!? Me or him? *Me or him!?*" Grabbing her by the throat, he pulls her close and whispers in her ear. "Remember what you told me? Well, it's time to keep the promise." He slides his hand to her shoulder and pushes down, trying to force her to her knees. Her legs are buckling, but at least she's resisting.

"Fight him, Nora!" I call out, only a few feet away.

"Last warning," he says as he points the gun at me. Turning back to Nora, he makes sure I get a good look. With a tight grip on her throat, he slides his gun toward her mouth. "Do you want me to get mad at you? Is that what you want?" As he presses the barrel against her lips, she shakes her head no. He pushes harder. The tip of the gun scratches against her gritted teeth. Her knees start to give way. "Please, Nora . . . it's me. It's just me. We can . . . we can fix it—like it was." She looks up and all she sees is him. Slowly, she lets the gun slip between her lips. A tear runs down her cheek. Lamb smiles. And Nora gives in. One final push sends her crumbling to her knees.

Slumped down, she's sitting next to the loose files. Lamb steps back and leaves her alone on the floor.

"You know what to do," he says.

Nora looks down at the lighter, then over at the files.

"Here's your chance," he adds. "Make it right."

"Don't listen to him!" I shout.

Without warning, Lamb turns to me and fires. The gun goes off with a silent hiss. Next thing I know, something bites through my shoulder. I slap myself like I'm going after a ten-ton mosquito. But when I pick my hand up, it's covered in blood. Warm. It's so warm. And sticky. There are dark red speckles all over my arm. Without thinking, I go to touch it. My finger goes straight in the bullet hole. Up to my knuckle. That's when I notice the pain. Sharp. Like a thick needle jammed in my shoulder. It pulses down my arm with an electric shock. I've been shot.

"See what he made me do?" Lamb says to Nora. "It's just like I told you—once it gets out, it all falls apart."

I want to scream, but the words don't come.

"Don't let him confuse you," Lamb adds. "Ask yourself what's right. Would I ever put you at risk? Would I ever do anything to hurt our family?"

From the blank look on her face, I can tell Nora's lost. As shock sets in, the throbbing in my shoulder is excruciating.

Continuing to hammer away, Lamb motions to the lighter in her hand. "I can't do it without you, Nora. Only you can fix it. For us. It's all for us."

She looks at the lighter, her eyes filled with tears.

Lamb's voice stays cold and steady. "It's in your hands, honey. Only yours. If you don't finish it now, they take it all away. Everything, Nora. Is that what you want? Is that what we worked for?"

Her answer is a trained whisper. "No." Refusing to look up, Nora opens the lighter and flicks on the flame. She holds it for a moment, staring at the fire as it shakes in her hand.

"Keep—your—promise," Lamb says with his teeth clenched.

"Don't!" I call out.

It's too late. She picks up the folder and brings it slowly toward the flame.

"That's it," Lamb says. "Keep your promise."

"Nora, you don't have to—" Before I can finish, she dips the corner of the folder into the orange flame. The thin file catches fire easily, and within seconds, the entire edge is lit up like a torch . . . Wait a second. The *Request Memos* file was an inch thick. This one's—

Nora shoots me a look, and with a flick of her wrist, hurls the burning file straight at Lamb. A blazing rocket, it hits him square in the chest as fiery pages fly everywhere. His tie, his jacket—both start to catch fire. Screaming at the small flame, he pats down his chest and fights his way out of his jacket. The flames go out quickly. The file folder, smacked through the air, lands near the guardrail surrounding the stained glass. Right at my feet. I'm still lying on the floor, but if I scooch forward . . . I can just about . . . There. Ignoring the pain in my shoulder, I stamp out the flame, pick up the charred remains of the folder, and read the label. *Radio Addresses.*

I look up at Nora, who, with tears streaming down her face, is already racing at Lamb. *"You fucking asshole!"* she screams as her fingernails slash a deep cut into his cheek. *"I'll kill you! You understand me, you vampire? I'll kill you!"* Clawing and punching in every direction, she's like an animal unleashed. But the louder she screams, the more the tears flow—launched through the air as her head whips back and forth. Every few seconds, she sniffles it all in, but moments later, a burst of shrieks and saliva sends it right back out. She grabs him by the hair and pounds him in the ear. Then she lifts his head and jabs him in the throat. Blow after blow, she goes straight for the soft spots.

As always, though, Nora takes it too far. Looking down, she realizes Lamb is still somehow holding on to his gun.

I clutch the guardrail around the stained glass, struggling to get to my feet. "Nora, don't!" I call out.

She doesn't even hesitate. Letting go of Lamb's hair, she reaches down for it. That's all the time Lamb needs. He lashes out with a backhanded fist and the barrel of the gun catches her in the side of the head. *"How dare you touch me!"* he screams in a mad rage. *"I raised you! Not your father! Me!"* Grabbing her by the front of her shirt, he pulls her in and pounds the butt of the gun against her face.

"Nora!" I shout. She falls to the floor and I hobble to her side.

"Don't move!" Lamb threatens before I can take a step. Once again pointing his gun, he waves it back and forth between us. He looks at her, then jerks his head back to me. Then back to her. Then back to me. Never together.

"I'll kill her," he warns. "You touch her again and I'll kill her." His shirt is charred black at the chest; a cut on his cheek is dripping blood. Looking into his frozen blue eyes, I know he means it.

"Larry, you don't have t—"

"Shut up!" he shouts. "It's up to her."

Shaking off the blow, Nora's still on the floor. Her right eye is already starting to swell.

"Are you okay?" Lamb asks.

"Drop dead, asshole," she shoots back, wiping her mouth with the back of her hand.

"It's not too late," Lamb says, sounding almost excited. "We can still make it work—just like I said. We stop him; we're heroes. We can do it, Nora. *We* can. All you have to do is say the words. That's all I ask, honey. Tell me I'm not alone."

I nod at her to play along. She won't even look at me. She takes one final sniffle and the tears are gone. Her eyes burn at Lamb. She licks her lips. With the taste of freedom on her tongue, Nora Hartson wants out.

I make one last attempt to get her attention, but she turns away. This isn't about me. It's about them.

"We can do it, Nora," Lamb says, as she climbs to her feet. "Just like always. Our secret."

Staring straight at her family's closest friend, Nora stays silent. She's trying to hide it, but his argument's wearing her down. I see it in the rise and fall of her chest. Hunched over, she's still breathing heavily. It'd be so easy to give up. Surrender now and blame everything on me. Searching for an answer, she touches her swelling eye. Then slowly, right in front of her face, she raises a defiant middle finger. "Rot. In. Hell," she snarls.

When I turn to Lamb, his eyes, cheeks, lips . . . all his features fall. I expect him to lash out, completely crazed.

Instead, he's silent. Even more silent than usual. Clenched jaw. Stabbing stare. I swear, the room gets colder. "I'm sorry you feel that way," he eventually says without a hint of emotion in his voice. "But I want to thank you, Nora. You just made the decision that much easier." Without another word, he turns the gun toward me.

"Michael!" Nora screams as she starts running.

As Lamb's gun swings across the horizontal plane, I barely register what's happening. I'm gaping down the barrel of the gun, and the whole world hits Pause. Out of the corner of my eye, I see Nora launching herself at me. Frozen solid, I struggle to turn. There's a coughing fluorescent light right over her head and a clear plastic fork discarded on the floor. A silenced shot explodes just as she crashes into me, face-to-face. I raise my arms, trying to catch her. A second shot erupts. Then another. And another.

Her head jerks back as she's hit from behind. One. Two. Three. Four. Her body jolts as each one connects. We're both thrown back by the impact, crashing into the guardrail.

"Nornie?" Lamb cries out, lowering his gun.

Falling to the floor, I barely notice him. "Nora, are you . . ."

"I-I think I'm okay," she whispers, struggling to raise her head. As she looks up, blood slowly creeps out of her nose and the corner of her mouth. "Is it bad?" she asks, reading the look on my face.

I shake my head, fighting against the tears that fill my eyes. "N-No—no. You're gonna be fine," I stutter.

Sinking in my arms, she ekes out a tiny smile. "Good." She tries to say something else, but it gets lost. I cradle her head as she coughs blood all over my shirt.

Across the room, Lamb just stands there. Shaking. "Is she . . . is she . . ."

I look back down, unable to think. "Nora—Nora—

Nora!" She's like a sack in my arms, but she manages to glance up at me. "I love you, Nora."

Her eyes are fading. I don't think she hears me. "Michael . . ."

"Yeah?" I ask, leaning over.

Her voice isn't even a whisper. Her breathing's down to a low wheeze. "I . . ." Her body heaves and the words stop. I shut my eyes and pretend to hear every syllable.

Trying to make it easier for her to breathe, I carefully lower her to the floor.

"I-Is she okay?" a voice cries out.

I slowly look up and my fists tighten. Straight ahead, all I see is Lawrence Lamb. Paralyzed, he's still just standing there. His gun dangles from his fingertips. His mouth gapes open. Rooted in place, he looks devastated, like his whole world just evaporated. But the moment our eyes meet, his brow contorts in an angry furrow. *"You killed her!"* he growls.

Inside my chest, a volcano of rage explodes. I freighttrain toward him as fast as I can. He raises his gun, but I'm already there. My good shoulder collides with his chest and sends him crashing into the wall. The gun goes flying.

Refusing to let up, I slam him back against the wall and punch him in the stomach. Lashing out, he takes a wild swing that connects with my jaw, but I'm way beyond the pain. "You think that's gonna hurt me?" I shout as my fist crashes against his face. Over and over, I pound at the cut Nora opened on his cheek. Again. And again. And again.

Older and far slower, Lamb knows he can't win a fight with someone half his age. Realizing he's trapped, he circles away from the wall, back toward the center of the room. His eyes search wildly for the gun. They don't find it. Gone is the stiff-jawed confidence that comes with being the President's best friend. He looks like he's about to fall over. The gash on his face is a bloody mess. "She never loved you," he says, holding his cheek.

He's trying to distract me. I ignore it and hit him in the jaw.

"She didn't even pick you," he adds. "She would've dated Pam if I said so—"

Cutting him off, I pound him again in the stomach. And the ribs. And the face. Anything to shut him up. Bent over in pain, he staggers back toward the recessed section of stained glass. I know it's time to stop, but . . . next to the railing is Nora's nearly lifeless body—she's on her back, a pool of her own blood still growing below her. That's all it takes. Barely able to see through the tears, I throw everything I have into one last punch. It connects with a thunderclap and knocks Lamb backwards a good four to five feet.

He hits the guardrail completely off balance, and like a human seesaw, flips over the railing and heads straight for the enormous stained glass panels that are built into the ceiling of the room below. I close my eyes and wait for the sound of shattering glass. But all I hear is a dull thud.

Confused, I rush over to the guardrail and look down. Lamb, dazed, is lying across the wide-paneled glass flower at the center of the glass. It didn't break. Directly below him, on the other side of the glass, the crystal chandelier is swaying from the impact.

"Hhhh." He lets out a haunting sigh as a cold chill runs down my back. He's going to get away with this.

Suspended above the Indian Treaty Room, he cautiously rolls over, turns himself around, and slowly, carefully, crawls back on the glass toward the guardrail.

Desperately, I look around for the gun. There it is—

right next to Nora's shoulder. Soaked in blood. I run and grab it, whirling back to point it straight at Lamb.

He stops in his tracks. Our eyes are locked; neither of us moves. Suddenly, he purses his lips.

I pull back on the hammer.

"Spare me the dramatics, Michael. You pull that trigger, no one'll ever believe you."

"They're not going to believe me anyway. At least this way, you're dead."

"And that's going to make it all better? Some quick revenge for your imaginary girlfriend?"

I look over at Nora, then back at Lamb. She's not moving.

"Come on, Michael, you don't have it in you—if you did, we never would've picked you."

"*We?* You destroyed her . . . controlled her . . . She never took part in the planning."

"If that's what makes you feel better . . . but ask yourself this: Who do you think that gun's registered to? Me—the confidant trying to protect his goddaughter? Or you—the killer I had to stop?"

My hands are shaking as I slide a finger around the trigger.

"And let's not forget what happens to your dad when they put you in jail. Think he'll make it on his own?"

A single shot—that's all it takes.

"It's over, Michael. I can already see tomorrow's paper: *Garrick Kills President's Daughter.*"

My eyes go dark. The gun's pointed right at his forehead. Just like he did to Vaughn—and blamed on me.

Watching me twist, Lamb flashes a cold smile. It digs straight into my shoulder. I tighten my grip on the trigger. Every muscle in my body tenses. My eyes narrow. The chandelier sways.

"Say good night, Larry," I say. Holding the gun at arm's length, I use both hands to steady it. I sight along the barrel. There he is. For the first time, he loses the grin. His mouth gapes open. My finger twitches against the trigger. But the harder I pull . . . the more my hand shakes . . . and the more I realize . . . I can't. Slowly, I lower the gun.

Lamb lets out a deep cackle that rips through me. "That's why we picked you," he taunts. "Forever the Boy Scout."

That's all I need to hear. Lost in adrenaline, I raise the gun. My hands are still shaking, but this time, I pull the trigger.

The gun hiccups with a hollow little click. I squeeze it again, hard. Click. Empty. I can't believe it's empty!

Lamb laughs, low and then louder. Crawling toward the railing, he adds, "Even when you try, you can do no wrong."

Enraged, I hurl the empty gun at him. He lowers his shoulder at the last second, and the gun just misses, skipping across the stained glass like a flat rock across a wide pond. Slamming into the recessed glass casing, it eventually lands on the far side of the enormous mosaic. Lamb's sick giggle is replaying in my head. It's all I hear. And then . . . there's something else.

It starts where the gun first hit the glass floor. A small pop—like an ice cube dropped into warm soda. Then it gets louder, more sustained. A slowly growing crack on a windshield.

Lamb looks over his shoulder. We both see it at the same time—a fracture moving like lightning across the wide panels of glass.

The whole moment plays in slow motion. Almost sentient in its movement, the crack zigzags from the gun toward Lamb, who's still at the center of the rosette. Panicking, he scrambles toward the railing. Behind him, the first piece of glass shatters and falls away. Then another. Then another. The weight of the chandelier does the rest. Like a giant glass sinkhole, the center of the mosaic crumbles. The chandelier plummets into the Indian Treaty Room. Piece by piece, thousands of shards follow. As the shock wave widens from ground zero, Lamb scrambles to avoid the undertow. He reaches up and begs me to help him.

"Please, Michael . . ."

It's too late. There's nothing I can do, and both of us know it. Below us, the chandelier hits the floor with a wrenching crash.

Once again, our eyes meet. Lamb's not laughing anymore. This time, his eyes are filled with tears. The glass rains down. His floor disappears. And gravity grabs him by the legs. Sucked down into the ever-widening hole, he still struggles to claw his way up. But you can't avoid the epicenter.

"*Miiiaaaaaeeeeeee—*" he screams the entire way down.

Then he meets the chandelier. The crunching sound alone will give me nightmares for years.

As the last shards fall, a high-pitched alarm screams out of the Indian Treaty Room. I lean forward over the railing. The stained glass is almost completely gone, leaving a gaping hole. It'll take forever to fill. On the floor below, amid the shattered glass, are the broken remains of the man responsible. For Caroline. For Vaughn. And most of all, for Nora.

Behind me, I hear a soft moan. Spinning around, I rush to her side and drop to my knees. "Nora, are you . . ."

"I-I-Is he gone?" she whispers, barely able to get the words out. She shouldn't be conscious. Her voice gurgles with blood.

"Yeah," I say, once again fighting back tears. "He's gone. You're safe."

She fights to smile, but it's too much of a strain. Her chest convulses. She's fading fast. "M-M-Michael . . . ?"

"I'm here," I tell her, gently lifting her in my arms. "I'm right here, Nora."

The tears roll down my face. She knows this is it. Her head sags and she slowly gives in. "P-P-Please . . . ," she coughs. "Please, Michael . . . don't tell my dad."

I take a sharp gulp of air to keep myself together. Nodding vigorously, I pull her close to my chest, but her arms just dangle behind her. Her eyes begin to roll back in her head. Tailspinning, I furiously brush her hair from her face. There's a final twitch in her torso—and then—she's gone.

"No!" I shout. *"NO!"* I grab her head, kissing her forehead over and over. "Please, Nora! Please don't go! Please! *Please!*" None of it does any good. She's not moving.

Her head slumps against my arm and a rasping, ghostly wheeze releases the final air from her lungs. With the lightest touch I can muster, I carefully close her eyes. It's finally over. Self-destruction complete.

CHAPTER 40

They don't let me out of the Sit Room until a quarter past midnight, when the empty halls of the OEOB are nothing more than a bureaucratic ghost town. In some ways, I think they planned it on purpose—this way, no one's around to ask questions. Or gossip. Or point at me and whisper, *"He's the one—that's him."* All I have is silence. Silence and time to think. Silence and . . . Nora . . .

I lower my head and shut my eyes, trying to pretend it never happened. But it did.

As I make my way back to my office, there're two sets of shoes echoing through the cavernous hallway: mine, and those of the Secret Service agent directly behind me. They may have patched up my shoulder, but when we reach Room 170, my hand still shakes as I open the door. Watching me carefully, he follows me inside. In the anteroom, I flip on the lights and once again face the silence. It's too late for anyone to be here. Pam, Julian—they both left hours ago. When it was still light out.

I'm not surprised that the place is empty, but I have to admit I was hoping someone would be here. As it is, though, I'm on my own. It's going to be like that for a while. Opening the door to my office, I try to tell myself otherwise, but in a place like the White House, there aren't many people who'll—

"Where the hell've you been?" Trey asks, bounding off my vinyl sofa. "Are you okay? Did you get a lawyer? I heard you didn't have one, so I called my sister's brother-in-law, Jimmy, who put me in touch with this guy Richie Rubin, who said he'd—"

"It's okay, Trey. I don't need a lawyer."

He looks up at the Secret Service agent who just stepped in behind me. "You sure about that?"

I shoot a look to the agent. "Do you think we can . . ."

"I'm sorry, sir. My orders are to wait until you're—"

"Listen, I'm just looking for a few minutes with my friend. That's all I ask. Please."

He studies both of us. Eventually, he says, "I'll be out here if you need me." He heads back to the anteroom, closing the door as he leaves.

When he's gone, I expect another onslaught of questions. Instead, Trey stays quiet.

On the windowsill, I glance at the toaster. Nora's name is gone. I stare down at the remaining digital green letters, almost as if it's a mistake. Praying it's a mistake. Slowly, each line of glowing letters seems to stare back—blinking, blazing—their flickering more pronounced now that it's dark. So dark. Oh, Nora . . . My legs give way, and I lean back on the corner of my desk.

"I'm sorry, Michael," Trey offers.

I can barely stand.

"If it makes you feel any better," he adds, "Nora wouldn't have . . . It wouldn't have been a good life. Not after this."

I shake my head unresponsively. "Yeah. Right." With a deep swallow, it once again all goes numb.

"If there's anything I can . . ."

I nod a thank-you and search for control. "You heard that Lamb . . ."

"All I know is he died," Trey says. "It's all over the news, but no one has the hows and whys—FBI scheduled the briefing for first thing tomorrow." He's about to say something else, but his voice trails off. I'm not surprised. He's too connected to be in the dark. He knows what the rumors are; he just doesn't want to ask. I stare at him across the room, watching him fidget with his tie. He can barely make eye contact. And even though he's right in front of the sofa, he refuses to sit down. But he still won't ask. He's too good a friend.

"Say it, Trey. Someone's got to."

He looks up, measuring the moment. Then he clears his throat. "Is it true?"

Again, I nod.

Trey's eyebrows go from arched curiosity to rounded shock. He lowers himself to the couch. "I-I waited in my office for her—just like you said. While you and Pam were digging through files, I had all these different ways to keep her busy—fake folders to search through, fake phone records to check—it would've been perfect. But she never showed."

"She knew what we were up to—she knew all along."

"So Lamb . . ."

"Lamb deleted the request from Caroline's computer, but he didn't know she was anal enough to keep a hard copy. And the FBI didn't need them—they had the actual files. To be honest, I think Nora knew where they were. Maybe it was her insurance, maybe it was . . . maybe it was something else."

Trey watches me carefully. "It was definitely *something else*."

I grin, but it quickly disappears.

"Was she . . ." he stutters. "Was it . . ."

"As bad as you think, it was worse. You should've seen her . . . when Lamb walked in . . . he'd been doing it since she was eleven. Sixth grade, Trey. You know what kind of monster you have to be? Sixth-fucking-grade! And when Hartson got elected—Lamb was there full-time! They thought he was doing them a favor!" My voice picks up speed, blurring, rambling, flying through the rest of the story. From Lamb's gun, to the stained glass; from being grilled in the Sit Room, to Adenauer's overlong apology, it all comes vomiting out. Trey doesn't interrupt once.

When I'm done, both of us just sit there. It takes everything I have not to look at the toaster, but the silence is starting to hurt. She's no longer there.

"So what happens now?" Trey eventually asks.

I head for the fireplace and slowly remove my diploma from the wall.

"They're scapegoating! Even though you didn't do it, they're hanging you out to—"

"They're not hanging me anywhere," I say. "For once, they believe me."

"They do?" He pauses, cocking his head. "Why?"

"Thanks a lot," I say as I lower my diploma to the floor and rest it against the mantel.

"I'm serious, Michael. With Nora and Lamb both dea— Without them, all you have is a file request with Lamb's name on it. Where'd they get the rest? Debits in Lamb's bank accounts?"

"Yeah," I shrug. "But they also . . ." My voice trails off.

"What?"

I don't say a word.

"What?" Trey repeats. "Tell me."

I take a deep breath. "Nora's brother."

"Christopher? What about him?"

My voice is dry monotone. "He may be in boarding school now, but he was around for junior high. And for every summer."

The stunned look on Trey's face tells me this is the first he's heard of it. "So he . . . Oh, sick— Does that mean we'll—"

"The press'll never hear it. Hartson's personal request. However she lived, Nora Hartson's going to die a hero— giving her life to catch Caroline's killer."

"So she and Lamb . . ."

"You only heard it because you're a friend. Understand what I'm saying?"

Trey nods his head and gives me the rub. A quick one. More unnerved than upset. Unless I bring it up, that's the last I'll hear of it.

Turning back to the wall above the fireplace, I stand on my tiptoes to reach the court artist's rendition of me at the moot court finals. Trapped behind a huge piece of glass, it's even bigger than it first appears. Deeper too. It takes me a second to get both hands around it.

Trey rushes to my side, helping me get control of it. "So what'd they do?" Trey asks as we lean it against my diploma. "Fire you or force you to resign?"

I stop where I am. "How'd you know?"

"You mean besides the oh-so-subtle clue of you dismantling your office? It's a crisis, Michael. Lamb and Nora are dead, and you were sleeping with her. When it gets that hot, this place goes running for shade."

"They didn't fire me," I tell him.

"So they asked you to leave."

"They didn't say the words, but . . . I have to."

He stares out the window. There're still a few reporters

doing stand-ups on the lawn. "If you want, I can help you with some media coaching."

"That'd be great."

"And I can still get you into all the really cool events— State of the Union, Inaugural Ball—whatever you want."

"I appreciate it."

"And I'll tell you what else—wherever you apply for your next job—you better believe you're getting a recommendation on White House stationery. Hell, I'll steal a whole pack of it—we can write letters to all the people we hate: meter maids, men who call everybody 'Big Guy,' people in retail who act like they're doing *you* a favor, those bitchy stewardesses on the airplane who always lie and say they're out of those Chicklet pillows—'One per person' my neck-cramped little ass—like I'm denying them a patio on their pillow fort."

For the first time in two days, I laugh. Actually, it's more like a cough and a smile. But I'll take it.

Catching his breath, Trey follows me to my desk. "I'm not joking, though, Michael. You name it; I'll get it for you."

"I know you will," I say as I quickly flip through the piles of paper on my desk. Memos, presidential schedules, even my wiretap file—none of it's important. It all stays. In my bottom left drawer, I find an old pair of running shorts. Those I'll take. Otherwise, drawer after drawer, I don't need it.

"You sure you're gonna be okay?" Trey asks. "I mean, what're you gonna do with your time?"

I pull open the top right drawer and see a handwritten note: "Call me and I'll bring Chinese." Below it is a tiny heart, signed by Pam.

I stuff the note in my pocket and close the drawer. "I'll be fine. I promise."

"It's not a question of being fine—it's bigger than that. Maybe you should speak to Hartson . . ."

"Trey, the last thing the President of the United States needs right now is a constant reminder of his family's worst tragedy walking the halls. Besides, even if he asked me to stay . . . it's not for me . . . not anymore."

"What're you talking about?"

With one swift tug, I pull the photo of me and the President off the wall behind my desk. "I'm done," I tell him, handing Trey what's left of my ego wall. "And no matter how much you moan and groan, you know it's for the best."

He looks down at the photo and pauses a second too long. End of discussion.

Reaching down for my diploma and moot court sketch, I slide my fingers under the picture frame wire, and with a half-fist, lift them up and head for the door. As I walk, they bang against my calves. It may be the last time I'm ever in this place, but as I leave the office, Trey's right behind me.

Shooting him a quick look, I ask, "So you still going to call me every morning to tell me what's going on?"

"Six A.M. tomorrow."

"Tomorrow's Sunday."

"Monday it is."

EPILOGUE

A week and a half later, my car turns off I-95 and heads back to the quiet, rural roads of Ashland, Virginia. The sky is crystal blue, and the early-fall trees blush in yellow, orange, and green. At first glance, it's just like before—then I take a quick peek in the rearview. No one's there. That's when I feel it the most.

Every time I come out to horse country, I notice the sweet smell of wildflowers. But as my car twists and turns past an amber thicket, I realize it's the first time I've actually seen them. It's amazing what's right in front of your face.

Taking in every yellow stalk in every wide-open field, I wind my way past the farms and toward the familiar wooden fence. A quick left takes me the rest of the way. The thing is, the gravel parking lot, the ranch house, even the always-open screen door—for some reason, they all look bigger. That's the way it should be, I decide.

"Look who finally made it," Marlon says in his cozy Creole accent. "I was getting worried about you."

"It always takes me longer than I thought. It's the side roads that mess me up."

"Better late than never," Marlon offers.

I pause to think about it. "Yeah. I guess."

Marlon stares down at the newspaper that's sitting on the kitchen table. Like every conversation over the past few weeks, there's an awkward pause hanging in the air. "Sorry about Nora," he eventually says. "I liked her. She seemed like a real brawler—always calling it like it was."

I pause on the compliment, seeing if it fits. Sometimes the memory's better. Sometimes, it's not.

"Is my dad . . . ?"

"In his room," Marlon says.

"Did you tell him?"

"You told me to wait, so I waited. That's what you wanted, right?"

"I guess." Heading to the room, I add, "You really think I'll be able to—"

"How many times you gonna ask me this?" Marlon interrupts. "Every time you leave, all he wants to know is the next time you're coming. Boy loves you like all-you-can-eat ribs. What else you possibly want?"

"Nothing," I say, fighting back a smile. "Nothing at all."

"Dad?" I call out, knocking on the door to his room and pushing it open. There's no one inside. "Dad, are you there?"

"Over here, Michael! Over here!" Following his voice, I look up the hallway. At the far end, on the back porch, my dad's standing on the other side of a screen door, waving at me. He's wearing wrinkled khakis and, as always, his Heinz ketchup T-shirt. "Here I am," he sings, his feet shuffling in a little dance. I love seeing him like this.

The moment I push open the screen door, he grabs me

in a bear hug and lifts me off the ground. I jump up to help him along. "How's . . . this?" he asks, spinning around and planting me on the porch. The moment he lets go, I see what he's talking about. Beyond the picnic tables where we all ate that day is the yawning field of the farm next door. Under the blinding glow of the honey-gold sun, four horses run wild through the crisp, green fields. The whole scene—the sun, the horses, the colors—it's breathtaking— as breathtaking as the first time I saw it, the day I came to examine the group home, a week before my dad moved in.

"Isn't it pretty?" my dad asks in his slurred voice. "Pinky's the fast one. He's my favorite."

"Is that him?" I ask, pointing to the chocolate-brown horse who's way out front.

"*Nooooo*—that's *Clyde*," he tells me as if he's said it a thousand times. "Pinky's the second to last. He's not trying today."

As I step farther onto the back porch, he stares back inside the building, checking the hallway. It's like he's looking for—

"Where's Nora?" he blurts.

I knew he was going to ask. He liked her too much to forget. Easing into an answer, I sit down on the porch's wooden swing and motion for my dad to join me.

He reads the look on my face. Bad news coming. "She didn't like me?" he asks, stroking his bottom lip with stubby fingers.

"No, not at all," I say. "She loved you."

He goes to sit on the swing, but he's too caught up with Nora. His weight crashes down and we slam back into the wall of the house. Sensing the tantrum, I put my arm around him to allay his fears. Within seconds, we're lightly swaying back and forth. Back and forth, back and forth, back and forth. Calm slowly returns.

"She really loved you," I repeat.

"Then why didn't she come?"

I practiced this one the whole way up. It doesn't help. "Dad," I begin. "Nora's . . . Nora had a . . . an accident."

"Is she okay?"

"No," I say, shaking my head. "She's not okay. She's . . . she died, Dad. She died a week and a half ago."

I wait for the fallout, but all he does is stare down at his shirt, picking at the black letters. Lifting his upper lip, he lets his top teeth show. Like he's smelling something; or trying to figure it out. Slowly, he starts rocking back and forth, his lonely wide eyes studying the upside-down logo. He knows what death is—we went through it years ago. Eventually, he looks up at the porch ceiling. "Can I say goodbye to her?"

He wants to go to the cemetery. "Of course," I tell him. "In fact, I think she'd like that."

He nods his head diagonally—making ovals with his chin—but he won't say anything else.

"Do you want to talk about it?" I ask.

Still no response.

"C'mon, Dad, tell me what you're thinking."

He searches for words that are never going to come. "She was nice to me."

"I'm telling you, she really liked you. She told me so."

"She did?" he whispers, still looking away.

"Of course she did. She said you were smart, and handsome, and what a good father you were . . ." I'm hoping to get a smile, but he still won't face me. I reach over and once again put my arm around him. "It's okay to be sad."

"I know. I'm not that sad, though."

"You're not?"

"Not really. There's a good part to dying too."

"There is?"

"Sure. You're not in pain anymore."

I nod. At times like this, my father's absolutely brilliant.

"And you know what the best part is?" he adds.

"No, tell me the best part."

He looks up at the sky with a wide, toothy grin. "She's with your mom. Philly. Phyllis. Phyllis."

I can't help but smile—it's a wide grin. Like my dad's.

"I told you it was the best part," he laughs.

Swaying in the swing, he starts to giggle. He found a way to make it all okay—his world still exists. "So have you spoken to the President lately?" he asks. When it comes to jokes, that's his old faithful. Strength in repetition.

"Actually, Dad, that's the other thing I wanted to talk to you about—I left my job at the White House."

He lowers his feet and the swing stops. "What about the President?"

"I think he'll be . . . better off without me."

"Marlon said he's going to win for re-President."

"Yeah. Real big winner."

Still not facing me, my dad starts flicking his pinkie and index fingers against his thumb. "Did you get fired?" he finally asks.

"No," I say, shaking my head. "I just had to leave."

He knows I'm alluding to something—he can hear it in my voice. The flicking gets quicker. "Does that mean you're going to move again? Does that mean I have to leave too?"

"Actually, you can stay here as long as you want. Of course, I was hoping . . . well, I was wondering . . . Would you like to come live with me for a while?"

The flicking stops. "Live with *you*?" he asks, turning around. His eyes flush with tears. His mouth is gaping open. "Together?"

I think back to my first encounter with Nora. How everyone stared at me when she crossed the room and approached me. Just me. That was the moment. When I was with her, as long as she was there, I was what I wanted. Now I want something different. All the secrets are out. I don't need to be a bigshot.

I look over at my dad. "If you'll have me, I'd love to have you."

Once again, I get the toothy grin. This is all he wants to be. Included. Accepted. Normal.

"So what do you say?" I ask.

"I'm going to have to think about it," he says, chuckling.

"Think about it? What do—"

"You don't even have a job," he blurts with a laugh.

"And that's funny to you?"

He nods his head vigorously, over and over and over. "Unemployed lawyers are no good."

"Who says I'm going to be a lawyer?"

He stops, surprised. "You're not going to be a lawyer?"

I think back to the small crowd of reporters that still camp outside my building. It's going to take years before it gets easy. It doesn't matter. That's not what's important anymore. "Let's just say I'm looking at all my options."

He likes that answer. Anything's possible. "Look," he adds, pointing down at his feet. "Just for you." He picks up his pant leg, and I expect to see a dark black dress sock inside his white sneakers. Instead, he reveals a bright white sock. "They don't stay up," he says, "but they look nice."

"They sure do—but I think I like the black ones better."

"You think so?"

"Yeah. I think so."

Shrugging, my dad lifts his feet and sends us swinging

through the afternoon breeze. Straight ahead, the golden sun is shining directly in our eyes. It's so bright, I can't see a thing beyond the porch. But I see everything.

"Y'know, Mikey, the 57 on the ketchup bottle stands for fifty-seven varieties of tomatoes."

"Really?" I reply, taking it all in. "Tell me more."

I'm still afraid of letting my father down, the cancer that killed my mother, dying unexpectedly, dying for a stupid reason, dying painfully, and dying alone. But for the first time in a long time, I'm not afraid of my past. Or my future.

I know where I'm going. And I know who I want to be. That's why I took the job in the first place . . . and why, four years later, I still put up with the clients. And their demands. And their wads of money. Most of the time, they just want to keep a low profile, which is actually the bank's specialty. Other times, they want a little . . . personal touch. My phone rings and I tee up the charm. "This is Oliver," I answer. "How can I help you?"

"*Where the hell's your boss?*" a Southern chainsaw of a voice explodes in my ear.

"E-Excuse me?"

"Don't piss on this, Caruso! I want my *money*!"

It's not until he says the word "money" that I recognize the accent. Tanner Drew, the largest developer of luxury skyscrapers in New York City and chief patriarch of the Drew Family Office. In the world of high-net-worth individuals, a Family Office is as high as you get. Rockefellers. Rothschilds. Gates and Soros. Once hired, the Family Office supervises all the advisors, lawyers, and bankers who manage the family's money. Paid professionals to maximize every last penny. You don't speak to the family anymore—you speak to the Office. So if the head of the clan is calling me directly . . . I'm about to get some teeth pulled.

"Has the transfer not posted yet, Mr. Drew?"

"You're damn right it hasn't posted yet, smart-ass! Now what the hell you gonna do to make that right? Your boss promised me it'd be here by two o'clock! *Two o'clock!*" he screams.

"I'm sorry, sir, but Mr. Lapidus is . . ."

"I don't give a raccoon's ass where he is—the guy at *Forbes* gave me a deadline of today; I gave *your boss* that deadline, and now I'm giving *you* that deadline! What the hell else we need to discuss!?"

My mouth goes dry. Every year, the *Forbes 400* lists the wealthiest 400 individuals in the United States. Last year, Tanner Drew was number 403. He wasn't pleased. So this year, he's determined to bump himself up a notch. Or three. Too bad for me, the only thing standing in his way is a forty million dollar transfer that we apparently still haven't released.

"Hold on one second, sir, I . . ."

"Don't you dare put me on h—"

I push the hold button and pray for rain. A quick

extension later, I'm waiting to hear the voice of Judy Sklar, Lapidus's secretary. All I get is voice-mail. With the boss at a partners' retreat for the rest of the day, she's got no reason to stick around. Crap. I hang up and start again. This time, I go straight to DEFCON One. Henry Lapidus's cell phone. On the first ring, no one answers. Same on the second. By the third, all I can do is stare at the blinking red light on my phone. Tanner Drew is still waiting.

I click back to him and grab my own cell phone.

"I'm just waiting for a call back from Mr. Lapidus," I explain.

"Son, if you ever put me on hold again . . ."

Whatever he's saying, I'm not listening. Instead, my fingers snake across my cell, rapidly dialing Lapidus's pager. The moment I hear the beep, I enter my extension and add the number "1822." The ultimate emergency: 911 doubled.

". . . nother one of your sorry-ass excuses—all I want to hear is that the transfer's complete!"

"I understand, sir."

"No, son. You don't."

C'mon, I beg, staring at my cell. *Ring*!

"What time does your last transfer go out?" he barks.

"Actually, we officially close at two . . ." The clock on my wall says a quarter past three.

". . . but sometimes we can extend it until four."
When he doesn't respond, I add, "Now what's the account number and bank it's supposed to go to?"

He quickly relays the details, which I scribble on a nearby Post-it. Eventually, he adds, "Oliver Caruso, right? That's your name?" His voice is soft and smooth.

"Y-Yes, sir."

"Okay, Mr. Caruso. That's all I need to know." With that, he hangs up. I look at my silent cell phone. Still nothing.

Within three minutes, I've paged and dialed every other partner I have access to. No one answers. My hands are soaked with sweat. This is 125 million-dollar account. I pull off my coat and claw at my tie. With a quick scan of our network's Rolodex, I find the number for the University Club—home of the partners' retreat. By the time I start dialing, I swear I can hear my own heartbeat.

"You've reached the University Club," a female voice answers.

"Hi, I'm looking for Henry Lapi—"

"If you'd like to speak to the club operator or to a guest room, please press zero," the recorded voice continues.

I pound zero and another mechanized voice says, "All operators are busy—please continue to hold." Grabbing my cell, I dial frantically, looking for anyone with authority. Baraff . . . Bernstein . . . Mary in Accounting—Gone, Gone, and Gone.

I hate Fridays close to Christmas. Where the hell is everyone?

In my ear, the mechanized female voice repeats, "All operators are busy—please continue to hold."

I'm tempted to hit the panic button and call Shep, who's in charge of the bank's security, but . . . no . . . too much of a stickler . . . without the right signatures, he'll never let me get away with it. So if I can't find someone with transfer authority, I need to at least find someone in the back office who can—

I got it.

My brother.

With my receiver in one ear and my cell in the other, I shut my eyes and listen as his phone rings. Once . . . twice . . .

"I'm Charlie," he answers.

"You're still here!?"

"Nope—I left an hour ago," he deadpans. "Figment of your imagination."

I ignore the joke, "Do you still know where Mary in Accounting keeps her user-name and password?"

"I think so . . . why?"

"Don't go anywhere! I'll be right down."

My fingers dance like lightning across my phone's

keypad, forwarding my line to my cell phone—just in case the University Club picks up.

Dashing out of my office, I make a sharp right and head straight for the private elevator at the end of the dark mahogany-paneled hallway. I don't care if it's just for clients. At the keypad above the call buttons, I enter Lapidus's six-digit code and the doors slide open. Shep in Security wouldn't like that one either.

The instant I step inside, I spin around and pound the Door Close button. Last week, I read in some business book that Door Close buttons in elevators are almost always disconnected—they're just there to make hurried people feel like they're in control. Wiping a forehead full of sweat back through my dark brown hair, I push the button anyway. Then I push it again. Three floors to go.

"Well, well, well," Charlie announces, looking up from a stack of papers with his forever-boyish grin. Lowering his chin, he peers over his vintage horn-rimmed glasses. He's been wearing the glasses for years— way before they were fashionable. The same holds true for his white shirt and rumpled slacks. Both are hand-me-downs from my closet, but somehow, the way they hang on his lean frame, they look perfect. "Look who's slumming!" he cheers. "Hey, where's your *'I'm no longer a member of the proletariat'* button?"

I ignore the jab. It's something I've had to get used to over the past few months. Six months, to be exact—which is how long it's been since I got him the job at the bank. He needed the money, and Mom and I needed help with the bills. If it were just gas, electric, and rent, we'd be fine. But our tab at the hospital—for Charlie, that's always been personal. It's the only reason he took the job in the first place. And while I know he just sees it as a way to pitch in while he writes his music, it can't be easy for him to see me up in a private office with a walnut desk and a leather chair, while he's down here with the cubicles and beige Formica.

"Whatsa matter?" he asks, as I rub my eyes. "The fluorescent light making you sick? If you want, I'll go upstairs and get your lamp—or maybe I should bring down your mini-Persian rug—I know how the industrial carpet hurts your—"

"Can you please shut up for a second!"

"What happened?" he asks, suddenly concerned. "Is it Mom?"

That's always his first question when he sees me upset—especially after the debt collectors gave her a scare last month. "No, it's not Mom . . ."

"Then don't do that! You almost gave me a heart attack!"

"I'm sorry . . . I just . . . I'm running out of time. One of our clients . . . Lapidus was supposed to put through a transfer, and I just got my ass handed to me because it still hasn't arrived."

Putting his clunky black shoes up on his desk, Charlie tips his chair back on its hind legs and grabs a yellow can of Play-Doh from the corner of his desk. Lifting it to his nose, he cracks open the top, steals a sniff of childhood, and lets out a laugh. It's a typical, high-pitched, little-brother laugh.

"How can you think this is funny?" I demand.

"That's what you're worried about? Some guy didn't get his walking-around money? Tell him to wait until Monday."

"Why don't you tell him—his name's Tanner Drew."

Charlie's chair drops to the floor. "Are you serious?" he asks. "How much?"

I don't answer.

"C'mon, Ollie, I won't make a big deal."

I still don't say a word.

"Listen, if you didn't want to tell me, why'd you come down?"

There's no debating that one. My answer's a whisper. "Forty million dollars."

"*Forty mil?*" he screams. "*Are you on the pipe?*"

"You said you wouldn't make a big deal!"

"Ollie, this isn't like shorting some goober a roll of quarters. When you're talking eight figures . . . even to Tanner that's not spare change—and the guy already owns half of downt—"

"*Charlie!*" I shout.

He stops right there—he already knows I'm wound too tight.

"I could really use your help," I add, watching his reaction.

For anyone else, it'd be a moment to treasure—an admission of weakness that could forever retip the scales between walnut desks and beige formica. To be honest, I probably have it coming.

My brother looks me straight in the eye. "Tell me what you need me to do," he says.

Sitting in Charlie's chair, I enter Lapidus's username and password. I may not be squatting at the top of the totem pole, but I'm still an associate. The youngest associate—and the only one assigned directly to Lapidus. In a place with only twelve partners, that alone gets me further than most. Like me, Lapidus didn't grow up with a money clip in his pocket. But the right job, with the right boss, led him to the right business school, which launched him up through the private elevators. Now he's ready to do the same for me. As he taught me on my first day, the simple plans work best. I help him; he helps me. Like Charlie, we all have our ways of getting out of debt.

As I scooch forward in the chair, I wait for the computer to kick in. Behind me, Charlie's sidesaddle on the armrest, leaning on my back and the edge of my shoulder for balance. When I angle my head just right, I see our warped images in the curve of the computer screen. If I squint real quick, we look like kids. But just like that, Tanner Drew's corporate account lights up the screen—and everything else is gone.

Charlie's eyes go straight to the balance: $126,023,164.27. "*A la peanut-butter sandwiches!*" he shouts. "My balance is so low I don't order sodas with my meals anymore, and this guy thinks he's got a right to complain?"

It's hard to argue—even to a bank like us, that's a lot of change. Of course, saying Greene & Greene is just a bank is like saying Einstein's "good at math."

At its core, Greene & Greene is what's known as a "private bank." That's our main service: privacy—which is why we don't take just anyone's money. In fact, when it comes to clients, they don't choose us; we choose them. And like most banks, we require a minimum deposit. The difference is, our minimum is two million dollars. And that's just to *open* your account. If you have five million, we say, "That's good—a nice start." At ten million, "We'd like to talk." And at twenty-five million and above, we gas up the private jet and come see you right away, Mr. Drew, sir, yes, sir.

"I knew it," I say, pointing at the screen. "Lapidus didn't even cue it in the system. He must've forgotten the whole thing." Using another one of Lapidus's passwords, I quickly type in the first part of the request.

"Are you sure it's okay to use his password like that?"

"Don't worry—it'll be fine."

"Maybe we should call Security and Shep can—"

"I don't want to call Shep!" I insist, knowing the outcome.

Shaking his head, Charlie looks back at the screen. Under *Current Activity*, he spots three check disbursements—all of them to Kelli Turnley.

"I bet that's his mistress," he says.

"Why?" I ask. "Because she has a name like *Kelli*?"

"You better believe it, Watson. Jenni, Candi, Brandi—it's like a family pass to the Playboy Mansion—show the 'i' and you get right in."

"First of all, you're wrong. Second of all, without exaggeration, that's the stupidest thing I've ever heard. And third . . ."

"What was dad's first girlfriend's name? Lemme think . . . was it . . . *Randi*?" With a quick shove, I push my chair back, knock Charlie off the sidesaddle, and storm out of his cubicle.

"Don't you want to hear her turn-ons and turn-offs?" he calls out behind me.

Heading up the hallway, I'm lost in my cell phone, still listening to recorded greetings of the University Club. Enraged, I hang up and start again. This time, I actually get a voice.

"University Club—how may I assist you?"

"I'm trying to reach Henry Lapidus—he's in a meeting in one of your conference rooms."

"Please hold, sir, and I'll . . ."

"Don't transfer me!" I interrupt. "I need to find him *now*."

"I'm just the operator, sir—the best I can do is transfer you down there."

There's a click and another noise. "You've reached the University Club's Conference Center. All operators are busy—please continue to hold."

Clutching the phone even tighter, I race up the hallway and stop at an unmarked metal door. *The Cage*, as it's known throughout the bank, is one of the few private offices on the floor and also home to our entire money transfer system. Cash, checks, wires—it all starts here.

Naturally, there's a punch-code lock above the doorknob. Lapidus's code gets me in. Managing Director goes everywhere.

Ten steps behind me, Charlie enters the six-person

office. The rectangular room runs along the back wall of the fourth floor, but inside, it's the same as the cubes: fluorescent lights, modular desks, gray carpet. The only differences are the industrial-sized adding machines that decorate everyone's desks. Accounting's version of Play-Doh.

"Why do you always have to blow up like that?" Charlie asks as he catches up.

"Can we please not talk about it here?"

"Just tell me why you . . ."

"Because I work here!" I shout, spinning around. "And you work here—and our personal lives should stay at home! Is that okay?" In his hands, he's holding a pen and his small notepad. The student of life. "And don't start writing this down," I warn. "I don't need this in one of your songs."

Charlie stares at the floor, wondering if it's worth an argument. "Whatever you want," he says, lowering the pad. He never fights about his art.

"Thank you," I offer, heading deeper into the office. But just as I approach Mary's desk, I hear scribbling behind me. "What're you doing?"

"I'm sorry," he laughs, jotting a few final words in his notepad. "Okay, I'm done."

"What'd you write?" I demand.

"Nothing, just a . . ."

"What'd you write!?"

He holds up the notepad. "*I don't need this in one of your songs*," he relays. "How good of an album title is that?"

Without responding, I once again look back at Mary's desk. "Can you please just show me where she keeps her password?"

Strolling over to the neatest, most organized desk in the room, he mockingly brushes off Mary's seat, slides into her chair, and reaches for the three plastic picture frames that stand next to her computer. There's a twelve-year-old boy holding a football, a nine-year-old boy in a baseball uniform, and a six-year-old girl posing with a soccer ball. Charlie goes straight for the one with the football and turns it upside down. Under the base of the frame is her username and password: marydamski—3BUG5E. Charlie shakes his head, smiling. "Firstborn kid—always loved the most."

"How did you . . . ?"

"She may be the queen of numbers, but she hates computers. One day I came in, she asked me for a good hiding spot, and I told her to try the photos."

Typical Charlie. Everyone's pal.

I turn on Mary's computer and glance at the clock on the wall: 3:37 P.M. Barely twenty-five minutes to go. Using her password, I go straight to *Funds Disbursement*. There's Tanner's transfer queued up on Mary's screen—waiting for final approval. I type in the code for Tanner's bank, as well as the account number he gave me.

"*Requested Amount?*" It almost hurts to enter: $40,000,000.00.

"That's a lot of sausage," Charlie says.

I look up at the clock on the wall. 3:45 p.m. Fifteen minutes to spare.

Behind me, Charlie's once again jotting something in his notepad. That's his mantra: *Grab the world; eat a dandelion.* I move the cursor to *Send.* Almost done.

"Can I ask you a question?" Charlie calls out. Before I can answer, he adds, "How cool would it be if this whole thing was a scam?"

"What?"

"The whole thing . . . the phone call, the yelling . . ." He laughs as he plays it out in his head. "With all the chaos blowing, how do you know that was the real Tanner Drew?"

My body stiffens. "*Excuse me?*"

"I mean, the guy has a Family Office—how do you even know what his voice sounds like?"

I let go of the mouse and try to ignore the chill that licks the hairs on the back of my neck. I turn around to face my brother. He's stopped writing.